"I THOUGHT I SAID YOU SHOULDN'T BE KEEPING AN EYE ON ME?"

Though she didn't manage to put the heat behind the words she probably should have.

"I have a problem with listening," Maverick said with a smirk.

"No kidding." Alexa planted her hands on her hips.

"Besides, I like keeping my eyes on you," he said with a wink. His gaze swept over her in a slow, satisfied up and down. Heat rose into Alexa's cheeks, because he'd said the words jokingly, but there was an intensity and a seriousness to his expression that made her think of dark rooms and frantic kisses and messed-up sheets. Molten-hot memories of the two of them together—memories she'd kept boxed up tight for the past five years—threatened to come roaring back.

By Laura Kaye

LAURA KAYE

Ride
ROUGH

A RAVEN RIDERS NOVEL

AVONBOOKS

An Imprint of HarperCollinsPublishers

"Hard Ever After" was originally published as an e-book novella in February 2016 by Avon Impulse, an Imprint of HarperCollins Publishers.

"Hard Ever After" copyright © 2016 by Laura Kaye.

First Avon Books mass marketing printing: May 2017

ISBN 978-0-06-240338-4

Avon Trademark Reg. U.S. Pat. Off. and in Other Countries, Marca Registrada, Hecho en U.S.A.
Avon, Avon Books, and the Avon logo are trademarks of HarperCollins Publishers.
HarperCollins® is a registered trademark of HarperCollins Publishers.

17 18 19 20 21 QGM 10 9 8 7 6 5 4 3 2 1

*To everyone who needs the encouragement
to fight for what your heart most desperately wants,
this book is for you.*

CHAPTER 1

Alexa Harmon tore out of her car and ran into the house, her high heels clicking against the concrete of the three-car garage and then the travertine tiles of the hallway and kitchen. She was late getting home from work, and that meant she was going to be hard-pressed to get dinner on the table on time.

She beelined for the bedroom, already working at the buttons on her silk blouse. Despite being under the gun, she took the time to hang up her work clothes and put everything away in the walk-in closet that was nearly as big as her childhood bedroom had been.

Grant didn't like mess or clutter. Everything had to be in its place. Always.

Slipping into a pretty blue blouse, jeans, and her ballet flats, Alexa's gaze cut to the alarm clock on her nightstand. She had twenty-five minutes. Twenty-five minutes to make sure her lateness didn't ruin their whole evening.

Damnit, Alexa. You should've kept your eyes on the time better.

It was true. She'd just been elbows deep in materials arriving for the model home in Grant's newest development. This was the first time he was letting her take the lead on the interior design of a model, rather than hiring their usual outside contractor, and she wanted it to be good. Oh, who was she kidding? She wanted it to be perfect.

More than that, *she* wanted to be good. Good enough. No, she wanted to be *perfect*. For Grant.

Grant *really* liked perfection.

Alexa got it. Her fiancé Grant's perfectionist tendencies went a long way toward explaining how he'd built Grant Slater Enterprises, the biggest real estate development and management company in Western Maryland. Though he'd come into some kind of a trust fund when he was younger, he'd built most of his success with his own hard work and smart investments. Now, Frederick was almost a company town, at least where real estate was concerned. There were more developments in the area with the words *Grant* or *Slater* in their names than she could count. Their own neighborhood was a prime example—Slater Estates.

Running back out to the kitchen, a low pleading *Meow* caught Alexa's attention.

"Come on, Lucy. Come with Mama," Alexa called, heading straight for the cat's bowl. She poured dry food into the dish, spilling a little in her haste. The hairless sphynx brushed against her leg in a show of affection. Alexa gave Lucy's sweater-covered blue-gray body a quick pet as she scooped up stray morsels of food with her other hand.

The clock on the microwave told her she had twenty-two minutes now.

She grabbed the package of two filet mignons from the fridge, along with a bag of fresh asparagus. Moving as fast as she could, she found the grill pan for the meat and the sauté pan for the asparagus, and got that much going. The baked potatoes she'd planned weren't going to be possible with this little time, and trying to boil water for corn on the cob would be pushing it. Her stomach knotted as her pulse raced. She buttered thick slices of Italian bread and seasoned them with garlic, then slid them into the warming oven to brown.

As soon as she turned the filets, she was back in the fridge. When her gaze settled on the container of chickpea salad from the weekend, relief flooded through her. She'd forgotten they had that. Finally, she threw together a green salad with chunky fresh vegetables.

Keeping a close eye on the time, she set the dining room table—Grant always preferred to eat in the formal dining room. She made sure to align the flatware just so, just as he liked. And then she was pouring the wine and plating the food with two minutes to spare.

Alexa might've fist-pumped if she wasn't so anxious about almost having been late. Her stomach was in so many knots she wasn't even sure she'd be able to eat. Though it was her own damn fault.

Six o'clock came and went. Six-oh-five. Six-ten. Sitting alone at the dining room table, Alexa frowned. Finally, her phone buzzed an incoming text message from Grant.

I've got a dinner meeting tonight. Don't wait up.

Alexa stared at the screen for a long moment, then found herself blinking away threatening angry tears. She stuffed down all the things she wanted to say—and all the things she felt—and replied simply, *Okay xo.*

Look on the bright side, she thought. Okay. On the bright side, she'd now have time she hadn't expected to work on her final project for her senior seminar.

Still . . .

She let herself fume and wallow for several more minutes, and then she shook her head. "Stop it, Al," she said out loud. God, she really was overemotional lately, wasn't she? Just like Grant said she was.

Between her job, designing the model home, her class project, her recent move into Grant's house, and their upcoming wedding, there was just so much going on. She felt like she should be juggling it all with more grace and enthusiasm. Instead, what she *really* felt scared her. Scared her bad.

Dread. Skin-crawling, stomach-dropping, run-while-you-can dread.

It was ridiculous.

Alexa was on the cusp of having everything she'd ever dreamed about. A beautiful home she could be proud of, a secure job that she loved, a man who wanted to be with her every moment he wasn't working, and more money than she'd ever be able to spend. She wasn't greedy; that wasn't where her interest in money and a nice house came from. Instead, it came from the way she'd grown up. Her father leaving her and her brother with nothing but a seriously ill mother, how *little* she'd had as a kid, how terrible the conditions in the trailer she'd grown up in had been—against all of that, it was simply amazing to think about how much she had now.

And hard to believe. A lot of the time, she was sure she didn't deserve it. And a part of her couldn't quite accept that it would last. Grant was Armani suits and Ivy-League education and million-dollar bank accounts, while Alexa was mall clearance racks and part-time evening classes and life lived paycheck to paycheck. At least, that had been her before they'd gotten serious. She didn't need Grant to tell her how lucky she was that he'd wanted her, although he did sometimes tell her just that.

Mostly, she was grateful beyond imagination. Grateful to

be safe and secure. Grateful not to be ashamed and embarrassed of where she lived. Grateful to be able to afford to take care of her mom, who suffered from an array of mental health problems and needed all the help Alexa could give her, which had been more and more since her older brother, Tyler, died five years before. Alexa was grateful to Grant for making so much possible that she never would've been able to accomplish on her own.

Which made the dread seriously ridiculous.

It was just wedding jitters. Totally normal.

Sighing, she surveyed the beautiful dinner she'd managed to throw together. Given how scarce food had been when she was younger, Alexa absolutely hated to waste anything. Problem was, her appetite had been all over the place lately. Either she couldn't stomach the thought of eating or she was binge-eating a bag of potato chips while Grant was at work.

Knock, knock.

The quick raps on the front door pulled Alexa from her thoughts. She crossed the dining room to the wide oval foyer framed by a grand curving staircase. A glittering chandelier hung from the ceiling, casting colorful prisms here and there from where it caught the late-day sun through the large picture window above the door. Out on the front porch, Alexa found a stack of packages. She gave a wave to the UPS driver as he pulled out of the end of their driveway.

With just over two weeks until the wedding, presents from the registry had been pouring in every day. Grant had so many friends, colleagues, and contacts that she'd never met, Alexa didn't know who most of the gifts were from.

She carried in two smaller ones, then two medium ones, and then found herself struggling to move the large square box on the bottom. It was too deep to get her arms around and not easily pushed. What the heck could it be?

She crouched behind it to try to gain leverage, and was just about to give up when a strong breeze blew her hair across her face, and she heard a soft click.

Her gaze cut to the front door.

"Oh, shit," she said. Knowing what she was going to find, she tried the knob anyway. Locked.

She was locked out, and Grant was away until who knew what time. She couldn't easily go anywhere because her purse, car keys, and phone were all inside. And she didn't know her neighbors yet because she'd just moved in.

"Shit, shit, *shit.*"

So much for getting work done tonight.

She sat heavily on the stupid box and dropped her head into her hands. And burst into tears.

Not because of being locked out. But because being . . . trapped with no easy way out of the situation? Suddenly, that felt like a crazy accurate metaphor for her life.

If she was being honest with herself.

Which she really, really didn't want to be.

"Stop it, Al," she said in a rasping voice. "You're not trapped. Stop thinking that." Except, just then, she leaned her left cheek too heavily against her hand. She sucked in a breath at the smarting of the healing bruise there.

The one from the fight she and Grant had last week. The fight that had started with Alexa leaving a big mess in the foyer from where she'd been unboxing another delivery of packages and had escalated into a huge argument, culminating in Grant saying Alexa was just like her mother—something Grant knew cut her deep on so many levels. The fight had ended when Alexa told him he was being mean and he'd kicked a box at her. When she'd tried to duck out of the way, she tripped over another box on the floor and fell, hitting her head against the leg of a console table in the foyer, giving her some nasty bruises.

Alexa had been totally and absolutely stunned, especially

when Grant hadn't helped her. Instead, a bitter, humorless laugh had spilled out of him and he'd said, "Way to prove my point, Alexa. I don't know why I put up with your shit. If you can't show me and my house a little respect, you can leave," he'd said, and then he'd stormed out.

His house? Granted, she'd only moved in a few weeks before, but she'd moved in for keeps.

Shocked, she'd lain there for long minutes, completely confused and overwhelmed by the pain and his cruel words. So she'd done what he said. She'd fled. To her past. To Maverick Rylan, her dead brother's best friend, and the man who'd once been her closest friend and lover. It had been pure instinct to seek him out at the clubhouse of the Raven Riders Motorcycle Club. Despite everything that'd happened between them, no part of her had doubted that he'd help.

And he had. Or, at least, he'd tried.

But Maverick represented a past she'd left behind for a whole lot of very good, logical, and well-thought-out reasons. So she hadn't stayed. And she hadn't answered his questions.

By the time she'd finally returned home, all she could see were the million mistakes she'd made—making that mess, overreacting, going to Maverick and opening that door to the past that she'd kept closed tight for so long. For years. She'd been prepared to plead for Grant's forgiveness, sure he was going to be done with her once and for all. But he'd surprised her. Because Grant had apologized so profusely he'd gotten down on his knees, his head buried in her lap.

Never before in the nearly five years they'd been to-gether had Grant ever hurt her. At least, not physically. He could be short with her and more controlling when he was stressed, and occasionally his criticism bordered on the mean side. But the truth was Alexa *could* be messy, which *was* why she'd tripped, and she could be disorganized and she could be forgetful, all things that drove him crazy. At the same time, Grant could also be generous and sweet and he'd done so much for her and her mother, things Alexa wouldn't have been able to do on her own. Their lives were better because of Grant Slater.

The night of their fight, things had just gotten out of hand, for both of them. And it was behind them now, so there was no point in dwelling—

"Alexa?" came a deep voice.

Prickles ran up her spine as she pulled herself from the bad memories and lifted her head—and found herself staring at her past, into the dark blue eyes of Maverick Rylan.

Alexa jumped up off the box, her heart suddenly in her throat. She swiped at the wetness on her face half sure she was imagining this man. This man she'd done her best to avoid—for years—until last week.

With his longish sandy-blond hair and his square jaw and his ruthlessly masculine features and his Raven Riders cutoff jacket hanging on those broad shoulders, Maverick was the sexiest man she'd ever known. Had been when they were together five years before, still was even now. No, he was hotter now. More muscular. More rugged somehow. More self-possessed. Utterly desirable.

"You okay?" he asked, stunningly dark blue eyes looking deep into hers.

Snap out of it, Al! Right. Because clearly she wasn't hallucinating. And that . . . that was a problem.

Releasing a shaky breath, Alexa met his gaze head-on. She had to know. "Maverick, what in the world are you doing here?"

CHAPTER 2

Alexa glanced up and down the quiet street with its manicured lawns and huge colonials and didn't see any cars that didn't belong—or any motorcycles. "Where did you even come from?"

Maverick's gaze narrowed on her face. "You're crying," he said, like that explained anything.

"No, I'm not," she said, brazening it out despite the wetness clinging to her eyelashes. "Seriously, why are you here?" She stopped short of saying he *shouldn't* be there, because she suspected that would make him dig in his heels and want to stay. Even though he really shouldn't be there. Grant wouldn't like it. Oh, God, why had she gone to Mav for help?

Maverick's head tilted the smallest amount, like he was assessing her, or challenging her. "You know why I'm here, Al."

Al. No one in her life called her by that nickname anymore. Tyler had almost *always* called her Al, which was where Maverick had picked it up. Of course, very few people from her *before Grant* life were still around either. Somehow, her relationship with Grant and the work they did together had taken over everything until she'd all but lost touch with her friends.

"No, I don't." She shook her head not just in answer, but against the old longing she felt for Maverick. In high school, Tyler and Maverick had been thick as thieves, which meant despite their four-year age difference, Alexa had known Maverick long enough to have crushed on him forever, pretty much. It seemed like some part of her had *always* yearned for him—and always would.

But that didn't mean there hadn't been problems, too. For a woman who'd grown up wanting nothing more than stability and respectability, a guy who built his life around a motorcycle club engaged in at least some questionable activities didn't seem most likely to offer that. And then Tyler had become a prospective member of the Raven Riders, following Maverick as he always did—until her brother had wiped out on a rainy mountain road one night and died on the way to the hospital. Mixed in with her soul-deep grief over his loss was a red-hot rage that his recklessness had made him leave her when she needed him so much. When their mother needed him.

Tyler's death had thrown a stark clarity on all the reasons that being with Maverick was problematic. She couldn't be with someone who lived such a dangerous life and couldn't offer her the security her mother required. Because Alexa was the only one left to take care of her. And it wasn't like Mav had ever talked about settling down, despite being together for three years. They'd just been having fun, hanging out. But mired in her grief and fear, she'd needed more than that. So she'd broken up with him. Just went cold turkey. Not that Maverick accepted that.

He'd pursued her. Hard. Dropping by her house, coming to her work, calling, texting. Trying to convince her to change her mind. Until he'd found her at Tyler's grave on what would've been his twenty-eighth birthday, and they'd had it out.

"Why are you doing this, Alexa? Why are you pushing me away?" Maverick asked, the two of them standing on either side of Tyler's burial plot as if it were a wall between them.

Alexa drew on everything she had to hold back her tears. "My mother is a wreck, and taking care of her is all on me. I have to focus on her now, and I have to do what's best for her. She needs stability, and I need to figure out how to give it to her, and I . . ." She peered up at him. "I need it, too, Maverick."

He grasped her hand. "So I'll help."

"But for how long?" she blurted. He frowned like he was trying to make sense of her question. And then her fears poured out of her. "How long until you wreck? Or some club business goes bad and you get hurt? Or you don't want me because—"

"Don't want you? Where the hell did that come from?" he asked, anger flashing in his eyes.

Grief was like a lead blanket wrapped around her shoulders, heavy and suffocating. And it hadn't escaped her notice that he hadn't addressed her fears about staying safe. Because he couldn't. "Maverick, losing Tyler was the last thing I ever imagined happening. I can't handle anything else. I need certainty right now, permanence, security." Forever. She needed forever. Once, she'd hoped Maverick would want it, too. With her, someday. But now what he did and who he was scared her. Especially standing there at Tyler's grave.

"And you don't think I can give that to you?" he asked, anger sharpening the angles of his ruggedly handsome face.

"Can you?" she whispered.

The silence that had followed had been her answer.

So Alexa had made her choices long ago.

"Yes, you do. You know exactly why I'm here." Maverick stalked toward her, his big body bearing down on hers in a way that set her heart to racing. With a gentleness that seemed impossible, given his size and all his rough edges, he grasped her chin and turned her face so that the side that had been bruised was toward him. "You came to me." He nailed her with a stare.

Hugging herself, she pulled her chin free from the heat of his fingers. "I'm sorry I bothered you last week. I shouldn't have gone to the clubhouse." She'd just been so shocked by the fight with Grant and his words and his storming out that she hadn't known what else to do. Going to her mother's would've just made things worse, and she felt too out of touch with all of her old friends to go to any of them. Not to mention too embarrassed.

She'd felt so alone.

She still wasn't sure why she'd driven out to the Raven Riders' compound on the edge of Frederick. Once there, she'd worried she'd unnecessarily complicated her life a whole lot by mixing the past with her present and future. The longer she'd stayed at the clubhouse, the more certain she'd been that Grant really was done with her. Scared that she'd ruined everything, she'd left without explaining what'd happened to her, but not before Maverick had seen her face.

Now, him standing on the front porch of the house she shared with Grant? That was all kinds of complicated.

"If you think coming to me was a bother, maybe you never knew me at all," he said, the muscle in his jaw clenching. He stepped away, his gaze fierce.

His words set off a pang in her chest. She *did* know him. His protectiveness, his possessiveness, his goodness—

despite his club not being totally aboveboard. Although, from what she understood, their less-than-legal activities funded the Ravens' quiet mission to defend those who couldn't defend themselves . . .

Wait. Was *that* why she'd gone out there?

The question was like a sucker punch to the gut. Alexa wasn't someone who couldn't defend herself. She wasn't in an abusive relationship like the women the Ravens helped. It had only been that one time and Grant had apologized over and over again. And she'd been the one who tripped, after all.

"Maybe I . . . maybe I didn't," she said, her voice not much more than a whisper as the thoughts settled uncomfortably deep inside her.

"Fine. Have it your way," he said, his voice like gravel. Just when she thought he would leave, he stepped up to her front door and pulled something from his back pocket.

"What are you doing?" she asked, moving to his side.

"Letting you back into your house." He worked a silver tool that looked like a pocketknife at the door handle.

"Are you picking my lock?" She watched in fascination as he quickly manipulated the tools and turned the knob, opening her front door.

"I'm letting you back into your house." He flipped the little tool set closed and slipped it into his pocket.

"You carry lock picks on you?" she asked. Her night had gone from stressful to surreal.

"Yes. You're welcome." His right eyebrow arched, just the littlest bit. And it was so damn sexy. Her blood heated, her nipples hardened, her pulse raced. She and Maverick had always been good at fighting. And even better at making up afterward. Her body clearly remembered . . . and hungered.

She blinked as he pushed open the door. "Um. Okay. Thank you."

He stepped away from the opening, and Alexa slipped into the spot where he'd stood, the word *Good-bye* on the tip of her tongue.

But he still didn't leave. He heaved the box off the porch and turned to her, the muscles of his biceps and in his neck popping out.

"You don't have to do that," she said, even as she backed into the house to get out of his way. As he passed her, she noticed a band of black fabric tied around one of his arms. She nearly gasped as memories again sucked her five years into the past. To Tyler's funeral. He'd been a prospective member of the Ravens, and they'd honored him by wearing strips of some of his cut-up T-shirts around their arms. Who'd died now?

Mav lugged the box inside. "Where do you want it?" he asked, pulling her from the memories.

"Maverick—"

"This thing is really fucking heavy, Al." He stared at her expectantly.

"Right around the corner in that room," she said. Her office had become the holding area for all the wedding gifts as they came in. Which suddenly made her uncomfortable about having sent Maverick in there. She followed him in and watched him settle the unwieldy box next to the long credenza filled with unwrapped gifts. China and picture frames and vases and luxurious linens, to name a few. "Thank you."

His gaze surveyed the wedding gifts, but he didn't make a comment, and she couldn't read his expression. At least, not until he looked at the project boards hanging over her desk, one filled with plans for the model home job and another filled with her work on a design project for her senior capstone. Then his expression became interested. "That for school or a job you're doing?" he asked, eyes still on her work.

"Both." What did he see when he looked at her design ideas? Maverick had always had an eye for design and an appreciation for aesthetics—it was one of the things that made him such a talented and sought-after custom bike builder.

He nodded. "Pretty cool," he said in a quiet voice. Before she'd started her interior design program, he'd been a big supporter of her going to school and pursuing her dreams. Now she was only her current course and one internship away from finishing after all these years of working full-time and pursuing her degree and accreditation part-time.

The sincerity of his words and in his expression did funny things to her chest. "Yeah?"

His gaze cut to her. "Yeah."

They stood looking at one another a long moment until Alexa's heart was thundering against her breastbone with an unnamed need. She shoved the desire back. She'd made her choice for a man and a life—and it hadn't been with Maverick. But being in his presence messed with her head . . . and her body. Clearly. Which was why she'd stayed away . . .

God. I should've stayed away.

"Your arm," she said, staring at that black band and trying to distract herself from the way he made her feel. Still.

Maverick frowned, and for just a second his true feelings reached the surface of his eyes. Grief. Anguish. Rage. "A friend," he said.

"I'm sorry." When he didn't say anything more, Alexa hugged herself. Despite their long estrangement, she hated seeing him in pain, but it wasn't like she could comfort him either. Finally, something occurred to her. "Hey, how did you know I was locked out? And that I couldn't move the box?" Voicing the question gave rise to goose bumps on her arms.

He just looked at her, that little eyebrow arch making itself known again.

"No, Maverick." She shook her head as realization set in. "Oh my God. You can't do that. You can't be . . . hanging around and watching out for me."

"Someone has to—"

"Grant. Grant watches out for me," she said, the words falling uncomfortably from her tongue.

"Is that what he was doing when that happened?" He nodded toward her, his gaze locked on her face, and she knew he was talking about the bruise on her cheek. What wasn't faded was fairly well covered with makeup, but they both knew it was there.

"Maverick—"

"Look, I don't want to fight," he said, closing the distance between them.

He stood so close she had to tilt her head back to keep eye contact. So close that all she'd have to do was reach out her hand and he'd be hers again. The thought came entirely out of left field and nearly made her dizzy. She hadn't thought of Maverick that way in years.

What was wrong with her? She was over him. Had been for a long time. For a lifetime.

Shaking her head, she managed, "Good. Me, neither." But that didn't mean she wouldn't find a way to get him to stop watching out for her. If Grant found out, he'd know she'd gone to Maverick or suspect she was still seeing Maverick, and neither would be good for her. Or Maverick.

The universe of strings Grant could pull—or have pulled—was bigger and scarier than she liked to think about. She didn't know many specifics because he shielded her from them, but she'd heard rumors and rumblings. Payoffs. Threats. Intimidation. Though maybe none of that was true. Maybe such things were rumors spread by competitors trying to take Grant down a notch, just like he said when she once asked about the things she'd heard.

Looking down at the space between them, Maverick planted his hands on his hips. "Damnit Alexa, you deserve better—"

She gave in to the dangerous urge to touch him and laid a hand on his chest. She wasn't sure what else he'd planned to say, but suddenly she couldn't bear for him to finish that sentence. With a quick shake of her head, she said, "Don't, Maverick. Okay? If you say anymore, we'll just end up fighting."

Maverick huffed, his gaze absolutely on fire as it raked over her face and settled on her lips. He leaned toward her, just the littlest bit, and her heart lurched into her throat. She was suddenly sure he was going to kiss her. And, *oh, God*, she wanted him to. She should push him away, say no, but she didn't know how to say no to him, never had, and especially not with five years of suppressed need roaring through her. She licked her lips, her breath catching, her mouth hungry for a taste . . .

Meow.

Lucy wound her body around Alexa's legs, and Alexa jumped back, breaking the spell that had wrapped around them. God, what was she thinking? Needing a shield, Alexa scooped the hairless cat into her arms and hugged her tight.

Mav eyeballed the cat and made a face. "What the hell is that?" he asked, more than a little amusement in his voice. He stepped back from her, like maybe he needed the space from whatever had just happened between them.

"It's Lucy," Alexa said, kissing her soft head.

"But . . . what is it? Or . . . happened to it?"

Alexa rolled her eyes. So her cat was bald. And had wrinkly skin. And was wearing an argyle sweater. And had the world's disproportionately biggest ears. "It's a sphynx cat. They're hairless. And they're awesome. Coolest cat you will ever know."

"It's really—"

"Don't you dare say she's ugly." Alexa nailed him with

a stare. The house she'd grown up in had been so cluttered and filthy that Alexa had developed terrible allergies and asthma, so hairless cats were the only kind she could have. She'd adopted Lucy from an animal shelter less than a month after Tyler died.

Maverick chuffed out a small laugh. "So ugly she's cute?"

Shaking her head, Alexa held back the smile that threatened. "I suppose that's acceptable. Just."

Giving Alexa a wink, Maverick held out his hand to the cat's nose. Alexa braced for Lucy to freak out and bolt, but though her little muscles did tense, she merely sniffed at Maverick and then turned away.

Whoa. Grant couldn't get within ten feet of Lucy. "Wow, she likes you."

"Of course she likes me. I'm awesome." He folded his arms, his expression full of challenge and humor.

Joking around with him felt all too comfortable, easy, relaxed. Which was really, really not good.

Alexa gave Lucy another kiss and turned away. Maverick needed to go—and he needed to stay gone—so that whatever had just nearly happened between them didn't happen again. "Well, thanks for your help," she said. "I'll walk you out." In the foyer, she dropped Lucy to the floor and opened the door.

All the easy affability faded from Maverick's expression, and the hard-ass biker was back in its place. "I'm worried about you, Alexa."

She ignored the pang in her chest caused by his concern. "There's no reason to be."

"Think Tyler would agree with that?" Maverick's gaze was filled with as much skepticism as his tone.

"Tyler would believe me," she said, knowing deep down that her brother would've flipped his shit if he'd seen her face. But he wasn't here now, was he? And she had responsibilities she had to take care of on her own. Still,

Maverick's question set off an ache inside her—an ache for what used to be, and maybe even for what might've been. "Because I'm good. No, I'm great."

She would have to do better if she was going to keep Maverick from coming around.

Her stomach knotted as words came to mind, and then she let them fly. "But if you hang around and Grant finds out, you're going to mess things up for me. So please, don't come here again. I made a mistake coming to you last week, and I'm sorry. It won't happen again either."

Now Maverick's expression was rankly pissed off. He stared at her a long moment, like he was debating how to respond. "Fine," he finally said, his voice like it had been scoured with sandpaper. "Have a good life, Alexa. Hope it's what you really want." He wrenched open the door and stalked out.

The silence seemed loud all around her. She quietly closed and locked the door, then turned and leaned her back against it. "Me, too, Maverick. Me, too."

CHAPTER 3

Sitting under the blue tent, his brothers gathered all around, Maverick couldn't hear the pastor's words. Mav's head was too full of churn and burn. Over the loss of one of their own. Over the attack on his club just last week. Over confronting Alexa an hour before. Damnit, why had he gone over there when coming to this funeral already had him so torn up?

You know why. Something's not right. She's not safe.

The bruises she'd had—that she *still* had—proved that. Whether she wanted to admit it or not. And he couldn't let it go, not when he might be able to do something about it.

Heaving a deep breath, he stared at the flower-draped casket and hoped this was the last funeral he and his brothers had to attend for a long damn time. This loss hit him and everyone in the Raven Riders Motorcycle Club particularly hard—because it had happened on their own turf. Inside their own clubhouse. And the victim—

prospective member Jeb Fowler—had been too young and too good to get taken out in cold blood.

The proof of Jeb's goodness was sitting right beside Maverick. Bunny McKeon, Maverick's mother, whose face still bore the bruises and scratches from where she'd been struck and her mouth duct-taped. But she was alive because Jeb had taken the bullet intended for her when a group of low-life criminals had broken into the clubhouse looking for something—or *someone*—that wasn't theirs.

Mav's gaze slid over to his right, where the club's president, Dare Kenyon, sat with his girlfriend, Haven. Three days out of the hospital, Dare's face was pale, and dark circles ringed his eyes. He'd been shot twice in the same attack that had hurt Bunny and killed Jeb. An attack by Haven's abusive father meant to kidnap her and force her back under his control by whatever means necessary. An attack that had ultimately failed, despite the losses the Ravens had sustained.

It all could've been so much worse.

A sentiment that had his thoughts returning to Alexa. Last week it had been a few bruises, a busted lip. What would happen the next time her bastard of a fiancé "took care" of her? That very question was why Mav had been shadowing her ever since she'd shown up bloodied and frightened at the clubhouse. Which was how he'd known she'd locked herself out. Seeing her looking so defeated had reached inside his chest and hauled him to her side. And seeing her cry made him not care that he'd just blown his cover. He couldn't have stayed away at that point if he'd tried.

The service concluded and people around Maverick rose to their feet. Despite the evening hour, the June air hung humid and gray. Almost oppressive. The weight of it was fitting. It was as if their collective grief had taken on a physical form.

Maverick held out his hand to Bunny. With her white-blond hair and dark blue eyes, she was still as pretty as she'd ever been. And every bit as feisty. Well, usually.

Accepting his help, she gave him a sad smile and rose. Her husband, Rodeo McKeon, steadied her from her other side.

"Thanks, Maverick," she said, stepping toward the casket. She pulled a long-stem red rose out of the arrangement and brought it to her nose. A moment later, she laid it on top of the lid by itself, her hand resting there for a moment.

When she turned away, her lips trembled, and when she made eye contact with Maverick, her whole expression crumpled.

Maverick pulled her into his arms, her tears like ice in his veins. "It's gonna be okay, Mom," he said, uttering a name for her he hadn't used regularly in years. *Everybody* called his mother Bunny, and somewhere along the way it had stuck for him, too.

From behind her, Rodeo rubbed her back. Mav met the older man's gaze and saw reflected at him the same pain and regret Maverick felt. Normally, Bunny was the youngest sixty-something you'd ever meet, but the attack and Jeb's death had left her fragile. And Maverick fucking hated it. Not because he thought her shakiness wasn't warranted, but because it reminded him of another time. When Bunny's first husband—Maverick's father—had finally beaten her so badly she ended up in the hospital for days.

That had been seventeen years before when Maverick had just been a kid in high school, but not a day had gone by when he hadn't blamed himself for not realizing what was going on, not being there, not protecting her. *Oh, I just fell, hon. I just tripped/bumped my head/slipped in the shower.* He'd believed every lie, swallowed every excuse.

And damn if Alexa wasn't giving him déjà vu.

Sonofabitch.

Maverick's gaze slid over Rodeo's shoulder to the casket. *I will find a way to avenge you, Jeb. And you can believe I'll never forget.*

"I'm okay," Bunny said, wiping at her cheeks. She patted his chest. "Thanks, hon."

Rodeo gave Mav a nod that said he had her, and Maverick didn't doubt it. Not only was Rodeo one of his brothers in the Raven Riders, he was also the best thing to ever happen to Bunny.

"Are you coming to the clubhouse?" Maverick asked, trying like hell to keep the rage out of his voice. Bunny hadn't been back since the attack the week before, which was totally unlike her. Normally, she spent part of every day there, often cooking one or more meals for whichever Ravens happened to be around or drop by.

"Yeah," she said. "We'll see you there."

"Okay," he said. With a last look at Jeb's casket, Maverick turned for the drive that wound through the rolling hills of the cemetery. Motorcycles formed an unbroken wall of steel and chrome almost forty deep. The whole club had turned out to pay its respects. As it should be when a brother took his last ride.

As vice president, Maverick's bike was at the front. Normally, he'd be riding third position behind Road Captain Phoenix Creed and Dare, but the gunshots to Dare's side and arm meant that he'd only be driving four-wheel vehicles for the immediate future. So Maverick was second in line. Still standing, he brought the bike to life on a low growl. One by one, all the Ravens' bikes rumbled until the cemetery nearly vibrated with the sound. Turning to the brother beside him, Maverick waited for Phoenix's command.

Like the black bands they wore on their arms—made of

thin strips torn from a couple of Jeb's Harley T-shirts—
they had traditions they honored when one of their own
died.

A few years younger than Maverick's almost thirty-five,
Phoenix normally wore a mischievous, good-humored expression. Not today. Not when they were burying one of
Phoenix's closest friends just a month after Phoenix had
buried his cousin, too. Their road captain had taken a beating the past few weeks, and it showed in Phoenix's unusual
frown and his lack of joking around.

When everyone else had started their engines, Phoenix
finally started his own. Then he turned his throttle and
revved his engine until it roared.

Every biker except one joined in.

Roar, roar, roar, roar, roar.

The five thunderous revs lodged a knot in Maverick's
throat. Because the Last Rev was meant to alert heaven
that a biker was on his way home.

And then all the bikes quieted to a low idle—except one.
The one that had remained silent before now roared out.
Ike Young, the Tail Gunner of the procession, revved his
engine five times, as if Jeb was answering the club's call
and saying his good-byes. One last time.

When the Last Rev ended, everyone mounted their bikes
and the procession got underway.

Quietly and slowly, they made their way home—back
to the Ravens' compound on the outskirts of Frederick,
Maryland. Maverick knew he had to at least make an
appearance at the reception, though his gut had him wanting to head back to Alexa's. Because instinct said the worst
was yet to come, and experience had taught him that abusers didn't abuse just once.

Her brief reappearance into his life had reminded him
of promises he hadn't been well tending and triggered
every one of his protective instincts, not to mention stirring

up all kinds of shit inside him he thought he'd boxed up tight.

And as if Maverick hadn't already been climbing out of his skin with worry over Alexa—whether she wanted him worrying about her or not—Bunny's attack whipped up all the old guilt inside him and made him *need* to know that Alexa was okay.

Or, if need be, *ensure* that she would be okay. Whatever that took.

After all, once, he and Alexa had been tight—not just lovers, but friends. Alexa had gone from the kid sister who clearly worshipped her big brother and his best friend, to the teenager with the smart mouth and the quick wit who loved to keep him and Tyler guessing what she'd get into next, to the ambitious woman who worked two jobs to put herself through school while bearing most of the burden of taking care of her sick mother. She was giving and tough and had always made him laugh and smile—even when shit at home had made that damn difficult. All of that *plus* the fact that they were together as a couple for three years before it all fell apart, and Maverick couldn't let what'd happened to her go unaddressed.

Because she was the first and only woman he'd ever loved. The fact that she'd broken up with him and moved on without him? That didn't matter if her life was on the line.

At the very least, Maverick owed it to Tyler Harmon to take care of his little sister. After all, it wasn't like Tyler could do that job himself. And Mav had once promised Tyler he'd always look out for Alexa.

But even more than that, Maverick needed to watch out for Alexa because he'd once failed his mother when she'd been in a similar situation, and that failure ate at him a little bit every day, like a slow dripping leak of acid deep inside his veins. Even all these years later.

Then, Maverick had been young and naïve and weak. He hadn't realized all the kinds of evil that lurked in the world. But that wasn't him anymore. Now he knew. And he refused to ever make that same mistake again.

"WHAT THE HELL'S the matter with you?" Dare asked as he joined Maverick for a drink.

Maverick had been sitting at the far end of the bar in the Ravens' clubhouse for the past few hours, in the midst of the party celebrating Jeb's life but not really a part of it. The driving bass beat of a rock song blared out all around him, and people laughed and joked, but Maverick barely heard anything.

"Nothing," Mav said, staring down at his whiskey.

"I excel at moody motherfucker, remember? I know it when I see it." Dare wasn't just the club president, he was also Maverick's cousin, though for years they'd been as tight as brothers. Calling each other out on their shit went with the territory.

"The past is a pain in the ass, that's all," Maverick said.

"Well, that's the goddamned truth." Dare grimaced as he slid onto a bar stool and flagged down Blake for a drink. Jeb had been his best friend, and the prospect served up the whiskey with bleakness in his eyes. Prospects were probationary members who wore the club's cutoff jackets but without the club's colors and patch on them—those had to be earned through loyalty and dedication to the club and were a privilege of full membership.

"How you feeling?" Mav asked his cousin when Blake stepped away. Dare was only five days out from multiple gunshot wounds and surgery, but he'd thrown himself back into club business as quickly as he could. It showed in the darker-than-normal rings around his brown eyes.

"I'm feeling like I might kill the next sonofabitch who asks me how I'm feeling." Dare raked his dark hair back off his face and gave Mav a look.

And Maverick got it. He did. But that didn't mean he wasn't going to try to shoulder as much of the burden around here as he could until Dare was on his feet again. Which was why he'd already pushed off the delivery of his current custom bike order by two weeks. He'd offered the customer a twenty percent discount for his inconvenience, and that'd smoothed over any hard feelings. And Mav had enough cred built up in the business to take the hit. "Yeah, well, I won't ask how you're feeling if you don't ask me what bug crawled up my ass." He smirked and tilted out his glass.

Dare chuffed out a laugh and clinked. "I'll drink to that."

The hot bite of the whiskey felt good against the back of Maverick's throat. A couple more of these and maybe he could convince himself he didn't care about Alexa Harmon anymore. About the fact that her slick scumbag of a fiancé had hurt her. About the fact that she'd so easily dismissed Maverick earlier. About the fact that his fucking blood had been on fire in her presence. Just like old times.

Exactly. Just like old times, she'd made her choice today. And it wasn't him. Not that he'd expected anything else.

"I'd like you to call a special meeting of Church as fast as you can get it pulled together," Dare said, yanking Maverick from his thoughts. Church referred to the club's monthly membership meetings, though recent crises had them meeting more often than usual. "After the shooting at the track, we need to talk damage control where the races are concerned. And we need a plan to deal with the Iron Cross once and for all."

Maverick nodded. "Yeah, we do. A plan that involves burning their fucking world to the ground." Stock-car racing and betting were their biggest businesses, and part of the attack on the club last Friday night had happened at the Green Valley Race Track that they operated on the edge of the Ravens' huge tract of land. The Iron Cross was an up-and-coming gang in nearby Baltimore that was tryͥ to take over the city in the wake of the recent destruction of what had been Baltimore's most powerful gang. And it was more than a little likely that they'd had a hand in helping Haven's father and his men attack the Ravens. That shit couldn't go unaddressed, despite the fact that the Iron Cross denied being involved.

What the fuck else were they going to say?

"I hear you, Maverick. I only regret that I was laid up in the damn hospital and couldn't act sooner. We're not letting this go. Trust me." Dare's gaze was ice cold.

"Not your fault, D," Maverick said.

The expression on his cousin's face said he didn't agree.

Maverick cleared his throat. "Since we're on the same page, I'll put in a call to Nick Rixey in the morning to see what else he and his men might've gathered on the Iron Cross's involvement." Nick was the leader of a team of former Army Special Ops guys who were opening a security services firm in the city. The Ravens and Nick's men had worked together on several occasions now and had become tight allies.

"Good. Do that," Dare said, throwing back a gulp of whiskey. "Because whether the Iron Cross actually told Haven's father where she was or not, they tried to blackmail us to keep her whereabouts quiet, and in doing so they risked her life. You threaten one of us, you threaten all of us. That's all I need to know."

Maverick nodded, the other man's words reflecting so much about who the Ravens were and what they stood for—family, brotherhood, loyalty. They didn't usually go on the offensive, but they sure as hell defended their own. On top of that, Dare had a protective streak a mile wide, one he'd come by painfully when his father had killed his mother and brother twenty-plus years before. Add to that Mav's own father had done to Bunny, and it explained club was in the business of standing up for people who couldn't do it for themselves. But Maverick had never seen Dare as fiercely protective as he was of Haven Randall. Then again, Maverick had never seen Dare in a serious relationship before, either.

And Maverick was happy for him. He really was. The guy deserved a little slice of happiness, and after everything she'd been through, so did Haven.

Which had Maverick thinking about Alexa again, and about the fact that she deserved happiness, too. Despite her comfortable circumstances now, Alexa had grown up poor and with a mother who had issues—issues that had gotten worse when Tyler died five years ago. And Maverick felt at least some responsibility for that since Tyler had picked up his love of motorcycles from Maverick. Hell, Tyler had become a prospective member of the club at Maverick's encouragement.

On some level, Mav couldn't help but wonder if Alexa blamed him for Tyler's death. Maverick had always wondered if that hadn't been part of her reason for dumping his ass. He wouldn't blame her if she did feel that way, because even if he hadn't been responsible for Tyler's death, Maverick had sure as hell played a role in setting that particular chain of events into motion. A rock dropped into his gut as the old guilt dug its claws into his skin.

He was damn near an expert at failing those he cared about, wasn't he?

"Hey," Dare said, grimacing as he shifted on the stool. "Did you ever get around to informing Mike Renner that you were sponsoring his prospective membership?"

"Fuck," Maverick said. "No, but I'll call him in the morning." Mike Renner was a Hang-Around, or friend of the club, that the Ravens had approved for prospect status at one of their last meetings. "I know he's eager."

"Eager's good," Dare said with a smirk.

Chuckling, Maverick nodded. "Yeah." Prospects had to

put up with a lot of bullshit from fully patched members and did a lot of the club's grunt work. It could be a pain in the ass sometimes, but the process helped determine if the guy was a good fit for the club. And they'd all been there.

Jeb had been a damn good prospect. Everything had rolled right off that guy's back. He worked hard, showed up, pitched in, and did it all with a good attitude and a fucking smile. He would've made a great addition to the club. Maverick looked at Dare as an idea came to mind.

"What?" Dare asked.

"D, we should make Jeb a fully patched member," Maverick said. "Like, as an honor. In protecting Bunny's life he more than earned it."

Dare's expression was thoughtful, and he nodded. "A posthumous award. That's a damn good idea, Maverick."

"Yeah. I have them every once in a while," he said, though the humor didn't quite reach his voice. Granting Jeb full membership didn't make up for much, but it was something, and it would be one more way to make sure Jeb—and what he'd sacrificed—was never forgotten.

"I'll put it to a vote at the meeting," Dare said.

"Hey," Haven said, coming to stand alongside Dare. Though she'd come out of her shell a lot since first arriving at the Ravens' compound over a month before, she was still soft-spoken and a little shy. But quiet didn't mean spineless, not by a long shot. Maverick could easily picture her from the night of the attack on the club—crouched over Dare's unconscious body, gun drawn against anyone else who might try to hurt him. She'd killed her own father to keep him from killing Dare and kidnapping her. She'd already been well liked by the club because she was a fucking amazing cook, but now she was damn near revered.

Dare's whole demeanor changed as he turned to her. Smiling, he sat up straighter, and then he slid his hand into Haven's light brown hair and pulled her in for a kiss.

As her arms slid around his cousin's neck, Maverick found himself needing to look away. Not because he was embarrassed by the display of public affection—that was kinda par for the course around here, especially on party nights. Instead, his discomfort came from the goddamned jealousy slinking through his blood.

Maverick wanted someone who looked at him with the kind of unconditional love he read in Haven's blue eyes when she looked at Dare. And he wanted the soul-deep solace he could see on Dare's face when the guy was in Haven's presence. Maverick wanted to fucking *belong* to someone. Well, to someone who wanted to belong to him, too. Fact was, someone had owned him for years.

Alexa fucking Harmon.

"Can I ask you a question, Haven?" Maverick said, swirling the last of his whiskey in the bottom of his glass.

"Sure," she said.

Mav debated exactly what he wanted to ask and finally found the words. "If you thought someone was in trouble, in a relationship that was maybe abusive, but that person told you to keep your nose out of it, would you?" No doubt Haven would realize he was asking about Alexa since Haven had helped clean her up after Alexa had come to the clubhouse last week. Remembering the blood and bruises on Al's face still made Maverick's chest hot with rage.

"I can't speak for everyone," she finally said. "But sometimes people tell you to stay out of it because they're afraid of how hard it will be to get out of the situation. Or they're afraid that having asked for help will get back to the abuser. Or they believe that they're not worth the risk that helping them might pose to someone else. I know I felt all of those."

Dare's jaw ticked as he listened. He slid his arm around Haven's shoulders, the gesture full of reassurance.

After a moment, Dare's dark eyes cut his way. "Question is, are you okay backing off if there's a chance she's feeling even a little of that?" Dare didn't need to clarify who he was talking about. Despite how hard Maverick had worked to keep that shit buttoned up, his cousin knew what Maverick felt for Alexa.

And the answer was a total gut check. *Absofuckinglutely not.*

What the fuck was he doing sitting there? Wallowing. Instead of doing what his instincts had been telling him for over a week to do—protect Alexa. Or, at least, be ready to do so if something else happened. That's why he'd started surveilling her after she'd left the clubhouse that day, insisting what'd happened had been a misunderstanding but refusing to actually explain what kind of misunderstanding led to a banged-up face.

Maverick pushed away the not-quite-empty glass of whiskey and slid off his stool. He needed to send out a meeting alert to the brotherhood, and then he needed to get his ass to Alexa's house. He clapped Dare on his good shoulder and pressed a quick kiss to Haven's temple. "Thank you," he said to her. She gave him a shy smile as pink filtered into her cheeks.

"Hey, where's my kiss, asshole?" Dare asked.

Maverick threw a look over his shoulder and flipped Dare the bird, but the approval he saw in the other man's gaze told him he was doing the right thing.

Because Dare was right—if there was any chance that Alexa was pushing him away out of fear, Maverick couldn't stay away. She could be pissed at him. Hell, she could hate him. As long as she was safe and sound, he could stand just about anything else.

CHAPTER 4

T he air was tense and weighted as everyone filed into
the Ravens' meeting room at seven the next evening for Church. Maverick took the seat next to Dare's at
the head of the long rectangular table. The room had probably been a lounge back during the inn's heyday, which
explained the cabin-like floor-to-ceiling stone fireplace and
the exposed wooden beams on the ceiling. The Raven's
logo hung on a carved panel of wood above the mantel.

Ride. Fight. Defend.

Dare banged an old, beat-up gavel against the table and
eased into his seat. "I'm calling this meeting of Church to
order." Everyone settled into chairs at the table or along the
side walls. They had a decent-sized crowd here today.

Clearly, Maverick wasn't the only one who wanted revenge for the attack on their people and property.

"Dare, it's good to see you and Meat here and in one
piece," Bear Lowry said. Maverick nodded in agreement

with the Old Timer who also was one of the club's founders. Bear had served as the secretary/treasurer for years because Dare and Doc trusted him implicitly, not to mention he had a damn good head on his shoulder for investments.

The guys on either side of Meat, whose real name was Craig Miles, clapped him on the shoulder, and he gave a nod. The night of the attack, Haven's father had shot Meat point-blank in the abdomen to prove that he was serious about his intentions to take out innocents for every ten minutes that passed without the club delivering her up.

And the Iron Cross had been the ones to send that ass-hole their way.

Dare shifted uncomfortably in his chair, whether from his injuries or his unease at the attention, Maverick didn't know. Raking a hand through his brown hair, Dare looked down at the table, his brow furrowed. "What we faced at the track that night . . ." He shook his head. "It was unprecedented. And what you did"—he looked up, his dark gaze intense—"what *all* of you did was above and beyond. It—"

"No, D," Meat said, looking the club's president in the eyes. "It was *exactly* what we should've done. Exactly what we should *always* do. Nothing more."

The visible emotion on Dare's face reached inside Maverick's chest. Because he couldn't agree with Meat more. Maverick only wished that he could've gotten to Dare to shield him from those bullets, or at the very least gotten to Haven before she'd been forced to kill her own father to protect them both. And God knew he wished he could've kept his mother from getting hurt. Mav knew that his cousin was shouldering a shitload of guilt over all the people who'd been hurt that night. They were alike that way. Not that Maverick thought any of it was Dare's fault, because it wasn't.

Only two groups were to blame. Haven's father's crew, who were all either dead or in jail. And the Iron Cross.

Sitting at the far end of the table, Doc nodded. "Meat's got it right. This is a family. And every man here is your brother. You can *always* count on us having your back. And that goes for everyone here. That's what the Raven Riders are about. That's why we exist." Frank "Doc" Kenyon was Dare's grandfather, the club's founder, and co-owner with Dare of the Ravens' property, which the older man had inherited decades before. Doc was also Mav's uncle. With whitish hair and beard that made him a shoo-in for playing Santa for the kids among the club members' families, Doc was fiercely protective of the club and every-one in it.

So Dare came by that naturally. Mav did, too.

"That's right," Maverick said. "Now we focus on getting justice for Jeb and for everyone else who got hurt." Mur-murs of agreement circled the room. And even though his focus needed to be right here on these men, he couldn't help but think of Alexa. Because she'd been hurt, too. And Maverick hadn't yet thought of a way to make that right for her. It was eating at him like an itch he couldn't reach.

"Which brings me to some news from Baltimore," Dare said, opening the folder of intel Maverick had received from Nick Rixey. "Off the record, Nick shared that the Feds are running some kind of undercover operation targeting Bal-timore's gangs. Ongoing investigations into narcotics and especially heroin. Long story short, in the week since every-thing went down, the Feds have tightened the noose around the Iron Cross as the primary player in that market, so it's very possible the Feds are about to take them out all on their own."

"Well, that's . . . kinda fucking unsatisfying," Phoenix said.

"'Possible' isn't good enough for me," Maverick said. "And letting the Feds do it does nothing for avenging our-selves and defending our reputation."

"I agree on both counts," Dare said.

Doc sat forward in his seat. "Given everything this club's been through the past six weeks, first with the fight over at Hard Ink and then with the attack here, we do not need more good people put in harm's way." He'd been leery of getting involved with the Iron Cross in the first place. Well, they all had. Maverick sure knew he'd been. But those mother-fuckers hadn't given them much choice if they didn't want to make an enemy of a new player in the region. Turned out they had anyway. Which pretty much proved that the road to hell was paved with good intentions. "I get that the Iron Cross is a problem that has to be resolved, but if someone else is willing to do the dirty work, I say we let them."

"All due respect, Doc," Maverick said, the anger inside of him hot and thick like the June night outside. "We sit back, even if the Feds do their job here, we pretty much invite every other fucker who wants to make a name for themselves to do it on our backs. They invaded our terri-tory. Attacked our home. Hurt and killed our people."

"I agree with Maverick," Caine McKannon said, his ice-blue eyes slicing toward Dare. Low murmurs of agreement rumbled around the room. Wearing a black knit cap over black hair and with black gauges in both his ears, Caine served as the club's sergeant-at-arms, which put him in charge of rule enforcement. The guy radiated a quiet in-tensity you didn't want to cross. Maverick had *never* heard the guy raise his voice, and could only imagine what kind of pissed off he'd have to be to do so. Of the six men who made up the club's board of directors—Dare, Maverick, Bear, Phoenix, their Race Captain Jagger Locke, and Caine—Caine was by far the one Maverick knew the least, despite having known him for *years*.

"So, what are we talking about here?" Phoenix asked, face set into an unusually serious frown.

Considering glances were traded around the table until Dare finally spoke. "Here's what I suggest. We're not typically into offensive assaults. But we have to assume that the Iron Cross will keep coming at us, because they made it clear they want to push us around until they push us out as a player in the power dynamics in this area. In my view, going after them would be a defensive preemptive strike." More murmurs of agreement. "I say we make a statement that hurts them where they live—we attack their clubhouse, clean them out until they're left with nothing, and then burn their world to the ground. And if that sonofabitch of a leader Dominic gets in the way, so much the better."

"And how do you think Haven will feel about you doing that?" Doc asked.

Dare's dark gaze cut to meet his grandfather's. "This is *club* business, Doc. But if you really want to know, I told her this was the likely reality. Don't think for a minute she doesn't understand our world after the one she grew up in, nor that this is still her father's mess that needs to be cleaned up. She'd be on the back of a Harley helping us do it if she could. Haven Randall is a hundred percent behind every one of us. Always."

Maverick surveyed his brothers' faces and saw the bone-deep respect they held for Haven. By saving Dare's life, she'd more than earned it.

"So we're going after property, not bodies," Phoenix said, eyebrow arched.

"That's what I'm proposing." Dare looked from one member to the next. "Discussion?"

"It may not be a long-term solution," Caine said, eyes narrowed.

The concern echoed Maverick's own thoughts; then something else occurred to him. "But think about this. If the Feds take out the Iron Cross after we take them down, then maybe it's the best of both worlds. They're out of the picture *and* we protect our rep and make it clear that fucking with us comes at a cost. A big one."

"Exactly," Dare said with a nod, his whole face set in a frown. "Anyone else?" When the room remained silent, Dare heaved a deep breath. "Let's put it to a vote. Raise your hand if you support going after the Iron Cross." His gaze sliced through each and every one of them, because they all knew he was asking them to cross some lines. But sometimes, that shit couldn't be helped.

"Goddamnit," Doc bit out, fisting his hands on the table.

Nearly every other hand went up. Dark satisfaction rolled through Maverick's gut. Maybe that made him a terrible person. He didn't know, but so be it. Because he'd seen two good friends shot and hospitalized, another murdered, and his own mother bound and gagged and stuffed in the back of a car. And that was all besides the harm done to the club's reputation and livelihood.

Dare let the weight of their decision hang in the air for a long moment before he spoke again. "We need to be the ones to do this, but I want the Hard Ink team to help strategize, especially since we're using intel they collected. We good with that?" Nods all around. Dare placed a call and let the ringing sound out on speakerphone.

Nick's voice mail answered, and Dare left a message. "Nick, I need your help ASAP. Gimme a call."

"Fuck, I hate waiting," Jagger said, his fingers moving in a perpetual progression of invisible guitar chords against the table top. Their race captain was brilliant with his hands—musical instructions, engines, it didn't matter—and was nearly single-handedly responsible for every good thing that happened down at the racetrack. A big fucking deal since that provided the club's main income stream.

"Well, we have other business to pass the time," Dare said. "Maverick came up with something else we can do to honor Jeb. Mav?"

Nodding, Mav glanced around at all his brothers. "I

move that we posthumously vote Jeb Fowler in as a fully patched member. He gave his life for my mother, for Rodeo's wife. He more than earned his place among us."

The group's discussion was quick and in full agreement, and then Dare put it to a vote. "All in favor?" Dare asked.

Without a word, Maverick rose to his feet. Then Rodeo did. Then Meat and Bear and all the others until every man in the room stood in honor of their fallen brother. A knot lodged in Mav's throat—pride that these men were his family.

Dare stood, too. "It's unanimous. Jeb Fowler is a fully patched member of the Raven Riders Motorcycle Club."

Silence hung thick and laden with emotion for a long moment, because the words highlighted the fucking tragedy of it all, and then Bear's quiet voice broke the tension. "I'll get his picture up," he said, referring to the wall of honor in the clubhouse's lounge where photographs of every member hung.

"Yeah," Dare said, sitting again. "That's good." Everyone else sat, too, and for a moment, quiet conversations filled the room. Dare banged the gavel, his gaze latching onto his phone like he could will it to ring. "We've got two more issues to discuss. First, Phoenix and Caine, a heads-up that county social services has reached out to us with a new protective assignment. I e-mailed you all the information before the meeting. Assess and see what the situation is going to require."

As the road captain and sergeant-at-arms, respectively, Phoenix and Caine took point on organizing the club's protective efforts, whether the cases came the Ravens' way through social services, the sheriffs' office, or local people who knew what the Ravens were willing to do for those who couldn't protect themselves.

"What are the basics?" Phoenix asked.

"It's a child abuse situation," Dare said, his expression

grim. "The mother's getting heat from several directions to keep it quiet."

"We'll handle it," Caine bit out, his tone like ice.

"Good." Dare slapped the folder closed in front of him and sighed. "Last thing. We've got a major fucking PR problem at the racetrack now following the shootings. Given that we missed five weeks of racing while we were tied up in Baltimore, and then a sixth week this weekend as the police wrap up their investigation, we can't allow our income stream to be further compromised. Ticket sales are down, and even though the club was cleared of wrongdoing, the press hasn't helped the situation with their continued coverage of what happened. So we need to stop the hemorrhage and restore the public's confidence in the safety of our events. To that end, Jagger has an idea he wants to propose."

Jagger raked his hands through the length of his brown hair, his gaze fixed on a sheet of paper in front of him. "So, this idea comes from the position of you gotta spend money to make money."

"How much money?" Bear asked, his voice skeptical.

Jagger shoved the paper in the treasurer's direction. "I'm proposing we do a big family weekend with half-price adult tickets, free tickets for kids under sixteen, and paid uniformed security. A carnival, a dunking booth, a fucking petting zoo. We get all the local businesses in here with their food trucks which motivates them to promote the event, too. With no vendor fees. Maybe we give away some prizes of season passes or photo ops with drivers. We go all out to get people here and make them see there's nothing to worry about. And, if we wanted to be really ambitious about it—"

"This number is pretty damn ambitious already," Bear said, studying Jagger's proposal.

Jagger shrugged. "Yeah, it is, but if we think of it as

buying a publicity campaign and not giving a bunch of shit away for free, I think it could be worth it."

Nodding, Maverick agreed with Jagger's thinking. Having lived in Frederick his whole life, Mav knew that they were going to have to make amends with the community. Frankly, he didn't have a problem with that. The Ravens took care of the local community and the town took care of the Ravens in return. Well, most of the town did, anyway.

They had a couple of perpetual thorns in their side. Like fucking Slater, who hated them because he wanted to develop the prime real estate they held. And because the Ravens had once successfully campaigned against one of his developments on environmentally fragile land adjacent to their own that might've impacted the zoning for their races. And because Maverick had been balls deep inside his wife-to-be. Maverick wasn't sure which one of those made Slater hate them more. But, mostly, the Ravens had a symbiotic relationship with their neighbors, one that needed to be nurtured.

"So, what would be even more ambitious than all of that?" Mav asked.

"Donating all profits from the weekend to a local charity," Jagger said. Bear looked a little like he might have a heart attack.

"How quickly could all that be pulled together?" Dare asked. They couldn't wait too many weekends to get back up to their regular numbers, that much was clear.

"I've got a carnival company available the last Thursday through Saturday of the month, which would give us two weeks to plan."

The first thought that Maverick had was *perfect*.

The second? That Saturday was Alexa's wedding day. For fuck's sake. At least he'd have something to do besides sit around and resist driving to the church so he could raise his hand when the preacher asked if anyone had any reasons why the happy couple shouldn't marry.

Conversation pretty quickly fell in support of Jagger's idea. The club had a rainy-day fund for exactly this kind of thing. Protecting their livelihood was more than a good enough reason to dip into it. Without their activities at the Green Valley Race Track, things would get tight fast. Certainly, the funding for their protective mission would largely disappear.

"The only hitch is that the county wants to move up our annual inspection before the event. I actually think it's a good idea. Get our permits and paperwork in order. Have the county sign off that everything is as it should be," Jagger said.

"Sounds like one more thing in our favor," Dare said. "Let's vote." The vote was overwhelmingly in favor.

"I'll get on it," Jagger said.

"Talk to Haven," Dare said. "Bet she'd make a bunch of stuff for a bake sale."

Jagger winked. "Already did, and she already agreed." Dare grinned, pride clear on the man's face.

"Can I just buy everything she makes now?" Phoenix asked, feigning as if he was taking out his wallet. Maverick laughed, and everyone else did, too. You never had a better cookie or cinnamon bun than what Haven made, that was for sure. And damn, it was good to hear everyone just laughing and shooting the shit. With everything they'd been through, they hadn't had nearly enough of that lately.

"You can," Dare said. "But I have it on good authority that she, Bunny, and Cora are making dinner for us, so—"

A cell phone rang out, immediately silencing the ruckus that had risen up in the room. Dare's expression revealed who it was before he even answered. "Nick, thanks for calling back so fast."

"Of course," he said, his voice sounding out through the speaker. "Sounded urgent."

"It is," Dare said. "I need to know if your contact has specifics on the Iron Cross's whereabouts. Hangouts, headquarters, meeting places, that kind of thing."

"Marz actually just got some new intel from our guy this morning." Nick spoke to someone on his end for a minute. "He's emailing it to you right now. Why? What's going on?"

"I won't draw this out," Dare said. "We're going after the Iron Cross. To be clear, we don't want you involved, but we'd appreciate your team's thoughts on carrying it out."

Silence for a long moment. "Shit, okay," Nick said. "I can't say that I blame you, but this is complicated by the Feds. They have undercover agents on the inside."

"Then you need to talk to your contact and get them out of there before it goes down. We're not going for body count but that doesn't mean there won't be collateral," Dare said, echoing Maverick's own thoughts. "Just telling it straight up."

"I hear you. I'm just not sure how much sway I have, Dare." The concern was clear in Nick's voice.

"I know you understand honor, justice, and loyalty, Nick. I've seen you live by it. Fight for it. Be willing to die for it. We might not have worn a uniform, but our code's not all that different." Dare's expression was fierce, unyielding. Maverick couldn't help but nod.

"Fuck, all right. I'll see what I can do. And I'll talk to the team and get you some thoughts."

"Good. And Nick? Don't wait. We're riding on this as soon as possible."

They hung up, and Dare tossed his phone to the table. "Board members and anyone else who can stick around to plan this thing out, stay here. Everyone else is dismissed. But be prepared to ride within the next twenty-four to forty-eight. We'll stay in touch." Eight members remained after the others filed out, and Dare nodded to the door. "Let's head to my office and take a look at what Nick sent."

It turned out to be gold.

Standing behind Dare's desk chair while his cousin opened files revealing locations, layouts, numbers, and more, Maverick already felt the adrenaline of the coming fight surging through his blood.

Dare sat back in his chair, his gaze glued to the monitor. "Their headquarters is in the middle of a largely abandoned industrial area right on the water, and they're not going to be there tomorrow night because they've got some big deal going down that the Feds are focused on."

"That's fucking *perfect*," Maverick said. For what they had planned, it was exactly what they needed.

"Jesus, if I was a religious man I might almost say this was providence," Phoenix said. Everyone nodded.

"Moving this fast makes me itchy as hell," Caine said in a quiet voice. "But we might not get this kind of opening again."

"The faster we get it done, the better," Dare said. "Maximum impact with minimum possible risk."

"Unless everything goes tits up," Jagger said.

"As tits are wont to do," Phoenix agreed.

Hands clasped over his belly, Dare nodded. "Then we spend tonight and tomorrow working on contingencies. But otherwise, let's get the word out to all the brothers." He peered up at Maverick. "We ride tomorrow night."

Satisfaction was a tight coil in Mav's gut. "This is the right call, D."

His cousin nodded, and then he looked back to the open documents on the computer screen. "I know. I just hope it doesn't cost us too much, because I'm not sure how much more we can stand to lose."

CHAPTER 5

"Why are you up so early?" Grant asked, coming up behind Alexa where she stood at the bathroom mirror carefully brushing on mascara. His arms wrapped around her stomach.

"This is the morning I have to take my mom to her doctor's appointment," she said, capping the tube.

"Mmm, that's right," Grant said, something that sounded like disappointment in his tone. He was estranged from his parents and had been for way longer than she'd known him, though he wouldn't talk about why so she didn't know what'd happened. But it meant he didn't really get her relationship with her mother. Mostly, he tolerated it. He settled his chin on her shoulder, and it was possible that the phrase *tall, dark, and handsome* had been coined just for him. Even just out of bed he was undeniably attractive, with his square jaw, his classical profile, his calculating brown eyes, and his stylishly cut short brown hair. "You came to bed too late."

"I know," she said, feeling the sleepy weight of having gone to sleep after two in the morning. "I'm sorry. I was working on my project. A rough draft is due two weeks after the wedding, so I'm trying to get ahead so most of it is done beforehand."

His hands roamed up to palm her breasts through her shirt. Pressing a kiss against the side of her throat, he said, "I need you."

Alexa watched him in the mirror, kissing her, grabbing her, rubbing against her. In another moment, it might've been sexy, but she didn't have time to have sex, which he would know if he remembered any of the three times she'd told him that she'd be late to work on Friday morning because of her mother's appointment. And now he was putting her in the position of turning him down, which he wouldn't like. Which he *never* liked.

She leaned into his kiss and put on a smile. "I would like nothing more than to be with you, but I'll be late."

He hugged her harder, grinding himself into her rear, and sucked her earlobe into his mouth. "We'll be quick." His hands slid down to her skirt and grasped it. Slowly, he worked it up.

"Grant," she said, her tone full of regret, a niggle of dread stirring in her belly.

He rucked her skirt up around her waist. Pushed her panties down. Slipped his fingers between her thighs.

"Honey, this feels good, but I'm gonna be late," she said, gently grasping his wrist, trying to still his movements.

"You've got time," he said, twisting his wrist out of her hold. "Her appointment isn't for an hour and a half."

So he *did* remember. "I know, but you know how my mother is." Her mother had anxiety about all kinds of things, including leaving the house and going to the doctor, which meant she was going to need lots of coaxing and reassuring just to get her out the door. There was no such thing as rushing Alexa's mother to do anything.

He pressed his fingers more firmly against her core, firm enough that the sensation went from arousing to uncomfortable. "Grant—"

"Fine," he said, stepping away so abruptly that Alexa stumbled back a step. Without another word, he opened the glass shower door and turned on the water.

Something that felt inexplicably like humiliation rolled through her as she awkwardly pulled her panties into place and smoothed down her skirt. Quickly, she bagged up the last of her makeup, knowing he didn't like anything out of place. "I'm sorry. Please don't be mad. It's just my schedule . . ."

"I know," he said, not sounding particularly convinced. Or appeased.

She walked to him and kissed his bare shoulder, torn between feeling guilty for upsetting him and feeling upset for having to apologize. "I promise to make it up to you tonight," she said, making her words upbeat and playful. Flirtatious. Sometimes stroking his ego was enough to make his mood rebound and smooth things over.

He looked at her, one eyebrow arched, his expression fierce, masculine, intense. "Yeah?"

She smiled, wanting so much to make him happy again, needing so much to be enough for him. Just as she was. "Yeah. Okay?"

For a long moment, he just stared at her. Then, in one quick motion, he turned, grasped the back of her neck, and hauled her into him. The kiss was aggressive, claiming, possessive. His hold was tight, his mouth hard, his tongue penetrating. Grant liked to be rough, and she usually found pleasure in it, too. Though lately, that's all their lovemaking ever was—rough, aggressive, quick. The slow, exploring, sensual sex they'd sometimes had earlier in their relationship had largely disappeared from his repertoire. Not that she'd complained. Because she couldn't begin to imagine how she'd ask for something different in bed. There was almost no chance he'd take it as anything but criticism.

Alexa barely had time to react to it before Grant released her again. "You *better*." The corners of his mouth tilted upward, like he was teasing, but his eyes were dead serious.

She ignored his eyes and kept up with the flirtation. "You know I will."

He grinned, and it was the smile that had helped win her over to him years before, when he'd pursued her maybe harder than any man ever had. The more she'd held out—worrying over the fact that he owned the company she worked for, then as an administrative assistant for a sales manager several levels down the corporate chain—the more Grant seemed to want her. "I'll look forward to that, Alexa." He dropped his boxers and stepped into the shower, his gaze latched onto her.

"Good," she said, giving him a smile and a sultry look. Playfully, she blew him a kiss. And then she was out of the bathroom and closing the door between them.

And feeling the oddest sensation of . . . relief.

Ugh. It was just the stress of dealing with her mother and knowing it wasn't going to be easy, on top of being late to work and knowing how that was going to make the rest of her day a scramble to catch up. Nothing more. Besides, no one liked starting out their day in a tiff with their partner. She was just relieved that things seemed okay between them now.

In the foyer mirror, she fixed her lipstick, and then she grabbed her purse and made her way to the garage. The Acura SUV she drove was another of her many gifts from Grant. She'd never minded the old Toyota sedan she'd driven for years—in fact, she'd been proud of the fact that she'd bought it and paid it off entirely with her own money. But a year ago, she'd finally given into Grant's insistence that she needed something safer and nicer and accepted his gift of a car.

As she backed out of the driveway, her phone dinged an

incoming message. She braked and grabbed the cell, then brought the screen to life.

MAVERICK: Can't stop thinking of you, Al. Want you to be okay.

On a gasp, she did a scan of the neighborhood around her, but didn't see Maverick's motorcycle or the old pickup he had. Or anything else that looked out of place in the upscale Slater Estates.

Heart racing in her chest, she stared at the text unsure what to do. Because she'd pushed him away, and here he was still trying to take care of her. After what'd happened in the bathroom just now, the point of comparison wasn't a comfortable one. And it meant a lot. It meant . . . maybe even more than it should.

Which made it hard to know how to respond.

She *should* just delete the message and pretend she never got it. But instead she found herself wanting to keep it, wanting to be able to reread it, wanting to know it was there. She slipped her phone back in her purse and put her car into reverse again.

Maybe Maverick would hear her silence and stay away. Just like she'd asked.

Is that really what you want? a little voice whispered inside her.

It didn't matter. This was about what was right. Because if Grant ever found out that Maverick had been inside their house, let alone that he was texting her, she was certain there wouldn't be much she could do to smooth that over.

On a sigh, she deleted that message after all.

FROM OUTSIDE, THE house appeared perfectly normal. A brick-and-siding rancher on a quiet street in a quiet neighborhood. It was a house Grant had bought and renovated to flip—but when the trailer where Alexa had grown up got condemned as uninhabitable, Grant had done what he always did and came to their rescue after Alexa had promised she wouldn't let his house get so bad. Grant agreed in part because he said he couldn't stand to see the mother of his soon-to-be wife living in squalor.

So her mother had been living here, rent free, for almost two years. Though part of Alexa felt bad that Grant was supporting her mom this way, his help ensured that she lived in a nice, safe place and allowed Alexa to cover the food and medical expenses her mother's disability checks couldn't.

It would've been so much harder to support her mom alone, even with her salary and the remainder of Tyler's small life insurance policy. With that, Alexa covered what she needed for her mom, paid for her own tuition, and saved as much as she could in case of emergency.

At the front door, Alexa took a deep breath and braced herself for how bad it might've gotten since her last visit two weeks before—she hadn't come the previous week because of how fresh the marks from her fall had still been on her face. She knocked twice and opened the door. "Mom? I'm here."

"In the kitchen," her mother called.

Alexa closed the door behind her and stepped from the small, tidy foyer—the foyer was *always* tidy to keep up appearances—into the living room. Her shoulders fell. The piles were . . . everywhere. Piles of stuff. *All kinds* of stuff. Waist-high and worse. Clothing. Boxes of pictures and keepsakes. Used furniture. Lamps. Pictures and mirrors that weren't hung and would never get hung. Garage sale and flea market finds, some of them not even taken out of the bag—because it seemed to be the acquiring and possessing of stuff—rather than the actual items themselves—that her mother prized and needed.

Her mom called what she did collecting, and she considered herself a pack rat. But, really, Alexa's mother was a hoarder. Had been for as long as Alexa could remember. Her mother hoarded everything and anything to fill the empty spaces inside her—empty spaces caused by her mother dying when she was young, her husband leaving her, and her only son dying in a motorcycle accident.

Wearing an old stained house robe, Cynthia Harmon came into the living room from the kitchen on the opposite side of the room. "Don't look like that. It's not so bad," she said. She ran her fingers self-consciously over unkempt shoulder-length gray-brown hair. Wrinkles cut into her plump fifty-eight-year-old face. She walked a little stooped over, the result of being really overweight and having a bad back she always complained was sore. Anxiety and hoarding and irregular stints on antidepressants hadn't been kind to her.

Queasiness curled into Alexa's stomach. How had the piles in here grown *so much* in just the last two weeks? *This* was why Alexa tried to get over here for at least a few hours every Saturday . . . She shook her head, refusing to get sucked into an argument about the house the second she walked through the door. "Why aren't you dressed? We need to leave soon."

Carefully picking her steps, her mother made her way through a narrow path lined with stacks of newspapers, magazines, junk mail, and years and years' worth of photo albums, to her favorite recliner and sat down. Alexa couldn't remember a time when her mother didn't keep herself surrounded by those photographs. "I was thinking I might not feel up to going today." She sniffed and pushed herself back in the overstuffed chair, almost knocking over a full ashtray resting on the arm.

Alexa wasn't surprised by her mother's words—it was normal to have to convince her to do things she needed to do. But offer to take her to a yard sale or a flea market or an after-Christmas sale and she was dressed and ready to go faster than you could blink. "Mom, you need to go. We already canceled this appointment once, and I've scheduled off work this morning to take you. I'll choose an outfit for you if that will help," she said, moving farther into the room toward the hallway that ran to the bedrooms.

"No, I don't want you to do that," her mother said, shooting out of her chair. The ashtray toppled over onto a stack of newspapers. "I don't want you back there. I don't need you to pick my clothes."

Alexa frowned and gingerly stepped out of the way so her mom could get around her, and nearly tripped over the broken poles of a lamp as she did so. Making decisions as simple as what to wear sometimes caused Mom a great deal of difficulty, so her strident refusal to let Alexa help probably meant her bedroom was as bad as the living room. Or worse. Alexa had been so busy getting settled into Grant's house—well, *their* house now—that she hadn't spent the time she usually did over here cleaning and trying to cull through the piles. It was only through Alexa's constant battles with her mother that the place had remained as livable as it was for as long as it had. Left to her own devices, her mother would've filled the place floor-to-ceiling by now. Just like when Alexa and Tyler were kids.

It was why her father had left them when Alexa was almost nine and Tyler was thirteen. Their dad hadn't been able to deal with the hoarding. Alexa could still remember them fighting about it. After each new loss, it just got worse.

"Have you eaten breakfast?" Alexa asked. Entering the kitchen, she cursed under her breath as a rancid smell hit her smack in the face. Dirty dishes filled the sink and spilled over onto the adjacent counter. She *hoped* it was just days' old food causing the smell and not a dead mouse somewhere.

"Yes," her mother called back.

Alexa opened the refrigerator, which was emptier than she usually let it get. She mentally added a grocery trip to her to-do list for the weekend. "What did you eat?" she asked loud enough for her mother to hear.

"A frozen breakfast. Now get out of my fridge," came the agitated reply.

Rolling her eyes, Alexa closed the bottom door and opened the upper freezer door. A few frozen meals remained. She hated that her mother's diet consisted largely of microwavable food, but considering that the stove was often covered in crap—like today, for instance, when there was a huge bag of . . . something sitting on it, the microwave was often the only accessible means she had of cooking anyway.

Between her mother's habit of stacking things on the stove and her smoking, Alexa was terrified that her mom was going to accidentally start a fire and get trapped inside the blaze by the mountains of junk. A fire had broken out in their place when Alexa was fifteen. Luckily, Tyler and Maverick had been at the house that day and had been able to put it out before it damaged much more than the kitchen, but Alexa still sometimes had nightmares about it. Sighing, she lifted the bag off the stove and put it on the floor.

"Now it's in the way." Her mother appeared in the kitchen doorway wearing a floor-length black maxi dress and a pair of flip-flops. She'd pulled her hair into a neat, low ponytail and put on a pair of earrings and a matching necklace.

"It's not safe to put things on the stove like that," Alexa said.

Waving a hand, Mom shook her head. "It's not like the stove can magically turn itself on."

Alexa didn't take the bait. "Better safe than sorry, that's all. Unfortunately, I don't have time to do it today, but tomorrow I will come back with groceries and do a little cleaning for you." *Do a little cleaning* was code word for *get rid of as much stuff as I can without causing you to have a panic attack*, and her mother knew it.

"You don't have to do that," her mother said as she tried to stack a few of the dirty dishes from the counter into the too-full sink.

"You know I don't mind," Alexa said. It wasn't exactly the truth. There had been a time when she first moved out of her mother's house when she'd sworn to never deal with hoarding again. As a kid, not even her bedroom had been safe from storing the unneeded and unwanted things her mother brought home. At one point, she'd lost the use of her bedroom closet because she'd put all the stuff her mother kept dropping into her room in there until it was filled to the top.

"Still, I don't need you to take care of me. I'm fine on my own. Always have been." Mom shuffled to the kitchen table and retrieved her purse from the back of a chair. Grocery bags filled with things Alexa couldn't make out buried the table next to the chair.

Her mom's words were a lie and they both knew that, too. "Well, I like to take care of you, so it's no problem. You letting me help makes me happy."

For just a moment, her mother gave her the softest, most sincere smile. "You're a good girl."

"I try, Mom."

"I know." Her mother came right up to her and did something she didn't do often—she hugged Alexa. "My baby."

Closing her eyes, Alexa soaked in the unusual show of affection. After Tyler died, her mom had become anxious about being touched. She only seemed to tolerate it from people she knew well, and even then, she allowed it infrequently. Just another of the issues that had manifested as she'd tried to cope with Ty's loss. Unlike her mother, Alexa never had the luxury of falling apart because someone always had to hold Cynthia Harmon together. More often than not, even when Tyler had still lived, it had been her.

"You ready?" Alexa asked quietly.

"I hate doctors," Mom said, pulling away.

Alexa nodded. "I know you do."

"But whatever. I'm ready. The sooner we leave, the sooner we get back. I don't want to miss my shows." As she moved toward the kitchen doorway, her purse caught a cracker box stacked in a recycling bin on the floor, causing an avalanche. "Just leave it," she said when Alexa went to right the pile.

"Okay," Alexa said. She stepped over the mess. She could deal with it tomorrow. Besides, there were only so many battles she was willing to fight today.

CHAPTER 6

The Ravens rolled into Baltimore under the cover of darkness on Friday night, the warm, humid air crackling with the electricity of an approaching summer storm. They'd ridden in six groups of five, each set of riders set to converge on one of two agreed-upon meeting points from different directions to hopefully make their approach less noteworthy. Maverick wasn't usually one to believe in fate or any of that bullshit, but it was at least lucky that the weather might offer them some additional cover.

Maverick pulled his Harley into an underground parking garage about four blocks from their target, the Iron Cross headquarters, joining two groups that had arrived before his. A box truck waited nearby to carry any acquisitions home. Their engines rumbled inside the subterranean space, but it was far enough away to be secure, to give them a place to wait, and to make sure their efforts were coordinated with the team meeting in the second location.

Their plan wasn't particularly sophisticated—they'd converge at one time on the location from two different directions. Infiltrate the building via multiple entrances, acquire any assets inside, and then set the place on fire, leaving the Iron Cross with nothing and pulling the rug out from underneath their efforts to take control of the city's underworld. More than that, their loss of power would encourage the city's other criminal elements to pick them off like sitting ducks—exactly what'd happened to the Church Gang. Hopefully the Feds would take care of the rest. And if they didn't, the Ravens just might have to come back for more. And put these fuckers to bed once and for all.

Maverick dismounted as Dare did. They tugged off their helmets and joined the guys milling about at one end of the lot.

The cold, hard press of his handgun in the small of his back felt too damn familiar. He usually only carried when they were actively involved in a protective situation with a client, but lately it'd been one shit storm after another that'd demanded they ride hot. It was hard as hell in Maryland to get a license to carry, but the Ravens had a friend and ally in the sheriff's department who'd helped a number of them get a permit over the years because of the protective work the club did. Not that a permit would've been important for a night like this, because carrying without one would be the least of the lines they were crossing.

"The storm will work in our favor," Mav said.

"I was thinking the same thing," Dare said, wincing and holding his arm close to his side. Maverick was worried about the guy. His injuries and surgery were too damn recent and he wasn't supposed to be riding, but Dare wouldn't hear of staying behind or driving his truck. Mav couldn't really blame him on either account. "Shit, hold on." On a grimace, Dare yanked his cell out of the pocket of his cut. "Nick, not a good time, man," he said by way of answering.

Maverick frowned.

"*What?*" Dare whipped around to look at the entrance through which they'd all come. "Who?" Pause. "Sonofabitch." Another pause, and the adrenaline Maverick had been riding all day turned pause by pause into anger. What the fuck was Nick doing? "I'm not making any promises." Dare hung up, his hand going as if to tug at his hair, an old habit, despite the fact that it was covered by a black bandana.

"What the hell was that?" Maverick asked, the guys circling around them.

"We're about to have company," Dare said. The words were hardly out of his mouth before a nondescript sedan eased down the ramp and into the level where they were. Raindrops had pebbled on the car's surface, evidence that the storm was starting, which should've been perfect. Maverick bit out a curse and wondered what the hell was coming at them now.

The car parked nearby, and a single man got out. Maverick peered into the car, but didn't see anyone else.

"Chen," Dare said as the man approached. Navy pants, white button-down, short brown hair, the guy's looks were total Middle America.

"Who?" Maverick asked, heaving an impatient breath. "Dude, we don't have time for this."

"Well, you'll be making it, Mr. Rylan," the man said, his voice even, neutral, dispassionate.

Maverick's eyes narrowed. "Do I know you?"

"No," Dare said on a sigh. "But he knows us. Don't you, Mr. Chen?"

"Indeed. Dare, good to see you again." Chen gave a nod.

"Somebody want to explain what the fuck's going on right now?" Phoenix said.

"Meet the Hard Ink team's contact," Dare said, looking over his shoulder at the gathered Ravens. "I met him at the end of their investigation."

This guy was from the CIA? Well, fuck. This was going to be a pain in the ass, no doubt.

"So, what, did Nick tell you where to find us? Or did you strong-arm that information out of him?" Phoenix asked. Maverick nodded, his gut not yet sure who to be pissed at in all this. Thunder rumbled loud enough for the sound to reach them.

"Nick passed on your message about getting my men out, but we've been watching you since the assault on your place last week. Figured it was only a matter of time before you responded." Chen laced his hands in front of him. The guy didn't look like he could hurt a flea, but Maverick had a strange feeling that was a façade. He *wanted* to be under- estimated, to be thought little of, and maybe not to be thought of at all.

"And you're here now, why exactly?" Maverick asked, planting his hands on his hips.

"To ask you to stand down."

All hell broke loose behind him, and Maverick under- stood the rage and aggression washing off the other men. He felt it, too.

Chen held up a hand. "Not for good. Temporarily. Hope- fully just a few hours."

Dare crossed his arms, his face set in a deep scowl. "Ex- plain why we should even consider waiting."

Maverick nearly growled in frustration. "D—"

"Hold on, Maverick." Dare put a hand to his chest. "We should at least hear him out."

"Thank you," Chen said. "You're going to want to hear this since your intel is already outdated."

Fucking hell. Mav traded an agitated glance with Dare.

"Welcome to tits up," Phoenix bit out.

Chen ignored the comment. "The Iron Cross has moved the location of their deal to their headquarters. Everyone will be converging there within the next fifteen to thirty. We're not sure what's behind the switch because communication with our agents is limited. If you go charging in now, you risk an all-out gang war and we lose our shot at acquiring the intelligence our investigation needs. An investigation that would be near to your heart, Dare, I should think."

"Meaning?" Dare asked. A crack of thunder split the awkward silence.

"The Iron Cross hasn't just picked up the Church Gang's heroin activities. They're reviving their human trafficking trade, too. Tonight's deal is their first sale and our shot at blowing this ring apart. And we have good reason to believe we have what we need to do just that. You strike now, and we lose intel on the players involved and the chance to rescue those women."

"Fuck," Maverick bit out. That tugged just as hard as his conscience as it likely did at Dare's. Especially given that the now-destroyed Church Gang had kidnapped Haven and her best friend, Cora. Anything might've happened to those two, women who'd become an important part of the Ravens' community, if the Hard Ink team hadn't stumbled upon them during their investigation weeks ago. So this hit too close to home.

"Exactly," Chen said.

"Where are the women now?" Dare asked.

"Presumably in transport but we don't know from where," Chen said. "So here's what I propose. Wait until I get the signal from my men that they're clear and have the women, intelligence, and evidence we need. When the club empties out later tonight, you do your thing."

Maverick's mind chewed on this new plan, not bothering to wonder how this guy knew their intentions. He was clearly one step ahead of them. Waiting sucked, but if it ensured their own safety *and* helping a group of innocents, what choice did they have? Though something about this bugged him . . . "Why are you willing to allow us to do anything here?"

Chen turned that too-observant gaze on Mav. "Shared liability. The more someone else does to take them out, the less my shop has to do."

"I thought the CIA wasn't supposed to do this shit inside the U.S. at all," Phoenix said, scowling.

Chen shrugged and gave him a droll stare. "I work for the government."

"And the government sanctions . . . this?" Phoenix asked, the arch of the eyebrow making the scar on the side of his face look more severe.

"The world's a complicated place, Mr. Creed. Given what happened to your cousin and your friend recently, I think you'd know that as well as anyone. These are bad men who want to be worse. And they're involved in more than I'm even sharing. They're on a crash course with fate one way or the other. Let's leave it at that."

"So, what? We're partners now?" Phoenix asked, arms crossed.

Chen shrugged with one shoulder. "In a manner of speaking."

Chen's words brought Maverick around more and more. The Ravens could help these women. They'd have the cover and assistance Chen and his men could provide. And it all still achieved their objectives. Mav turned to Dare. "I hate it, but I think we gotta wait."

Dare nodded and nailed Chen with a stare. "We'll wait. But this needs to happen tonight. We want to use the cover of the storm, and we want to be fast asleep in our beds well before dawn." He arched a brow. Thunder rumbled again as if to emphasize the point.

"I think that can be accomplished," Chen said with a nod.

"Given we're stretching this out now, you got a way to keep the police out of the situation until we're clear?" Maverick asked.

"Yes," Chen said, offering nothing more. Well. There ya go.

"Fine," Dare said. "We'll play it your way. For now. But if things don't go down like you said, we're still doing this. So you keep up your end of the bargain, and we'll keep up ours."

THE SIGNAL FINALLY came at quarter after one.

"We're about to be clear," Chen called from where he'd been sitting in the driver's seat of his car. "Get the word to your men. There might be a few Iron Cross left behind but it broke up about a half hour ago."

"Doing it right now," Dare called, his face already in his phone.

"Jesus," Maverick said, shaking off the lethargy that hours of waiting had caused. Not hard, because the imminence of the fight fired up his adrenaline again. A few Iron Cross was worse than they'd hoped but better than if they'd gone in there hours before with the wrong intelligence. All around him, last-minute plans were being confirmed, and men were mounting up, checking their weapons, and starting their engines. He turned to Dare, gingerly straddling his ride. "D, for real. Be careful." Maverick nailed him with a stare.

"I hear you," he said.

Maverick grasped his cousin's good shoulder. "I'm serious, Dare. It's storming like a motherfucker, we're about to ride into God knows what, and you have someone to go home to." The sentiment made him think of Alexa, even though she wasn't his. Still, he had promises to honor—promises he wouldn't be able to keep if he got his ass killed tonight. And the thought of never seeing Alexa made him fucking *ache*. How had she gotten so far beneath his skin again in so few days? Or maybe she'd always been there, and he'd just been ignoring it.

"I *hear* you. And we all do. I'll be careful." Dare tugged his helmet on, the action clearly causing him pain.

Stubborn bastard. Family trait, though, wasn't it?

Cursing under his breath, Maverick made for his own ride. The Night Rod came to life underneath him, the rumble of the engine sounding like an old friend saying hello.

Phoenix and Dare led them out, headlights dark, the echo of their collective engines drowning out the storm raging outside. And then they were out in it, rain lashing at them and pretty much instantly soaking through Maverick's jeans and shirt. The visor on his helmet kept his eyes clear and hid his face, too, but the rain still limited his vision through the shield. His cut grew wet and heavy on his shoulders, but Mav didn't mind. He liked the reminder of who he was and why they were doing this tonight.

Within a few minutes, they were in position in hiding places along the derelict street and around the edge of the waterfront compound, surveying the site and preparing to converge. The storm would no doubt prove a lifesaver, because there was plenty of evidence of unfriendlies on site. Four cars sat between his position and the building, and two Hummers sat close to a side entrance. More problematic, three men hung by the water at the back door of the long two-story building covered in old white siding. The remains of ancient signage under an old metal lamp revealed that the place had once housed some sort of shipping facility. The deluge obscured everything else.

Mav's heart was a freight train in his chest as he positioned the semiautomatic he'd had stowed in his saddlebag. How ironic that this was one of the weapons they'd taken off the Church Gang weeks before and that the Iron Cross had more recently tried to twist their arms into selling to them. Fuckers. Time seemed to drag out as he glanced between his cell and the warehouse before him, waiting for Dare to give the signal.

His cell buzzed in his hand. Finally. Dare's command simply read, *MOVE IN*.

Maverick took off, moving fast and low, pausing for cover where he could—at a fence, behind one of the cars. He was aware of the movement of the others only because he knew they were there. Otherwise, the rain was doing what they'd hoped and cloaking their approach as they tightened the noose around the building.

This was the part that was going to suck. Crossing the big open stretch between the last of the cars and the building. Surveying the wide expanse again, Maverick double-checked the position of the men by the water and found them still seemingly oblivious. Which meant, fuck it, time to go.

He cut around the bumper and broke into a sprint, weapon in hand and at the ready.

Boom.

Maverick paused, wondering—

BoomboomBOOM!

The shock wave of the explosion knocked Maverick back on his ass. He landed hard, his head cracking against the pavement and making his ears ring. A fireball rose to the sky as debris launched into the air, falling into the water and the parking lot all around him.

"Jesus Christ," Maverick said, dodging a flaming board that landed too fucking close for comfort. Heart in his throat, his brain slowly came back online. He found the weapon he'd dropped and surveyed the scene like he was stepping out of a fog, just able to make out some of his brothers' movement through the deluge. Oxygen-stealing heat roared off the blaze like an impenetrable wall, the fire engulfing nearly the whole structure, particularly the end closer to the water. Weapon in shaking hands, he retreated, wanting to return to the cover of the car until he could—

Automatic gunfire erupted, the sound just audible over the storm and the inferno. Maverick dove for the ground and caught a flash of motion near the Hummers. Survivors. Fleeing the building. And coming out shooting.

A hail of bullets sailed over his head, and Maverick soldier-crawled through the mud and grime and puddles to the closest car. Rounds ricocheted off the metal as he got closer, and he wasn't sure if they were shooting *at* him or if it was just his own dumb bad luck. Fuck. This took *tits up* to a whole new level. Where were the others? Had any of their men made it to the building before the explosion? How many of them were caught out in the open like he'd been?

Maverick didn't have time to worry about any of that just then, because the two Hummers lurched into drive, a piece of burning siding on the hood of the first. Time slowed to a dreamlike crawl as he slid under the car, using the tire for cover from the shots and the heat. He couldn't tell how many people were in the vehicles careening around the flaming debris. Mav only knew that the Iron Cross refugees were still spraying bullets like they thought they had to shoot their way through. And then the Ravens started to return that fire. The storm couldn't quite hide the sound, but it hardly mattered. Because everyone in the city would've heard that explosion, and there wasn't anything Chen could do to cover their asses now. They just needed to get out as fast as they fucking could. Setting up a shot, Mav debated what to do—

Another explosion erupted from inside the building. Maverick felt it in his chest against the pavement. The heat was searing.

"Fuck," he said, flinching and watching as the second Hummer spun out of control and crashed into the closest of the parked cars. The first one had been clear of the building when the new detonation occurred, but it suddenly spun out of control, too—and it was coming right for him.

Rolling hard and fast, Mav made for the opening on the far side of the undercarriage and had just about made it when the collision occurred. Metal scraped upon metal like a building was coming down on top of him. The Hummer pushed the sedan so hard that the far tire he'd just been hiding behind settled against his shoulder again.

He'd barely managed to swallow his heart when movement caught his eye and someone spilled out of the Hummer's driver's side maybe ten feet away. The man hit the ground hard, but Mav knew he remained lucid when he adjusted the grip on his weapon and scanned the scene with wide searching eyes. Pissed-off eyes. Then those eyes found Maverick through the darkness, and the man raised his gun.

Maverick got a shot off first because he'd had his weapon at the ready. It was the only thing that saved him. He knew the slug found its target when the man's head and arms slumped. Mav didn't feel great about that, but the situation was too hot to sit and spin on it. And no one made it through life without losing a few pieces of themselves along the way, did they?

He waited for another moment, making sure no more Iron Cross were going to come out that side door that the flames hadn't yet reached. But all was suddenly still. *Time to fly.*

He'd no more had the thought when his phone buzzed in his back pocket. Maverick looked at it to confirm the message.

Pull back. Follow assigned route home.

No kidding.

Racing to his Harley, his boots hit deep puddles and slipped on the grass, but then he was astride the bike and underway. Hauling ass away from the blaze. Maverick looked back once more in time to see one of the walls collapsing inward in a loud crack of flying sparks and flame.

Despite Chen's assurances, Maverick expected the authorities to appear on their tails at any second. The only comfort was in seeing the groups of motorcycles forming up—each complete group of five a reassurance that their men had survived. It wasn't until they were out on the open highway and heading west toward Frederick that Mav believed that they were truly free and clear.

The Bluetooth inside his helmet picked up an incoming call. "What?" he answered. He heaved a breath, trying to shake off the stress of the night.

"You okay?" Dare asked.

"Fuck, I don't even know. Yeah. You?"

"I'm good," Dare said. "So, that was some shit."

"What the hell happened?" Maverick bit out, dark farmland flying by on both sides of the highway.

"I talked to Chen. He said there was some sort of power play inside the Iron Cross that tilted the whole fucking night on its axis, for starters. He's not sure why the initial blast occurred like that, though they had a meth lab and were building explosives. For what, he wouldn't say. They also had some kind of fail-safe destruct system hardwired in, which they apparently tripped," Dare said, his voice sounding tired. Or maybe that was just their connection.

Building explosives? So the Iron Cross were into even more bad shit than they knew, just like Chen said. That lightened a little of the darkness inside Maverick's chest over the man he'd taken out tonight. He sighed and shifted in the saddle, his back aching after being knocked on his ass.

"Are we whole?" Mav asked, still worrying about their men even though the bike count had been right on the way out of the city.

"Two not serious GSWs. Joker and Bandit. Otherwise, yes." Dare's voice didn't sound like they weren't serious. But the guy felt every hit the Ravens took personally and always had.

"Damnit," Mav said. "Did Chen mention the women?"

"His men got them, and took a number of other Iron Cross out in the process," Dare said. "They apparently got what they needed before it all went down."

"Good. That's good." Those women could've been Haven. Cora. Alexa. Goddamnit.

"Yeah. Tonight sure as fuck didn't go like we'd planned but hopefully it did what we needed it to do," Dare said.

Well, that was an understatement if Mav ever heard one, but his cousin was right. "I'm just glad things might be settled with the Iron Cross now," he said on a troubled sigh. "For Bunny, for Jeb, for all of us."

They hung up, and Maverick tried to embrace the peacefulness of the open road for the rest of the trip. All told, it wasn't long. Just about an hour door to door. Usually, having his fists and knees in the breeze was the surest path to chilling his ass out when life had him wound tight. Tonight was no exception, though perhaps he was wound a little tighter than normal.

Because of their own dead and injured. Because of what they'd just done. Because of his worry for Alexa.

He really was worried about her, and equally worried that there wasn't much he could do. Not if she wouldn't let him.

But at least with tonight behind him—with the Iron Cross finally out of the picture, Maverick could put his focus on watching out for her without feeling like he was letting the Ravens down.

He couldn't do more to help those women, but he could help Alexa. And he would.

If she needed him, he'd be ready. That was all he knew. And for now, that would be enough.

CHAPTER 7

Dealing with her mother two mornings in a row was a special kind of hell. Guilt gripped Alexa for feeling that way, but she couldn't help it. Yesterday after the doctor's visit, her mother had broken down into hysterical tears that were, Alexa suspected, a ploy to get her to stay at the house longer. Which she'd done, making herself even later for work. Of course, Grant hadn't appreciated that.

This morning, Alexa had brought over an order of groceries just like she'd promised, but getting any cleaning done was proving harder and taking longer than it had in a long time.

So far, Alexa had washed and put away the dirty dishes and washed several loads of laundry, and every step had been filled with tears, negotiations, and protests. Her mother hated having things put away because then she couldn't see them, and she fiercely resisted any attempts to throw things away, even stuff that was obviously trash.

"Okay, Mom," Alexa said, coming into the living room again. "We need to make more of a walkway in here for you so you don't fall. Why don't you keep the last week of newspapers and the last month of magazines and catalogs and let me recycle the rest?"

Wearing a T-shirt and a pair of capris, her mother sat in her recliner wringing her hands. A pile of used Kleenex sat on the chair beside her. "I need my magazines. They have coupons and recipes and good stories, and I haven't read them all," she said, voice filled with threatening tears.

"Then how about I recycle the newspapers and catalogs and you hold on to the magazines for now?" That would get rid of three huge stacks of paper. A small victory, but a victory nonetheless.

"Oh," her mother said, frowning. "Oh, I don't know." She sighed as she grabbed a photo album and pulled it into her lap. She'd always found comfort in pictures of the past, and her needing to hold that album revealed her escalating stress level. "I guess."

"Okay, thank you," Alexa said, moving before her mother changed her mind. She grabbed a black trash bag and crouched next to one of the piles. Halfway through, a headline from last Saturday's local paper caught her eye.

5 KILLED IN ATTEMPTED KIDNAPPING AT GREEN VALLEY RACE TRACK

Alexa's gaze raced over the story. Green Valley belonged to the Raven Riders, and Alexa had spent many weekend nights there with Maverick watching stock-car races or the occasional demolition derbies the club hosted. Maverick's uncle had inherited the track and the huge piece of property that surrounded it, all of which the motorcycle club now called home.

According to the article, a gang of out-of-state criminals had tried to kidnap a woman under the club's protection, causing a shoot-out in the middle of a race.

The black band she'd seen tied around Maverick's arm . . .

What if he'd been one of the five?

She shuddered as goose bumps erupted over her arms. *But he wasn't. You saw him with your own eyes. He's fine.*

"What are you looking at there?" her mother asked.

"Oh," Alexa said, holding up the paper. "The shoot-out at the race track. I hadn't seen this." Which made her wonder why. They got the newspaper at her house, but she hadn't seen one around in more than a week.

Her mom shook her head. "Terrible what happened. That Kenyon boy got shot and Maverick's mother got hurt, too."

"Oh, God. Are Dare and Bunny okay?" Alexa asked. Suddenly, she remembered the anguished look Maverick had worn that day in her office when she'd asked about the band he wore. An ache took up root in her chest for him. He'd lost a friend, and his mother and cousin had been hurt, too? And here Alexa had told him to stay away. Worse than that, she'd told him his presence could ruin things for her. Nausea curled through her belly.

"I don't know the specifics, but I think so," Mom said. "Bunny was treated and released. I think Dare was in the hospital for a few days. How have you not heard about this? It's been all over the news."

"I . . . I don't know," Alexa said. She didn't always read the newspaper, but Grant usually left it on her desk after he'd read it in the morning. Seeing this made her realize he hadn't done that all week, and in the midst of everything— including the aftermath of their fight, Alexa hadn't noticed. Was it possible he'd taken the papers so she *didn't* see this? No. Surely not. Frowning, Alexa stuffed the paper she'd been reading in the trash.

Before long, the papers filled the bag, so she grabbed a second and turned to the stack of catalogs.

"I want my catalogs," her mother said in a small voice. "I like to look."

No, she liked to shop. "Mom, there are so many of them."

"I like my catalogs," she said, her voice rising. "I don't know why that's so much to ask."

"You don't need them. You order from the internet anyway," Alexa said, grabbing a handful.

"But I like to look at the bigger pictures in the catalogs first," her mom said.

Don't lose your temper, don't lose your temper. The minute Alexa did, her mother would burst into tears and refuse to make another concession for the rest of the day. And that would be totally counterproductive. Alexa needed to keep this place clean—not just for her mother's health and safety, but because Grant would flip if he ever saw exactly how bad the inside of this house sometimes got. It was why Alexa came over here most Saturdays to clean. He'd been inside this house exactly one time since she'd moved in, and he'd nearly had a panic attack at seeing it— and that had been early on, before it had really gotten bad. So he didn't help because he couldn't stand the mess and didn't like to spend time with her mother, anyway—he said she made him uncomfortable, and his discomfort made her mother nervous and anxious. It was just better to keep them separate, even though it made Alexa sad.

"Let me take these, Mom. You'll get more in the mail. By the end of the week, you'll have half this many right back again. You won't miss them. Please," she said, giving her mother a pleading look. "I worry you'll trip and fall with so much right around the foot of your chair." Especially since the pillow and folded blanket stacked next to her meant that she was sleeping in the chair again, too. More evidence that her bedroom had probably become unlivable.

"Why do you make me do this, Alexa? You know I like my things," her mother said. It wasn't a no. Progress.

"I know. But I love *you*. And I want you safe. It's not safe to have all this in here." She held up a handful of catalogs. "Okay?"

Her mom hugged herself and waved her hand dismissively.

It didn't take long to fill the second bag. Though getting rid of the newspapers and catalogs did clear some floor space, their removal hardly made a dent in the overall state of the room. "I'm going to take these outside. Be right back."

It was always best to remove things from the house after getting her mother to agree to part with them; otherwise Alexa would turn around and find her mom pulling stuff out of the trash. With more than a little difficulty, Alexa hefted the bags over her shoulders so they would clear the piles of junk she had to navigate on her way to the foyer.

Awkwardly, she made her way through the front door and then she walked the bags to the end of the driveway, her biceps burning. She set them down with a groan next to a row of other bags she'd brought out earlier. Catching her breath, she braced her hands on her bare knees and enjoyed the warm June breeze blowing across her neck. She'd been working for a little over three hours and she was beat.

She needed to get back into her routine of doing the elliptical a few times a week. Really, she had no excuse not to since Grant had a fully decked-out workout room in the basement. Well, no excuse except for the fact that her final project and all the last-minute wedding planning took up the time she might otherwise have devoted to the elliptical. Still, Alexa had a wedding dress to fit into in just two weeks. And Grant seemed to notice the minute her weight fluctuated more than a few pounds. Of course, she wasn't sure she knew someone more fit than Grant, who ran on the treadmill and lifted weights almost every morning.

"How 'bout I give you a hand?" came a voice from behind her.

Alexa whirled, heart in her throat. "Oh my God, Maverick. Don't sneak up on me."

"I wasn't sneaking," he said, looking sexier than any man had a right to look in a pair of jeans, a white T-shirt, and his Ravens cut hanging on those broad shoulders. And here she was, sweaty, grimy from cleaning her mother's house, and with her hair thrown up in a messy knot. Not that her appearance mattered, of course.

"Then where did you come from? Again?" She arched her brow and gave him a look. "I thought I said you shouldn't be keeping an eye on me?" Though she didn't manage to put the heat behind the words she probably should have.

"I have a problem with listening," he said with a smirk.

"No kidding." Alexa planted her hands on her hips.

"Besides, I like keeping my eyes on you," he said with a wink. His gaze swept over her in a slow, satisfied up and down. Heat rose into Alexa's cheeks, because he'd said the words jokingly but there was an intensity and a seriousness to his expression that made her think of dark rooms and frantic kisses and messed-up sheets. Molten-hot memories of the two of them together—memories she'd kept boxed up tight for the past five years—threatened to come roaring back.

She couldn't let them, so she changed the subject. "Hey, how's your mom? And Dare? I'm sorry I didn't ask the other day. I didn't know what'd happened."

The amusement melted off Maverick's rugged face. "Both doing better. They'll be okay."

Relief flooded through Alexa. "Oh, thank God. I was worried."

Lips pressed into a tight line, Maverick nodded as his gaze drifted toward the house. "How's your mom?"

"Oh. She's . . ." Alexa shrugged. She couldn't help but

be struck by another comparison. Grant rarely asked after her mother, except to ask how long Alexa would be gone on Saturdays. "You know. Pretty much the same." As much time as Maverick had spent with Tyler and her over the years, he would know what she meant. In that moment, Alexa realized Maverick was the *only* other person left who truly understood Cynthia Harmon's problems—and what it took to deal with them.

"Yeah. So let me help." The sincerity in those dark blue eyes reached inside her chest and played with long-buried needs and desires.

"Okay," she found herself saying. She shook her head, confusion swamping her even as she went with it. "Yeah. Sure. Um." She gestured toward the house. "Come say hi?"

Maverick smiled. And holy *wow*. It had been a long time since Alexa had seen him smile that way. It stole her breath. Because Maverick Rylan smiling was stunningly gorgeous. The smile brought out deep dimples on both sides of his mouth, and combined with the stubble covering his jaw and those blue, blue eyes—

"We going in?" he asked, one eyebrow cocked.

So busted. "Of course," she said, hugging herself and looking down at the blacktop of the driveway as she led him toward the house. "When we get inside, let me give Mom a heads-up that you're here in case she wants to put herself together a bit. Or something."

"Sure," Maverick said from beside her. Out of nowhere, Alexa was swimming in the most overwhelming sensation of déjà vu. How many times had Maverick come to visit her mother with Alexa? How many times had he helped drop off groceries or take out trash or sat and chatted with her mom while Alexa took care of something that otherwise would've caused her a lot of stress? Him being there was suddenly so familiar *and* so foreign—because it had been a long time since she'd felt like she had any companionship in dealing with her mom. Going all the way back to Tyler's death.

A weird little knot of tension settled into Alexa's gut.

She opened the front door and stepped inside, Maverick right behind her. She held out a hand to him and moved to the living room doorway. "I have a surprise for you," she said to her mother. "Someone came to say hello."

"Who?" Her mom ran her hands over her hair. "I look a mess, Alexa."

"It's just me, Mrs. H," Maverick said.

"Oh!" Alexa hadn't seen her mother's face light up like that in a long time. "Oh, Maverick Rylan, you come in here and see me right now."

Grinning, Maverick slid past where Alexa stood in the doorway. Though it was soft and quick, the slight brush of his body against hers flashed heat through Alexa's body. Just that little touch. Just that promise of something more. And that knot in her belly got a lot bigger and a lot more uncomfortable. Because barely touching Maverick made her hot with want, but just last night she'd had to pep talk herself into keeping her promise to make her rushed morning up to Grant.

"Hi, Mrs. H," Maverick said, crossing the room to her.

"Oh, Maverick. What a sight for sore eyes you are," she said, standing up. She held her arms out to him, and Maverick didn't hesitate for a second. He not only hugged her, but he lifted her off her feet, making her mother laugh like a girl. "Put me down before you break me," she said, not meaning a word of it.

"It's good to see you." Maverick carefully put her back down. "How have you been?"

"Same old. You know." Mom sat again. "You here to help Alexa straighten me out, then?" she asked with a sniff.

Maverick laughed. "I'm here to help Alexa with whatever she needs help with," he said, looking over his shoulder at her. His expression revealed that he meant that in all kinds of ways Alexa didn't want to think about. *Shouldn't* think about. Since she was engaged to another man and all. And had given Maverick up long ago.

Regret crept across her skin in a shiver, but Alexa refused to give it a second thought. "Well, if you wouldn't mind helping me in the kitchen, then?"

"You're the boss," he said.

"Ha. Says the man who doesn't listen to me." Alexa threaded her way through the room, glad that needing to be careful of her steps meant that she had a good reason not to make eye contact with Maverick.

"You be nice to him, Alexa," her mother said.

"Yeah, be nice to me," Mav whispered. The sexy bastard.

In the kitchen, Alexa pointed her finger at him and raised an eyebrow. A silent command to be good.

"What?" he asked, his mouth sliding into a cocky half grin. She wanted to kiss it off of him.

"What are you going to do in the kitchen?" her mother asked from the other room.

Alexa shook away the troubling impulse. What was wrong with her? "Just dealing with the trash and recycling, Mom. Don't worry," Alexa called. Even though Maverick had been in their trailer many times and knew just how bad their mother's hoarding could be, Alexa found herself really glad that she'd taken care of the dishes earlier. The room didn't smell nearly as offensive now. And luckily she hadn't found any buried critters—so far, at least. She looked at Maverick and spoke in a near whisper, "Sure you don't mind doing this?"

"I never have," he said.

She knew that was true, and it poked at something deep inside her. Alexa nodded. "Then we gotta work as fast as we can in here. She was getting pretty anxious earlier."

"I hear you," he said. "Just tell me what you want me to do."

CHAPTER 8

Maverick had never been happier to do grunt work in his whole damn life. But he was doing it with Alexa, and that made a fucking difference. Not just because he was with her. But because she'd invited him in and welcomed his company. More than that, she seemed to be enjoying it.

It felt damn close to old times. The *good* old times.

An hour passed in the blink of an eye as they worked together. The happiness flowing through him made him feel damn pathetic, truth be told. But he ignored it in favor of letting himself enjoy what might be one of the last days he'd be spending with her. Ever.

He followed Alexa out to the curb with what was going to be their last bags of trash. Mrs. H had blown up at them moments before and made them promise to stop, so she was clearly at her limit. Not that it was any skin off Maverick's nose. He'd seen it all before going years back. And, anyway, being a hoarder was a lot better than being an abuser like his father, so it wasn't like he had any room to criticize anyone else's parent.

Alexa dropped her bag into the big pile at the curb with a groan. She planted her hands on her hips, emphasizing her mouthwatering curves there. "I'm really sorry Mom yelled at you." She wiped at her brow on a long sigh. Even with little makeup, her hair thrown up in a messy bun, and being dressed down in a pair of jean shorts and a form-fitting black tank top, she was still the most beautiful woman Maverick had ever known. Damn it all to hell.

"You don't owe me any apologies, Al. I know how it is." He dropped his bags at the curb.

"I know you do," she said quietly. Her expression was thoughtful. Maybe even a little wistful. And it made him want to argue, convince, hell, even *plead* if it had a chance of making things different between them—all shit he should've done more of five years before.

"Can you?" she'd asked that day at Tyler's grave. He'd heard everything she'd asked without her needing to say the words. Can you be there for me? Can you give me what I need? Can you commit? Can you do forever? And he'd frozen. Like the damn fool, like the *damn immature kid*, he'd been. It was a moment he'd replayed so many times, wishing he could do it over each and every time.

Alexa pulled her cell from her back pocket. "Maybe I can get one of Grant's guys to come haul these bags away. If I leave them here 'til Monday morning, Mom will end up going through them and taking stuff back inside."

The mention of Slater's name was like nails against a chalkboard and hauled Maverick right back to the present. He grasped her hand. "I'll take care of it," he said a little more harshly than he intended.

As if it wasn't bad enough that Maverick had lost Alexa to the wealthy asshole, Grant Slater was one of the few businessmen in Frederick who thought that the Ravens' racing activities at Green Valley weren't good for the town. The Ravens had allies among the restaurant, hotel, and retail store owners who benefited from the out-of-town visitors who came to see the races, and lots of locals supported the Ravens because of how many people they employed during racing season. But Slater argued that the races were detrimental to luring yuppies looking for an escape from city life into one of his developments of Mc-Mansions. So of course he'd jumped on last week's crisis at Green Valley to get face time with the local news that he used to criticize the club. Worse than that, his wealth gave him influence, including with the mayor, who was so far into Slater's pocket it wasn't funny.

So Maverick had all kinds of reasons to want Alexa away from him. Not that it was his choice, was it?

"I'll run to the house and get my truck. I can be back in twenty," he said.

"Oh. Really?" Alexa asked, those hazel eyes wide with surprise.

Maverick just looked at her. Because no way he was opening his mouth and chancing revealing how deep it cut when she doubted him. Especially since he knew that her not believing in him—in his ability to take care of her—was part of what made her choose the wealthy, seemingly respectable asshole over him. And if that wasn't enough, her doubts poked at his own fears about himself, born when he'd failed to take care of his mother years before.

"Okay. Wow. Um, are you sure? I can't imagine you intended to get hung up here all day."

"I don't say what I don't mean, Alexa," he said, nailing her with a stare.

"I . . . I know. It's not that. It's just . . ." She shook her head. "You know what? Never mind. Thank you for offering. If you got your truck, that would be great, actually."

Maverick nodded. "You got it." He made for the street, and then an idea had him stopping in his tracks and turning back to her. "What are you going to do?" He'd spent enough time with Alexa and her mom to know that Alexa could only take so much of her mother at a time.

Alexa shrugged and looked maybe just a little lost. It made Maverick want to hold her, claim her, tell her she was fucking found. Forever. Which was a problem given that she was engaged to be married in just two weeks. If his gut wasn't so sure she was in trouble, he'd cut himself off from seeing her again. Because on one level he was just torturing himself by coming around. "I don't know," she said with a rueful chuckle. "Fall down on the grass right here and take a nap maybe?"

"I got a better idea," he said, a yearning planting itself in his gut. *Could be the last time . . .*

"Oh, yeah? Do tell," Alexa said with a smirk and an arched eyebrow. And fuck it was sexy when she came at him with a little playful attitude like that. Always had been.

"Ride with me." The words flew out of his mouth, and he didn't want to take them back even though, *fuck*, it put him out there to be smacked down again. But damn if it wouldn't be worth it to feel her holding him, pressed up tight against him, laughing in his ear.

She hesitated and maybe even looked a little nervous, but Maverick could see the interest in the liveliness of her eyes.

"Don't think. Just say yes," he said.

Alexa tilted her head and narrowed her gaze at him, and then she smiled. "Okay. Yes."

That's my girl. He kept the sentiment to himself, but he felt it down deep. *His* Alexa was in there. The one who could throw caution to the wind and have fun doing absolutely nothing. The one who laughed freely and bantered relentlessly. Maverick gave a single nod.

"Let me tell Mom. Be right back," she said.

"I'll bring the bike around." Maverick took a step backward, but then paused when Alexa turned and hurried toward the house. His gaze traced her curves and lingered on the bare skin of her thighs. Thighs that were going to be wrapped around him in just a few short minutes. Thighs that *had been* wrapped around him in all kinds of ways many times. *Many* times. Fuck.

A few houses down, Maverick straddled his Harley Night Rod Special and brought the engine to life on a low rumble. He pulled the bike to the curb in front of the Harmon house and waited. He didn't have to wait long.

Alexa came flying out through the garage. She made eye contact with him and it fucking seared his blood. For some reason this ride felt weighted with a significance he couldn't put into words. And he wasn't trying. He was just going to enjoy the hell out of it. Because Maverick knew her agreeing this one time didn't change anything. Not anything important.

By the time she reached him, Alexa was smiling even though he could tell she was trying to hold that shit back. But she couldn't, and that got to him, too. For a moment, she hesitated, like she wasn't sure what to do. No way that was it, though, because even though it had been years, she'd been in his saddle as many times as his bed. He suspected the real issue was giving herself permission to do what she was gonna have to do—get close and hold tight. To him.

Something she hadn't done in years.

But then she did it.

She braced one hand on his shoulder and climbed onto the small leather seat behind him. Her thighs hugging his ass. The softness of her breasts against his back. Her breath against his neck.

Fuck. The good old times once more.

He slid on a pair of sunglasses, then handed her his helmet. "Put this on."

"What about you?" she asked as she took it.

"I'll be careful." He looked over his shoulder at her, and she gave a nod when she had it secured. "Ready?"

"Yeah," she said, and he didn't think he was imagining the anticipation in her voice.

The moment her hands came around him, Maverick pulled away from the curb. And the rightness of having her on his bike again made him want to drive up into the mountains for the rest of the day. Fists and knees in the breeze for a long ride. Find a quiet spot by one of the lakes. Fuck like a couple of kids against a tree or in the grass. They'd done it before. More than once.

But that wasn't who they were anymore, was it?

And he was working on accepting that once and for all.

But not today.

THIS WAS PROBABLY a big mistake. Huge. Gargantuan, even. But that didn't keep Alexa from getting on the back of Maverick's bike and holding him tight.

One last time . . .

And it was just a ride. For old time's sake. For *fun*, something she hadn't prioritized in so long. And for her mom. Couldn't forget that, either.

So, yeah. It was just a ride.

A shiver ran through her that had nothing to do with the air rushing over her skin. It was Maverick. His heat, his muscles, his long hair that she'd always loved running her hands through. It was his rough masculinity and his daredevil attitude and his fierce loyalty.

It was Maverick that had her body getting hot and feeling needy. She found even the leather Raven Riders' patch on the back of his cut alluring, which made no sense since it was his membership in the club that had been one of her rationales for pushing Maverick away. But holding him as she was, all she could think about was how that same image was tattooed on his broad back. Watching the raven perched on a dagger move as his naked body did had *always* attracted her to him, even if everything the tattoo represented had sorta scared her.

Alexa closed her eyes and heaved a deep breath. Why was she torturing herself like this? She'd made her choice. Her future was set. Her future was *Grant*.

This? This was just a ride with someone she used to know.

Alexa groaned to herself. She might not want to admit the truth out loud, but it wasn't like she could hide from herself. And if she was being honest, she hadn't accepted the ride just to get a break from hanging out with her mother, although that had been part of it. She'd also *wanted* to ride with Maverick. Deep down, a part of her hadn't wanted to spend the minutes apart that it would take for him to get his truck and return. Because she wouldn't have many more—if any—opportunities like this again, not with her wedding just two weeks away. Now, experiencing all these feelings welling up inside her, it made her remember something she hadn't thought of in a really long time.

Being with Maverick . . . just made her want to be with him even more. It had *always* been like that between them.

Which was one of the reasons, five years before, that she'd broken things off with him cold turkey. No friendship, even though they'd started out as friends. No hanging out casually or with groups of mutual friends, even though they'd done that all the time before they ever started dating. No asking for his help with her mom, even though he'd done it so many times and she could've used the help after Tyler died. She'd just been overwhelmed with grief and anger and responsibility, and it had been too hard for her to be around Maverick and not want him. Even if she'd been convinced he couldn't give her everything she and her mother needed.

It hadn't been easy. In fact, it'd hurt almost as much as Tyler's death had. And that'd made her feel maybe more guilty than she ever had in her life.

And then Grant had stepped in, offering her kindness and support and help. Even as Maverick made a few last attempts to bridge the gap between them.

At first, staying away from Maverick had been her idea—all self-preservation. So it hadn't mattered when Grant had made it clear early in their relationship that he didn't want Alexa seeing Mav—or any of the Ravens, really—anymore. In her grief for her brother, she was already avoiding Maverick. In her need to focus on taking care of her shattered mother, she'd already cut him off. So honoring Grant's preference had been easy because it went along with her own intentions. Either way, it'd been a long time since she'd spent any time with Maverick like this.

And staying away from him had worked. It had made it easier to avoid feeling what she most desired where Maverick was concerned. Which was *him*. Had always been him. Since she'd been a girl who was way too damn young to be crushing on a teenager, and then a man, who was four years older than her. A man whose lifestyle had scared her on so many levels and made her choose what seemed like the more rational—safer—choice.

Grant Slater.

But now . . .

Today was the third day in a little over a week that Alexa had seen Maverick. And *damn* if that desire wasn't still there. Even after all this time.

And that was a total sucker punch because she'd convinced herself a long damn time ago that she was totally and completely over this man. Emotionally. Physically. In every way.

Maverick took a fast turn, tilting the Harley at what seemed to Alexa to be a dangerously low angle. It'd been years since she'd ridden a motorcycle, but when they'd been together she'd done it all the time with him. As if on instinct, her body leaned the way it needed to handle the turn. Still, she clutched her arms and legs around him tighter, and his laughter floated back to her on the wind. And even though her heart was racing and her belly was flipping from the unexpected move, Alexa had a big smile on her face, too.

She and Maverick had sometimes butted heads, but mostly things between them had been easy, natural, effortless. She hadn't realized just how true that was, but being with him again held a mirror up to her relationship with Grant. And maybe the comparisons were unfair since they were working on merging their lives as soon-to-be husband and wife, something she and Maverick had never broached during their time together, something Maverick had said he wasn't sure he'd ever even want. Not after how his parents' marriage had turned out. And it was far easier to be fun and lighthearted when forever wasn't on the line. Right?

Right. *Stop talking yourself into thinking there are problems where none exist, Alexa.* Maybe Grant was right. He said all the time Alexa worried and overthought things too much. This sure seemed like proof.

Gah. Why hadn't she just stayed at her mother's?

"You up for going fast?" Maverick's voice yanked her from her thoughts.

Without really thinking, the old answer she used to give when he asked that spilled out of her mouth. "Always."

Nodding, Maverick smiled over his shoulder, and then he turned off the busy commercial route that led most directly to the Raven Riders' compound and toward the more rural back way to his house. It didn't take long to reach the open country road, and then they were *flying*.

The roar of the engine. The rush of the wind. The sheer power and speed of the bike.

Joy bubbled up inside Alexa until she was smiling and laughing. She wished she could throw out her arms and tilt her head back and let herself just float on the wind. She settled instead for letting out a loud *woohoo* that made Maverick laugh and had him giving the bike just a little more speed.

A nagging voice in the back of Alexa's head reminded her how dangerous a bike could be. Doctors didn't call them "donor cycles" for nothing. Motorcycles versus . . . just about *anything* was more likely than not going to be worse for the motorcycle, which Tyler's death had proven. It had just been him versus a wet mountain road and a guardrail. And he hadn't survived it. Once, that had terrified Alexa for Maverick. Made his bike-riding a risk her heart couldn't tolerate. And there was still some fear there.

But there was more than that. There was just a sheer exhilaration, too. When was the last time she'd felt this alive, this free, this . . . happy?

Maverick slowed the bike as they approached the back driveway into the Raven Riders' compound, off of which his house sat. Maverick was one of the few members of the club who lived on the Ravens' compound, a privilege reserved for those related to the club's founder, who was also Maverick's uncle. Though she'd been young, Alexa could still remember the day Maverick and his mother moved into the old cottage on the club's land to get away from his abusive father. Bunny had moved out years ago into her new husband's house, but Maverick had stayed here, content to keep his life centered around the club and starting his then-new custom bike-building business.

The forest hung all around them as they approached a secured gate. Maverick swiped a card and they sailed through, then took a turnoff that went farther up the mountain. The trees opened up on Maverick's house, an old two-story white cottage with a killer view over a small pond and the valley below.

Alexa hadn't been there in years, which meant every change Maverick had made to the place jumped out at her. The house had a fresh coat of paint and a new roof. New landscaping lined the front of the house. The circular driveway had been paved. The detached garage had new doors. The place looked . . . fantastic. Homey and comfortable and charming.

The bike came to a stop in front of the garage as one of those doors rolled up, and then Maverick eased it into the empty space inside and killed the engine. Alexa pulled her helmet off and handed it to Maverick.

He smiled at her as he helped her off, his big hand warm and strong around hers. "Good time?"

She couldn't help but smile back. "Really good time."

"Good." He dismounted the bike and raked his hands through his hair, and everything about his actions was so freaking sexy. The way his big body moved. The way his T-shirt rode up, revealing a sliver of toned abs and a dark blond happy trail just above the waistband of his jeans. The way he grinned at her all smugly and annoyingly and knowingly when he caught her watching him.

Alexa turned toward the open garage door, needing a break from touching and admiring Maverick freaking Rylan. She scanned her gaze over his house and yard. "Your place looks great, Maverick. You've been doing a lot of work."

He came up beside her. "Checking things off my project list one at a time."

The house had always been charming, but the TLC he'd put into updating it gave it a curb appeal it never had before. "It really shows."

"Yeah?" he asked, pride clear in his tone. "You should see the inside."

Truth be told, the designer inside her was seriously tempted. As was the woman who'd spent many nights here in another lifetime. But Alexa had told her mother she'd be back in less than a half hour, and a part of her also wasn't sure it was a great idea to be alone with Maverick at his place. Not after what she'd been feeling while riding with him. What she was *still* feeling . . . "I'd love to, but—"

"Right. I know," he said abruptly. "We gotta get back. Another time. Maybe." He turned toward the pickup.

A ribbon of guilt curled inside her belly. "Yeah," she said, not at all believing there'd be another time. Which was probably for the best.

Heading to the driver's side of his old truck, Maverick said, "Well, hop in and we'll take off. Not as fun as the Night Rod but it'll get the job done."

Alexa slid into the passenger seat and closed her door. "That's all that matters. If I don't keep things under control at the house, Mom will just fill it up. So it's good to get rid of what we took out right away. I can't afford for her to lose this place, too."

Maverick gave her a hard look. "Why would she lose it? I thought Slater owned her place."

Alexa didn't bother to ask how he knew that. The one thing Grant and Maverick had in common was that they were both networked into just about everything that happened in Frederick. Grant because of his business activities. And Maverick because of the Ravens' businesses, not to mention the club's long history in the area. "He does," she said. "But he doesn't know just how bad it can get. It makes me worry."

Maverick frowned. "Well, there's no way he'd ever put her out on the street. She's your mother. He has to know how much she means to you, so I can't imagine you need to worry. You're finally set where she's concerned, Alexa. I know that means a lot to you."

The words nearly stole Alexa's breath. Mav didn't like Grant. It didn't take a genius to figure that out or know why.

So it was a really generous thing for him to say about her fiancé—and really . . . mature, too. She wasn't sure the old Maverick could've offered her that kind of understanding. It meant a lot to her. More than that, it almost sounded like he understood why she'd made the choices she'd made. Or maybe that was her wishful thinking reading into what he'd said. She hoped he did understand. Because Alexa had never wanted to hurt Maverick, even though she knew she had.

Hell. She'd hurt herself, too, hadn't she? She knew that. Now. Being around him again made her wonder how she'd ever forgotten just how much.

Alexa just hoped Maverick was right about Grant. She wished she knew for sure. The fact that she *didn't* know? She refused to analyze too closely what that meant. So she just said, "Yeah. Thanks."

"Don't have to thank me," he said, turning the key. The engine echoed inside the old garage as he backed out of the spot. Then he was putting the truck in Drive and pulling around past the front of his house.

"I do," she said, studying his roughly handsome profile as he sat behind the wheel. "You didn't have to do all this today. I appreciate it." She hadn't realized how much she needed some support in taking care of her mother until she had Maverick working at her side.

Mav gave her a long sideways glance. "You know I'm always here for you and your mom, right? You and her and Ty were like family to me for a lot of years. That didn't end just because we didn't make it. Understand?"

After a moment, Alexa gave a tight nod, and then she had to look away, out her window at the passing trees. So that Maverick didn't see just how much his words meant to her. Or ask why she suddenly had tears in her eyes.

Because she wasn't sure she knew, either.

CHAPTER 9

I have a surprise for you," Grant said almost as soon as Alexa returned home that afternoon. Wearing an expensive blue dress shirt with the sleeves rolled up and the collar open, he met her in the kitchen and pulled her into a hug and a long, lingering kiss.

Registering his good mood—for which she was grateful given how much later she was than usual—Alexa relaxed into his embrace. "You do?" she asked.

"Mmhmm." Finally, he eased away from the kiss. Tucking some loose strands of hair behind her ear, he smiled. "You're always so stressed when you come home from your mother's, so I'm whisking you away for an overnight getaway. We'll relax, eat great food, take a sail. Just you and me."

"Wow, really? That sounds amazing," she said. And so much like the kinds of things he planned for them early in their relationship. He used to take her away on trips and weekend getaways all the time the first year or two that they dated. Weekends in New York City, Atlantic City, and the Massanutten ski resort in the Shenandoahs, and surprise weeks in Mexico, Paris, Rome, to name a few. They still traveled sometimes, but now his business and her school and job responsibilities made it harder to get away as often.

"Having you all to myself is what sounds amazing," he said, nailing her with an intense stare. "No wedding planning, no jobs, no school, no mother, no life obligations at all. Just you and me."

A fleeting wave of stress passed through her, because she had been planning to spend Sunday running errands for the wedding. Picking up gifts for Grant and the bridesmaids, who were mostly colleagues at work. Dropping by the reception venue to finalize menu details. Finding a few last things to pack for their honeymoon in Cozumel, the first place they'd ever traveled out of the country together years before. Neither of them having parents who could help with the planning was a mixed blessing—on the one hand it meant they didn't have to try to please a bunch of people besides themselves, but it also meant she didn't have any help. And all of that was in addition to the reading she still had to do for Tuesday night's class. The list was never-ending.

But Grant was right. They could use some time in the midst of all the madness to just focus on each other. And it would help screw her head back on right, too. "That *does* sound amazing. Thank you, Grant. This is so thoughtful." She pressed her lips to his. "I'll just pack a quick bag."

"Already done," he said, nodding to something behind her.

She turned to see two overnight bags in the doorway to the foyer. Alexa laughed. "My, someone *is* eager, isn't he?"

He kissed her roughly, in a way that made her feel claimed. "Where you're concerned? Always." He swatted her on the butt. "Now go get pretty: I'll pack up the car."

After cleaning all morning, Alexa guessed she must look a mess. "Okay, I'll do that." Excitement and anticipation flitted through her. No doubt wherever he was taking her would be romantic and luxurious and sure to take all her cares away. With a quick last kiss, she pulled away.

He caught her wrist and gave her an intense look. "And wear that white sundress for me."

"You like that white one, huh?" she asked, batting her eyelashes.

"I like tearing that one off of you," he said. "I like playing with the knot at your neck and imagining undoing it whenever I want to. Wherever I want to." His gaze flashed hot, and her belly answered with a flutter of butterflies. Whether nerves or arousal, she wasn't sure. "Now, go."

In their room, she found the dress, a pair of panties, and a pair of tall wedges set out at the bottom of the bed, all folded and lined up with excruciating precision. It reminded her of his desk at work, where the few items he kept out on it had exact placements, everything all symmetrical and aligned. She smiled and shook her head. Pure Grant. Dotting every i and crossing every t, and not leaving anything to chance. In his personal life just as in business, he took charge and control of every detail.

She quickly showered, dressed, and styled her hair in a chignon that allowed her to get away without blowing it fully dry. Grant had left her makeup bag on the counter, so she put on her face and a pair of earrings, and then she was ready to go.

Alexa gave herself a once-over in the bathroom mirror. She looked summery and put-together. She wasn't a hundred percent comfortable going without a bra, but the halter top and low back on the dress didn't really allow for one.

And Grant *really* liked that about the dress, anyway. So she could be okay with it for the day.

"I'm ready," she announced when she returned to the kitchen.

Grant gestured with his finger for her to turn for him. She did. "Even more beautiful than I remembered you being in that dress," he said.

The ride was easy and the time passed quickly with Grant filling her in on how a couple of his projects were developing. The only weirdness happened when she brought up something she probably shouldn't have.

"Hey, I meant to ask you. What happened to all the newspapers this week? You never left them for me."

"What do you mean? They were on the desk in the kitchen," he said.

Alexa frowned. "Really? I didn't see them. You usually put them on my desk when you're done with them."

"Well, forgive me for being a little busy, Alexa." He gave her a look.

"No, no, of course. I'm sorry. I didn't mean anything by it. It just occurred to me that I hadn't seen them." She grasped his hand and gave it a squeeze.

"Why is it such a big deal, anyway?" he asked, gaze straight ahead.

"Oh, I just happened to see one of the papers at Mom's and I hadn't heard anything about that horrible shooting and attempted kidnapping incident that happened out at Green Valley. That's all. I was just surprised I hadn't seen anything about it."

He shrugged. "The Ravens are such bad fucking news for this town. Violence at their hands is hardly a surprise."

Schooling her reaction, Alexa swallowed. "I was just curious about it. That's all."

"Well, I can't help it if you didn't see the papers. It's not like I was hiding them from you," he said. His cell rang, and he picked it up on the car's Bluetooth. "Grant Slater here."

When he hung up a few minutes later, she apologized again, wanting his good humor back more than anything. Then she steered the conversation to safer subjects, and his mood rebounded.

Two hours later, they were driving through the quaint, small town of St. Michaels on the Eastern Shore of Maryland. They passed antique shops and small eateries on the main street and finally turned onto a long brick-paved and tree-lined driveway that eventually opened up onto a broad courtyard surrounded by a series of white buildings.

"Oh my God. Is this where they filmed *Wedding Crashers?*" Alexa asked, peering out the window as Grant pulled the car up to the lobby.

Grant laughed and gave her a teasing look. "Leave it to you to know a pop culture reference for one of the nicest resorts in all of Maryland."

The valet opened her door. "Welcome to the Inn at Perry Cabin," a man wearing a gray-and-black uniform said.

"Thank you." She accepted his hand to rise out of the Mercedes.

Grant came around to guide her through the doors with a hand low on her bare back. As they walked inside, he leaned down and pressed his mouth close to her ear. "Every man is looking at this dress and wishing they could be the one to take it off of you. But that pleasure is mine alone. *You* are mine alone."

"Of course," she said with a shiver as she peered up at him.

"Don't ever forget it," he said, his expression serious, his gaze piercing.

Before she could respond, they were standing at the reception desk and Grant was checking them in. His words echoed over her body along with a rush of goose bumps. His claiming words had been arousing, but that last line left her feeling . . . odd. Why had he felt the need to say that? She'd been with him for nearly five years. She worked for him, lived with him, wore his ring, and planned to marry him. There wasn't one part of her life that wasn't bound up with his. *Of course* she was his.

Except, just then, images of another man flashed through her head. Maverick. Hugging her mother. Smiling over his shoulder at her on his bike. Raking his hands through his hair. *Oh, God. Does he know Maverick was at my mother's today?*

Fear and guilt sloshed through her belly. Although, why should she feel guilty? She hadn't invited Maverick to come, and certainly nothing had happened between them. *Then why aren't you volunteering that you saw him?*

"Alexa?" Grant asked.

She blinked up at him, and the look on his face told her he'd called her name more than once. "Sorry," she said. "Lost in a daydream."

Grant shook his head and gave her an indulgent smile. "You? Always. Let's check out our suite," he said. "I've reserved a private dining room for us and we have dinner in an hour."

"Wow, you didn't have to do all that, Grant. I'm sure the regular restaurant here is lovely," Alexa said, taking in the light and airy décor. It was a mix of colonial charm and nautical colors and accents. Large windows provided expansive water views throughout the whole back side of the building, and comfy sitting rooms and reading nooks appeared around every corner.

"Of course I didn't have to," Grant said as they made their way down a long hallway, "but tonight I don't want to share you. I just want you all to myself." Finally, he gestured toward a door. "This is us."

The suite was beautiful and spacious. The large sitting room with overstuffed couches and chairs arranged around a fireplace opened onto a porch that overlooked the water. A bowl piled high with fresh fruit sat on the coffee table. Italian marble covered every surface in the bathroom, and a massive four-poster king bed dominated the bedroom. "This is amazing, Grant."

He came up behind where she stood in the doorway to the bedroom. His hands circled her wrists. "If I wasn't so hungry, I'd have half a mind to handcuff you to that headboard for the rest of the night and have my way with you."

Alexa leaned back against him. "You don't need hand-cuffs to have your way with me," she said, putting a light-ness in her tone she didn't quite feel. Grant had always made comments about not wanting to share her and want-ing them to be alone, but suddenly it felt different. Less sexy than controlling. Less about desire and more about ownership.

"You know what? You're right." He grasped her by the shoulders and manhandled her into the bathroom.

Laughing, Alexa worked to keep from tripping in the high wedges. "What are we doing?"

"Getting what you wouldn't give me yesterday morn-ing," he said, pushing her in front of one of the sinks in the long vanity. Confused, Alexa could hardly keep up with the rush of his movements. And then he was flipping up her skirt and tugging at her panties and pushing her upper body down with a palm planted in the center of her back.

She braced her hands on the marble. "Grant—"

"Been thinking about this," he gritted out. "I need it, Alexa. Just like this. Give it to me."

The blunt head of his erection pushed against her core, driving into her. Or trying to. She wasn't ready and her body wasn't opening for him. He pushed harder. As hot as his urgency and need were, the friction was uncomfortable and his words were confusing.

Grant smacked her ass, once, twice, and the sound reverberated within the room. "Let me in, goddamnit." He surged forward, penetrating her.

On a whimper, she pulled away, or tried to, but she couldn't move much with the way he had her pinned against the sink. If he'd just give her body a chance to respond. "Grant, wait—"

"Be still," he said roughly, his hand pushing her down harder. He withdrew, and she heard him spit. And then he was right back inside her again. "Don't make this harder than it has to be." Her fingers clenched and unclenched against the smooth surface of the counter, and she let out a moan at the burning friction. Her thoughts were a confusing, conflicting whirl, her heart raced in what felt a lot like fight or flight, and she almost perceived the moment as if she were watching what was happening rather than experiencing it.

What *was* happening?

Finally, her body provided the slickness that eased the way, but the soreness didn't fade. "There it is," he groaned, palm still holding her down.

He tugged hard at the tie of her dress around her neck, the falling material exposing her breasts, and then his hand fisted in her hair, forcing her head back and her gaze to the mirror. "I put you together. I can mess you up, too," he said, meeting the reflection of her gaze. A cold sweat broke out across her body, making her dress cling. "So fucking hot." He slapped her ass again. Hard. The sting made her cry out.

But otherwise, Alexa was . . . frozen. She couldn't talk. Despite the emotions blowing up inside her, she couldn't cry. She couldn't even make sense of what they were doing, exactly. It had started out kinda hot, but it was also . . . scary. She liked rough sex and she loved a man who took command in the bedroom, but why was that the only way they ever came together anymore? And why did this feel like something else?

Like . . . punishment.

Like control.

Like he was showing her who had it. And that she didn't.

Except that was ridiculous, wasn't it? She liked it rough. She liked hair pulling and spanking and being restrained and having it hard and fast. Exactly what this was, and what they'd done many times. And Grant was her fiancé. They were getting married. She loved him.

Hand tight in her hair, he drove into her again and again, his expression harsh, his pace fast and frenzied, her hips and thighs knocking into the front of the counter each time. She could already tell that she'd be bruised. And sore. Despite the fact that she was wet, arousal wasn't a part of this for her. Shouldn't it have been?

Finally, Grant finished with a groan, his grip almost painfully tight on her hip. Panting, he held himself inside her for a long moment. Then he bent over, pressing her into the hard counter, and kissed her shoulder. "Dinner's in a half hour, so you have time to get cleaned up," he said. He pulled out, causing her to wince, and then he stepped to the toilet.

"Okay," Alexa whispered. She grabbed tissues from the fancy silver dispenser on the counter to clean herself up, avoiding her own gaze in the mirror as she did.

Because she wasn't sure what she'd see in her eyes, or how her expression might reflect the queasiness taking root in the pit of her stomach.

"Alexa?" Grant asked from behind her. She whirled, startled. "Everything all right?"

"Yeah," she said, clutching the counter behind her to hide her shaking hands. "Just catching my breath." *And trying not to lose my mind.*

He gave her a wolfish grin. "Okay," he said, and then he walked out into the sitting room.

Alexa stared at the empty place where he'd been standing. *Pull it together, Al. You're fine. Everything's fine.*

Except that feeling of dread she'd been flirting with for the past couple of weeks was stronger than it had ever been before.

CHAPTER 10

The biker rolled into the big parking lot in front of the Raven Riders' clubhouse and brought his Harley to a stop. Maverick gave a wave and waited as their newest prospective member hung his helmet on his handlebars and dismounted.

"Maverick, thanks again for sponsoring me, man," Mike Renner said. Stocky, with reddish-brown hair and a close-shaved beard, the guy was a few years younger than Maverick's thirty-four and had been a club Hang Around for almost a year. Mav had met him about three years before when he'd bought a custom bike from him, which was when Mike had first become interested in the club.

"Glad to have you," Maverick said, shaking Mike's hand. "Do me proud."

Mike grinned. "I will."

Nodding toward the front steps of the big two-story clubhouse, Maverick led Mike inside. "The induction ceremony is pretty low-key. Some words from the prez, advice from some of the patched members, and then you get your cut." Maverick winked at the other man. "And then the hazing—I mean, the fun, begins."

Laughing, Mike nodded as they stepped into the big front lounge that had once served as the lobby and reception area to the inn when it had been the center of a mountain resort decades before. On the wall by the mess hall hung all the members' photos, including Jeb's. Above the old registration desk, foot-high words carved into the wood spelled out the club's motto, *Ride. Fight. Defend.*

Tempting smells that had Mav's stomach growling came through the mess hall door—proof that Bunny, Haven, and Cora were putting together a fantastic, celebratory Sunday dinner—but Maverick led Mike in the other direction, toward the big rec room where about thirty Ravens were waiting.

A round of applause and cheers erupted as Maverick and Mike walked into the big rectangular room and made their way toward Dare, standing in front of the bar.

"Dare," Maverick said when the ruckus died down, "I'm proud to sponsor Mike Renner for prospective membership into the Raven Riders Motorcycle Club." After the insanity of Friday night's raid on the Iron Cross, it felt really fucking good to have something positive for the club to focus on.

Dare reached behind him and grabbed a denim cutoff jacket with black leather patches sewn on here and there. "Mike, are you interested in becoming a member of the Raven Riders?"

"Yes, I am." Wearing a black button-down shirt and jeans, he stood solemnly with his hands clasped in front of him.

"Are you committed to learning about the club, supporting its activities, being a brother in actions, not just name, protecting the club and its business, and putting your loyalty to the Ravens above all else?" Dare asked, nailing the younger man with his dark stare. The words sucked Maverick back into his own induction ceremony at the age of eighteen. He could still remember the pride he'd felt at standing next to Dare as Doc asked them these same questions and they became brand-new prospects together.

Mike nodded, his expression serious. "I am." An approving murmur rolled through the group.

"The Raven Riders is more than just a club. It's a brotherhood of men who share similar interests, interests that include standing up for those who can't stand up for themselves. It's a family of choice, made up of the brothers and their kin—a family that protects and takes care of its own. We ride, we fight, and we defend as one. If you want to be a part of the Raven Riders, declare your intentions and accept your prospective status by putting on this cut." Dare held up the jacket for all to see. Unlike the cuts of the fully patched members, a prospect's cut lacked the Raven Riders' patches and name and location rockers, or badges, on the back. Instead, both the back and the chest simply read, *Prospect*. The full patches had to be earned. "Wearing it proclaims your loyalty and membership until such time as we deem you fit for fully patched status."

Mike stepped forward, and Dare slid the cut onto his bulky frame. Maverick grinned as welcoming cheers broke out all around.

The prospect came to Maverick first. "Thanks, Maverick. Really proud to be here."

"We're glad to have you," Mav said, glad to have something to celebrate, something that let them all focus on the future. One by one, everyone shook Mike's hand and personally welcomed him, and grabbed one of the beers Blake had served up on the bar.

"Words of wisdom for our new brother?" Dare called out.

"The more you contribute, the easier it'll be to become a full member," Bear said. Words of agreement rang out.

"Don't be a fuckup," Phoenix said with a grin. He raised his beer in a salute and gave the man a wink. Guys raised their beers all around to that one, and Mike took it in good humor, laughing and nodding.

A man of few words, Caine shifted on his boots. His ice-blue eyes zeroed in on Mike. "Never discuss club business with anyone. Keeping your mouth shut is always the wise choice if you're not sure."

Doc rose out of his chair, no doubt the hip and knee he'd had replaced a few years before bothering him as they often did late in the day. He ran his hand over the white hair of his beard as he looked at Mike. "As Dare said, this is a family. So start by getting to know everyone. Learn their names, and the names of their wives and kids. Figure out who can use a helping hand, and offer it. If a brother breaks down at two in the morning, go help, no questions asked."

"Amen," someone said. Others echoed the sentiment.

"Always have your brothers' backs," Jagger said. "No matter what."

Maverick nodded, agreeing down deep. The loyalty and brotherhood he'd found in this club were just two of the reasons he'd built his life around it. He hadn't had a good relationship with his father, which just proved that you could create a family just as well as be born into one. No doubt many of the guys felt the same way because there were a lot of loners, outcasts, and men estranged from their families for all kinds of reasons standing in this room.

Mav turned to Mike. "Whenever you're wearing that cut, you're not just representing yourself. You're representing the club. And me. And every man in this room. Never forget that."

Mike nodded, taking it all in.

Dare raised his beer. "To brotherhood, club, and family."

"Brotherhood. Club. Family," everyone called out, following the toast. Maverick took a long pull off his beer and clapped Mike on the back. "Welcome to the Ravens."

The man smiled and nodded, and soon got pulled into a conversation with a couple other brothers. Music turned on. Laughter rang out. On the other side of the room, someone racked up the balls on one of the pool tables.

"The club needs this," Dare said, coming to stand beside Maverick. Was his face pale, or was Mav just imagining it? The guy hadn't seemed himself since Friday night's fight. "New blood. Especially with everything that's gone on."

"Yeah," Maverick said, eyeballing his cousin. "Fresh enthusiasm never hurts. Especially after the other night."

"Amen to that," Dare said. "At least it appears we put the Baltimore issue to bed once and for all. Nick emailed news from Chen this morning. They've confirmed that most of the Iron Cross are either in custody, dead, or scattered."

Mav sighed as a weight lifted off his shoulders. Having that threat gone? Knowing those who'd hurt his mother wouldn't be able to do it again? Yeah, he couldn't help but feel good about that. "Glad that's behind us."

Jagger joined them, his fingers tapping out a beat against the back of an iPad he held.

Maverick clasped hands with the guy. "What's up, Jag?"

He raked longish brown hair back from his face. "The carnival's what's up. And I'm nailing down volunteers for shit while everyone's here."

"Damn, Jagger. You work fast," Maverick said. The guy always went above and beyond for the club, which was why their operations at the racetrack were such a success, recent catastrophe notwithstanding. "What do you need?"

"Eh, it's not all me. I've had help," he said, tapping on the tablet. "Okay, I have tickets, parking, and meeting the race car drivers almost covered. But I need setup and tear-down and dunking booth victims." Jagger smirked.

"Count me out for that shit," Dare said, and then he rushed to add, "Wound. Very serious wound. Can't get it wet. Doctor's orders."

Maverick threw him a look. "Doctor also said to keep your stubborn ass off your ride. Expect me to push on that next time." Dare flipped him off, clearly pleased that he had a reason not to get wet. Shaking his head, Mav said, "Count me in for the damn dunking booth. And put both of us down for setting up." Dare gave a nod.

"Done," Jagger said, then he threw Dare a mischievous grin. "Oh, by the way, D."

"Yeah?"

"Haven volunteered for the dunking booth."

As Dare's expression visibly darkened, Jagger winked at Maverick and took off. Dare mumbled something under his breath about good hearts and wearing a parka that made Mav laugh.

Dare scrubbed at his face and released an agitated sigh. "You heading out?"

To Alexa's hung unspoken in the air between them. Maverick tipped the bottle to his mouth and took a long draw. "Nah. Here with all you ugly motherfuckers is where I want to be for right now." Seeing her yesterday had been fantastic, but it had left him feeling hollower than he wanted to admit. And he wasn't leaving Dare when the guy looked like hell.

With a wry grin, Dare clapped him on the back. "Good. Then let's find a place to plant our asses, because my goddamned side is killing me."

The admission caught Maverick by surprise. "You—"

"Fine. Just overdid it. Which makes me sound like a fucking geriatric," Dare groused as they cut through the crowd to one of the big groupings of leather couches.

"A geriatric dating a twenty-two-year-old hottie. Not bad," Maverick said with a wink.

Dare glared at him. "Shut the fuck up." He dropped into the corner of one of the couches on a grimace.

Maverick looked at him, and the realization hit that Dare

wasn't joking around like he had been. "Shit, D. You know I didn't mean anything by that." He sat facing Dare. "You gotta know I respect the hell out of Haven. As long as I live, I will *never* be able to forget seeing her save your life and protect your body with hers. Damn. I'm sorry."

Waving him off, Dare shook his head. "Forget about it."

"You're really serious about her." Maverick knew he was, but he hadn't realized just *how* serious. Clearly. Dare just eyeballed him. "How serious? Talk to me, man."

Dare nailed him with an assessing stare, then gave a little shrug with his uninjured shoulder that belied the significance of what came out of his mouth. "Forever serious."

The words impacted Maverick square in the chest. "Have you asked her—"

"No," Dare said, glancing around to see if anyone might be listening in. But the music and other conversations gave them cover in the midst of the chaos. "I'm in no rush. Neither is she. But when the time is right . . ." He shrugged again.

"Fuckin' A," Maverick said, managing a smile. "I'm damn happy for you. For both of you." He meant it, especially since not two weeks ago, Dare had convinced himself that he'd have to send Haven away—to keep both her and the club safe. Now, nothing stood in their way. Just as it should be.

Which just cast a big, ol' glaring spotlight on all the things Maverick didn't have, didn't it? Probably made him an asshole to spend one second of time feeling regret in this moment when his best friend admitted to having found everything he ever wanted. Maverick knew it did. But he couldn't help it.

"Thanks," Dare said. "But do me a favor and keep your trap shut about it. I don't want anyone teasing and making Haven feel uncomfortable. Or whatever." Mav nodded. "And besides, we got word on Friday that Haven may be due some inheritance from her father's estate, assuming it gets released by the Feds. So we got things to work through."

"Ain't that some shit," Maverick said. "What's she thinking?"

"She was stunned at first. Then said she wanted nothing to do with anything that'd been his. But then she asked me if the Ravens could use the money to help our protectees." Pride and affection came over Dare's expression.

"And then she was willing to consider it?" Mav asked. It was just like Haven. He still remembered watching her tend to Alexa's wounds the day she came here. He'd already liked Haven then, but that was the day she earned his undying loyalty.

"Yup," Dare said. "Cora told her she should use it to open her own bakery business, which I think is fucking brilliant, but Haven said she'd rather use it to help other people like herself. We'll see. Either way, it's up in the air for now."

"You got a good one, D. For real." Maverick took another pull from his beer.

"The best." On a sigh, he relaxed back into the leather.

"Hey, speaking of Cora, where has she been?" Maverick asked. "I haven't seen her around lately." Cora Campbell was Haven's best friend from back home in Georgia. The pair of them had run away together from some bad situations and landed with the Raven Riders last month. From what Maverick understood, Cora had played a big role in helping Haven escape from her father, and she was also sarcastic and funny as hell. What Maverick knew of her, he liked.

Dare peeled at the label on his beer bottle. "She's been at Slider's place watching the boys. He got in a jam because the lady who usually watches Sam and Ben has been sick."

"Huh. Kinda awesome of her to help out like that," Maverick said. Sam "Slider" Evans was a longtime member who'd lost his wife to breast cancer three years before. As

far as Maverick could tell, the old Slider they'd all known—
the one who'd wiped out on his bike without injuring himself or his ride and got up laughing about it—no longer
existed and never would. The guy's pain was so tangible
that he wore it like a shadow. He hadn't attended Church
on Thursday or participated in their ride to Baltimore that
next night, and Mav hadn't been the least surprised at
either. His two boys seemed to be the only thing that kept
him functioning.

"That's for damn sure." Dare nodded, his concern about
Slider clear in his expression. "Haven said Cora's happy to
do it. And I appreciate the hell out of anything that takes
even a little weight off of Slider's shoulders."

"Damn straight," Maverick said. And the fact that Cora
was doing just that was one more reason to like her.

Dare shifted and propped his boots up on a table, his
ankles crossed. "I'm thirty-fucking-seven, Maverick. I
didn't think anything like what I have with Haven would
happen for me. In fact, I was sure it wouldn't."

Maverick sagged back, his hands clasped across his
stomach. "Yeah."

"Hey," Dare said, tagging his arm. "You get what I'm
saying?"

Frowning, Mav just stared at the guy. He wasn't the
slightest bit interested in having this conversation.

Rolling his eyes, Dare nailed him with a pointed stare.
"When you gonna fight for what you want?"

Like it was that easy. "Come on, D." Maverick looked
away, not wanting his cousin to see the resentment he
probably wore for even bringing it up. For making Maverick confront yet again the fact that he'd given his heart
to someone who didn't want it. And he couldn't seem to
get it back.

Dare heaved a belabored breath. "Fine. I'm just saying."

"Well, don't. Let's move on to religion or politics or

something." Because hell if he wanted to keep pricking at all the sore places inside himself.

"All right," Dare said, and the concern and resignation in his voice was a total kick in the ass. But whatever. Mav's life was what it fucking was. And for the most part, it was good. Damnit, before Alexa had shown up the week before last, he probably would've said it was great. This place, these men, Bunny and Rodeo and Doc and Dare—*this* was Maverick's home, his family. He didn't need a woman to give him a sense of belonging.

He really didn't.

And it made him resent her for stirring up all this shit for him again after so long. For reminding him of the feeling he'd battled five years before that a part of him had died and been put in the ground right alongside Tyler. Because he'd lost his friend. And then he'd lost his woman. And his love for her had been killing him ever since.

That resentment? That was good. He clutched onto it. Because it was a helluva lot easier to be angry than to be hurt. It was that anger that had him making a resolution, one that self-preservation meant he was gonna have to stick to once and for fucking all.

He'd do right by Tyler's memory and the history he shared with Alexa and keep an eye out for her as much as he could. Just in case his gut was reading things right. But in thirteen days, she'd be walking down an aisle and into another man's arms.

Which meant Maverick had just under two weeks to let Alexa Harmon go. For good. Because he couldn't keep wanting something he could never have.

CHAPTER 11

The gown was quite possibly the most beautiful thing Alexa had ever seen. Standing on the raised step in front of the angled mirrors, Alexa couldn't stop admiring her wedding dress. It had a voluminous A-line skirt made of tulle, a long chapel train, a satin bodice with a flattering sweetheart neckline, and a wide champagne-colored ribbon at the waist. Classic. Romantic. Ungodly expensive, but Grant wanted to spare no expense on their wedding.

Pick something beautiful. Something that will make me proud.

That's what he'd told her as she'd set out to shop for a dress, a personal shopper he'd hired at her side. The woman had steered Alexa away from what she'd deemed the *pedestrian* dresses to more exclusive, one-of-a-kind designer gowns—following instructions Grant had apparently given her. He wanted their wedding to be the swankiest social event Western Maryland had ever seen. And since so many business associates would be there, she understood why, even though all of it was so much more than what she needed to be happy. Alexa had dreamed of having a beautiful wedding as much as any other woman, but it was the marriage that came after and the joy of building a life together that was most important to her. Because she wanted what her own parents never seemed to have had.

The seamstress inspected each alteration she'd made and frowned as she examined the hidden back zipper. "It is a little snug here," she said, running her fingers down Alexa's spine.

The French fries Alexa had gotten at the drive-thru on the way to the fitting sat like a rock in her stomach. Snug . . . because she'd been eating junk food nonstop the past three days. Ever since having sex with Grant in the bathroom at the inn had left her feeling so strange. So unsettled. So . . . unsure.

Even more than she'd already been. She just wasn't sure if she was making something out of nothing. *Or allowing Grant to walk all over me*, a little voice whispered.

The older woman met Alexa's eyes in the mirror. "Hmm. Maybe I should—"

"Don't worry," Alexa said, shaking her head and putting on a smile despite the tendril of panic snaking through her veins. "We just did some celebrating this past weekend. I overindulged a little. But it'll be fine by the wedding." Alexa would make sure of it. Grant wanted everything to be perfect—including her. Maybe even especially her. And she certainly wouldn't make him proud if she was busting out the seams of her six-thousand-dollar gown.

So stupid. Why hadn't she thought more about the fitting today?

"Okay, then. If you're sure," the seamstress said with a smile. "Let's get this off of you. You're all set."

An hour later, Alexa was back at the office, that rock still heavy in her stomach.

"Hey, sweetie," Christina Lee said from behind the ornate reception desk as Alexa entered the building. Alexa and Christina had started working at Slater Enterprises at nearly the same time—about a month before Tyler's death, and they'd been friendly ever since. Friendly enough that Alexa had asked her to be her maid of honor, and Christina had agreed. They might've even become much closer, but Grant's pursuit of Alexa back then seemed to have scared some people off of befriending her, like they were afraid Alexa might report back on them to the big boss. But that was better than the people who resented her for their relationship. "How'd the fitting go?"

Alexa leaned against the high desk. "Good. It's so gorgeous I can barely stand it."

"Of course it is," Christina said, grinning. "Less than two weeks now."

Something which should've unleashed excitement inside of her, but . . . didn't. "I can hardly believe it," she said, forcing a smile of her own.

"What's left on the list that I can help with?" she asked.

"Honestly, not too much. I visited the venue yesterday and confirmed the menu and did a little shopping last night. So things are on track, but let me check with Grant about his schedule. We should get together for dinner one night this week." Assuming he had a late meeting so she wasn't taking time away from him.

"You know I'd love that," Christina said. A phone call came in through the switchboard. "Oh, duty beckons."

Alexa gave a little wave and made her way to her office on the second floor. She probably ought to search out Betsy, Maggie, and Ellen, other lunch friends at work who had agreed to be bridesmaids, to keep them in the loop of wedding goings-on, but she found that she wasn't as up to it as she wanted to be. There'd be other chances to tell them about her fun weekend and the amazing party favors that'd finally come in and just how gorgeous her dress really was another day this week.

Instead, she dropped into the chair at her desk and threw herself into reviewing the construction punch list from the model home she was decorating. The place was amazing— the kind of home she'd always dreamed of living in. Spacious and light and airy, comfortable and well designed, chic without being stuffy. She'd spent the morning on-site doing a walk-through with the foreman and compiling the list which noted incomplete installations that needed to be corrected and incidental damage that needed to be fixed. Furniture to stage the model would be arriving this Thursday, so she was hoping the guys would work through most of the list before the deliveries began. All of which was leading up to her deadline next Wednesday to have the place ready for Grant's stamp of approval. That gave her eight days. And today was half gone.

Her gaze slipped to the clock display at the bottom corner of her computer screen. *Maybe I should skip class tonight.*

She twisted her lips as she debated, and quickly ruled it out. It might only be her one-credit professional development course, but she was already going to miss one class during their honeymoon. And since the class only met once a week, not going would be the equivalent of missing a whole week's worth of material.

Knock, knock.

Grant stepped into her office wearing an exquisitely cut navy blue suit, his hand behind his back. "Alexa."

"Oh, hey," she said, smiling. "I wasn't sure if you were back yet." She'd known he had plans this morning to be out of the office inspecting an apartment complex he was considering buying and rehabbing. Alexa got up and came around her desk to him.

"I am, though I have another meeting off-site shortly. But I wanted to catch you before you left for class," he said. "And I brought you something." He handed her a single long-stemmed red rose.

The gesture reached right inside her chest. "Aw, Grant. This is so sweet," she said. It was just the pick-me-up she needed. She grasped the flower and brought the velvety petals to her nose. "Thank you."

"Anything and everything for you, babe. You know that." He pressed a kiss to her cheek, her jaw, the corner of her lips. And then his mouth came down on hers as his body boxed her in against the desk. Alexa's gaze strayed to her open office door and she ignored her discomfort over the possibility that someone might see them. It wasn't like everyone didn't know they were together, but Alexa still didn't like to flaunt it in front of their colleagues. It was one of the reasons she still drove herself to work, and definitely why she'd refused a bigger office in the executive suite. What she got here at work, she wanted to have *earned*. Maybe she'd feel differently after they were married. Or maybe not. Just when she was going to pull away, Grant did instead. "Any chance I can talk you into staying home tonight?" he asked, a mischievous smile on his face.

"I wish. But I don't want to get behind before we leave on our honeymoon. Then I'm all yours." She gave him a sweet peck on the cheek. "Thank you again for the rose. You made my day."

He stepped away and smoothed a hand down over his red silk tie. "Just as well, I suppose. The mayor's having a reception, and I should probably put in some face time."

"He's a good friend to you," Alexa said. "So go and enjoy. I won't stay after, though. I'll come right home."

"You do that," Grant said as he stepped to the door and made to leave. Then he peered back in, his smile sexy and playful. "I'll be waiting."

Alexa grinned as Grant left, pulling the door shut behind him. He could be so charming, so attentive, so thoughtful—qualities that had attracted her from the beginning. She hadn't realized how much she needed that side of him today. And it made her want to show him how grateful she was.

Which made her even more eager to have class over with.

But, fine, she'd go. At least now she had something to look forward to when she got home.

TIRED FROM CLASS and from driving home in the pounding rain, Alexa came in through the garage door to the dark kitchen and dumped her purse and messenger bag on the counter. Seeing Grant would make her feel better. Hands free, she flicked on the light.

"Grant? I'm home," she called. Her gaze snagged on the desk built into one wall of the kitchen because . . . it was totally reorganized. The mail had been sorted by size, shape, and color, the edges of the envelopes lined up exactly parallel to the edge of the desktop. The pins in the corkboard were all in neat rows, sorted by color. Grant did things like that every once in a while, but she'd learned to just take it in stride after asking about it had once caused an argument.

She turned to find Lucy curling her sleek body around the corner of the island, meowing a greeting at her.

"Hi, baby," Alexa said, crouching to give her little one some love. Sometimes it seemed that Lucy was the most dog-like cat Alexa had ever known. Lucy came when Alexa got home and when she called. She loved to play. Was generous with her affection. And pretty much always wanted to be where Alexa was.

So as Alexa went in search of Grant, Lucy padded behind her. The house felt unusually still. Quiet. The steady drumming of the rain on the roof was the only sound she heard. Grant wasn't in the living room, nor the media room, nor their bedroom. She knocked on his mostly open office door. "Grant?" she said as she peered into the darkness. His car was in the garage, so he had to be here somewhere. Her heart tripped into a sprint as worry lanced through her.

The chair at his carved mahogany desk sat empty.

Lucy hung back in the hallway as Alexa made her way across the room, turned on the desk lamp, and pulled her cell out of her back pocket.

"Just who is it you're calling?" came a voice from behind her.

Alexa nearly screamed. She jumped and whirled, her heart in her throat, the phone clutched tight in her hand. "Grant! Oh, my God. You scared me. Are you okay?" She rushed across the room to where he sat in the big wingback leather chair in the corner. Leaning over him, she cupped his face in her hand. "Why didn't you answer me?"

He stared down at a tumbler in his hand that Alexa hadn't noticed he was holding. Bourbon, if she had to guess. A quick glance to the Chippendale table next to the chair revealed a mostly empty bottle. His lips pressed into a tight line and his brow slashed downward. He tilted the glass in his hand as if watching the amber liquid was somehow mesmerizing. When he finally peered up at her, it was as if he'd turned into another man.

Grant's expression was like a storm descending—dark, twisted, calculating. "Did you think I wouldn't find out?" he asked, the words gritty and harsh.

"Find out what?" she asked, her thoughts frozen, her stomach dropping.

"Don't play coy with me, Alexa," he said, batting her hand away from his face.

Stepping back, Alexa shook her head, dread a living thing inside her. "Grant, I don't—"

"Don't fucking deny it!" he roared, lunging up from his chair. He grabbed her by the biceps and got right in her face.

"Grant, stop. Deny what? What happened?" she asked as she curled in on herself. His fingers dug into her arms like hooks.

He shoved her free and brushed his hands down his shirt as if to straighten himself, and then he glared at her. "How do you think it felt to have one of the sheriffs tell me, in front of the mayor, that he saw you riding on the back of Maverick Rylan's motorcycle? A goddamned degenerate Raven Rider piece of shit." He spoke with a quiet reserve that was somehow scarier than when he'd raised his voice.

Alexa broke out in a cold sweat as nausea swept through her. "I . . . I can explain."

"I'm sure you can."

She shook her head and held out her hands. "It was innocent. He was helping me—"

"Oh, I'll bet. I know *exactly* what Rylan wants to help you with." He picked up his glass off the carpet and poured just enough bourbon in it to finish in one big gulp. She hadn't even seen the glass fall, he'd moved so fast.

Alexa's mouth was so dry it was hard to talk. "He rode by my mom's house on Saturday morning and happened to see me hauling trash to the curb. I was doing some cleaning for her, and I wanted to get rid of the garbage instead of letting it sit there in a big pile. He offered to get his truck to take the stuff to the dump for me. That's all."

"What do you take me for, Alexa?" he asked.

"I don't . . . Nothing. It's true. I only went with him to get his truck because things had been really tense with Mom and I wanted a break before we got into an argument. You know how she is," Alexa pleaded, her head spinning, her heart thundering in her chest.

"Oh, I do. I live with her daughter, after all." He chuffed out a humorless laugh and shook his head. Paced back to the table and poured himself more liquor.

His words hit her like a body slam, knocking the breath out of her. Regret and guilt twisted inside her. "That's all that happened. He was just helping me."

Grant turned to her and glared, his face flushed. From anger or the alcohol, Alexa wasn't sure. "You made a fucking fool of me. Twice. First, by parading around town with a known criminal. And second, when I refuted the sheriff's words, saying, *oh, no, that must've been someone else because Alexa was at her mother's.* Only to have Davis insist he'd seen your face clearly while you'd been waiting at a red light on 15. Hanging all over another man."

"I'm sorry," she said, tears pricking at the backs of her eyes. "It didn't mean anything. He used to be very close to my mother because of how long he and Tyler had been friends. He was just helping. That's all it was." She heaved a breath, trying to calm herself down, trying to keep everything from falling apart.

"It's not how close he is to your *mother* that worries me," Grant sneered.

Alexa's stomach dropped to the floor. "Seriously?" she asked, the thought voicing itself without her permission.

His head tilted as his eyes narrowed. "You don't agree that sneaking around behind my back and lying warrants suspicion?"

The air felt thick as she drew it into her lungs, as if her sensation of dread had taken on a physical form all around them. "I wasn't sneaking around. And we weren't doing anything wrong. We were in public. In broad daylight."

"And by your own admission, you went to his house," he said, his tone like he'd just produced the smoking gun.

Alexa put her hand to her forehead, absolutely at a loss for how to pull this back from the brink of disaster, and beyond stunned at how different this night was going from what she'd planned. She'd expected to come home and seduce Grant, to show him her gratitude for his thoughtfulness earlier, to make love to him slowly and thoroughly until they were both sated and sleepy. "I . . . I don't know what else to say. I'm sorry I didn't mention seeing him. I should have, and I'm sorry. Frankly, I didn't want it to cause a fight when seeing him had been completely random and unlikely to happen again. And honestly, I was so surprised by the trip you planned for us that all my thoughts were focused on being with you and us being together."

"At least you don't deny lying to me. I'm giving you all this"—he gestured with outspread arms at the room, the house, the physical proof of his wealth and power— "and lies and deceit and betrayal are what you give me in return." He braced his hands on his hips and shook his head, disgust pouring off of him.

The guilt inside her twisted, morphed, flashed hot. Anger took root in the center of her chest. "I don't need all this, Grant. I need a man who trusts me. Who doesn't assume the worst of me. Who knows I can be in the room with another man, even someone I used to date, and remain faithful. I give you that kind of trust, and what you're giving me in return is suspicion and accusation." The more she spoke, the faster the words spilled out of her, and the stronger the anger grew inside her. And, oh, man, the well of anger inside her was deep. So deep. *Scary* deep. How had she not seen that before?

Color raised higher in his cheeks and his eyes blazed with anger and outrage. "Oh, you don't need all this? Is that it? You'd rather go back to the shithole of a life you had before me? Is that what you're saying? You have *nothing* without me. You *are nothing* without me."

Oh, my God.

"How could you say such a horrible thing?" she whispered, calling him out in a way she never had before. "How could you even think it?" Nausea rolled through her at his words. Was that what he really thought of her? *Why are you so surprised, Alexa? And how much more do you need to hear before you grow a spine?*

"Truth hurts, sweetheart." He glared at her. He stared at her like she was trash, which was exactly how he was trying to make her feel. But she wasn't feeding herself his running commentary this time. Not this time.

"Yeah, I guess it does," she said, staring at everything she thought she'd wanted. And seeing for the first time that it had all been a pretty charade. A pretty charade she'd let herself believe in with all her heart. "You know what? Let's take a break before one of us says something else we don't mean." Because she needed a moment. Just one. To decide whether to try to fix what was broken . . . or start packing her bags.

Do you really *need to think about it?* She suddenly felt like she was standing on the edge of a tall cliff and about to plunge into a free fall.

"I mean every word I'm saying, darling. Count on it."

The hollowness in her chest hurt so damn bad. What a fool she'd been. What a blind, stupid doormat. Maverick was right—Tyler would've killed her if he knew what she'd let Grant get away with. "Wow. Okay," she said, shaking her head. She made for the door.

"Don't walk away from me, Alexa," Grant growled.

She kept going. As she rounded the corner toward the kitchen, she nearly tripped on Lucy who was hiding in the shadows as if she'd been listening to them fight, but from a safe distance. Alexa caught herself on the wall and leaned down to scoop up the cat, needing her warmth and her unconditional love. Alexa's stomach was jiggly and her knees were weak and her heart hurt so damn bad she could barely breathe. Nothing felt real.

Fingers wrapped around Alexa's arm, squeezing a gasp out of her. The grip was hard. Painfully tight.

"Wha—"

Grant tugged and dragged her, not saying a word.

Alexa stumbled until her feet caught up with his pace. "Grant, stop. *Stop.* You're hurting me."

He pulled her through the hall and into the foyer. Lucy growled and her claws dug into Alexa's shoulder in response to being jostled.

When they got to the front door, Grant pushed her against it roughly, hand still like a manacle, her shoulder and the back of her head making contact with the hard wood. Lucy struggled in her arms, but Alexa was so stunned that she hung on.

"You don't need all this? You don't think I'm good enough for you?" His chuckle held absolutely no humor. "Then you're fucking free to go," he seethed, his face looming over hers.

"What that's suppo—"

"Enjoy seeing what life would be like without me, Alexa." In one fast movement, he yanked her to the side, pulled the door wide, and then pushed her through the opening onto the front porch, giving her a rough shove when he finally let go of her arm. Lucy did break free then, her back claws catching Alexa on the neck as she jumped.

Alexa was so shell-shocked that she barely felt it. "What in the world are you doing?"

"Nothing you didn't ask for." The door slammed in her face. A metallic click told her he'd thrown the dead bolt for good measure.

She stared at the door in disbelief. "Are you fucking kidding me?" she yelled, pounding on the door with her fist. "Grant! Open the damn door." She pounded again. "Grant!"

The porch light shut off, and then what lights had been on inside went out, too.

"Grant!" She pounded again. "You're being a lunatic!"

She blinked at the darkness, at the craziness of what was

happening to her life. Of what she'd *let* happen. Her fiancé had thrown her out of their house. Out of her own house. Over a motorcycle ride.

Alexa stepped back, the whole world feeling like a Tilt-A-Whirl. It wasn't until the thunder cracked that she even realized it was still raining. The porch roof protected her from the deluge, though the air was humid with it. Lucy sat as far away from the front door as she could get while still being under the porch's cover. Her tail flicked in agitation.

Alexa's fiancé had thrown her out of the house in a storm. At ten o'clock at night. Because she'd gone on a motorcycle ride.

It was so ridiculously unbelievable that for a moment she was frozen standing there, no idea what to do, unable to think. Remembering her cell phone, she fished it from her pocket and immediately found and pressed Grant's number. She hugged herself as she placed the cell to her ear and listened to the ringing.

Four rings. Voice mail. Thunder crashed above her. For a moment, lightning lit up the night. She hung up and redialed. Two and a half rings. Voice mail. Which meant he'd declined the call. *Asshole.*

Mind in a spiral, Alexa hugged herself and stared down at the floor. And was suddenly sucked back to Saturday afternoon in that fancy bathroom. Feeling sore and upset and *used*. Violated, if she really wanted to be honest. Why hadn't she been honest before?

How long had she been hiding from the truth?

And now this.

"Oh, my God," she said, pressing her palm against her forehead to ward off the headache blooming there.

Weeks' worth—hell, maybe even months' worth—of nagging doubts and quiet misgivings roared into her thoughts next. The way he always made her feel like she needed to apologize. The way he so often made her feel like she was crazy or irrational for asking a question or having a different point of view or even remembering something differently. How he so often made her feel guilty and like she wasn't good enough, and how he'd left her feeling in that bathroom.

The horrible things he'd said to her in his office. The way he'd manhandled her. The fact that he'd locked her out of her own house to prove a point, to make her grovel to be taken back, to punish her.

"I can't do this," she whispered, shaking her head. Tears welled until the porch went blurry. "I can't." She took one step back from the door, then another. "I'm *not* doing this," she said louder, though the rain swallowed up the words. The weight of everything crashed over her like a wave, and a sob broke free. "*Fuck this*," she rasped. "I'm not begging to be taken back. I'm not standing out here waiting. I'm not . . . I'm not . . ." Her hands fisted. She bit back the tears, because she wasn't crying over this asshole either. She'd already given him enough pieces of herself as it was.

It was time to start taking them back.

Starting with her dignity.

Trembling with shock and anger, Alexa crouched and held out her hand toward Lucy. Slowly, the cat came to her and sniffed at her fingers, and Alexa scooped the sphynx into her arms.

Alexa made for the steps, and then something occurred to her. She paused. Considered. And then turned back to the door. Juggling the cat, she tugged the diamond off her ring finger, too numb to know if the relief that washed through her was real or confusion resulting from this insanity. Not that it mattered. She wasn't changing her mind.

She dropped the ring over the top of one of the pointed brass leaves on the pineapple door knocker.

Without even one more thought, she walked off the porch into the storm, not looking back even once.

The rain immediately drenched her straight through, but she didn't care. Especially given how fast her mind churned. Alexa had no idea where she was going, or what she was going to do, or how she was going to figure out what happened next.

All she knew was that she had to get away. Everything inside her was screaming for that. *Had been* screaming for that for so long. Only, now, she was finally hearing it. She was finally *listening to it*. Where the hell had she been? The real Alexa. The *old* Alexa.

She was four houses down the street when a flash of lights from behind her illuminated the sidewalk. Dread ignited inside her. If it was Grant, what would she do?

Panic nearly making her take flight, she looked over her shoulder. It was just a pickup, not Grant. Relief surged through her, and then an even bigger wave of it hit as she realized.

Maverick. It was Maverick.

The truck pulled to a stop beside her and the passenger door pushed open. "I've got you, Al. Get in."

CHAPTER 12

Maverick was nearly shaking he was so pissed off.

From the moment he'd seen Alexa walk off her front porch into the rain, his body had gone on high alert. Because there hadn't been a damn thing normal about that. And when she'd rushed down the street in the darkness, in the middle of a goddamned storm, he'd known. Some kinda shit had gone down.

Thunder cracked so loud it rattled the old truck's windows. For a long moment, he concentrated on the roads, the traffic, just getting her away. "I know it's a stupid fucking question, but I gotta ask it anyway. Are you okay? Are you hurt?" He tried really hard to keep the rage out of his voice.

"He didn't hit me," she said, her voice barely audible over the rain and the windshield wipers. "Can we just . . . not? Not yet?" The anguish in her pretty eyes nearly slayed him.

He gave a tight nod. But that didn't mean he wasn't

dying to know what the hell had happened. That Slater hadn't hit her was the only thing keeping the asshole above ground right now. But she hadn't said she was okay, had she? In the light that shone into the cab from oncoming cars, her skin appeared pale, her eyes unfocused, and there were angry scratches on her neck. Though given the constant low yowls coming from the cat curled in her lap, maybe the strange-looking thing had been responsible for those.

All she left with were the clothes on her back and her cat.

What. The. Fuck.

When they came up along the outskirts of the Raven Riders' property, Alexa finally spoke again. "Where are we going?" she asked.

"I'm taking you home." Maverick felt the rightness of those words down deep, even if she wouldn't hear them the way he felt them. And even if he couldn't keep her.

"Home." She said the word with so much hollow despair that it made him need to touch her. He reached across the old bench seat and grasped her cold hand in his. She clutched him right back. Which was when he realized that she was shaking.

Everything inside him wanted to go ballistic. But he had to keep the urge to flip the fuck out under control. Whatever had happened hadn't been pretty, and he didn't need to make things worse for her. Because the only other time he'd seen Alexa Harmon look so fragile, so vulnerable, so lost, was when Tyler had died five years before.

Maverick had known Alexa Harmon long enough to know that Ty's death had been the worst moment of her life. And it had changed everything—about her life and about his own. Which meant whatever had happened tonight had been bad.

But Mav would have to let her open up at her own pace, because pushing her to explain what had happened hadn't worked worth shit two weeks before when she'd shown up at the clubhouse with a bloodied face.

Soon, he was parking on the circle as close to his front door as he could. "Sorry. We're gonna have to get wet to get in."

She shook her head. "God, Maverick, please don't apologize." For a moment, she stared out the rain-blurred window at his place, and then she hugged Lucy close and opened the door. She moved mechanically, like her brain wasn't fully connected to her body.

Marrow-deep concern lanced through him as he hauled ass around the truck, the rain pelting his face and drenching him straight through in seconds. Under the cover of the porch, he opened the screen door and unlocked the front, and then he pushed it open for Alexa and gestured for her to go first.

They stepped inside, both of them dripping all over the place. "I'll get some towels." He rushed into the hall bathroom and grabbed two, then returned to find Alexa standing right where he'd left her by the door, her nose pressed to the cat's head.

"You can put her down if you want," he said as he offered Alexa a towel. He was trying like hell to do what she needed, even though what he really wanted to do was haul her into his arms and make sure she was okay with his hands and his mouth and his body.

Alexa placed Lucy on the floor and grasped the terry cloth, pressing it to her face, squeezing it around her hair, and wrapping it around her shoulders like she was cold. Or like she needed the fabric to hold her together.

Fuck.

"Alexa—"

"Please." She gave a quick shake of her head, and those hazel eyes cut up to his.

Not knowing what she was asking for, Maverick just

nodded as he gave his face and hair a quick swipe of the towel. "Do you want to, uh, sit? Or have something to drink? Or . . ." He shifted feet and dragged a hand through his wet hair.

"I'm soaked," she said, looking down at herself. When she looked up again, she had a strange expression on her face, one that quickly shifted into amusement. Laughter spilled out of her, and she slapped a hand over her mouth. "I don't—" More laughter, this time with a slightly hysterical tinge to it.

Maverick frowned.

"Oh, my God," she finally said. She cupped her hand to her forehead. "I don't have . . . anything. I don't have clothes or my purse or my keys or my schoolwork. I literally have nothing." She peered up at him, her expression full of incredulity.

Anger lanced hot and fast through Maverick's blood. "Anything you need, I will give you or help you get," he said, meaning in the short term, but he wasn't opposed to meaning it otherwise, too.

Alexa let go of the towel, dropping it to the floor, and pressed both of her hands to her mouth—and that was when he noticed. She wasn't wearing that big-ass rock. Her ring finger was bare.

Chaos erupted inside his head.

He couldn't help it. Maverick stepped closer and gently grabbed her left hand. For a long moment, he looked down at the pale indent where the ring had been, and something that felt dangerously like hope flared through him. Except he beat that shit back—hard—because he couldn't afford to make assumptions here. He wouldn't survive it. And that wasn't what she needed right now anyway.

Finally, he looked up at her, the air between them heavy with so much. Unanswered questions. History. Desire.

Alexa's grip tightened around his hand, her eyes shiny

and bright as she looked into his. And then her whole face crumpled and she burst into tears.

Maverick finally gave in to what he'd been wanting to do and hauled her into his arms. "Fuck, Alexa," he said, stroking her wet hair with one hand while holding her tight to him with the other. The rightness of her against him made his body fucking sing. "Whatever it is, I'll help you figure it out." He wasn't even sure she heard him over her wracking sobs. Sobs for another man. Desire, his ass. On his part, maybe.

Don't lose sight of what's going on here, Maverick. She didn't come to you. She didn't call you. You picked her up.

Which was all true. The only good thing about how upset she was right now was that it forced him to keep his feet planted squarely in reality. A reality where she was crying over her troubles with another man.

Standing there holding her, her body tucked tight against his, her hands fisted in his T-shirt under his Ravens cut, he pushed everything else away and focused on her. A million years ago, they'd started off as friends—good friends.

That's what he would be to her once again.

ALEXA HATED THAT she was crying, but there was so much noise inside her that she'd just needed to let it out. She wasn't crying over Grant, exactly, but over the loss of the life she thought she was building. And, even more, over the humiliation and soul-deep disappointment she felt in herself for tolerating all the things in their relationship that had made her feel so bad for so long. She was just so fucking *mad*.

Old, long-ingrained thoughts tried to sneak in around the anger. Thoughts that made excuses and put blame on herself and tore herself down. Thoughts she'd learned the past five years, from Grant. Thoughts she'd made a very bad habit of taking to heart and making her own.

How had that happened? Why had she let it? How long had it been going on?

Who the hell had she become?

"Whatever you need, Al. Just name it," Maverick said, his big hands giving her so much comfort.

She forced a deep breath. And another. Trying to rein herself in. She scrubbed at her face and leaned her forehead against his broad chest. She breathed him in, her heart and her body recognizing his scent, all leather and soap and Maverick. And she wondered if just a few of her tears weren't for the relationship she'd walked away from five years before out of grief over losing Tyler to the thing Maverick loved most, fear of getting hurt even worse if she lost Mav, too, and the crushing weight of responsibility for her mother.

Right there in that moment, Maverick was her rock. Dependable, reliable, and certain—all things she'd doubted about him five years before. All things she'd believed Grant absolutely guaranteed.

The weight of all her mistakes was almost too much to bear.

She looked up into Maverick's dark blue eyes, so filled with concern for her, and whispered a confession. "I've been so wrong about so much for so long."

He cupped her cheek in his hand and swiped at her tears with his thumb. His calluses were rough against her skin, but it was the most amazing thing she'd felt in a long, long time. She couldn't resist leaning in to his touch. "No fucking way this was your fault. Tell me what happened."

"Grant accused me of cheating on him with you," she said.

Rage flashed through his blue eyes, but his hands remained gentle, soothing, caring. It made her heart ache and soar at the same time. "Go on," he whispered, his voice raw.

"One of the sheriffs saw us on your bike and told Grant. Nothing I said mattered. No, it was worse than that. He twisted everything I said. Threw my words back in my face." Anger rose up inside her again and she shook her head as Grant's voice echoed inside her mind. *You have nothing without me. You are nothing without me.*

"No doubt it was Curt Davis. He's so far up Slater's ass it's a surprise you don't hear Davis's voice when Slater talks." He chuffed out a humorless laugh. "All this over a fucking bike ride," Maverick said under his breath. "Damnit, I'm sorry. That's my fault."

Alexa braced her hands on his chest, his warmth seeping inside her where she was so cold, so lonely, so alone. "No, Maverick," she said, the anger coming through in her voice. "It's neither of our faults. That's the thing. There were *so many* things I couldn't do, or shouldn't do, or he would get mad. So much that was better left unsaid because it would cause a fight. I knew he wouldn't like knowing I'd ridden with you, but we didn't do anything wrong. You were just helping me. And I needed you—"

She cut herself off, the words taking her by surprise. How long had it been since she'd last let herself think that thought? That she'd *needed* Maverick Rylan.

He gave a tight nod, his eyes on fire with emotions she didn't dare to guess at.

"And then he threw me out." How humiliating was that to say out loud? Just voicing it made her stomach toss.

Maverick's eyes narrowed. "He kicked you out of the house?"

"He literally grabbed me and threw me out the front door," she whispered, barely able to give voice to such an ugly truth. "To punish me."

"Sonofabitch," he bit out, his gaze searching hers. "I'm going to kill this motherfucker. I swear to God."

"*No.* Promise me. You will *not* go after him. You're right.

He has friends in lots of places around town, including the sheriff's and mayor's offices. You lay one finger on him and he'll find a way to get you arrested. *Promise me*." She held his stare, all the while realizing she never would've talked this way to Grant. Well, not before tonight.

Maverick looked like he wanted to murder someone. Well, obviously, he did. "He threw you out of your own house, Alexa. In a goddamned storm. He hurt you."

"I know. But I refuse to let him hurt you. Promise me." She grasped Maverick by the edge of his cut and shook him. "*Promise*."

His eyes were blue fire. And, God, even rankly pissed off, he was so freaking hot. And it wasn't just his looks, though those were damn fine. It was his sense of honor. His protectiveness toward her. His basic decency. When had she stopped valuing that? "Fine. I promise. *For now*."

"Maverick—"

"Tell me what happened the day you came to the clubhouse." He arched a brow at her.

"He didn't hit me," she rushed to say.

The brow went up a little higher. "Hanging on by a very short thread here, Al."

"We got in a fight over a mess I made. He kicked a box at me and I jerked back out of the way and tripped. I fell and hit my head on a table. He told me it was my own fault and stormed out. I . . . I freaked out." The words spilled from her in a rush.

"Please tell me you realize that none of that is normal. None of that is the way normal people react to a mess or seeing someone with an ex or having a fight. Right? You get that?" The concern was back in his expression again. It only took a little of the edge off the anger, not that his anger bothered her. And it certainly didn't scare her. Because Maverick Rylan would never intentionally hurt her. It wasn't even a question.

"I know," she said on a sigh. Her shoulders fell and she ducked her chin. Unthinkingly, she rubbed her fingers over the indent where her ring used to be. "I *do* know. I knew as it was happening, although he always made things feel like they were my fault. Or I always found a way to rationalize what'd happened. *I* was the one who tripped on the box. *I* was the one who made the mess in the hall. *I* was the one who went on a bike ride with another man and didn't tell my fiancé." She shook her head. "I don't know when I started thinking that way. I was thinking about it on the ride here and I can't pinpoint exactly how it happened. Things were good between Grant and me at first. And then . . . it was like he changed, but only in bits and pieces that I learned to live with one at a time, until he'd become someone else and I'd accepted it all." She shook her head, so disappointed in herself. "What happened to me?"

Maverick caught her chin in his fingers and made her look up at him. "Abusers know they have to work up to the bad behavior. Suck you in. Make you feel special. Get you acclimated to the abuse a little at a time. Wear you down more and more until you not only can't fight back, you don't fight back," he said, voice gritty and raw. "I saw that shit with my mother, but I didn't recognize what it was. My father did that shit with me, too. Abuse is insidious, Alexa. That's why it's so effective at tearing you down and stripping you of your defenses, your support system, your independence."

Alexa nodded, surprised to hear Maverick talk about what had happened to Bunny. He'd never said much about it even when they'd been close. She often wondered if he'd said more to Tyler. But she knew it ate at him and always had. "Well, no more. I'm done. I left my ring and walked away, and it was the first smart thing I've done in so damn long even though I have no idea what it means for my life. But I can't be with someone who treats me that way. And I certainly can't marry him. I won't." She clutched her stomach as a wave of anxiety washed through her, the sensation almost as if she'd nearly been in a terrible accident. She fell back against the front door. "Oh, God, I can't believe I came so close to marrying him."

Maverick stepped in close. "He doesn't know that part, though, right?"

"Not unless he opened the door and saw I wasn't there, saw the ring." She blew out a breath. "But I don't care. I'm done."

"He's not going to let you go that easily," Maverick said, peering down at her.

Her stomach flipped again as she nodded. Maybe. Probably. This was likely just the beginning of some hard days. But it was also the beginning of something new—a new life. What exactly that would be, who exactly *she* would be, she didn't know. "What am I going to do? My entire life is wrapped up in him. My job. Where I live. My car. Where Mom lives. *Everything.* Oh, God. This is going to be a nightmare, isn't it?"

Maverick grasped her hands. "One thing at a time. You're out. You can stay here as long as you need to. I have plenty of room. I'll help you through it. That'll give you time to figure out what it is *you* want. There's no rush."

"Okay," she said. "Okay. God, thank you." A shiver raced over her skin.

"You don't have to thank me. I'm so relieved for you that I might fall the fuck over," he said, his thumb rubbing over her knuckles. She almost managed a little smile. "Your hands are like ice, Al. I shouldn't have made you stand here all this time when you're soaking wet."

Alexa shook her head. "It felt good to get it out, Maverick."

"Glad to hear it. Would a hot shower make you feel better? I can find you a T-shirt and a pair of boxers to change into while your clothes dry."

All the TLC and understanding he was giving her reached right inside her chest. When was the last time someone had taken care of her this way?

The last time you were with Maverick. The truth of that thought made her breath catch. "Yeah. I'd like that," she managed.

He gave a tight nod and stepped back, and she missed his heat immediately. "Uh, good. That's good. You remember your way around?"

"Of course," she said. How much time had she spent here over the years? Even before they dated? At one point, Maverick's place had practically been a second home. Though, as she'd finally calmed down enough to take note of her surroundings, all the changes he'd alluded to the other day jumped out. The hardwoods were refinished, new drywall replaced the old, dark paneling, and the fireplace had been redone with gorgeous stonework. The finishes, fixtures, and décor were a fantastic mix of modern and lakeside cottage.

"You okay?" he asked, watching her.

She pushed off the door. "I don't know yet," she said, coming to him. "But what I do know is how grateful I am to you. For everything. For being there when I told you not to. For listening. For just . . . being you."

"Always." He crossed his big arms and ducked his chin, like something about the exchange made him uncomfortable.

"I mean it," she said, and then she pressed onto tiptoes and kissed his cheek, his stubble tickling her lips. "You saved me tonight."

"No," he said, eyes flashing, one brow arched. "You saved yourself, Al. I was just your getaway driver."

Staring into one another's eyes, the tender moment stretched out, morphed, suddenly flashed hot. Being so close to him set her body on fire, and *finally* she could actually consider acting on it. Need roared through her, a living, breathing thing. "Maverick," she whispered.

"Fuck, Alexa, I think you better go take that shower," he said, his jaw ticking. "Now."

She released a shaky breath and nodded. He was right. Of course, he was.

So, showering. She could handle that.

Afterward, God only knew what she was going to do.

CHAPTER 13

Alexa woke up in the middle of the night and immediately knew where she was—and where she wasn't. She was in Maverick's guest room, not in her own bed at home. Though, she supposed, she actually didn't have a home right now, did she?

Annnd that thought pretty much ensured she wasn't going back to sleep.

Part of her was surprised she'd fallen asleep in the first place, because her thoughts were a stressed-out, confused mess. But then she'd emerged from the shower feeling like she was carrying a lead blanket on her shoulders, and it had been all she could do to keep her eyes open. Maybe her brain had just needed to shut down. Maybe her sanity had just needed a break from this new reality. One where she had almost nothing.

The only saving grace in the whole situation was that she hadn't yet combined her savings account with Grant's, which meant she at least had some money to provide a cushion. Not that it was huge, but it was at least something.

She threw back the covers, got up, and made her way out to the kitchen in the dark. Lucy hopped off the end of the bed and padded after her. After a moment of fumbling for a light switch, Alexa found it, and then she was squinting against the brightness while her eyes adjusted. Standing at the sink, she filled a glass with water.

"You okay?" came a voice from behind her.

"Oh, hey," she said, the glass nearly slipping from her hand in surprise. Maverick stood at the edge of the room, sexy as all hell with his sleep-mussed hair and wearing an unbuttoned pair of jeans and nothing else. Which reminded her that he liked to sleep naked. Or he used to. His tattoo-covered muscles were lean and hard, and her brain unhelpfully supplied her with the memories—so many molten-hot memories—of how all that hardness felt against her. "Did I wake you up? I'm sorry."

"Wasn't asleep." He crossed his arms and leaned against the corner of the wall, the position emphasizing the bulge of his biceps and drawing her gaze to the maddening opening at his fly. Dark blond hair ran in a line down his abdomen and under the denim. And damn if her mind didn't help-fully supply her brain with all kinds of images of exactly what lay beneath. She swallowed hard. "You neither?"

"I slept for a little while." Sighing, she finished her drink and placed the glass in the sink. Everything inside her wanted to go to Maverick and burrow in against him. And at least a little of her wanted to go to him and push those jeans off his hips and down his thighs. Maybe re-acquaint her mouth and fingers with every tattoo he had. The *Live Free/Ride Free* and crossed wrenches tattoos on his chest, the tribal black motorcycle on his arm that morphed into black flames, the black-and-white checkered flag that wrapped around his ribs on one side, the big piece on his shoulder that looked like he was mechanical under his skin—that one was new. Well, at least since they'd been together. But she'd lost the right to do any of those things. Worse, she'd thrown that right away.

"You gonna try to sleep some more?" he asked, dragging a hand through his hair. Hair she knew was so soft.

What was wrong with her? The last thing she needed to be doing right now was drooling over another man, but she couldn't seem to stop noticing all the things that had always driven her crazy about Maverick Rylan.

"Al?"

"Huh?" Her gaze snapped to his, and found that dark, dark blue absolutely blazing. "Oh, uh. I'm not sure there's much point. Maybe I'll just watch some TV. Or something."

He nodded toward the living room. "Maybe there's something good on HGTV," he said with a wink. "Probably not, but . . ."

Alexa chuckled. "Don't say that like you don't like a lot of those shows, too. You know you do."

"Do not," he said, shuffling toward the living room and yawning.

Walking out of the kitchen, she came up behind him. And the sight of his back nearly took her breath away. She'd forgotten how sexy his massive tattoo there was. The words *Raven Riders* arched across his shoulder blades, and below, a huge black raven clutched at the hilt of a blade stabbed through the eye of a skull. The club's logo. Every fully patched Raven had one like it. Mav's muscles rippled under the ink, making the big black bird seem alive.

"How much of the work around here did you do yourself?" she asked, glad when he dropped onto one end of the charcoal-gray couch, breaking her view of his impressive ink. She sat away from him, but not all the way at the other end either. She hugged her legs to her chest as Lucy perched on the rug on the other side of the coffee table and stared at them.

"I had some help, but I had a hand in all of it." Mav flipped on the TV and changed the channel to a show about fixer-uppers.

"Uh-huh. Don't worry, big bad biker. Your love of HGTV is safe with me." She gave him an innocent look, but inside this all felt so familiar that she could almost pretend that the last five years hadn't happened. She and Maverick had always shared an interest in design. Interiors were her first love and building custom bikes was his, but they'd watched more than their fair share of shows about rehabs, renovations, flips, and more. They both liked learning new things and neither was afraid to try to do something themselves. She'd always loved refinishing and repurposing old furniture and, as the updates to his place proved, he had more than a little handyman skill. She used to enjoy watching him work on his bike projects in the chop shop at the Ravens' clubhouse. She'd always found competence and confidence sexy as hell—and Maverick had both in spades.

"It's a good thing I like you," he said, yawning again. He stretched his legs out in front of him and settled his big body into the cushion behind him.

Alexa chuckled, but her smile slipped right back off her face. Because the past five years *had* happened. She couldn't pretend they hadn't, after all. More than that, she was going to have to deal with a whole host of consequences for all the things she'd let get so out of control.

They watched the show for a couple minutes, but as soon as a commercial played, her thoughts raced. Laying her head against her knees, she peered at Maverick. "I don't know what to do about work in the morning."

Maverick gave her a serious look. "Do you have any kind of a contract?"

She shook her head. "I'm in the middle of a huge project,

though. The deadline's next week. God, I don't even have any clothes to wear."

"I can run you home in the morning, Alexa. But if he's realized you left your ring there, that you intend to leave him for good, you gotta prepare for him to be vindictive. And that maybe means violent, too. He's already shown he's not above that. But don't worry. I can bring some of the guys if I need to." Maverick shifted toward her, crooking one of his legs up on the couch. The position pulled the gap at his waist open, and her gaze couldn't help but lock on the fascinating strip of skin it revealed.

"Yeah?" she said, looking back to his face. "Okay." The heat in his gaze said he'd caught her admiring him. She pressed her fingers into her neck and massaged a knot there. "You don't have to stay up with me, you know."

"I don't mind." His gaze flicked to her hand. "You hurting?"

She gave a little shrug. "I'm just a ball of stress."

"I'd say you came by that honestly, Al." He sat up, bringing his body closer to hers, and then he pushed her hand out of the way. "Lemme."

Maverick's big, warm hand gripped the back of her neck and massaged her sore muscles. She groaned and buried her face in her knees.

"Too much?" he asked, his voice gravelly.

"It's perfect," she said. And it was. Warm, firm, strong, his touch felt so damn good it was all she could do to keep from moaning.

"Turn your back to me."

She did, and then both of his hands fell on her skin where the opening to his too-big shirt hung wide on her shoulders. He kneaded at her neck, dragged his fingers against her scalp, and pressed delicious circles against her upper back. His big hands spanning her body, he pushed his thumbs into the muscles running down both sides of her spine.

Alexa did moan then. Heat licked over her body. From

her embarrassment at the sound that had just spilled from her throat. From his warmth and closeness against her back. From his hands on her skin.

The quiet suddenly felt weighted, heady, full of anticipation. Was that her imagination? Or did Maverick feel it, too? She held stock-still, both because she didn't want him to stop *and* because she felt like if she gave even the slightest indication that she wanted more, this moment would explode into something she maybe wasn't ready for. Certainly not tonight.

Which made Maverick massaging her the sweetest torture. Because his touch brought her body to life like she'd been hibernating for the past five years. Her skin became hypersensitive. Her nipples hardened. Her core ached with need.

She shivered from the intensity of the arousal suddenly flooding through her.

"Cold?" he asked, hands smoothing up her back again.

"No," she said.

"Tired?" The timbre of his voice was low, rough.

"I don't know." She peered over her shoulder. Maverick's eyes were hot and intense, though she wasn't sure what to make of that, or whether she was projecting her own desires onto him. "I don't want to sleep again, though. I'd rather not be alone with my thoughts right now."

He looked at her for a long moment, and then he pushed himself back into the corner of the couch. Regret at losing his touch rushed through Alexa until Maverick held open his arm to her. "Come here."

Alexa didn't let herself second-guess it. She moved into the space along the side of his body. Her head on his chest, her chest against his side, her legs pressed along his. The sensations were familiar and new at the same time.

His arm came around her shoulder. "Sleep, Alexa. Everything else we can figure out in the morning."

"I hope so," she said.

"I know it." He gave her a squeeze.

His warmth and his scent and the lulling grumble of his voice made her eyelids sag and then close altogether. Maybe everything would look better in the light of day. She could only hope.

IT WAS ONE of Maverick's favorite dreams.

He and Alexa had gone up to Swallow Falls in Western Maryland for a weekend getaway and were staying in one of the mini cabins at the state park. After a day of hiking and swimming and picnicking outside, they'd come back to their cabin tired and ready to crash, but getting naked for showers had sidetracked them for hours. And even once they finally fell asleep, Maverick was hard and ready every time he woke up, and he took her again and again, falling asleep still buried inside her . . .

And fuck if he wasn't ready right now.

He burrowed his face in her soft hair and banded his arm around her stomach. His hand filled with the soft mound of her breast. He pulled her back against his chest and ground his erection against the swell of her ass.

"Maverick," she moaned.

Hell, yeah. He nuzzled her neck, kissed her there, tasting and nipping and sucking. God, he needed in her. "Fuck, Alexa," he whispered.

Her hand gripped his. "Maverick."

He rolled her under him and crawled on top of her, his body falling into the cradle of her spread thighs.

"Uh, Maverick."

He frowned and kissed her jaw, her cheek, her mouth.

It was the kiss that did it. Something wasn't right. The memory playing out in his sleep-fogged mind didn't feel like the reality confronting his physical senses. His eyes blinked open.

And he found himself lying on top of Alexa. Not in the cabin at Swallow Falls years before. In the gray morning light of his house. Her wide hazel eyes stared up at him.

He reared off of her in an instant. "Fuck," he said, coming to stand by the couch. Alexa looked stunned—and so fucking sexy that Maverick barely resisted crawling back on top of her. She lay on her back in *his* clothes, on *his* couch, her knees drawn up and falling out, her hair sleep-mussed and sexy. Jesus. He adjusted himself, unable to hide his raging hard-on, and scrubbed at his face. "Goddamn dream. I'm sorry, Alexa. I didn't mean to do that."

"You . . . you were dreaming. Of me?" she whispered.

His gaze narrowed. "Don't ask a question you don't want the answer to."

She swallowed and licked her lips. "What if I do want it? The answer," she added.

Years of need and longing roared through Maverick like a drug he'd mainlined. His thoughts spilled out unfiltered. "Damnit, Al. You're laying there in my clothes in my house with your thighs spread after I've just woken up holding you. My skin smells like you. And I'm sporting an erection because of you. Don't fuck with me." The words came out harsher than he intended, but she couldn't play with him. Not on this. Not when he cared so much. Not when he *wanted* so much.

Her mouth dropped open and her chest rose and fell a little quicker. "I'm not playing a game. I want to know."

Planting his hands on his hips, Maverick studied her. Her beautiful, languid body. Her pretty, open face. Her eyes, honest and free of pretense. He felt pulled in a million directions. Between wrong and right, between taking advantage and taking care, between giving in and opening himself up to a world of hurt. "I was dreaming of you. Of us. Up at Swallow Falls."

"That night we—"

"Yes," he growled.

"Maverick—"

"*Fuck*." He dropped his chin to his chest and closed his eyes. Trying to be bigger than his base needs. Trying to put her before himself. "Whatever is about to come out of your mouth is *not* a good idea."

"Mav—"

"I mean it, Al—"

"Maverick!" she nearly yelled. "Listen to me."

His gaze cut up to hers in time to see her sit up a little and take off her shirt. Well, his shirt. Then she laid back again, her eyes on him, drinking him in, *inviting* him in. "What if I do want it?" she whispered.

Something inside him snapped.

He was on her in a second. Body covering hers. Hands going to her warm skin. Mouth tasting her everywhere— her shoulder, her throat, her cheek. His chest pressed against her breasts, her hard nipples evident, her excitement palpable. And then his mouth found hers. On a triumphant groan, he claimed her, his lips sucking, his tongue penetrating. His big hand found her breast and kneaded at the soft mound.

And Alexa was right there with him. Moaning, kissing him, clutching on to him. Her thighs wrapped around his hips and her fingers twisted in his hair.

Bad idea bad idea such a fucking bad idea.

Why did bad ideas have to feel so good?

"Fuck, I want you," he said, grinding his cock against the soft, welcoming spot between her thighs.

"I want you, too. Feels like I've been wanting you my whole life." She peered up at him, her eyes so vibrant they were nearly green.

Maverick pulled back, her words hitting him in all kinds of places, some comfortable, some even healing, but some less so. "You can't toy with me, Alexa. Not when I've wanted you for so long. Not when I never wanted to let you go in the first place. This . . . this can just be fucking. But don't you dare say anything you don't mean."

She stroked his hair. "Truth?"

He gave a tight nod and prepared for the worst, even as he hoped for a shot.

"Truth is, I don't know what this means. Yet. I am so messed up right now. I'm not even going to hide that. But . . ." She tilted her head, and her expression was filled with something Mav didn't want to name, but it sure as hell looked like affection. "But I know I want this. I want *you*, Maverick. Right now. And wanting you feels like one of the smartest decisions I've made in forever. Everything else be damned." Her voice was shaky and breathy and her words were so full of dangerous, dangerous hope that Maverick didn't dare move.

His muscles nearly shook with the force of his restraint, because his body was literally screaming at him. Screaming at him to just let go. "Fuck, Alexa."

"I don't want to hurt you. I *never* wanted to hurt you. But I want you. I want you inside me right now more than I want my next breath."

Even though his mind was rolling out a list of *all the reasons why this was a no good what the fuck are you thinking very bad idea*, Maverick's body grabbed the reins. On a groan, he went in for a kiss, rougher than he intended, but the moan she unleashed when his mouth crashed down on hers told him she didn't mind. They fumbled with clothes. Her boxers. His jeans. Until they were both naked and pressed tight, all hot skin on skin, and his cock ground against her soft folds until she was mewling and writhing and silently pleading with the rough, desperate grip of her hands on his shoulders, his back, his ass.

A big part of Maverick wanted to pick Alexa up and carry her to his bed—where his heart said she belonged— but this wasn't about that. At least not yet, and he wasn't giving either of them any more time to think than he already had.

He needed her too damn bad. Just this once. In case that's all it was.

Taking his cock in one hand, he dragged his head against her pussy, the contact sending a ferocious need through his veins. He braced his other hand next to her shoulder and met her bright eyes. "You sure?"

"Now," she said.

"What about prot—"

She shook her head. "I'm covered. And I want you just like this."

"Christ," he bit out, the trust inherent in her words kinda blowing his mind. His cock found her opening, penetrated her, slid slow and deep. It was perfection of the soul-deep, bone-bending, never-get-enough kind. He'd been with other women since they'd broken up, of course. But being with Alexa again reminded him just how much every one of those experiences had paled in comparison to being inside this woman. Damn if it wasn't like coming home.

It took everything Mav had not to rut against her like an animal, not to just let his hips fly and pound, because that was the kind of urgency firing through his blood.

But she deserved better than that. She deserved his *care*. And he didn't want to rush this. He wanted it to last forfuckingever.

He came down on one elbow as his cock bottomed out inside her. Her head wrenched back as she cried out, the look of pleasure on her face so damn beautiful. "Oh, God," she rasped. "Oh, Maverick."

His name from her mouth licked heat over his skin. He withdrew slowly, then hammered home again. Alexa's eyes went wide. Her mouth dropped open. Maverick did it again and again. Slow withdrawal, fast penetration. Until her core was fisting around him and driving him insane.

"You gonna come for me, Al?" Their gazes collided as

his hips snapped against her clit. "Come for me." His hips hammered home again. Staying deep, he ground himself against her. That was all it took.

Alexa's whole body went taut as her mouth formed a silent cry and her eyes squeezed shut, her nails digging in to his arm and his side. Her core sucked at him over and over, and Maverick forced himself to move despite the utter fucking perfection of it, because he wanted it to be good for her. He wanted the goodness—the *rightness*—of it to mark and change her on the inside. The way it was doing to him. Because this was shining a spotlight on everything he'd been wanting for so long.

Her whole body shook and she finally found her voice, crying out and calling his name. He kissed her, deep and claiming, keeping their faces close, and wrapped himself around her. And then he let his body off its leash. He fucked her in a fast grind that quickly had them hot and sweaty and panting. Their gazes locked, she raked at his hair and pulled him in for a kiss they couldn't hold. Small needful whimpers spilled out of her, the sounds driving him wild. The closeness, the honesty, the need—it was the most intimate moment he'd had in years. Maybe ever. And it gave his body a giant shove toward release.

"Come again for me," he said. "Show me how good I'm making you feel."

"Maverick," she rasped.

"That's right," he said, tilting his hips to concentrate on her clit. "Give it to me, Alexa."

"Shit," she whispered.

Taking the hair at the back of her head in hand, he forced her to open to him as he bore down on her in a claiming, penetrating kiss, his body still moving in hers. "*Come*," he growled.

The cry started low and then turned into a guttural moan in his ear. "Mav, baby." The spasming of her core around his—again—was all he could take. Braced up on one arm, he let his hips fly, snapping against her and concentrating sensation into his balls. And then he was coming and cursing and shooting inside her. He moved through it, trying to drag it out for both of them as long as he could.

Because he didn't know what this meant. Or whether it would happen again. And Alexa hadn't made any promises. Neither of them had.

"Jesus," he whispered, pressing a kiss to her forehead. They stared at one another for a long moment. Not speaking or hiding. Just looking. And he felt it—a bunch of things she was maybe thinking and maybe even feeling, but not saying. He knew because he was doing the same thing. "You okay?"

The small smile she gave him was so damn pretty. "I'm . . . definitely better than okay."

He chuckled and nodded, affecting a nonchalance he didn't feel. "Good. That's good."

Soft fingertips dragged down his face, then pushed the length of his hair back. "Thank you."

"Yeah," he said. Not sure what more to say when there was so much he couldn't. Or shouldn't. Easing out of her, he immediately missed her heat and her touch. "How 'bout I make some coffee?"

Alexa nodded, her smile still small but turning playful. "Coffee is life."

"Coffee is life," he said on a nod. He scooped his jeans off the floor and forced himself to act all chill, to walk away, to keep his mouth shut.

Because what else could he do?

SITTING ON THE couch, the sounds of Maverick puttering around in the kitchen coming from behind her, Alexa quickly pulled on her clothes and made her way to the bathroom. She shut herself inside and pressed her face to the cool wood of the door. And let the quiet tears flow.

That . . . that had been the single most amazing thing Alexa had experienced in almost five years.

Everything she'd been wanting. Everything she'd been missing. Everything she'd been *needing*. Maverick gave it to her, not even realizing what he was doing, and how earth-shattering it truly was for her. He hadn't just held a mirror up to her relationship with Grant—because, Jesus, when she thought of what'd happened in that bathroom at the inn, it was *nothing* like this. Mav had taken a sledge-hammer to whatever last pieces of the charade of her life that she'd been clinging to. And in the process, making her see how much she'd tolerated that she shouldn't have, how little she'd accepted for herself, and how much she'd convinced herself that something existed where it didn't. And maybe never had.

Where had she been?

Why the hell had she given up on Maverick the way she had? Given up on *herself?* She'd had good reasons, right? Good, totally reasonable reasons. Except, what were they again? And why did they ring so hollow to her now?

God, she was a mess. And it was one problem too many for her to try to fix just then.

Shaking her head, she freshened up and met her reflection in the mirror. "Time to face reality, Al," she whispered to herself.

How Maverick fit into that reality, she didn't know.

Out in the hall, she found Lucy waiting for her and meowing repeatedly. The cat followed her to the kitchen, where Alexa found Maverick much as he'd been the night before—shirtless, jeans hanging on his hips, though buttoned this time, and sexy as hell. "Do you have some lunch meat or tuna I can feed Lucy? Just until I can buy her some cat food?" she asked.

"I have ham and cheese," he said, gesturing to the fridge. "Help yourself to whatever you need. I mean it, Al. Like it's your own house. Okay?"

She ducked inside the refrigerator, not wanting him to see just how much his words meant to her. "Okay, thanks." For the next few minutes, she diced lunch meat while Maverick made toast and fixed them both a cup of coffee. They worked in silence and the way they moved around one another reminded her of all the times they'd made meals here when they'd been together. So she really didn't need to ask how he knew how she liked her coffee.

When Lucy had her breakfast and Alexa had forced herself to eat a piece of toast, she sighed. "I should check my phone," she said, moving into the hall. In the guest room, she found her cell. "Holy shit," she whispered, her gaze latching onto the little notification numbers.

"What is it?" Maverick asked from behind her.

She turned, her stomach making a slow drop to the floor. "I have thirty missed calls and five messages."

Standing in the doorway, his big arms crossed, Maverick frowned. "Do you want me to listen to them first?"

"No." She had to face this. *She* had to be in control. For once. Sinking onto the edge of the bed, she shook her head. "You're not going to be able to shield me from all this, Maverick. It's my mess. I have to fix it. I have to face it." She wasn't sure what would be harder to hear—Grant yelling at her or playing nice. And she honestly had no idea which to expect. That said a heck of a lot, didn't it? Taking a deep breath, she played the first voice mail on speaker.

"Alexa, where the hell are you? Where did you go? I'll come get you. Call me." The tone was urgent, clipped, not obviously angered, but not just concerned, either.

"One down," she said, playing the next message. Adrenaline made her hands tremble around the device.

"Damnit, Alexa. This is ridiculous now. Where are you? I'm . . . I'm worried about you, babe. Call me."

She made a face at the phone. Was he really concerned about her? And did she care if he was?

Maverick blew out a long breath. "Fuck, Alexa. You're killing me."

"Why?" Her eyes cut up to his.

"Because I'm terrified that you're going to give him another shot." He braced his hands on the doorframe and hung his head for a moment. "And this isn't about what we just did. It's about what he did to you last night. For starters."

She pulled her gaze away from the fascinating movement of the tattoos over his muscles. "I'm not. No matter what he says."

Blue eyes flashed to hers.

"I may not know a lot yet, but I know that," she said. "I won't go back to him." It was a promise. A vow. To herself more than anyone else. But to Maverick, too. Because even though he'd said what they'd done could just be fucking— and it had been some mind-blowing fucking at that—it had felt like so much more. What she should do with that just then, she didn't know. But it didn't mean nothing, either.

The third message played, the tone much more conciliatory. "Babe, please tell me where you are. I know I lost my temper. Things are just really stressed right now. Come home. Let's talk this out. Like you said."

She wasn't sure how to read the tone, but what she could see was that every one of his messages was filled with commands. *Tell me, call me, come home.* And she also heard all the things he *didn't* say, too. No apology. No declaration of love. Or was she reading too much into it? God, after years of misreading Grant's words and intentions, she wasn't sure whether to trust her reactions.

Alexa sighed and dropped her forehead into her hand. "This whole thing is so crazy," she said almost to herself. "How is this my life?" Her fingers moved over the cell's screen to play the next.

"Goddamnit, Alexa. I'm calling the police. Come home." That one had the angriest tone of all.

"Great. You do that, I'll be happy to tell them you physically threw me out of the house," she whispered to herself. Although, if he called Davis, that guy wouldn't give two craps that Grant had hurt her. Maverick was right. Officer Davis was a total lackey. "Last one."

"Alexa, I love you. I'm . . . I'm sorry about last night. It won't ever happen again. Just let me know you're okay, babe. I need you so much."

She blew out a breath and dropped the phone onto the bed beside her.

Maverick crossed the room and sat next to her. "You okay?"

"Wanna know the sad thing?"

"Yeah," Maverick said, clearly trying like hell to keep his voice even.

"I'm not sure I know how to read those messages." She finally met his gaze. "I'm not sure I trust my own judgment about them."

Emotions rolled over Maverick's expression, and she watched him rein them in. "Okay. What do you think they might mean? What are you hearing?"

She swallowed hard and ducked her chin. "Well. I think he wants me back. But he didn't apologize or even say he loved me until the last message, so I think he's trying to tell me what I want to hear rather than what he really means. I think he wants to control me." She blinked up at him.

Mav tilted his head, and his hair fell across his eyes. "Sounds to me like you know more than you're giving yourself credit for, Al." He gave her a pointed stare, and she nodded. "Slater had two ways to play reaching out to you—attacking you and lashing out in anger, or appeasing you and luring you back in with what seems like worry and concern and remorse. What happened when you went back to him after the last fight?"

"He apologized. Said he hadn't meant for things to get so out of control. Said it would never happen again." She shook her head. "But it did."

"Yeah, it fucking did," he said, his voice like gravel. "Last night you said there are all kinds of things you're not supposed to say or do or he'll get mad. So, that means he likes to control you, yeah?"

"Yeah," she whispered, looking away.

"Fuck," he gritted out, huffing an angry breath. Mav grasped her chin and made her look at him again. "Well, he can't control you as easily if you're not living under his roof, so his first objective is to get you back home. No doubt he didn't expect you to leave, so he has to be on his best behavior now. Don't think for a second he doesn't know exactly what he's doing. Don't believe for even an instant he isn't calculating the best way to get what he wants. That's what guys like Slater do, Alexa. That's what he's been doing to you." He touched two fingers to her forehead. "Trust yourself in here." To her heart. "And in here." To her stomach. "And in here. You *know*."

Just then, her cell phone rang. Alexa flinched, then scooped it up off the mattress. "It's him."

"Of course it is," he bit out, anger giving his voice a harsh edge. "He won't give up 'til you give him what he wants."

She blew out a breath and her belly went on a loop-the-loop that left her a little queasy. "I guess I have to talk to him at some point, right?"

Maverick gave a tight nod, his face set in a scowl that was almost scary.

"Then here goes nothing," she said, answering the phone.

CHAPTER 14

G rant," Alexa said, hating the shakiness in her voice. Part of her wished she'd let the call go to voice mail so she had more time to gather her thoughts and come up with a game plan. Grant had always been an expert at litigating arguments and disagreements, managing to turn things around so that what had started out as a legitimate concern on her part ended up feeling silly and unreasonable and inconsiderate.

"Oh, thank God, Alexa. Where are you? Are you okay?" His voice, filled with a convincing concern, sounded out on speaker. Letting Maverick hear her life fall apart was about as comfortable as eating glass, but he'd already *seen* it fall apart. So what was the difference?

"No, I'm not okay," she said, her stomach tossing. But what more did she have to lose? If she wasn't going to speak the truth to him now, she never would. "You physically threw me outside in the middle of a storm late at night. I'm not okay."

"I know. I know. Things just got out of hand." In her mind's eye, she could almost see him pacing.

"Things didn't get out of hand, Grant. *You* got out of hand. With your suspiciousness, you mistrusting me, and you physically hurting me. Do you know how humiliating it was to be locked out of my own house? You were supposed to take care of me." The anger she'd felt the night before, the anger that had given her the strength and determination to leave her ring and walk off that porch, pooled in her gut once again.

"I didn't hurt you, did I? I didn't mean it," he said, an odd tone to his voice.

"I just said that you did, so yeah." Her gaze cut to Maverick, who was studying her, that scowl getting deeper, the look in his eyes totally lethal. Not that she minded any of that. Because she meant what she'd admitted to him— she didn't trust her own judgment where Grant was concerned. She needed him to be a sounding board right now. "My arm hurts from how you grabbed me and the back of my head hurts from you pushing me into the door. And this is just a few weeks after you promised that nothing like our last fight would ever happen again." She blew out another shaky breath. Adrenaline coursed through her. She *never* talked to Grant like this and her body was clearly preparing for the need to flee from the consequences.

"Yeah. Yeah. Uh, okay, Alexa. Can you please come home so I can make sure you're okay with my own eyes? I've been up all night worrying and imagining every nightmarish scenario. I need you to come home."

It didn't escape her notice that he'd brushed off her pain to list all the things he needed and had suffered. Had he always been this big of an asshole? "I don't think that's a good idea," she said, her voice less certain. Had he not found her ring?

"What? Why not?" he asked. The surprise in his voice

sounded so damn genuine that Alexa believed it. Which meant that he either didn't expect her to draw a line in the sand where his behavior was concerned or that he really didn't think he'd done anything so wrong as to warrant this reaction. Both possibilities left her feeling sad and defeated. How had she not seen this sooner? How had she let him get away with it for so long?

"Something clearly isn't working between us, Grant. It's getting worse and I can't take it anymore," she said. She felt the weight of Maverick's gaze, but couldn't let herself look at him. Not just then.

"Alexa, I can fix this," Grant said. "It was just a fight."

"I don't think so," she said. "And it was more than that to me."

"Damnit, Alexa—"

"You told me I was *nothing*, Grant," she said, shame making her face hot for having to say that in front of Maverick. "Who says that?"

"I know, babe. Things just got out of control."

Again with the *things*. He wasn't taking responsibility here, was he? She sighed and didn't answer. She'd already addressed this once.

"Well, uh." A long pause filtered down the line. "What about work? Are you planning to come in? The model home project won't get done without you. No one else could do it like you. And you love that project."

Relief lifted some of the weight pressing down on her shoulders. If he was asking her, then maybe he didn't see her being *with* him and working *for* him as being fundamentally linked. After all, she'd worked there initially before they'd become a couple. Maybe she'd be able to continue to work at Slater Enterprises and they'd be able to act like professionals and adults.

"I still have a job at Slater Enterprises?" she asked, figuring she might as well be direct about it.

"Of course you do, sweetheart. Yes."

She ignored the *sweetheart*. "Then I'll be in this morning, but I'll be late since I don't have any clothes with me."

"Whatever you need, Alexa. Of course. I'll see you later then?" he asked. Was that hope in his voice? Or something else?

"I'll see you at the office." A shiver rushed over her skin.

"I love you," he said.

For a moment, her tongue got tangled, because she couldn't say it—not just because of what had happened, but because she felt like she was talking to a stranger. Like she'd been loving and sleeping with a stranger. Not to mention that Maverick's burning blue eyes were focused so intently on her. "Okay," she finally managed. "Good-bye." She hung up without waiting for him to say anything else. Blowing out a breath, she scrubbed her hands over her face. "How'd I do? I know I didn't flip out on him," she said, chancing a glance at Maverick.

"You did fantastic, Al. I know that couldn't have been easy, but you stood up for yourself. You didn't let him get away with anything. And you set some ground rules for yourself." He nodded, his expression full of a pride that allowed her shoulders to relax and her lungs to inhale a deep breath. And God did it feel good to have someone in her corner. For once. She hadn't had that in so long. "I'm worried as fuck about you going back to work, though. I'm not going to lie. The idea of you being near him makes me want to smash things."

She sighed, as her belly did a little flip. "I know. I don't really want to be near him, either. But I have to work, especially given this situation. I have some savings, but I'm going to need more. Because almost everything I have is his. Including my mom's house. I don't even know if I'd get to keep my car because he convinced me to get rid of the one I had when he bought the new one for me, so it's in his name." Alexa hugged herself, sadness making her chest feel hollow. "I get that working for him long-term probably isn't realistic now. Even if we can manage a professional relationship, there's no way things won't be awkward. But I need to work there until I can find something else, at least. And seeing this project through to the end will give me a project for my portfolio I'll need to land a new job."

Mav bit out a curse under his breath and nailed her with a stare. "Fine. But I'm taking you and picking you up. At least until you get a better feel for how he's acting towards you. But I wouldn't trust good behavior for a fucking second."

Alexa thought about it for a moment and nodded. "I think that's probably a good idea. Thank you."

"You're welcome," he said, not sounding too happy about it.

The silence stretched out, and in that quiet, Alexa's mind returned to what had happened between them on the couch, to Maverick waking her up with his hands and his mouth and his body. Waking her up in so many ways.

Maverick Rylan was unquestionably masculine and un-apologetically rough around the edges, and she found it even sexier now than she had when they'd been a couple. Maybe she'd been too young to appreciate him all those years ago. Maybe she'd been too focused on the wrong things. Maybe she'd been too distracted by her grief and her fear to see what was standing right in front of her.

Well, clearly all of that had been the case, hadn't it?

How could she ever ask him to forgive her?

I never wanted to let you go in the first place.

The gravel of his voice played over again in her mind.

"When do you want to go?" Maverick asked. "It's eight-thirty."

His question pulled her from her thoughts. "Um, let's leave around nine? That'll make sure Grant's already left for work. I don't want to have to deal with him at the house.

Oh, wait. I . . . I don't—" Alexa bit back her words and smiled.

"What?"

"I was going to say I don't have a way into the house, but I have you." She grinned. "Oh master of lock picking."

"Like that idea now, do ya?" He smirked at her.

"It's proven to come in handy," she said.

Maverick nodded and rose, and Alexa couldn't help but stare at his Ravens tattoo as he crossed the room. Why didn't the sight of it rattle her like it once had? "I'll grab some coffee and a quick shower, then we can go. Your clothes from last night should be dry if you want to change." He left, then quickly peered back into the room. "And I like it when you call me master." He winked and left before she could throw something at him.

Her grin faded as her thoughts got all tangled up in the past. After losing Tyler, Alexa had thought she'd learned everything she could know about being scared. She'd been scared of how she'd manage to take care of her mother by herself. She'd been scared of how her mother would handle Ty's death, and then of how her mom had fallen apart and gotten sicker. She'd been scared that she'd never get the life she'd always dreamed of having. And she'd been scared of what would happen—and how it would feel—if she lost Maverick the same way, too.

Now she knew there was a lot about fear she hadn't known.

She'd learned that living your life guided by fear meant that a scary amount of your life passed you by while you weren't doing the things or being with the people you most wanted. She'd learned that there was more than one kind of loss. Death was the most catastrophic, obviously. But losing your friends and your independence and your faith in your own judgment were pretty damn scary, too. And she'd learned that sometimes playing it safe was its own kind of loss—representing wasted chances, unrecognized opportunities, and unrealized possibility.

Maybe . . . maybe things crashing and burning with Grant didn't represent so much of a loss as an opportunity?

From the direction of Maverick's bedroom, the hum of the shower water sounded out, and her mind couldn't help but conjure up a series of old, secret images. The water sluicing over all Maverick's hard edges and ink. Him taking her against the tile wall. Her on her knees on the shower floor, his cock in her hands, her mouth. A shiver raced through her.

Maybe losing the life she thought she was going to have with Grant could give her a second chance with . . . other things?

Lucy curled around Alexa's ankles and let out a pleading meow. On a sigh, Alexa bent down to give the sphynx some love. "Don't worry, Luce. Everything's going to be all right. We'll figure it all out. I promise."

Though Alexa didn't know who she was trying to reassure most.

"Want me to come in with you?" Maverick asked from the driver's seat of his truck.

Alexa looked out the window to the sleek glass building that housed Slater Enterprises. Would going inside feel as strange as going home had felt? Maverick had let her into her house so she could shower and change, and the first thing that had dropped a ball of nerves into her gut was that her ring hadn't been hanging on the door knocker. Which meant Grant had seen it after all. Which left her wondering even more about what he'd said—and what he hadn't said—when they'd spoken on the phone.

The second thing that had left her feeling uncertain was the question of whether she should take anything beyond Lucy's nearly empty food and kitty litter and her own clothes, toiletries, and things for school. She didn't even know whether to take her car. Maverick convinced her that she should, and he had a new guy who was joining the Ravens drive someone over who could take it back to Mav's house. Otherwise, she'd only taken what was definitely hers.

And Mav made sure she had *all* of it so she didn't have to come back. He'd personally carted loads of hanging clothes and suitcases full of personal items out to his truck himself until the other Ravens showed up to help.

The third thing that had felt so weird about returning was how much she didn't feel like she belonged there. It was almost like poking around a stranger's house, her nerves telling her she was going to get caught at any moment. She could almost imagine it'd been months since she'd last been there—years, even. It was more than a little surreal.

Finally, Alexa shook her head, her eyes still glued to the Slater Enterprises building. Wondering. Worrying. Debating. But she had to do this. She had to be strong. It was time. "No. It'll be okay. If I get worried, I'll call you to come get me."

"Look at me," Maverick said. Alexa's gaze cut to him. "Promise me." He arched a brow over dark blue eyes filled with fierce concern, his expression so serious it emphasized all the hard angles of his face. It made him beautiful to her, although he'd probably think that was a ridiculous thing to think about him. But how could she find his protectiveness, concern, and support anything but beautiful? She knew too well what the opposite looked like.

"I promise," Alexa said, making her words strong and sure when her insides felt a whole lot like someone was taking a mixer to them. But she was going to have to face Grant some time. No sense in putting it off, and doing it in public had all kinds of advantages over doing it privately.

He gave a tight nod. "I'll be here when you come out at five."

"Okay." She resisted the urge to lean over and kiss Maverick, because despite *the couch*, she had no idea what they were or weren't. She opened the door and climbed out. Hesitating, she looked back in. "Thanks, Maverick. You didn't have to do all this for me, and . . . yeah . . . just, thanks."

"That's bullshit," he said, eyes blazing with an intensity she didn't really understand. "You're family. It's what we do. But you're welcome." He winked.

For some reason his expression and his words made her ache with yearning—a yearning that there was more between them than just history. "Okay." With a little nod, she pushed the door shut and headed inside.

Alexa's nerves were on high alert as she entered the building, part of her sure some sort of trap would spring on her the moment she walked through the doors. But there was only Christina, smiling at her but her expression also a little concerned. "Hey. Your mom okay?"

Confused, Alexa nodded.

"It's just that you're never late unless your mom has an appointment," Christina said.

"Oh, uh, no. Mom's fine. Thank you, though." She debated what to say, and then decided it would be better not to say a word. Not yet. "I'm sorry to run, but I'm late for something." She thumbed over her shoulder as she moved away from the desk. "I'll see you later, though?"

"Okay," Christina said, clearly catching on to her weirdness. Not that Alexa could worry about it just then.

She made her way to her office, sure that everyone knew what'd happened, like everyone could just look at her and see that her world was falling apart. But she pasted on a smile, offered greetings as she passed her colleagues, and finally made it to her desk.

A gigantic over-the-top bouquet of fresh flowers in a thick crystal vase filled one whole end of her work space. Three dozen flowers in bold, bright colors, leafy foliage, and baby's breath made an arrangement so big it could've been for a wedding. Or a funeral.

She opened the card.

Alexa—

Come home to me where you belong.

Love, Grant

She sighed. It almost didn't matter that he hadn't given the flowers as an apology, because him apologizing wouldn't change how she felt. The note bothered her for other reasons. She was worried that it revealed Grant's stubborn unwillingness to hear what she was saying. That he was ignoring the fact that she'd taken off her ring. And it bugged her that he'd put her in the position of having to keep the flowers in her office or else give her coworkers a reason to wonder why she wasn't keeping such an exquisite gift from her fiancé less than two weeks before their wedding. She moved them to the credenza to get them out of her way and then dove into all the work the model home and a few of her smaller projects required.

Maverick texted her throughout the day making sure she was okay, and who knew that the word *fuck* could sound so sweet? *I'm fucking worried about you. He'll fucking pay if he hurts you. IS IT 5 OFUCKINGCLOCK YET?* That one came complete with a winky face. And when a big tough biker dude sent you shouty caps and a winky face, it could make you smile.

Otherwise, no one disturbed Alexa all day. It was four o'clock before she knew it. And she was both relieved and anxious about not yet having seen Grant.

Of course, his knock finally came.

"Alexa," Grant said, stepping into the office wearing an exquisitely tailored blue suit. His gaze cut to the flowers off to the side before he closed the door. "Did you like the flowers?"

"They're beautiful, but you shouldn't have," she said, not trying to hide the edge in her voice. She clasped her hands on top of the desk.

Grant came closer until he stood right in front of her, forcing her to look up to meet his eyes. "Of course I should. I'd do anything to make things right."

Her stomach dropped. "Flowers can't fix what's broken between us, Grant."

For a moment, she would've sworn the narrowing of his eyes and the tightness around his mouth foreshadowed building anger, but then it was gone from his expression and he shook his head. "I know. I just wanted you to know I was thinking about you, wanting you."

Nerves made her knees feel like jelly, but Alexa stood up anyway, needing to be on a more even playing field while she said what she had to say. "You need to stop wanting me, Grant. I know you found the ring." She shook her head and gathered her thoughts. "We're over."

Grant's eyes did narrow then, and he pulled something out of his pocket. Her diamond. It glinted in the sunlight coming through the window behind her. "Damnit, Alexa, this is *yours*." He nailed her with an intimidating stare. It was hard not to duck her chin. "You can't just end it. We have five years of history. You can't throw that away. Don't you think we deserve some conversation, some time to cool down and talk this out, some effort to fix things?"

"Grant—"

He stepped forward and she could've sworn he meant to grasp her wrist, but then he put the ring down on her paperwork. "I'm not letting you give it back. This isn't over."

She crossed her arms and arched a brow at him. "Yes, it is."

He scrubbed his hands over his face, then held them up as if in surrender. "Please, Alexa. You're important to me."

Frowning, Alexa shook her head. For one of the first times ever, she seemed to be able to hear what he wasn't saying as clearly as what he was, and it solidified that she was doing the right thing. "Please take it, Grant. I know it's really valuable. If you don't take it I'm afraid it'll get lost or stolen, because I won't be taking it either."

"I don't care about the ring," he said, his voice quiet but intense. Just like it had been in his office the night before.

"You say you care about me and you want to fix things, but you won't even honor what I want right now," she said, working to keep her tone even. "Take the freaking ring."

She had no idea how she held out in the staring match that followed. Her heart raced. Her knees felt like they could give out. She fisted her hands to try to hide her shakiness. Finally, he heaved out a long breath and scooped the diamond up again. "This isn't over," he said, and then he turned and stalked out.

The moment the door closed behind him, Alexa nearly collapsed into her chair.

She was shaky and a little woozy from the adrenaline pumping through her, but it still felt like a damn victory. That was quite possibly the first disagreement with him she'd felt like she'd ever won.

Despite his parting words.

But they didn't matter. Because she and Grant *were* over.

And there was absolutely nothing he could do to change that.

CHAPTER 15

Maverick was crawling out of his skin waiting for Alexa to walk out of work. Leaning against the front of his truck, arms crossed and eyes trained on the doors, it took everything he had not to march in there and escort her out.

He'd been a mess of worst case scenarios all day. Slater hitting her. Slater nabbing her and hiding her away. Slater snapping and taking them both out in some melodramatic murder-suicide. Even as the thoughts had been rushing through his brain, he'd known they were fucking ridiculous. Grant Slater was nothing if not image-conscious, which was the only thing that'd kept Maverick sane. The guy wasn't going to do anything obvious, not in public at least.

That hadn't made it any easier for Maverick to concentrate on the 1950s Copper Hardtail he'd been working on reengineering for a client. And that didn't mean her ex wouldn't go all stalker. Because Maverick believed he had that in him. And he didn't trust Slater's concerned act on that call this morning in the least.

He just hoped Alexa didn't either.

Then, finally, there she was. A beautiful vision in a pair of form-fitting black pants, strappy black heels, and a silky pale pink blouse. A *sexy* vision. Put together and polished and professional.

Unlike him. He was all ripped jeans, stained hands, and beat-up boots.

Did she care about that stuff?

Didn't she have to—at least on some level? Five years ago, she'd picked Slater over him, and he and Slater couldn't have been more different. Abusive-asshole factor aside, Slater was two-thousand-dollar business suits and high-end luxury cars and million-dollar mansions. From his own business and his cut from the Ravens, Maverick had money, but he didn't flash it. He was a jeans, T-shirt, bike kinda man.

Sonofabitch.

As she neared, Alexa smiled. And damn if that shit didn't light him up inside. "Hey," she said.

"Hey." He gave a nod as she came to stand in front of him. His gaze raced over her, checking for signs that anything bad had happened in the seven hours that they'd been apart. But she looked fine. She looked *perfect*. Need roared through him. "Everything okay?"

"Yep," she said, her voice cheerful. Too cheerful?

He eyeballed her. "Slater in there?"

Her smile slid away. "Yeah."

Maverick ground his teeth together as a fantasy flooded through his mind's eye. One he wanted that asshole to fucking see. "Know what I want to do?"

"You promised you wouldn't hurt—"

"No, that's not it. Well, it is, but it's not what I was thinking of right now," he said.

An uncertain smile crept back onto her pretty face. "Okay. Well, then, what do you want to do?"

One beat passed. And then another. And Maverick let the words that described his fantasy fly. "I want to pin you against my truck and kiss the fuck out of you. I want to put my hands on you. Everywhere. I want to push those sexy little pants off your even sexier ass and make you wet with my fingers until you're crying out my name. While all those eyes behind that dark glass are watching. While *Slater's* watching."

Alexa let out a shaky breath and her mouth dropped open. Heat slid into her gaze, making it harder for him to resist turning his words into actions. "Probably . . . um, probably not a good idea."

He chuffed out a little laugh. "Probably not." He reached for the handle and held the door open for her.

With a little nod, she got up into the truck's cab.

Maverick stepped into the doorway. "You really okay?"

"Yes," she said, her voice breathy.

"He talk to you?" She nodded. "He *touch* you?"

"No." Her eyes flashed to the building, making Mav's scalp prickle. He peered over his shoulder just to make sure Slater wasn't standing right behind him. "I told him we were over. He tried to convince me to at least talk it out. And then he gave me back my ring."

Maverick couldn't help it. His gaze dropped to her lap, where her hands were fisted against her thighs. No ring.

"I wouldn't accept it, though, and he finally had to take it back."

He met her eyes and what he saw there nearly sucker punched him. Pride. Strength. Courage. None of this was easy for her, and he knew that. It made him proud of her, too. And he wouldn't have been the only one. "Tyler would be proud of you."

She gave him a smile that was so sweet and so sad that

it felt like she'd reached inside his chest and squeezed. "That . . . that means a lot, Maverick."

"Just calling it like I see it," he said in a low voice. "He say anything else?"

She rolled her eyes. "Just that it wasn't over."

Of course it wasn't. The fucker. "We'll see about that."

The ride home was quiet, and then they were back at his house again.

"Your stuff's all in your room," Maverick said. He dropped his keys on the kitchen counter.

"You didn't have to unload it all. I would've helped," she said, placing her purse next to his keys.

He shouldn't like the look of that so much. Or the way it felt to have company in here at the end of the day. Or the way the clicking of her heels against the hardwoods echoed through the house.

"No biggie, Al," he said, grabbing a soda from the fridge. Just to have something to do with his hands that didn't involve getting them wet with the slickness he could draw out from between her legs. Yeah, they'd fucked this morning. But that didn't mean she wanted it to happen again. He needed to rein his damn self in.

"Gonna change. Be right back."

When she was gone, he raked his hand through his hair and mentally ran through his favorite parts of the rebuild he was doing. It had a copper-forged gas tank and copper-coated lower shock arms, rear fender strut, bar risers, and a bunch of other copper accents. When it was done, it was going to have a sweet throwback vibe.

Nope. Didn't work. He still wanted to follow her back to her bedroom. Especially since his brain knew that she was stripping down and baring all that warm, warm skin.

Goddamnit. He needed to knock his head against a wall somewhere. Because the last thing she needed was him coming on too strong. Or, frankly, coming on at all.

"Hey, Mav?" she called. "Do you see Lucy anywhere?"

He pushed off the counter and made for the living room. "Not in here," he said. He grinned to himself because he had a few surprises for Alexa where Lucy was concerned. He checked the hall bathroom next. As little as the thing was, she could be hiding just about anywhere. When he'd returned earlier in the day with Alexa's stuff, the cat had been standoffish at first, but once her mama's things started coming in, Lucy came closer, poking around and sniffing at Alexa's clothes and bags, until she finally let Maverick pet her and even pick her up.

And then, naturally, he'd needed to win over the fucking cat all the way. So when he'd gone to the grocery store to make sure he had some of Alexa's favorites in the house, he'd just happened into the pet aisle. Not seeing much, he'd stopped at the pet store, where a shit-ton of stuff had fallen into his cart. For fuck sake.

"Maverick?"

He followed her voice to the back of the house and found her standing in his bedroom doorway. She'd changed into a light green tank top and a pair of beat-up jeans that framed her curves perfectly, and put up her wavy brown hair into a ponytail. Standing there in bare feet, the threads of the frayed denim just touching the floor, she was the sexiest woman he'd ever seen.

"I can't believe it," she said, peering inside the room.

Lucy was curled up asleep on his pillow. "Why not?"

Alexa's eyes stayed on her cat. "Because Lucy was terrified of Grant. Wouldn't go near him. Bolted out of any room he came into. The only exception was at night. She slept under my side of the bed to be near me." Al finally met his gaze. "I thought she had a problem with men."

Mav smirked, even though the awe in Alexa's tone was doing shit to his chest again. "Only the assholes, apparently."

She burst out laughing. "Only the assholes."

A meow rang out from the bed, where Lucy was engaged in a long, exaggerated stretch.

"Hey, baby," Alexa said, crossing the room. "What . . . what are you wearing?"

Grinning, Maverick waited.

"Oh my God." She laughed and scooped the cat into her arms. "You bought her a sweater?"

He finally let his laughter loose. "I made her a badass." The sweater covered the cat's thin body from neck to back legs and was black with white skulls and crossbones.

Alexa kissed the cat's head, and Maverick could hear Lucy purring from several feet away. "She didn't mind you putting it on?" More of that awe.

"I wouldn't go as far as saying that she loved it," he said, moving closer and holding his hand out for the cat. Lucy forced her head against his palm. "But we made friends. Plus, um, I might've bribed her with treats."

Chuckling, Alexa shook her head. "I'm sorry I missed that." Lucy hopped out of her arms. Alexa's expression slowly changed and sadness filled her hazel eyes. "I'm sorry . . . for so much."

The word stirred up all kinds of things inside him, but Maverick just shook his head. "You're all about the future now."

"Yeah. Yeah, I am."

His cell buzzed in his pocket. Looking at the screen, he found a text from Bunny.

You coming to dinner tonight?

He hadn't planned to, not with Alexa here, but it wasn't often that his mother asked that outright. Which had him feeling like she wanted him there at the clubhouse. Rodeo had confided that she still didn't feel entirely comfortable being there.

"Everything okay?" Alexa asked.

He shrugged. "Mom. Asking if I was coming up to the clubhouse for dinner. She's, uh, she's still having a hard time."

"I'm sorry, Maverick. I can't believe everything that happened to her. You should go."

"You, uh, you wanna come?" he asked.

"Oh. Uh. Really?"

"Is that a no?" he asked with a frown. He hadn't realized how much he wanted her to agree until she'd answered.

"Not a no," she said. "More of a 'are you sure.' I remember how Dare looked at me when I was there a couple of weeks ago. I know after everything that happened between us that he's not my biggest fan." She hugged herself. "I don't blame him for that. Just stating the facts."

"My cousin's a pain in the ass," he said. He couldn't deny her words, so there was no point doing so. It wasn't that Dare didn't like Alexa; he didn't like the way things had gone down between them five years before. But that wasn't any of Dare's business, and he'd get over it in five seconds if Maverick wanted him to.

"No, your cousin's loyal," Alexa said. The characterization earned her some points in Maverick's book, not that she needed them. Just that he respected the hell out of her saying something nice about someone he cared about. And it was true, too.

"Come," he said.

Her eyes rose to his, and a beautiful blush bloomed across her cheeks. What the hell? And then he thought about his choice of words.

Come.

A slow smile slid onto his face, and he dragged his knuckles down her cheek. "Come," he said again, just to see if the blush would deepen. It did.

On a laugh, she knocked his hand away. "*Now* who's

being an asshole? Lucy's going to take her sweater off." She pushed by him, and it felt a whole helluva lot like she was running from the innuendo, which kinda made him want to keep teasing.

"So are you coming yet?" he asked, laughter in his voice now. He was cracking himself up.

"Oh my God," she said as she went into her room up the hall.

"You know you want to," he said as he leaned in her door. He found her unzipping a suitcase full of shoes.

"You want me to come?" she asked, smiling up at him as she slid on a pair of sandals.

Grinning, he nodded, loving that she was playing along. Loving *seeing* her happier. Because finding her in the rain the night before, her expression desolate, her voice anguished, had been a big part of the reason he hadn't been able to sleep. "Hell, yeah, I do."

She planted her hands on her hips and arched a brow, a blasé expression on her face. "Then why don't you *make me* come?"

It took half a second for the challenge to sink in, and then Maverick was crossing the room and tossing her over his shoulder. "Oh, Alexa. Don't issue a challenge you don't want answered."

She screamed and laughed, her hands smacking his back. "Put me down, Maverick Rylan."

He swatted her butt, loving every squirm of her body against his. "No fucking way."

"You better put me down right now!" she said, laughing harder.

"Oh, yeah? Why's that?" he asked, enjoying the hell out of himself as he grabbed the keys for his Harley off the counter.

"Because . . . because . . . if you don't, I'll make you pay!"

He chuckled. "I think I like the sound of that."

"Oh, my God," she said, as he walked them toward the door. "What is . . . Maverick, wait."

The change in her voice made him stop. "What?"

"Is that . . ." She twisted her upper body. "Is that a new climber for Lucy?"

"Oh," he said, glancing at the carpeted three-level contraption sitting in front of the big window that looked out onto the pond behind the house. Lucy lay in the top level, her gaze fixed on something outside. "Uh, yeah."

For a long moment, she didn't say anything else. Fuck. He'd gone too far, hadn't he?

And then her arms came around his stomach and she laid her head against his back in an awkward but awesome embrace. "Take me to dinner, Mav," she said softly.

Satisfaction roared through him. "You bet."

CHAPTER 16

The ride to the clubhouse wasn't long, but Alexa savored every minute on the back of Mav's Night Rod Special, which was quite possibly the sexiest bike ever made. The warm breeze across her skin felt like freedom, and riding gave her a totally legit reason to wrap herself around him. This man who was not only generously taking care of her, but also of her cat.

A cat climber was maybe a stupid thing to get choked up about, but she had anyway. Because it wasn't just a cat climber to her. It was Mav recognizing that something was vitally important to her, even if it wasn't to him, and treating it with care and respect. And that had touched her.

When was the last time I had this much fun and felt this carefree after coming home from work?

The easiness, the joking innuendos, him tossing her over his shoulder, them going for a ride. There was no stress about any of it. No right or wrong. No expectations to live up to. She had no doubt that she could've begged out of dinner, and Maverick would've been fine about it.

She could just be herself—wants, wishes, desires, needs, and all.

Which was when it occurred to her. How much acting she'd done in Grant's presence. The masks she'd donned and the roles she'd played. Ones he'd crafted for her slowly but surely over the past five years until she thought they'd been her own idea.

She released a deep breath, imagining as she did that she was letting go. Letting go of all that stuff that wasn't her true self. And just letting it blow away in the wind.

Before long, they pulled into the big parking lot in front of the Ravens' clubhouse. The building still had the charm of a mountain resort even with more than a dozen motorcycles parked in front of it. Maverick parked the NRS and the engine went quiet. As she dismounted and took off her helmet, her eyes strayed to the chop shop building across the way. Maverick did most of his bike-building work in there, and she'd spent many an hour watching him. Asking him questions about what he was doing and handing him tools.

"You working on anything fun right now?" she asked.

"Always," he said with a smile. "Although club business has been distracting me the past few weeks. I can show you after dinner if you want."

"Yeah," she said.

With a side nod, he gestured toward the door. "Ready?"

"Sure." Even though she was more nervous than she wanted to admit. The last time she'd come, she'd been so upset over the fight and her injuries that she really hadn't had time to think about how the guys might treat her. And even though she'd sensed a little wariness from Dare, he'd also been clearly concerned and ready to help her. Everyone had been kind. No one had been mean. In fact, a woman named Haven had not only tended to her wounds but made her feel welcomed, reassured, and so much calmer. So maybe she didn't have anything to worry about after all.

The thought didn't keep the butterflies from whipping around in her belly.

Inside, things looked pretty much like she remembered. Couches filled the big lounge in what had once been the inn's front lobby, and the registration desk still actually stood at the back of the room. Photos of the club members filled the wall by the mess hall door. And on the other side, she could just peer into the big rec room where the bar was and most of the partying happened.

Voices spilled out of the mess hall, and she followed Maverick in, those butterflies getting a lot more active.

A couple of the guys greeted Maverick right away. She hung back as he shook hands and gave a few of those one-armed hugs men did. He made introductions, or re-introductions in a few cases, and everyone acted totally normal towards her.

"Alexa?"

She turned to find a woman . . . who looked a lot different than she remembered. "Haven?"

Nodding, Haven laughed as she settled a big platter of grilled burgers, hot dogs, sausages, and chicken legs in the middle of the table. Beside her, a woman with shoulder-length blond hair was putting down an equally big platter of grilled vegetables. "The hair, right?" Haven asked, smiling.

"Yeah," Alexa said, remembering the hip-length pale blond hair she'd had when they'd first met. Now it was light brown and hung in soft waves to her shoulder blades. "It looks really great."

"Sometimes change is good," Haven said.

The words sure hit home for Alexa. "Yeah. Sometimes it really is."

"Alexa, this is my best friend, Cora," Haven said.

Cora's smile was immediate. "Hey, there. Nice to meet you." They shook hands.

"You, too. Can I help at all?" Alexa asked, feeling more and more comfortable with each passing minute.

"Sure," Haven said, waving her into the kitchen.

They passed through the swinging door, and then Alexa's gaze snagged on the chair where she'd sat that day, bruised and bloodied, while Haven knelt in front of her and cleaned her up. It felt like yesterday and years ago all at the same time.

"Alexa Harmon. How are you, honey?" Bunny asked.

"Hi, Bunny," she said, so happy to see Maverick's mother whom she'd always liked, even if she was also nervous about what the older woman thought of her. Despite having hair that was so pale blond it was nearly white, you'd never guess that Bunny McKeon was in her early sixties. She wore a stylish pair of dark wash jeans and a form-fitting black T-shirt. "It's really good to see you." Though it was equally hard to see the nearly healed but still visible scratches and bruises on Bunny's face.

"Well, come on over here and give me a hug, young lady. It's been too long," Bunny said, holding open her arms.

The welcoming gesture made the backs of her eyes prick with tears that Alexa blinked away. They hugged for a long moment. "I'm sorry for what happened," she said.

"It's a crazy world," Bunny said, her voice quiet.

Alexa nodded. "Yes, it is."

Bunny pulled back from the hug and held Alexa's face in her hands. Light blue eyes examined her. "You doing okay?"

"Much better now," Alexa said.

"Good. Well . . ." Bunny patted her shoulder. "Let's get these boys fed before there's an uprising."

They all laughed.

Dinner was a lively, raucous affair full of funny stories, snarky retorts, and at least one roll-throwing incident. Alexa hadn't laughed so much or so hard in a long, long time. God, she couldn't even remember when the last time was. Not that she'd ever had a big family, but that's what it felt like. And it made her even more certain that she'd misjudged things five years before. She wanted to go back in time and shake herself.

Emotion suddenly crashed over her, like a wave unexpectedly swamping her in the ocean. She excused herself from the table and rushed into the kitchen and then out onto the big back porch. Lounge chairs filled the long space, which had a stunning view of the mountain and the valley beyond. Bracing her hands on the railing, Alexa stared at the vista until it went blurry.

The screen door quietly closed behind her, and Alexa batted away the wetness on her face.

"You okay?" Haven asked.

Alexa released a long breath. "Mostly."

"Yeah," Haven said, coming to stand beside her. "Isn't this view the best? I love to sit out here."

"I've always loved it," Alexa said, her thoughts a jumbled mess. "I just wish it hadn't taken me so long to see it again." Not just talking about the view. Obviously. She could almost feel Haven's questions, and she finally turned to look at the other woman. Haven appeared younger than Alexa was, though there was something about her eyes— the brightest blue Alexa had ever seen—that read as older, like maybe she'd seen way more than she should've at her age. "Messing up really sucks."

Understatement of the century.

"It does," Haven said. "But sometimes it also makes what you should've done really crystal clear. And that at least gives you a direction to go in."

The words resonated with Alexa down deep and took a

little of the weight off her shoulders. Nodding, she said, "Just got a little overwhelmed in there."

Haven laughed. "They're an overwhelming bunch."

The affection in the woman's words made Alexa smile. "That's for sure." She turned to Haven. "Do you mind if I ask how you're connected to the Ravens? I'm just curious." When Alexa had been with Maverick, Bunny; Bear's wife, Margie; and Slider's wife, Kim, were the women she most frequently saw around the clubhouse, with a few other wives and girlfriends pitching in for bigger events and on race nights. But Margie and Kim were both several years' gone now. Alexa had seen their obituaries in the paper.

"Well, it's kind of a long story," Haven said. "My father was a bad man, and I ran away from him with Cora's help. When our truck broke down in Baltimore, the tow truck driver turned us over to a gang in the city. A couple days later, we got rescued, and then the Ravens agreed to take us in until we figured out what was next."

Alexa's mouth dropped open. And she thought she'd been in a tough situation. "Oh, God, Haven. I'm so sorry. That's terrible."

"Best thing that ever happened to me," Haven said, a little humor in her tone, but mostly it was clear that she meant it. "It led me to this place and these people. To Bunny, who's become like a mom to me. And it brought me to Dare." Her face went pink at the admission, and Alexa was kinda blown away to learn that Dare had a girlfriend. Back in the day, she'd never known him to be remotely interested in settling down. "And to making new friends like you."

The words reached inside Alexa and made her see the Ravens through Haven's eyes. As protectors, as heroes, as *family*. And that made Alexa realize again that in her grief and fear she'd focused on the wrong things five years ago. Or, at least, it felt that way now. She shook the thoughts away. Maverick was right. She was all about the future. "I could use a new friend."

"Good. Then, would you like to see my trick to getting a big group of scary bikers to eat out of the palm of your hand?" Haven asked, a mischievous sparkle in her eyes.

Laughing, Alexa nodded. "You've got me curious, so, yes."

"Come on." Haven led her into the kitchen. The guys were bringing in their dirty dishes and stacking them in the sink. On the far counter, Haven pulled out two big containers. "My secret weapons," she whispered, taking off the lids.

The most glorious smells wafted into the air. "My God, what is that?"

"Are you getting dessert?" came a voice from behind them. Alexa turned to find Phoenix Creed grinning at them. With all the time she used to spend out in the chop shop, she'd once known him pretty well. He was a jokester and a hopeless flirt and always made people laugh. Wearing a charming smile and a playful expression, he didn't appear to have aged one day.

"You best stay back, Phoenix," Haven said, pointing at the guy as if to ward him off. "You try to get a peanut butter cookie before Dare and I'm not responsible for what happens."

"Aw, come on, Haven. Help a brother out," he said, pressing his hands together like he was praying.

"You know that's not an idle threat about Dare," Alexa said. "Better listen."

"Aw, you, too?" He clutched his heart as Cora joined them, a smile on her face and her eyebrow arched like she was trying to figure out what was going on. He put his arm around Cora's shoulders and held out a hand. "Why do all the women around here gang up on me?"

"Uh, because it's super fun?" Cora said, sliding out from under his arm and giving him a look.

"It really is." Haven nodded.

Expression roguish as he came up behind Phoenix, Dare asked, "You hassling my woman?" His voice was stern, clearly unhappy, and he schooled his expression as Phoenix turned to him.

"Dude. Me? No. Of course not. Was I, Haven? Just ask her. I totally was not hassling her." Alexa laughed as his words spilled out in a rush.

"You know, the longer you all chatter at me," Haven said, "the longer it takes me to get everything ready."

Phoenix held up his hands. "I'll be out here waiting patiently. Like a good biker."

"Sorry," Dare said with a wink as he kissed Haven on the cheek. And stealthily snatched a cookie from one of the tubs.

"Hey!" she said, grinning and shaking her head.

Smiling, he took a bite. And then his dark eyes turned on Alexa and scanned over her face. And she just knew he was looking for signs of the injuries she'd had. Gone now. "Good to have you here, Alexa."

"Thanks," she said. "For everything."

He nodded, his expression open, his tone genuine. "Anytime." Eating his cookie, he made his way back out to the mess hall.

"Okay," Haven said, so clearly at home among these men. Alexa found herself envying that. How long had it been since she'd really belonged somewhere? "So we have chocolate and caramel chip cookies. Peanut butter cookies. And mocha s'mores squares. Have one."

"I kinda want to go put on some comfy pajamas, find a good chick flick, and eat every single one of these," Alexa said, taking a chocolate and caramel chip cookie.

"That sounds like the best night ever," Cora said, grinning and snagging a cookie for herself.

"I agree. I could totally make that happen," Haven said, "but only if I'm invited."

"Deal." Alexa nibbled at her cookie, so good she had to

close her eyes on the first bite, while she helped pile the treats on three big plates. "Is this your recipe? Because this is one of the best cookies I've ever had."

Cora chuckled and tucked her blond hair behind her ears. "And another one bites the dust."

Haven rolled her eyes. "Yeah, it's mine. Baking's kinda my thing."

"Clearly," Alexa said around her last bite, more than a little sad that her cookie was gone. Luckily, there appeared to be at least six dozen more left.

"It's not *kinda* your thing," Cora said, nailing the other woman with the kind of calling-you-on-your-bullshit stare that only a best friend can get away with. "It *is* your thing. Which is why you need to open your own bakery."

"Oh, are you thinking of doing that?" Alexa asked. Because she would buy the *crap* out of these cookies.

Haven sighed and returned her friend's stare in a way that suggested there was a whole lot of something Alexa didn't know. "We'll see. But either way, I'm not doing it tonight, so you guys take those two and I'll take the peanut butter," Haven said, smiling at Alexa. "They'll love you forever."

Cheers rose up as she and the other girls walked into the mess hall, arms laden with sugar. Alexa couldn't help but smile as the guys thanked them and dove in like they'd never seen a cookie before. When Haven placed her plate in front of Dare, he pulled her down into his lap and gave her a big kiss that earned a round of catcalls. Dare flipped his middle finger at the room while he was still kissing her, and she finally pushed him away, laughing and shaking her head. Her face was bright red but her expression totally happy.

And Alexa . . . Alexa wanted that. So bad it made her ache.

Her eyes drifted to Maverick, who was looking at her

like he was thinking the same thing. Her whole body flashed hot and everything else in the room faded away. God, what was happening between them? What *could* happen between them, given what a mess her life was? Would Maverick even want something with her again after what she'd done to him five years ago? She had no doubt that he'd be a friend to her. And obviously he was still attracted to her—though that had never been their problem. And it also wasn't the same as having a relationship and trusting someone not to shut you out.

He'd given her that trust once and she'd thrown it away. And she knew him well enough to know that had to be huge to him.

"Tell me you're going to have some dessert," Phoenix said from the seat beside where she was standing. "Here, take a load off." He pushed out a chair for her.

"Thanks." Smiling, she sat and forced the thoughts away. And then she remembered something she'd seen a few weeks before. She turned to Phoenix and placed her hand on his arm. "Hey, I was really sorry to hear about your cousin." He'd apparently died in some kind of explosion. God, the Ravens had really been through it lately, hadn't they?

He clapped his hand atop hers. "Thanks, Al." His voice was softer, lacking the usual Phoenix playfulness. "I appreciate that." His brown eyes were sad for a moment, but then it was like he forced it away. Which reminded her that she wasn't the only one going through something. You never knew what a person was carrying inside them. She thought back to being at work earlier today. No one there realized that she and Grant were imploding, at least, she didn't think so. "Now have a cookie," he said. "They'll probably be gone in about thirty-five seconds."

Grinning, she looked down the table to the plate in front of Dare. "I want to try a peanut butter."

"Good luck with that," Phoenix said, sniggering.

"Hey, Dare?" she said, swallowing her nerves. "May I please have one of your cookies?"

The room got quieter in a hurry, and Alexa looked around to see what'd happened. Everyone was staring at her, then Dare. She looked back to him.

The guy's face was serious, almost stern, and he had one eyebrow cocked and his eyes locked on her. Like he wasn't happy. Like he was *pissed*. And she couldn't believe that he—

Dare grinned and laughed. "Only because you called them mine," he said, pushing the plate to the guy next to him to pass down. Everyone burst into laughter.

Shaking her head, Alexa had to laugh, too. Because she'd totally fallen for it.

As if he'd get pissed off over a cookie. These men had their rough edges, but they were good guys. They'd always been good to Tyler and her when she'd hung out with them years before. And everything she heard about what they did for people who needed help in the community said the same, too.

Grant *looked* like Mr. Respectable, and yet, behind closed doors, he wasn't a nice person and he certainly hadn't been good for her the way she'd convinced herself he was. Meanwhile, sometimes Maverick looked like a total grease monkey and other times like a hard-ass biker who might kill you just as soon as ask your name, and yet he *was* a good person, a fair person, generous and kind.

Damn. She'd totally fallen for the façade, hadn't she? For the stereotype. Not the truth.

In not much longer than thirty-five seconds, the cookies and s'mores squares were all gone, and Alexa pitched in with the dishes. Maverick and Dare hung out while they worked, helping by putting away the bigger things as the women dried them. Alexa was glad for the time to hang out with Bunny and the girls some more, because she already liked Haven a lot and Cora seemed pretty great, too. More than once, Alexa felt Maverick's eyes on her. Sure enough, when she gave into the urge to look, he was watching her work, his expression intense and approving. She didn't know what to make of that, except that it made her belly flip every time.

"Hey, uh, Cora?" came a deep voice from the doorway.

As the man exchanged nods with Dare and Maverick, it took Alexa a few seconds to realize who the new Raven was. Slider. Except he didn't look anything like the person she'd known five years before. This man seemed to carry the weight of the world on his rounded shoulders. His eyes were shuttered, his mouth was set in a grim line, and his hair was much longer and hung in a manner that made her think it'd been a long time since he'd had it cut.

"Hey," Cora said, grabbing a paper towel to dry her hands. "I can be ready in two minutes. Do you want some dinner? I can pack up something for you."

Not quite making eye contact, Slider shook his head.

"For the boys then?" she asked.

"They had pizza," he said, turning for the door. "I'll be in the truck."

Cora sighed and squeezed Haven's shoulder. "See you tomorrow," she said.

"Okay," Haven said, her gaze equal parts sad and worried.

They were all quiet for a moment after Cora left. Dare heaved a long troubled breath. Alexa's heart hurt for the changes she saw in Slider. She'd never known him that well, but he'd always seemed happy—good to Kim and a proud dad to their two little boys. Kim had died a few years before, but clearly he was still torn apart.

"Okay, youngins, I'm beat," Bunny said, folding a hand towel.

"Thanks for everything, Bunny," Dare said. "Dinner was great as usual."

"It's my pleasure. You boys know that. Besides, these

girls did most of the work." She pulled her purse out of a cabinet in the corner and then gave a round of hugs and kisses before she left.

"I guess we'll head out, too," Maverick said, clasping hands with Dare. "You need anything?"

Dare shook his head. "Everything is quiet right now, which, knock on wood, will stay that way for a while." He rapped his fist against the closest cabinet.

"Amen to that," Mav said. "But just ask, okay? Don't be a fucking hero all the time." He turned to Haven. "Make him ask me for help."

She smiled and nodded. Dare gave him a shove. "Weren't you leaving?"

"Yeah, yeah," Maverick said, smiling at Alexa. "Still want to see the bike I'm working on?"

"Definitely," Alexa said. She turned to Haven and gave her a meaningful look. "Thanks for everything." She didn't just mean the awesome meal, but the pep talk out on the porch, the offer of friendship.

Haven seemed to understand. "You're welcome. Maverick has my cell phone number. Give me a call anytime." They hugged and said their good-byes.

And then it was just her and Maverick. Well, there were some other Ravens still around as they made their way through the clubhouse. But the moment Maverick placed his hand against her lower back, he was the only man Alexa could think about.

The only man she wanted.

CHAPTER 17

As they walked across the darkening parking lot to the chop shop, the evening air still warm, Maverick felt a little like he'd traveled back in time. Alexa was here. Hanging with him and his brothers. And it felt good, natural, *right*.

Only tonight had actually been better and worse. Better because Maverick was older now, old enough to know what he actually wanted out of life, old enough to know that he didn't want to come home to an empty house forever, old enough to understand down to his marrow how important family was—and that he wanted one of his own. He hadn't understood all of that five years ago. Not really. Not enough to fight for it the way he should've. Not enough to man up when she'd all but asked him to.

Not enough to ask her what he should've asked her.

Damnit. Why hadn't he fought for her—for them—harder? Why hadn't he laid it all on the line and gotten down on one knee? Especially when he'd known that in her grief over losing Tyler she wasn't strong enough to do it herself. But then watching her head get turned by Slater had fucked with *his* head. Maverick had let that shit happen. So that was on him.

At the same time, the night was worse because Mav had no fucking idea whether Alexa wanted any of that in return—with him. Sure, the chemistry between them was still off the charts. And the sex this morning had been phenomenal. Even better than he remembered it from before, and before had been fantastic. Worse because seeing Alexa at the clubhouse only made Maverick want her more, want her to see what he saw, want her for his, for keeps, forever.

And he knew it wasn't fair to even expect her to know what she wanted from or with him. Not when she was only a day into the implosion of the life she'd thought she wanted. There was no reason why she'd feel the same urgency he did. The urgency not to make the same mistake again, the urgency to hold tight and never let go. No matter how rough the ride got this time.

All of which meant it was going to fucking suck if he turned out to be her rebound man. And only her rebound man. And Maverick knew there was a chance that's all he was.

But, fuck, if that's all he could have of her, he'd take it. And deal with the fallout later.

The chop shop was a long building with four bay doors and an office at one end. He pushed in through the office door and hit the lights. The two desks in the room were primarily his and Phoenix's, though others used them sometimes. But this wasn't where Maverick did the lion's share of his nine-to-five. Instead, the last of the bays was his most regular domain. Kicking on lights as they went, he led Alexa through the shop past bikes other Ravens were working on to his space, separated from the rest by a cinder block wall. A sign over the door they walked through was the same as one that hung above the outside bay door and read, *Maverick Custom Cycles*.

"Everything looks the same," Alexa said, slowly glancing around the room. She shook her head.

"What?" he asked, trying to see what she was seeing, trying to understand where her head was.

She gave a little shrug. "Standing here . . ." She cleared her throat and met his gaze. And damn if her eyes weren't a little glassy. "It feels like I was *just* here. And it also feels like I've lived a whole lifetime since I was last here. I don't know." She looked away and moved closer to the bike he was working on.

So her head was kicking around some of the thoughts his was, then.

He watched her move around his space, liking seeing her there. How many hours had they spent here together? Her keeping him company when he was up late finishing something on deadline. Her singing along to the radio. Him teaching her about bikes and engines the way he'd been taught, and her being genuinely interested, asking a million and a half questions.

Them not being able to keep their hands off of each other, even when there were guys out in the rest of the shop working.

Heat rushed through his veins at the stream of memories that played against his mind's eye.

"I love the copper," she said, walking around the bike, running her fingers over the smooth, mirrored surface. "That really looks sharp. Kinda vintage."

She'd *always* gotten his love for making something custom, unique, one-of-a-kind. Even when she hadn't known what the parts were called or what they even did, she'd had a great eye for what looked good.

Unlike her, he'd been around engines since he was a kid.

He'd known the names of car parts before he'd been old enough to drive, courtesy of his mechanic father, who'd specialized in customizing trucks. Still did. Not that Maverick had seen him in a long time, because he avoided the sonofabitch as much as possible. It'd been the better part of a year since they'd last run into each other. Which was too recent for Mav's taste.

But the love of engines, of building and rebuilding, of putting your own custom spin on something? Yeah, he had to credit that to his old man. At least he had one positive thing that the guy did that he could point to.

Motorcycles, though . . . *that* he'd learned from Doc. Maverick had spent a lot of time with his uncle growing up, and Doc didn't believe in idle hands. Never had.

"Yeah, vintage is the goal," Maverick said, moving closer. The bike stood between them. "The base was actually a 2004 Chevy, but it's been reengineered so heavily you'd never know. The goal is something similar to a 1950s hot rod style chopper."

She grinned, her eyes flashing.

"What?" he asked, her smile beckoning his.

"It's been a long time since I've heard you talk bike makes and models." Her smile got considerably sadder.

In a weird way, that gave him hope. "Too long?" he asked. Pushing her. Just a little.

"Too long," she said. "Definitely too long." She turned away like maybe the admission had been a lot to make. But that didn't take away from the satisfaction he felt. Not one bit.

She wandered around the space a little, looking at a couple of decorative ornaments he had laying on one counter. Leaning in close to some photographs he had pinned to a corkboard. And coming to—

Shit. Why hadn't he thought about this?

"What's this one?" she asked, her hand grabbing the dusty drop cloth covering the bike.

"Alexa, don't—"

The black cloth puddled on the floor around Tyler's repaired bike. In the months after her brother died, but before it was clear that Alexa wasn't going to take Maverick back, he'd fixed the bike. It had felt like a way for him to pay respect to his friend, and he'd thought Alexa could sell the bike if she didn't want the reminder. He knew she could use the money. At least, back then. But he never even got the chance to offer.

Shit.

"This is . . . is this . . ." She shook her head, her back still to him. "It's Tyler's." She said her brother's name so low Mav barely heard it.

"Yeah," he said, coming up behind her and aching for opening her up to this right now.

"You fixed it?"

He hated that he couldn't read the emotion in her voice, and finally gave in to the need to see her face. Taking her by the shoulders, he turned her to him. "Yeah," he said, leaning down to meet her eye to eye.

"Why?" she whispered, those pretty hazel eyes glassy— and that glassiness gutted him.

"For him," he said. A tear finally fell, and he caught it with his thumb. "And for you."

Her bottom lip trembled. "But I . . . I hurt you." More tears fell.

He wasn't going to deny it. "You did."

"I'm so sorry," she said, her face crumpling. "I was such a wreck when he died." She shook her head. "And I made so many mistakes. And pushing you away was the biggest of them all. And I'm so fucking sorry, Maverick." She clasped her hand over a sob.

He pulled her into his chest, wrapped one arm around her back, and cradled her head in his other hand. "I know, Al. I get it. And I did then, even though I hated it." And, *fuck*, but hearing her words made him rage, too. Because he'd let himself be pushed away, hadn't he? He'd known she was a wreck, but hadn't done the hard work to stick it out and carry her through.

God, why hadn't he seen how much she needed him? Because hearing her now, it was so damn clear that he'd failed her.

And Tyler.

"I'm sorry, too," he said, his voice like gravel. Her tears scalded him with guilt and regret, but he'd take every one. For her. He stroked his hand through her soft hair, loving the way it felt. Loving the way *she* felt pressed against him.

"No," she said, her voice no more than a rasp. She lifted her eyes to his. "All on me."

"Fuck, Al. Rarely is anything in a relationship all on one person. That day in the cemetery . . ." He shook his head. "You have no idea how many times I've wished that I'd given you what you needed. That . . . that was on me."

Her mouth dropped open, like the admission surprised her. And then they stared at one another a long moment, Maverick swiping away her falling tears until they slowed, then stopped.

"Wanna head home?" he finally asked.

She released a halting breath, her eyes searching his. "You're a good man, Maverick Rylan. Better than I gave you credit for. But I see you now." She paused, and he hung on her words like they were the oxygen he needed to breathe. "I know it may be too late. But, God, I see you."

His heart tripped into a thunderous beat, one that pounded through his veins. His cock hardened at the sentiment and the raw emotion on her face. "Not too late," he managed, need putting him on edge. "But, Jesus, you need to stop looking at me like that."

"Like what?"

"Like you want to take a bite out of me."

"Why?"

"Because my bite will be fucking bigger."

She shifted against him, the friction of her belly turning his cock to steel. His hands tightened on her, a silent command to be still. Alexa licked her lips, and he saw his hunger reflected back at him. Her gaze dropped to his mouth. Lingered there.

"*Alexa*," he growled.

"You sure? Because I don't want a bite. I want the whole meal."

The words hit him like a blowtorch licking over his skin. Without thought, he kissed her. Hard and claiming and rough. He absolutely plundered her mouth, his lips sucking, his tongue penetrating. The whimper she unleashed shot to his cock as her fingers twisted in his hair.

In his head, he was pulling down those sexy beat-up jeans and bending her over his bike . . .

Bike.

Maverick's eyes flashed open . . . and his gaze landed on the handlebars of Tyler's motorcycle.

He pulled back from the kiss, his fingers going immediately to his lips. "Fuck."

"What?"

"We're not doing this," he said, anger making his words come out sounding harsh. Anger at himself for thinking with his dick, for thinking of himself, for taking advantage of the emotional wreck she'd been just five goddamned minutes ago.

"Why?" she asked, a tinge of hurt in her voice.

He grabbed her hand and pressed it to the painfully hard ridge of his cock. "Not because I don't want you. Understand?" He nailed her with a stare. He didn't know all the shit Slater had filled her head with, but he'd never make her doubt his desire for her. Maverick didn't have the patience, tolerance, or disposition for game-playing. Never had.

Finally, she nodded, but she didn't remove her hand. "Then why?"

He shuddered out a breath and forced her touch away, but he slid his fingers through hers to try to take the sting out of the gesture. "Because you don't need anything else that messes with your head right now. Being inside you this morning was the best fucking thing I've felt in five years, but it also complicates the shit out of what you're going through. And me bending you over a bike in my garage isn't going to help you figure things out." He stepped away as what he was saying to her sank in to his own brain. Yeah. This was the right thing to do. Keep his damn hands off until she figured her life out. "So, yeah." He raked at his hair.

"Oh." She hugged herself, but nodded. "I guess, yeah. Makes sense. Sorry."

He stepped back into her space and grasped her chin. Forced her to meet his eyes. "Stop apologizing for things that aren't your fault, Alexa. That's *him* talking and I won't fucking stand for it." He arched a brow until she agreed.

She did. "Okay. Should we go home, then?"

"Yeah," he said, his cock still rock hard. Traitorous bastard. "We should."

"ALEXA," GRANT SAID, walking into her office the next morning. Without knocking. He closed the door, then turned to her, his face set in a deep scowl. A shiver raced over her skin.

"Grant," she said, pulling her attention away from checking over the furniture deliveries scheduled to arrive at the model home beginning this afternoon. She forced strength and confidence into her voice, refusing to be cowed by the anger radiating off of him. "Can I help you?"

"Yes. By coming home. Today." He crossed his arms, his eyes set in a dark glare.

"We've already had this conversation," she said, her heart racing despite herself. He was back in that scary, quiet mode again. "Will there be anything else?"

He stalked toward the desk and braced his hands against it, and then he leaned down close. Too close. "Collect your belongings and *come home*."

Was that what this anger was over? He'd noticed she'd removed all her belongings? "I don't have a home right now," she said.

"Is that what this is still about? How many times would you like me to apologize?" he asked, no remorse in his tone whatsoever. So be it. Acting like this just confirmed that she'd made the right decision.

In fact, half of her wanted him to keep talking, to break into a full-out tirade, even. Because both of those were likely to further validate her choice to leave him. "One genuine apology would be nice. But there's a difference between apologies and forgiveness and forgetting or overlooking. I have no intention of doing the latter. So I won't be coming home. Or getting back together with you. Or marrying you. Which is why I returned your ring and packed my stuff." She clasped her hands on the desktop to hide how much they were shaking. "Perhaps we should talk about who is calling to cancel what. I could take care of the venue, the photographer, and the band if you'll cancel the honeymoon reservations, the florist, and the cake maker. And I assume you'd prefer to send out the email notifying the guests." At least they didn't have a slew of in-laws coming into town that they had to worry about disappointing. For once, neither of them having much in the way of family was an advantage.

His expression transformed, like he was confused and angry in equal measure. "Cancel the wedding? We'll do no such thing."

She blinked, because she'd been very clear on this already, yet he was acting almost surprised to hear it. "Grant, you're not listening to me. We're over."

The rolling changes to his expression were almost comical. She couldn't decide if he was trying to figure out how to play this or was actually this . . . emotionally out of control. It was so unlike him that all she could do was stare and wait for his reaction. Like watching to see which number the ball landed on in roulette.

"We are adults, Alexa. We will talk this out like adults," he finally said.

"There's nothing to talk about," she said, trying very hard to keep her frustration in check. But talking to him right now was a lot like talking to a brick wall.

"There's everything to talk about. There's *forever* to talk about."

"Grant—"

"What do you think is going to happen here, Alexa? That I'm just going to let you go? That I'm going to allow you to walk away from the life we've started building, the one that we've invited three hundred people to come celebrate and *witness* the start of in ten days? That you're going to shack up with a criminal biker gang and I'm just going to stand for it?" His volume escalated on those last few words, his anger finally coming through, and he leaned over the desk, invading her space until it was hard to breathe.

Needing distance, she pushed back in her chair, her scalp prickling and her hair standing up on end. She wasn't sure she'd *ever* heard rage in his voice as scary or as lethal as what he'd just spoken. Whatever sass had been on the tip of her tongue melted away. Where had these mood swings come from? Or had she just never noticed because she'd always gone along to keep the peace?

"Surely, you realized that I would find out where you were."

She had. Of course she had. It had only been a matter

of time, and Frederick wasn't that big—especially for Grant Slater. "If I was trying to hide where I was staying, I wouldn't have Maverick giving me rides to and from work," she said, hating the quivering in her voice. Maverick, who she'd had sex with. Maverick, who she wanted to have sex with again. Though she thought better than to share any of that with Grant. He probably wouldn't want her back if he knew, which could be good. Except she feared his reaction would be a whole lot worse—and more damaging—than that. And, anyway, she hadn't been with Maverick to get back at Grant, so she wasn't sharing that with him for anything.

He made a sound full of disgust. "You've made your point with this little stunt. I only have so much patience. And I'm not letting you go without a fight," he said, his tone seemingly calm but, to her, obviously razor sharp and ice cold.

"There's nothing left to fight about, Grant," she said, exasperated. How the heck was she going to get this through his head? "You said you wanted me to do this job for the model home, so would you please leave so I can do it? This conversation isn't getting us anywhere."

He jabbed his finger into the desk. "Agree to see me after work."

"No."

"Agree—"

"Grant, no."

"*Agree*, Alexa." His stare was like sitting under the lights in an interrogation room. Hot and uncomfortable.

"I can't see you tonight. My mother has an appointment," she lied, terribly, but she was desperate.

"Fine. Tomorrow night." He arched a brow.

"Grant—"

"I'm hardly being unreasonable. You *owe* me an hour of your time."

"No, I don't—"

"I swear to God." Anger washed off of him and over her. Despite the air-conditioning in the office, a trickle of sweat ran down the center of her back. He leaned closer and it seemed like his body vibrated with tension, like he might come right up over the desk at her. "Al—"

"Fine," she said, regretting it immediately. Especially when a smug smile spread over his face. "Just know that I will not be changing my mind. And there's nothing you can say to get me to. But out of respect for you and the time we shared, I will talk to you about our relationship. One last time. But please, stop doing this to me at work." The words rushed out as her heart hammered inside her chest.

"So be it. I won't bother you here again with personal conversation. But remember how persuasive I can be. I *will* change your mind." The smugness overtook his whole expression in an attitude that was supposed to come off as sexy but now just struck her as smarmy and purposely obtuse. Who *was* this man?

She took her seat and laced her hands together on the desk again. "Tomorrow night. Until then, good-bye."

His eyes flashed. If there was one thing Grant wasn't used to, it was being dismissed. But she was so angry at herself for agreeing to see him, and she'd had enough. "Tomorrow night," he said before finally turning on his heel and leaving.

On a heaving breath, Alexa bent over and rested her forehead on her hands. Why had she let him badger her into meeting? She didn't want to see him or spend time with him. She certainly didn't want to be alone with him. And it wasn't like talking was going to change anything anyway.

Damnit. Way to cave, Al.

And if all that wasn't bad enough, Maverick was going to freaking kill her.

The thought made her remember that Grant knew she was staying with the Ravens. Maverick at least needed to know that much now.

Grant knows I'm staying with you. She shot off the text.

Good, came Maverick's reply.

What if he takes it out on you? She hit *Send,* for the first time wondering about what the consequences could possibly be to the Ravens for offering her shelter.

I can handle Slater.

Her belly flipped at all the things that might possibly entail. *I don't want you to have to handle him.* Maverick didn't need Grant's kind of trouble, and after everything that Bunny and the club had been through recently, it was clear that none of them did.

Her cell rang. Maverick.

"Hey," she said. Her heart gave a little pang that he'd stopped what he was doing to call her.

"Hey. You okay?" he asked. And another pang over his concern. "What happened?"

"Yes, I'm okay, but it's a long story. Do you mind if I recount it all tonight?" she asked, not wanting to possibly start a second argument in five minutes. Plus, she really needed to get some paperwork finished so she could meet the general contractor over at the model home to go over room-by-room furniture layout.

"Fine," he said. "That's a plan. But listen to me, Al, and listen to me good. You're under my protection. You're under the protection of all of my brothers. Period. Something comes at you, it comes at all of us. We try not to go on the offensive if we can help it, but we sure as fuck defend our own. This is what we do. And that includes you."

His protectiveness chased away some of the anxiety that had settled into her muscles from the confrontation with Grant. "Okay," she said.

"Okay. You need me, you reach out. You hear?" he

said, the fierce urgency of his voice sending comfort and strength down the line to her.

"I hear," she said. "Thanks, Maverick. It was . . . it was good to hear your voice."

"Any time." He paused like maybe he wanted to say something more, but then he just said good-bye.

Alexa couldn't help but compare how she felt after talking to Grant and Maverick. Grant left her stressed out, anxious, angry at him and herself, and just drained, while Maverick built her up, made her feel secure and less alone, and eased some of her concerns. Hammering home how much she'd misjudged the two men five years before.

Enough.

Enough personal bullshit for one day. It was only nine-thirty in the morning, for crap's sake. And here she thought her day couldn't get any more awkward after running into Maverick in the hall this morning wearing only a towel, water droplets running down his bare chest and back from the ends of his freshly washed hair. She'd wanted to drop to her knees and reacquaint her hands and mouth with what was under that towel, but she'd been too worried that he wouldn't want her to. Not after he'd put the brakes on the night before out in his garage.

God, she really was a mess right now, wasn't she? Her whole life. Which probably made Maverick right in wanting to put on those brakes.

She just needed to do her job, take care of her mom, and figure out how to put her life back on track. So that's what she'd stay focused on doing.

CHAPTER 18

"You did *what*?" Maverick asked, standing in the doorway to her bedroom that night. "Because I know I didn't just hear what I think I heard."

Alexa had been sitting on the edge of the bed trying to work up the nerve to tell him that she'd agreed to meet Grant when he'd popped in and asked what was wrong. "I told Grant I'd meet with him. Tomorrow after work." She forced herself to look Maverick in the eye.

He raked his hands through his dark blond hair, the movement raising his shirt and exposing a sliver of lean muscle and inked skin above his jeans. "Why? Why would you do that?"

"I didn't want to—"

"Did he threaten you?" Maverick asked, coming to stand in front of where she sat. Agitation rolled off of him, but it didn't scare Alexa. It made her worry that he'd be disappointed in her, but didn't scare her.

She thought back over the interaction with Grant. There hadn't been an overt threat, but she certainly hadn't felt entirely safe, either. He *had* scared her, even though she hated it, so agreeing had seemed like the path of least resistance. "No, not really."

Mav held out his hands, still stained with grease around the tips of his fingers. "What does that mean, Al? Please, start from the beginning and tell me what happened."

She did, recounting everything she could remember. "So, no, he didn't threaten me. But he was really angry and I . . . I . . . just gave in. Okay? I hated it the minute I agreed, but now I'm stuck."

"Cancel. Tell him you're not meeting with him. It's bad enough you have to work with him. I don't trust him alone with you at all." Maverick paced in front of her.

"He won't let me cancel. I'm going to have to do this sometime. For closure. And stop pacing. You're making me even more nervous."

Oh a huff, Maverick crouched down in front of her, his hands on her knees. "Damnit, I don't mean to make you nervous. But my gut says this is bad news. Fucking Slater."

"Yeah." She shrugged and hugged herself. "But what's the worst he could do? It's not like he can lock me up in the basement."

Maverick's blue eyes flashed. "Don't even joke about that, Alexa. You'd be surprised what a control-freak with his reputation on the line might be willing to do to get what he wants. And I don't want to see that happen to you."

She let out a shaky breath. "So what do I do then?"

"Not you. We. You do this, we're going with you." He pulled out his cell phone and dialed.

Alexa's stomach flipped before the meaning of his words fully sank in, and by then, he already had Phoenix on the line.

"MAVERICK, I DON'T think this is a good idea," Alexa said when he picked her up after work at the model home she'd been designing. She was meeting with Slater in an hour, and Mav was kinda going out of his fucking mind about that.

Straddling his Harley parked in a driveway surrounded by newly laid sod, he handed her his helmet. "It's the *only* idea." It was the first day he'd picked her up on the Night Rod instead of in his truck, but for what was happening tonight, he wanted the NRS. No, he *needed* it. Needed Grant to see them two up on the back of the bike, Alexa with her arms and her thighs wrapped around Maverick.

Maybe it made him an asshole, but Maverick was worried about her being alone with Slater, and that had his protective instincts roaring to life. Being worried made Mav pissed off, too, and being pissed off made him feel all kinds of possessive and territorial. All of which meant he'd been a bear to be around the past twenty-four hours, something he'd apologize to Alexa for later. When all this was behind them and he knew she was safe. And this *would* be behind them, one way or the other. Because by the time this night was over, Slater was going to know Alexa Harmon wasn't his. Once and for fucking all.

"Take the damn helmet, Alexa," he said, nailing her with a stare. Somehow it didn't help his mood that she looked stunning in a pair of slim black pants, strappy black heels, a silky tank top and a little black jacket with leather accents all over it. She had her hair up in a high ponytail that made Maverick want to suck on her neck. Hard enough to mark it.

She sighed and took it. "I don't need you to be bossy."

"Why can you stand up to me but not him? Ever think of that?" he asked.

She froze with the helmet halfway to her head. "Because . . ."

"Finish that sentence," he bit out, his boot scuffing the pavement.

She licked her lips, and her eyes appeared golden in the late-afternoon sunlight. "Because I know you won't hurt me."

He grasped her by the front of her jacket and hauled her into his side. Their bodies collided, and she threw her arms around him to steady herself. Maverick grasped her tightly, probably too damn tightly, but he had to touch her. Had to feel her. Had to—

He kissed her. Hard. Just one long, thorough, breathless kiss. Finally, he pulled his mouth away from hers. "You're right. I won't. But the fact that we both believe Slater would is why we're doing this my way. Got it?"

"Yeah," she said. "Okay."

He gave a nod. "Okay. Now get your pretty ass on my bike and let's do this."

The minute she was straddling his ride, her arms and legs wrapped around him, he felt about a million times better. Her embrace, her heat, her heartbeat against his back, it was all proof of life. Proof that she was safe. Proof that she was right there by his side—right where everything in him demanded she belonged.

He backed out of the driveway of the big brick McMansion and made his way through the yet-to-be-built development to the main road. From there, it was less than fifteen minutes to his rendezvous point—a downtown restaurant called Dutch's. Maverick pulled his Harley in line with seven others waiting there. Eight members of the Raven Riders Motorcycle Club ought to make the point—and be more than able to handle any shit should it go down.

Turning off the engine, Mav gave Alexa a hand off. "We have a few minutes to kill," he said. He raked a hand through his hair as he dismounted.

She just nodded as she peered at the big picture window

that lined the street. His brothers were visible sitting at the counter just inside.

"Hey, com'ere." Maverick pulled her into his arms. More gently this time. "I know I'm being an insufferable prick, but just roll with it a bit longer. Please." He stroked his hand over the long, thick silk of her ponytail.

Alexa gave a little chuckle. "Can I remind you of that later?"

He bit back a grin. He liked Al when she was feisty. And he definitely liked her standing up for herself. "You really gonna listen if I say no?"

"Probably not." He felt her smile against his chest.

"That's my girl. Come on." He took her hand and led her into the diner. Dutch's sat on the corner, and had a long, narrow interior that filled the whole first floor of an old brick building. A Formica counter with spinning stools and red-and-white booths with juke boxes on the wall completed the old-timey look.

Somber greetings met them as they walked through the door, the bell jingling overhead. Phoenix, Caine, Jagger, Bear, Joker, Blake, and Mike Renner were all there— Maverick had insisted Dare keep his still-healing ass back at the clubhouse. His brothers were ready to stand with Maverick. Ready to fight with him, if it came to that.

Though the place used to be open later, because of Dutch's age, it now typically closed at five. But Dutch was a friend to the club and had agreed they could hang there for a bit after closing. The restaurant Slater had picked—after realizing he wasn't going to get Alexa to agree to come to his house—was only two blocks away.

"Maverick," Dutch said, extending his wrinkled brown hand across the counter. Despite owning a diner his whole life, Dutch Henderson was tall and thin. He had a friendly face and graying black hair, and he never forgot a name or a face. "Good to see you, son. How's your mother doing?"

"Better every day, Dutch. Thanks for asking," Maverick said. Dutch and his wife had been at the racetrack the night all hell broke loose, so he knew exactly what'd gone down.

"You tell her and Rodeo to come on in for some breakfast or lunch, and it'll be on me," he said.

"You bet," Maverick said. "She'll love that. But how are you? Dare said you've got a surgery coming up."

"Hip replacement," he said, patting his right hip. "Never get old, Maverick. Never get old."

"I'll remember that," Mav said with a grin. He turned to Alexa. "Dutch, do you know—"

"Alexa Harmon, of course I do. Though I don't think I've seen you in a whole lot of years."

"Hi, Dutch," Alexa said, giving him a smile. "Being here makes me remember how much I loved your milk shakes. Do you still make them with the whipped cream and the little cookies that slide over the straw?"

The question flashed a memory before Maverick's eyes. Him and Tyler and Alexa when she was seventeen or eighteen. Some asshole boy had spread a rumor around school that he'd scored with Al, and she'd come home upset but not wanting her mom to know why. So Mav and Tyler had brought her to Dutch's because she loved those damn milk shakes so much. They had the ice cream first, and then got dinner after. By the end, Alexa was smiling again. And the next day, Tyler put the fear of God into that kid. Best Mav knew, he never gave her another problem.

"I surely do," Dutch was saying. "I can make you one if you like."

"Oh, no," Alexa said, giving a quick shake of her head. "I don't think I can eat anything now. But another time."

"You know where to find me," he said with a wink.

"It's time," Caine said, icy blue eyes flashing.

"Let's do this," Phoenix said. "Fucking Slater."

"Fucking Slater," Jagger groused. Of anyone, Jag probably had to deal with Slater's bullshit the most. The wealthy prick hated the racetrack because it hurt his home-building business, or so he argued. He was constantly making noise—with the mayor, the city council, the sheriffs, the press—that the Green Valley Race Track was bad for Frederick. Occasionally, Slater managed to stir something up that would bring the sheriffs sniffing around. Once, he almost had the city council agree to debate zoning ordinances that would've seriously hampered the Ravens' business. And every time, Jagger had to deal with the brunt of the bullshit. Of all of them, the guy was probably the hardest to ruffle and the smoothest talker, and he'd memorized all the relevant rules, policies, and laws pertaining to the track like the brilliant motherfucker he was, so he thwarted Slater at pretty much every turn. It was a thing of beauty.

So Maverick nodded, joining in with the sentiment. "Fucking Slater." Everyone got up from their stools and moved toward the doors. Toward Alexa.

"Before we go," she said, bringing all the guys to a halt. Maverick eyed her, no idea what was about to come out of her mouth. "I just want to say thank you. For being here for me. And for Maverick. I know you're mostly here because he asked you, but I wanted to tell you that I appreciate it, too. I know I flaked after Tyler died"—she paused like it took something out of her to say her brother's name—"and I'm sorry for that. But that was more about me than it was about you. So, yeah, that's all I wanted to say."

"We're doing this for both of you," Phoenix said, giving her a flirty smile that under other circumstances Mav might've wanted to knock off his face. "Don't you worry none." The other men nodded.

Jagger rubbed her arm. "Losing Tyler was a damn shame, Alexa. We all regretted it. You were allowed to be messed up by that. No apologies needed here."

The men filed out, offering kind words that made Maverick proud to be one of them. Taking Alexa's hand, he squeezed. "Thank you for that."

"It was the least I could do," she said, her expression uncertain, maybe even a little overwhelmed. Had she expected them to do anything other than appreciate her gratitude?

He leaned down to look her in the eyes. "No, the least you could do was say nothing at all. Or, worse, disrespect them. Instead, you gave them your gratitude and respect. In our world, that means a helluva lot." When she nodded, he turned to Dutch, who was clearing the counter of a few soda glasses and coffee cups. Maverick put a hundred-dollar bill on the counter. "Thanks for always taking care of us, Dutch."

"Always," he said. It was just that simple. "Ride safe now."

Maverick gave a wave over his shoulder as he guided Alexa out the door.

And then they were on their way, riding through town in four sets of two. Maverick and Alexa rode at the front of the group with Phoenix at their side. They roared into parking spaces right in front of the restaurant's long windows. Eight Harleys. Eight bikers in full colors.

And what do you know? It was perfect timing. Because just then, Slater pulled up in his Mercedes and valeted the car. Alexa was standing at Mav's side, and he could feel anxiety rolling off of her. He wanted to take her into his arms and comfort her, reassure her, let her know that they'd be right there the whole time. But she knew that. They'd talked this through. And Maverick didn't want to do anything that might cause her dinner companion to get any more pissed off than he already looked.

Without a word, Alexa made her way up the sidewalk toward the front door where Slater stood waiting, scowling, looking like he wanted to break something with his hands. None of the Ravens moved. They just stood there watching.

When Mav and Alexa's abusive prick of an ex made eye contact, Maverick arched a single brow. *Touch her, hurt her, and I'll fucking make you pay.*

The guy's face was red and his mouth was pressed into a tight line. He bit something out at Alexa that Mav couldn't hear, and it took everything he had to keep his feet planted and let this bullshit play out. They disappeared inside, but only for a second. Because then they appeared in the window, visible behind the pale, sheer curtains. They stood there long enough that it seemed like some sort of debate was going on, and then Maverick smiled. Because they sat at one of the tables in clear view of the street. Of the Ravens. Just like they'd planned.

That's my girl, Al.

For the next forty minutes, the Ravens waited. They got a lot of strange looks from passersby on the sidewalk and traffic slowed as it went by as if trying to figure out what was going on, but he and the guys didn't pay attention to any of it. Maverick couldn't tell a lot about the conversation taking place inside because the curtains obscured facial expressions, but he could see Alexa. And that was all he needed. For now.

The brief, high-pitched *whoopwhoop* of a siren sounded out from just down the street. Maverick turned to see one of Frederick's finest rolling up behind the farthest of the bikes, lights flashing. And of course it was Davis behind the wheel. So Slater had called in his lapdog.

The guy got out, all five-foot-seven-inches of him, and glared at the lot of them. You never saw a man with a bigger fucking power trip than Curt Davis. The blowhard swiped his hand over his slicked-back brown hair and put on his cop hat. "Y'all need to move along."

Caine turned his lethal stare on the little weasel. "We're citizens peaceably inhabiting public property. What's the problem, officer?"

"The problem is *you*. All of you. We're getting complaints from business owners. You're loitering. And you're impeding the flow of traffic," Davis said, sounding a whole lot like he was trying to think of anything that might be relevant to harass them with. Maverick listened to the conversation, but mostly tried to keep his focus on Alexa. The cop's appearance wasn't really a surprise—it was a total Slater douche move—but it felt like a distraction. And distractions were dangerous.

Caine looked up and down the street, then back at the cop. "We all know who called you, Davis. You moonlighting as Slater's security detail while on duty these days?"

"That doesn't seem strictly kosher," Phoenix said.

"No, it doesn't," Caine said, arching a brow.

Davis planted his hands on his hips, though one fell on the butt of his holstered weapon. "Move on. Now. Or I'll add disturbing the peace and throw the lot of your sorry asses in jail."

"Remember when the football team stuffed his sorry ass in a locker?" Phoenix asked one of their brothers, just needling the cop.

As if Davis had no sense of self-preservation, he got up in Caine's face and spouted off with indignation and more threats.

"Go ahead. Try to arrest me," Caine said. "*Please*." If Davis couldn't hear the deadly intent in the Raven's tone, he was an idiot. And Maverick believed his brother meant it, which meant shit was about to escalate. Fast.

Inside, the curtains parted, briefly revealing Alexa's unhappy face, and then she pushed up from the table. Slater followed quickly after. As she spilled out onto the street, her ex grabbed her wrist. She stumbled as the asshole reeled her in against him.

Maverick saw fucking red, already moving to get her free.

"Oh, shit," someone said from behind him.

"Grant, let me go. Okay? Haven't you said enough?" she cried, her voice clearly upset.

"Don't forget what I said," he said. "And know that I'm dead serious."

"If you don't get your hands off of her, you'll be dead all right," Maverick said, coming up to them.

Alexa tugged her arm free and crashed into Mav's chest, pushing him back with both hands on his pecs. "No, Maverick. Don't."

He nailed the bastard with a murderous stare, letting Alexa hold him back. But just barely.

"Oh, please do, Maverick. By all means," Slater said. Arrogant goddamned sonofabitch.

Mav's blood fucking boiled with the need to take a swing at him. Which was exactly what he wanted.

"He's not worth it, Mav. Come on." She pushed him harder. "Come *on. This* we're doing my way. It's over. Let's go."

He pointed at Slater over Alexa's shoulder. "Hurt her again, I rain down twice as much hurt on you." Then he let himself be pushed, not waiting to see or hear what baiting comeback the asshole would throw at him. He hadn't heard the other Ravens gather around him, but they were all right there on his six and walking with him back to their bikes.

"Have a nice evening, officer," Jagger said with a smile as they all got on and started their engines. Alexa held Maverick tight, way tighter than on the way there, and he didn't know whether she was still holding him back from Slater or just needing to feel him there. Whether her touch came from protectiveness or need, both sent heat through his blood.

One by one, they pulled out. Caine glared at Davis, while Phoenix flipped him off with a grin. But Maverick only had eyes for Alexa's ex. Because that was not a man who thought this was over. Not by a long shot.

CHAPTER 19

The ride back to the Ravens' compound passed in a blur. Because Alexa had no idea how she was going to resolve the situation Slater had backed her into, or whether to believe he'd really do all the things he threatened to do.

As if he sensed her worry, Maverick squeezed her hand where it lay on his chest. She hugged him tighter, wishing she could get closer, needing him inside her, wanting him to just make all of this go away, even if for only a while.

His little gesture of caring escalated her worry on a whole other front—Grant was off-the-scale irate about what he deemed the Ravens' interference in his life and their relationship. In fact, she'd never seen Grant less in control than at that dinner. Obsessively arranging the flatware. Cutting the steak she hadn't stayed long enough for him to finish into precise, same-sized squares. At one point he'd actually stammered, his eyes blinking almost like a tic. The fact that he'd called in Davis at some point proved he wasn't going to let that interference go unaddressed.

It had been all she could do to keep Maverick from jumping Grant and beating him to a pulp right there in the middle of downtown Frederick. But then Maverick would've ended up arrested, shot, or dead. No doubt all things Grant would either like to see happen or maybe even was actively planning. Given what she could finally see about him now, Alexa wouldn't put such things past Grant. Not anymore.

If only she'd seen it sooner.

A nauseating flutter of nerves rushed through her when they returned to the clubhouse. The way Maverick had been when they'd left the restaurant, there was no way he wasn't going to be enraged at Grant's efforts to blackmail Alexa into giving in. And at the same time she hated to do anything that might pull the Ravens further into this mess.

But Maverick was like a dog with a bone. She knew he wasn't going to let this go, either.

"So what did he say?" Maverick asked when they got inside. The nine of them headed straight to the bar in the big rec room for a drink, and caught up with Dare, who was hanging there waiting for them to return.

"What happened?" Dare asked, rising from the couch where he'd been sitting with Haven and his grandfather.

"Exchanged some words with Slater and Frederick's very own Barney Fucking Fife," Mav said. "But nothing major. Except whatever happened inside. Alexa?"

Everyone looked to her.

She took a deep breath and tried to collect her thoughts. Alexa couldn't believe she had to give voice to Grant's wild demands. She was overwhelmed and worried and stunned. She should've been panicking about the implications of what Grant was trying to do. Instead, she was just . . .

shocked. All the noise inside her was too much. She'd gone numb. "I . . . he . . ."

"What?" Maverick asked, worry and a banked rage emanating from him.

Finally, she summed it up as succinctly as she could. "If I don't do what he wants, he's going to destroy me." She crossed her arms and squeezed, trying to hold herself together. How was this her life? *How was this her life?*

"Sonofafuckingbitch," Maverick bit out, raking at his sandy blond hair.

"And he wants?" Dare asked, his voice low and lethal.

"Me. To have me back. To marry me. Why would he want to marry someone who doesn't want to marry him?" She shook her head, "bewildered" too small a word for what she felt. "He could have anyone. Why would he go to all this trouble . . . over me?"

Maverick was in front of her in an instant. "One, because you're you. You're smart, you're caring, you're talented, and you're beautiful, and any man would want you. Don't ever let me hear you ask such a bullshit question again." He arched an eyebrow and nailed her with a fierce stare until she nodded, his words piercing a hole through her numbness and letting in a little heat and light. "Two, because he's a control freak, and you're denying him something he wants. That makes him want it even more. Three, because he doesn't want to lose face by having it known that you called off the wedding and broke up with him. I'm sure he wants to avoid the questions that will naturally arise from that, not to mention the personal embarrassment at having been jilted, and he's willing to do whatever it takes to do so."

"And four," she said, having to swallow around the knot of emotion in her throat. She met Maverick's intense blue gaze. "Because you're involved—all of you. He's crazy pissed about that, and he sees this as a competition with the Raven Riders. And Grant doesn't like to lose."

Maverick gave a tight nod. "Sounds about right."

"But I don't want anything bad to happen to you," she told him; then, she looked around at the group. "To any of you."

"If Slater throws something at us, Alexa, we'll handle it," Dare said. A low rumble of agreement went around the room. She appreciated the sentiment and the support, more than she could say, even though it made her worry more.

"Why did you say he was going to destroy you, Alexa?" Haven asked, coming to stand right next to her. "What does that mean?" Her eyes radiated concern, and her expression was full of strength and resolution. Haven rubbed her back, making Alexa realize how tense her muscles were, like she was braced against an oncoming blow.

Alexa's shoulders dropped as she released a long breath. "He didn't say it this starkly, but he threatened to report my car as stolen and take it away and evict Mom from his house. And he hinted that my job isn't safe, either. And I . . . I have no idea what I'm going to do."

I'd hate to see you lose everything you've worked so hard for, Alexa.

The memory of Grant's smug voice made her stomach roll. He'd clearly spent a lot of time thinking about what would devastate her the most, and his attitude was full of confidence that she'd cave. Just like she always did. And who knows, maybe she would've if she'd sat there long enough enduring the brute force of his badgering and withering stare. But then Davis had shown up and Alexa had been able to see that things were getting tense between the sheriff and the Ravens. Her worry for them had sent her fleeing from the table, wanting to save them from any further trouble and needing to be free from Grant's threats.

Any one of which would be a huge blow, but all of them together would be catastrophic for Alexa.

And the issue wasn't just financial—although it was

partly that, too. If Grant fired her, what would that do to her future prospects as an interior designer? She couldn't even fathom all the doors he could close to her. Even worse, her mother couldn't easily be moved from Grant's house. It wasn't just because she had a tractor trailer's worth of crap in her house to sort through, but because her mother wasn't going to want to go. Best case scenario, it would take some preparation and cajoling, and probably a little arm-twisting and bribing, too, to get her mother out of the house without sending her into a complete and total mental breakdown. And that was saying nothing of finding another place where a hoarder could live without good references or credit.

Oh, my God, what am I going to do?

"You're sure as shit not going back to him," Maverick said, as if she'd spoken the words aloud. Had she? The situation felt so surreal she wasn't sure.

Alexa met his gaze again and hated the doubt she saw there, and the little hidden sliver of fear. Maybe the others wouldn't have seen it, but she knew Maverick, and she did. "No, I'm not. I can't. Especially not now. But, Jesus, getting free of him means that my mom and me . . . we lose everything. How am I going to tell her? Where am I going to move her? Am I even going to be able to stay in this area if Grant ruins my career and reputation here?" She kneaded at the muscles in her neck. "What an arrogant, twisted asshole he is. I can't believe it's come to all this."

Maverick grasped her hand and leaned down until their eyes met. "We'll figure it out. Did he attach any sort of a deadline to his demands?"

She laced her fingers with his. "He wants me home—well, back to his place—immediately, but the real deadline is next Saturday."

"The wedding," Maverick said.

"Yeah. I don't show—"

"—and the shit hits the fan," Mav finished for her. She nodded.

"So we have a week to make arrangements for your mom," Dare said. "We *will* figure something out. That's a guarantee."

"Shit," Maverick said, his eyes going wide. He turned to Phoenix. "I hate to ask, man."

"What?" Phoenix asked. "Name it."

Alexa loved that about the Ravens. Always had. How they were there for each other, no matter what. Like a family.

"Any chance you'd be willing to let Mrs. Harmon use Creed's house?" Maverick asked. Alexa gasped. Creed was Phoenix's cousin who'd been killed a month or two ago in Baltimore. He was older, and she hadn't known him well, but she knew Phoenix well enough to know that he'd idolized Creed. Which meant Maverick asking him such a thing for her was *huge*.

She shook her head. "Oh, no, I couldn't—"

"Hey, that's actually a damn good idea," Phoenix said, nodding, his expression thoughtful. "I haven't touched it since Creed died, so it'll take some work, and it's not very big, but it's just sitting there."

The kindness they extended to her disproved stereotype after stereotype. Her billionaire businessman fiancé was a manipulative, abusive control freak, and her law-breaking motorcycle gang friends made a habit out of helping people who needed it. "That's an amazingly generous offer, Phoenix, but my mother's not the easiest person. She's not likely to take the best care of the place even with my help, and I don't even know what I can afford yet."

He gave her a look. "I'm talking about a gift, Al. I don't want your money. Or your mother's. Once we get it cleaned and fixed up, she could stay there as long as she wants. Creed always liked Tyler. I think he'd like this."

The man's generosity pierced more holes into her numbness. "Okay, well. Wow. I don't even know what to say. Thank you isn't enough."

"Yeah it is." He winked. Nodding, her thoughts raced. That potentially alleviated one big problem, assuming the work could be done within the next week, and assuming that Alexa could get her mother and all her crap out of Grant's house within that time frame.

Maverick turned to Phoenix and offered his hand. "I know what this means. Thank you. We owe you. Anything, anytime. Just name it." The men clasped hands for a long moment.

We owe you. We. Such a small word. Such a huge meaning. It shattered what was left of Alexa's numbness. Worry, fear, panic all came rushing in, but so, too, did courage, resolve, and—for the first time in a long time—the steadfast knowledge that she wasn't alone. We. She and Maverick. Whatever they were, he was in her corner. All of these guys were. After years of feeling so alone, that meant everything. She pressed a hand to her chest and nodded, emotion overwhelming her.

Maverick faced her again, his big hands going to her shoulders. And it was like his touch grounded her, shielded her, pulled all the disparate pieces of her together so she could stand strong. "The rest we'll figure out. I promise. But until then, no going out on your own anywhere. If you feel like you need to stick it out at work, I understand. But we keep with me dropping you off and picking you up." On their surface, his words seemed calm, but the agitation was clear in the tight clench of his jaw and the hot flash of his eyes.

"Knowing Slater, this will escalate before it gets resolved," Dare said matter-of-factly. In her heart, Alexa knew that was right. But what would that escalation mean? She couldn't stand the idea of anyone getting hurt because of all the mistakes she'd made.

Which meant she had to act. She had to do whatever she could to protect herself and her friends. "I need to get a lawyer first thing Monday morning. And maybe I should talk to Sheriff Martin this weekend, just to see what he thinks?" Alexa didn't know Henry Martin well, but she'd heard Grant grouse about a divide within Frederick's local police over the Ravens—and that Henry tended to fall on their side and even protect them. The details of those internal politics were a mystery to her, but certainly an enemy of Grant's could be a friend to her.

"Good. That's good," Maverick said, a gleam of pride in his gaze. "Touching base with Martin makes sense. Get you protected legally, too. Because this fucker's not going to get away with what he's trying to do. Just you wait."

No, he wasn't. At least, not without a fight.

Problem was, she feared into her very soul that she was going to have to pay in some way before everything was said and done. The only question was how great that cost would be.

CHAPTER 20

As it got later, more Ravens arrived at the clubhouse. Bunny and Haven laid out the fixings for beef tacos, and everyone dove into building a plate. Afterward, the atmosphere clearly veered in the direction of partying. Truth be told, Maverick had some adrenaline and not a little anger burning through his blood that could use being worked out. But then he found Alexa sitting at the kitchen table talking to Bunny and Haven, her knees drawn up to her chest. And even though she put on a smile for him, it was clear that she wasn't in the partying mood.

"Why don't I take you home?" Maverick asked, something deep inside him needing to not just protect her, but take care of her, comfort her. However she needed, whatever she needed.

"It's okay," she said.

"What do you want to do?" he asked, crouching beside her. He was aware that his mom and Haven were listening in, but didn't mind, didn't care. There was no shame in wanting to take care of what was his—even if she was only that in his stubborn fucking heart.

"I'll do whatever you want," she said. Her hand fell on his where it rested on her knee, and the touch shot heat through his blood.

He arched an eyebrow. "I want to know what *you* want."

She met his gaze for a long moment, then gave a little shrug. "I don't want to pull you away."

"I can give you a ride, hon," Bunny said.

Maverick shook his head. "Thanks, Bunny, but I got this. You want to go, Al, I want to take you."

Her expression went soft and sweet for him. "Yeah?"

His grip on her knee tightened. "Yeah."

"Well, whenever, then." Her fingers stroked over his.

Between the small touches and the way she was looking at him, all affectionate and even a little unguarded, his body came alive with need. He rose and held out his hand. "Let's go."

The smile she gave him told him it was the right call. She needed him more than he needed to blow off some steam. And that was that.

Maverick watched while Alexa hugged Bunny and Haven and said her good-byes, and he liked what he saw— Alexa being folded into the arms of his community, and embracing it right back. He liked it a lot. Fuck, it was too soon to be feeling this, to be *wanting* this—too soon for her. Just today, Grant had driven that point home with a goddamned sledgehammer. She was right in the thick of dealing with her ex. The last thing she needed was to deal with Maverick, too. For fuck's sake.

When you gonna fight for what you want? Dare's chiding voice echoed in his memory. The question—and the urgency to answer it—pulsed through his veins with every heartbeat.

"Ready?" she asked.

"Yeah," he said, shoving away the thoughts. He hugged Bunny and Haven.

"I make a mean cinnamon roll," Haven said to Alexa. "In case you want to come for breakfast. Maybe we could do that girls-only movie day."

"I just might take you up on that," Al said with a smile. And Maverick found himself grateful to Haven once again. Alexa needed friends and fun in her life right now, and he appreciated Haven making her feel like she belonged. He knew enough about how Al had grown up to know that mattered to her. So it mattered to him.

It took a couple of minutes of good-byes to make their way out of the clubhouse, but then Maverick was starting up the Night Rod and Alexa was sliding on behind him, her heat ramping up the arousal stirring in his body. Especially when she didn't just embrace him. Her hands gently rubbed his chest. The night air blew warm and inviting against them as they took the back way through the big Raven Riders tract to the pond and his house beyond.

Alexa didn't mean anything by the soft caresses against his chest, but it was driving him fucking crazy. His cock hardened against his thigh, setting off an ache that pounded in his blood. Finally, he stilled her hands against his sternum, but instead of that putting a stop to the rubbing as he'd intended, it set her hands off to *exploring*.

Up over his pecs, the heels of her palms dragging across his nipples. Down over his abs, turning his cock to steel. Down farther, onto his inner thighs. Her nails raked against the denim. And then her right hand found his hard length and tormented him with rubs and squeezes that had him spilling groans into the wind.

Christ, what was she doing to him? And should he let her do it?

By the time he pulled the NRS into his garage, he was

wrecked by lust and need, the adrenaline that had been surging through him since the confrontation at the restaurant finding an outlet his body liked. A lot.

He didn't kill the engine or flip out the kickstand. His boots braced the bike upright, the engine's vibrations spilling through him and winding him tighter. And then Alexa's fingers made quick work of unbuttoning his jeans. Unzipping. And pulling out his cock.

"Fuck, Alexa," he groaned as her hand wrapped around the thick column of his flesh. She reached to hang her helmet on the handlebar, and he helped her, wanting to know what she wanted, needing to see where she wanted to take this, unable to do anything but give in to the steady jerking of her hand around his hard length.

"Your voice is so sexy when you're turned on," she whispered against his cheek. "Makes me wet." Her tongue traced his ear, and then she was kissing him there, her hand on his neck, trying to make him yield to her mouth, her tongue.

"What else makes you wet?" he rasped. He should be questioning this, questioning her, not egging her on. But his body had taken over this train and pulled it right on out of the station.

Her fist gripped him tighter, pumped harder. She hummed low in her throat, her tongue dragging up his neck. "How hard your cock is. How it fills my hand. How I know it could fill me."

"Jesus," he bit out, needing to hear every filthy secret she'd share with him. "What else?"

"Your long hair. Your eyes. Your ink." She punctuated each pronouncement with a jerk and twist of her hand. "The feel of this bike rumbling between my legs," she offered without him asking.

He swallowed thickly, his thoughts trying to break through, trying to rein in the beast that wanted to break free. "I wasn't going to start this."

"That's why I did," she whispered, swiping her thumb through the wetness on the head of his cock.

Each word, each touch hammered another nail into the coffin of his restraint. "I've been trying not to take advantage of you, Alexa. You've got a lot coming at you right now." His head dropped back on her shoulder. He felt connected to her by her touch, their words, the bike's vibrations.

"It's not taking advantage if I want to be with you, too, Maverick. Just because my life's a wreck doesn't mean I don't know what I want. And I see it now with a clarity I haven't had in years. Please, don't take that from me," she said, her voice strong, but with just a hint of pleading. Her words hit him square in the chest, unleashing need and hope in a one-two punch that buried the last of his concerns, at least for tonight. But then she released him. "Unless you don't want—"

"Oh, fuck, no. I want." Twisting, he wrapped an arm around Alexa's slim waist and hauled her in front of him so that she was straddling his thighs, her front to his.

She gasped and grinned. "That was impressive."

"Not nearly as impressive as what I'm about to do," he said, lust making him feel desperate and crazed as he roughly unfastened her thin dress pants.

"What's that?" she asked, bracing her hands on the gas tank behind her, reclining away from him a little as he worked.

He reached into his back pocket, urgency fueling his plans. "Is your pussy wet for me, Al?"

She squirmed against his thighs. "Yes."

"Good, then you'll forgive this." His flipped out the pocket knife, grasped the open bottom of the fly, and carefully sliced at the seam that ran between her legs. A quick precise slash separated the flimsy silk of her wet panties, and then she was exposed to him.

"Holy shit, Maverick!"

In a quick move, he pocketed the knife, ripped the ruined seam wider, and lined his cock up with her wet core. And then he was sinking deep, shifting her forward on the bike just a bit so he could bear down on her. Her moan lanced heat through his blood, her body arching over the curved tank, her hair spilling fucking beautifully over the matte blank with its red accents. When he was balls deep it felt so good that he had to grip the handlebars to steady himself.

"Oh, my God, this is so fucking hot," she cried. Her hands joined his grasping onto the handlebars. "Please, Mav."

"Yeah," he said, his voice like gravel. He withdrew and thrust, the bike rocking under them, the engine adding a hot full-body sensation. Her pussy was wet and already tightening around him. He grabbed the knife again and fisted her little silk tank top. "Need all of you," he growled, slicing it from the low neckline to the hem. It was easy work to cut through the satin holding together the cups of her bra, exposing the mounds of her tits.

"Yes," she said. "Take what you want."

"What about you?" he said through a clenched jaw as he penetrated faster, deeper, riding her without mercy. Not that she was asking for any. "You gonna take me?"

"Yeah," she cried. "Oh, yes."

And God help him, he needed her to, to take all the adrenaline and aggression inside him. With each mind-blowing thrust, it was like she was sucking the poison of darkness and loneliness from his soul. "Yeah, you are. Take me, Alexa. Fucking take me."

"Maverick."

Her moan twisted up the tension gathering low in his gut. "That's it. Take all of me." He bottomed out inside her, then ground himself even deeper.

"God!" She reached a hand between her legs, and watching her work her own pussy while he fucked her on his bike was the single hottest thing he'd ever seen in his life. She screamed her orgasm, her whole body bowing over the gas tank, her thighs bucking over his. He planted his hand on the flat plane of her belly just below her breasts, steadying her and pinning her in place.

And then he shifted his stance so that he was hammering down into her, his pelvis crashing into hers on every thrust. Sensation was barreling down his spine and stealing his breath. "Christ, you're gonna take me, Alexa. You're gonna take everything I've got to give."

She grabbed his wrists. "Everything," she rasped.

The word tripped his orgasm, just ripped it right out of him until he felt turned inside out, raw and exposed, on top of the world. His shout echoed over the bike's low rumble against the garage's concrete, his cock kicking inside her again and again and again. It went on until Maverick saw spots around the edge of his vision, like he'd taken a drug that had sent him on the best, purest high.

When his body finally calmed, he lifted her against him until he was cradling her in his arms, her legs wrapped around his hips, their fronts pressed together, his cock still buried to the hilt. When he finally killed the engine, her arms wrapped around him on a sigh so contented he could've dedicated his life to making her sound that way over and over. She stroked at his hair as her whole body went lax against him. The silence was loud all around them.

"So good with you," she whispered.

"Always," he said, not sure if she meant the sex or how she felt or, just, all of it—the sex and the closeness and the fun times and the hard times and the boring minutiae of daily life. Which was how he meant it.

"I can't even be mad that you ruined my clothes," she said with a little satisfied hum. "Because it was too damn hot."

He chuckled and nodded. Someday he'd be eighty and

too arthritic to ride and too senile to remember what he was arguing about with Dare, but he'd sure as shit recall every detail of what'd just happened with her. It was seared into his very DNA. "I'll replace them."

She pulled back from the hug just enough to look him in the eye. "I don't care about the clothes, Maverick. I don't care about anything that's replaceable. Not anymore."

At just that moment, he realized that he'd made love to her without kissing her even once. His gaze dropped to her lips, and suddenly he was ravenous for a taste. He devoured her with a deep, slow, lingering kiss, full of tangling tongues and tugging lips. His senses were full of her, but not as full as his heart. So he kept right on kissing, because it ensured none of the words pinballing around in his head got voiced. Not yet.

Alexa shifted in his lap, emphasizing that his cock was hardening again inside of her. He gripped her hips and thrust himself as deep as he could go. Held himself there. His libido started making plans he wasn't sure either of their bodies was actually up to carrying out.

Just then, wind gusted a warm, humid breeze through the garage, and a thin spray of water blew over them.

Al squeaked and laughed. "When did it start raining?"

Maverick peered over his shoulder. "Hell if I know." A nuclear bomb could've exploded out there ten minutes before, and he wouldn't have realized it. She shivered, goose bumps rising up on her skin. "Let's get you inside." When she nodded, he eased out of her, helped her off the bike, and did up his jeans when he got off.

She tried to hold the pieces of her clothes together, but he'd literally ripped her to shreds. And he couldn't stop staring. "You are a wet fucking dream right now, Alexa. I'm not gonna lie."

"I am? I'm a disaster." Looking down at herself, she gave a little chuckle.

He shook his head. "A beautiful disaster, maybe. But all of us are sitting on some kind of disaster, Al. Some are just better at hiding it than others." He sure as hell was. The guilt over not protecting his mother all those years before still had the ability to steal his breath and trash his self-worth. He should've seen it. He should've acted sooner. He shouldn't have let it get so out of control. He shook away the thoughts and slipped out of his Ravens cut. "Here." He held it out for her to put on.

She put her arms through the holes and wrapped it around herself, and the denim and leather was so big on her that it hung to the tops of her thighs. And *fuck* if seeing her wear his colors didn't threaten to rev him up all over again.

An image flashed before his mind's eye—a black-and-purple tribal raven with a red heart tattooed on Alexa's fair skin. Marking her as one of them, as claimed, as *his*. The imagining made him think of his conversation with Dare, and that his cousin might actually get the pleasure of seeing such a thing on Haven's skin in the not-too-distant future. And Maverick had maybe never been more jealous of another human being in his life until that very moment.

Not that his cousin didn't deserve every bit of happiness he found with Haven. Because he did. They both did. But that didn't keep Maverick from wanting a little slice of that for himself. Wanting it *bad*.

"Maverick? Are you sure it's okay for me to wear this?" Alexa asked, her fingers stroking over his name patch and impacting him like it was his cock instead.

"It'll be fine," he said in a gruff voice. "Just 'til we get you inside. Come here." He bent and scooped her into his arms.

"You don't have to carry me." She grinned and wound her arms around his neck.

"Yes, I do. Because then I get to touch you." With that, he walked out into the gentle summer rain.

She laid her head on his shoulder. "Yeah, okay. Touching is good."

Hell, after years of thinking it would never happen again, touching her was everything.

And he didn't want to stop.

Inside, he carried her to her bed and stripped them both down. "I want you in my arms tonight. You good with that?"

"Yeah, Mav." She fit herself into the nook along the side of his body until there wasn't a breath of space between them. Her hand settled on his chest, and he folded his around it. "I'm great with that."

And even though they lay there perfectly still, perfectly peaceful—at least for that one moment—Maverick realized that Alexa Harmon was the best fucking ride of his life. And he never wanted it to end.

CHAPTER 21

Alexa first became aware of the delicious achiness of her body, an achiness that spoke of sex so hot just thinking about it made her sweat. Smiling, she kicked off the covers, her mind playing the highlights reel. The electrifying shock of Maverick cutting open her clothes. The deep satisfaction of him taking her in such a primal way. The rough need in his voice. But as raw as the sex had been, there'd been tenderness, too. The way he'd held her after, cradling her against him. How he'd covered her with his cut and carried her inside, his face nuzzling her hair. His tight hold all night long, his body molded to hers, his hand cupping her breast.

Except . . . her hands stretched out and found only emptiness.

Her eyes opened, confirming that she was alone. "Maverick? Hey, Maverick?" Pushing onto an elbow, a sheet of paper on his pillow caught her eye.

Hey Al—

The club got an emergency call at 5:30 A.M. so I had to ride. Hated to leave your bed without saying good-bye. Come to the clubhouse when you get up?

—Mav

Alexa pressed the paper to her chest as she fell back against her pillow. The man had spent last night protecting and helping her, and then he'd gotten up in the middle of the night to help a stranger. A warm pressure filled her chest, getting bigger and bigger until she knew.

She *knew.*

She still had feelings for Maverick—and maybe had never stopped having them in the first place. She still wanted Maverick. The clarity and growing certainty of her emotions was stunning and a little jarring after months of building questions and doubts.

Part of her worried that this was all happening too fast. Only days had passed since Grant had thrown her out. It *was* fast.

But everything that had happened between her and her ex these past weeks had snapped Alexa into a level of awareness she hadn't had in such a long time, like she'd suddenly awakened from a drug-induced sleep. Now it was like Grant had simply been an interruption to something that'd existed since she first became aware of the opposite sex—her attraction to Maverick Rylan. Her longing for him. Her need for him in her life. Either way, she felt miles away from the woman who'd stared in that bathroom mirror last weekend and tried to convince herself that there was nothing wrong with the way Grant had taken her.

She wasn't perfect, she wasn't flawless, and she was far from being as strong as she wanted to be, but she wasn't *that* Alexa anymore, either.

And now that she had that clarity, she wasn't wasting it. So once she'd dealt with the chaos of her life and finished fighting Grant, she was going to lay all her feelings and flaws out on the line and fight *for* Maverick. Because she wasn't making the same mistake twice in letting him get away, not if he was willing to give her a second chance.

Lucy leapt onto the foot of the bed, meowing as she walked up Alexa's body until she was demanding attention by lying on Mav's note and pushing her head into Alexa's hand. "Well, there's my baby. How are you today?" Purring was her only answer, and it was a good one, full of contentment and lazy satisfaction. Lucy liked it here. "I do, too," Alexa whispered, her mind wandering, building hopes and dreams she didn't know whether she had any business wishing for. For long minutes, she stroked her fingers over the softness of Lucy's head and big ears. "You need a bath, little one. We'll do it tomorrow. Okay?" That wasn't the only thing she needed to do. Her final project was due on Tuesday, and Alexa hadn't done five minutes of work on it all week. But even that wasn't the most important thing she had to do. "I need to take care of my mama today."

The words chased away some of the happiness Alexa had felt upon awakening. Telling her mother about the move was going to be hard. So hard that Alexa realized she'd need help to do it. She had to get her mom's case worker out to keep her calm and offer some support. Which meant Alexa had things to do.

"Okay, little friend, I have to get up and start my day." She slid Lucy off of her and pushed out of bed. The screen on her phone said it was nearly seven-thirty.

She typed out a quick text to Maverick. *Hope everything's okay. Be to the clubhouse in 30.*

Be better when you get here, was the quick reply. Well, now she wanted to hurry.

So she did. She rushed through showering, dressing, and

running some Google searches to make arrangements for moving her mom. She left a message with the case worker, hoping the lady could come out today. And then Alexa was heading out the door, eager to try Haven's mean cinnamon buns and see Maverick to make sure everything was okay.

When she arrived at the clubhouse, voices rang out from the big mess hall, indicating breakfast was in full swing. Alexa felt a little shy about walking in to a roomful of Ravens already sitting and eating, but she also wanted to be a part of it, too. A part of them. So she pushed through her anxiety and walked through the door.

She shouldn't have worried.

From among the dozen or so gathered Ravens, Phoenix and Jagger called out immediate hellos, and Bunny gave her a big smile and a wave. Haven rose from her seat next to Dare to give her a hug. "I'm so glad you came," she said.

"Thank you," Alexa said, feeling more comfortable by the second.

And Maverick . . . he came to her wearing a tired smile and eyes full of satisfaction. "I'm glad you came, too. Come, sit." He took her hand and guided her to the open seat next to him. A cinnamon bun already filled a big part of the plate. "I grabbed one for you because they never last long."

Aw, that was kind of crazy sweet. And thoughtful. And proof that he'd been thinking about her. All of which stirred up more of that warm pressure growing in her chest. For him.

"That's so sweet, Mav. Thank you," she said.

"Yeah, Maverick, that's soooo sweet. You're just the sweetest motherfucker I ever knew," Phoenix said in a singsong voice. He glared at Mav and eyeballed her cinnamon bun. Laughter rumbled around the table.

Maverick flipped his middle finger and gave Phoenix a big shit-eating grin, then he winked at her.

Smiling, she leaned a little closer to Mav. "Sorry," she said.

His hand fell on her bare thigh under the table. "Don't you worry about it," he said in a low voice full of humor.

Heat shot from his palm to her clit so forcefully her breath caught. And then that heat got amped up even further when Mav's gaze cut to her, his eyes full of blue fire, his expression smug and knowing. His fingers squeezed, his little finger slipping under the hem of her shorts.

"Yo, pass everything down for Alexa," he called out.

Warmth spilled into her cheeks as she accepted a platter of sausage and bacon from a younger guy with brown hair whom she didn't know. The patches on his cut indicated he was a prospective member. Like Tyler had been.

Thinking of Ty while sitting in the Ravens' clubhouse set off a small pang of longing in Alexa's heart, but it also did something she didn't expect—it made her feel a little closer to him. For the first time in a long time. Why hadn't she ever thought that could be the case? That being around the guys he'd so badly wanted to be a part of would allow her to be around a part of him, too? She was seeing all kinds of things in a new light lately, wasn't she?

"Thanks," she said to the prospect, taking a few slices of bacon. "I'm Alexa."

"I remember," he said, passing her a bowl. "Blake. Nice to meet you."

"Oh, have we met already? I'm sorry." She scooped scrambled eggs on to her plate next.

He shook his head. "Not officially. I was here when you—" He cut himself off and gave an awkward shrug. "A few weeks ago."

"Oh." So he'd been here when she'd shown up with the bloodied face. Awesome. "Right."

Maverick's hand squeezed again, softer this time, like he meant to reassure her.

Alexa dug into her food and listened to the banter that ran around the table. She remembered this, the rowdiness and camaraderie of meals at the Ravens' clubhouse. Her eyes scanned the room. It hadn't changed a bit. Two big long tables, one currently empty, filled the space in front of a large stone fireplace that harkened back to the building's past as an inn. A carving of the Ravens' raven/dagger/skull logo was mounted over the mantel, and POW/MIA flags hung from the rough-hewn exposed beams overhead.

She saved Haven's bun for last—a dessert for her breakfast. With as much icing as it had, it totally fit. "Oh, my God," she said around her first bite. Rich and creamy and sweet. She took another bite and moaned. She couldn't help it.

"Right?" Mav grinned at her, his gaze tracking her tongue as it swiped icing off her lip.

"This is amazing," Alexa said, leaning forward to see Haven at the far end of the table. She called the other woman's name. "Your cinnamon rolls are crazy. They're, like, happiness in food form."

Haven beamed as the men all joined in offering praise. "Why, thank you."

"You could totally sell these," Alexa said. "And those cookies you made the other day, too."

Sitting at the head of the table, Dare gave Haven a look, one eyebrow arched. "I agree," he said, his tone like they'd had this conversation before.

Just then, Alexa's cell buzzed in the back pocket of her shorts. She grabbed it. "It's my mom's case worker," she said, already rising. "Be right back." Putting the phone to her ear, she moved into the big, empty lounge so she could hear better. She explained the situation to the case worker, an older woman named Lillian Hite who Alexa hadn't had cause to call on in a while.

"I'm sorry to bother you on a Saturday," Alexa said.

"No, you were right to call me, dear. Cynthia's going to need some help adjusting to this news," Lillian said. "I could come around three, unless that's too late? Otherwise, I could be there Monday morning."

Relief flooded through Alexa. "Three today would be great. Thank you." The sooner she got things moving on that front, the better. She only had a week, so she couldn't afford to waste even one day.

Just as she hung up, the mess hall door swung open behind her. "Everything okay?" Maverick. Sweet, sexy Maverick.

"Yeah. I was able to get my mom's case worker to agree to come out this afternoon. So I guess I'm breaking the news about the move today."

Maverick rubbed her arms. "I know it sucks, Al. I'm sorry it's come to this."

"In the end, it'll be better to be completely free of Grant. It's just that Mom doesn't handle change well." The degree to which that was an understatement unleashed butterflies through her belly. This was not going to be an easy conversation.

"Can I come? Maybe another friendly face will help. Unless you think it would stress her out more for me to be there," he said, dropping his hands.

The offer reached into her chest and squeezed. "You're too good to me. I'd love to have you there."

Maverick's whole expression went stern as his hand cupped her face. "There's no such thing as too good for you, Alexa. When are you going to get that?"

She grasped his wrist like he was her anchor in the storm that was her life right now. And he was. "I . . . I'm sorry."

"I don't want you to apologize," he said, his eyes searching hers. "I just want you to believe I'm here for you. Whatever you need."

"God, Maverick. How could I not believe that? There's

not even a question in my mind," she said, knowing the truth of his words to the bottom of her soul, and needing him to believe she knew it, too.

His eyes smoldered, all that sternness shifting into desire. In her mind's eye, she saw him staring down at her as he took her on his bike, trapped between the hardness of steel and chrome against her back and his body over her. "Good. That's good."

She nodded. "I really liked last night," she whispered.

He made a sound like a growl under his breath. "I fucking *loved* last night. I can't ride the goddamned Night Rod now without picturing you laid out for me, hair all over the handlebars, legs spread, your clothes wrecked."

Need settled between Alexa's thighs as her heart pounded. "Good. Because I can't stop seeing you over me, *riding me*, fully clothed while I was all exposed, the hard vibration of the bike rolling through me as—"

Two Ravens Alexa didn't know spilled out of the mess hall. Maverick's eyes held frustration and amusement as he clasped hands and said quick good-byes to them. And then his hand was back on her face again, the touch tender and possessive at the same time.

"Now back to me riding you," he said when the guys left.

Chuckling, she turned her face in his grasp and pressed a kiss against his palm. As the heat in his gaze reignited, the moment felt weighted, significant, full of promise. She sneaked her tongue out to teasingly trace his palm. Mav's jaw clenched, the look he was giving her like he was a breath from devouring her. Her heart raced and her nipples hardened.

His hand slid from her mouth to her hair. His fingers dug in and hauled her close, her breasts crushing against his chest. Maverick kissed her on a groan she greedily swallowed as her hands went around his neck.

The door to the mess pushed open and a couple more

Ravens spilled into the lounge behind them. Alexa gasped into the kiss, instinctively trying to jump back, but Maverick held her fast. "Don't care about them. Not done with you," he whispered into her mouth.

A shiver ran through her whole body. The guys said good-bye to Maverick, but he paid them no mind, even when someone laughed good-naturedly at his expense. For her part, Alexa was hyperaware—of the hard press of Maverick's body against hers, of the shared sweetness of sugar and cinnamon on Mav's tongue, of being watched by the others.

When Maverick pulled his lips away, he wore the sexiest, most satisfied smile she'd maybe ever seen on his ruggedly handsome face. "Mmm, good morning."

She smiled and smirked at him. "Good morning to you."

"Yo, Mav," Jagger said, coming into the lounge. "I gotta head down to the track to check over a bunch of shit for Monday's license renewal inspection, but give me a call when you know when you need my help this week."

Maverick finally released Alexa from his embrace, though he kept her close with his arm around her shoulders. "Will do. We're heading over to Alexa's mom's today to start figuring things out so I should have more details in the next day or two."

"Good deal," Jagger said, his fingers tapping against his thigh. A memory came to her—listening to Jagger play his acoustic as a group of them sat at the fire pit out by Maverick's pond one fall night. The man was self-taught and absolutely amazing. She hadn't thought of that in years. "Just say the word. See ya, Alexa." He gave a wave as he headed out the front door.

"Bye," she said, trying to make sense of the exchange through the haze of lust and nostalgia clouding her brain. "Jagger's gonna help move my mom, too?"

Mav shrugged like it was obvious. "Of course. Everyone

will as much as they can. Before you arrived, Jag reminded me that he's got a cousin who owns one of those three-guys-and-a-truck moving companies. He's going to call in a favor to see if he can do the move. We got to talking that if your mom will agree to it, maybe we get her and her most essential things moved as fast as we can, and then we take our time going through the rest. That gets her out of Grant's crosshairs sooner."

"Wow. Yeah, that all sounds great, assuming Mom can be brought around to the idea," Alexa said, the realization sinking in that the Ravens had spent time talking about how to help her and coming up with an actual plan to deal with Grant's blackmail attempt. It was so unusual to feel like she wasn't alone that she barely knew what to do with the emotion welling up inside her. "Thank you."

More Ravens came into the lounge, headed up by Phoenix. He clapped Maverick on the back and gave Alexa a smile. "Okay, we're heading over to Creed's to get it ready for your mom. Should I leave the furniture or does she have enough of her own?"

Alexa's gaze scanned over the small group that included Phoenix, Blake, and a Raven she didn't know well whose cut read *Bandit*. "She does have a lot, but it's not all in the best shape. Maybe leave it until we see what she actually wants to move and what she might need?"

Phoenix nodded and waved, already heading for the door with the others. "That's a plan. Okay, then, we're outie."

"Thank you, Phoenix," she said, overwhelmed by the generosity all of these men were showing her. Which made her remember . . . "Hey, what was the emergency you had to leave for this morning?"

A storm rolled in over Maverick's expression. "The situation for one of our clients escalated when her estranged husband tried to break in. The mother called nine-one-one. Sheriff Martin knew she was one of ours so he called us in on it, too. The husband had never done anything like that before so we didn't have a twenty-four/seven detail on her." He shook his head, clearly frustrated. "We moved them up here to one of the cabins for the weekend because the kid is so spooked. As if it wasn't bad enough that the sick fuck had abused her, now she's scared of him crawling through windows in the middle of the night."

"Oh, God," Alexa said, her heart aching for the little family. What would people like them do without people like Maverick and his brothers in the club? What would *she* have done without them? Once, she'd thought she had nothing in common with the women and families the Ravens helped protect, but now Alexa knew that was just one more thing she'd denied because she hadn't *wanted* to see the similarities. "That's so terrible. Was anyone hurt?"

"Just rattled. Mostly." His dark expression made it clear there was more he wasn't saying.

"I'm glad you were there for them," she said. "Is there anything I can do to help?"

His gaze ran over her face, soft and searching. "No, but thank you for offering."

She nodded and heaved a deep breath. "There are some things I should do before heading over to Mom's this afternoon."

"Then let's get to it," Maverick said. "Because the faster we sever your remaining ties to Slater, the easier I'll be able to rest."

"And the less ways he'll have to try to hurt or control me," Alexa said in a low voice.

"Hey." Maverick tipped up her chin. "Over my dead fucking body is anyone going to hurt you." He arched a brow.

As much as Alexa appreciated the sentiment, the words unleashed an icy chill all down her spine. "Please, don't say that, Maverick. I couldn't . . . it would . . ." She shook her head, the horror of imagining him dying—or even getting hurt—stealing her ability to pull together her thoughts.

"I'm not going anywhere, Al. Don't you worry." He took her hand. "Come on."

But as they headed out into the already hot summer morning, that chill wouldn't go away. Because she didn't know what she'd do if something happened to Maverick because of her.

And she hoped she never, ever had to find out.

CHAPTER 22

Alexa was right.

Her mother took the news badly. She yelled, cried, and rocked in her chair, the nastiness of her rants and name-calling more a reflection of her stress than what she truly thought of her daughter. Intellectually, Alexa knew that. It still hurt to hear her mother accuse her of being selfish and stupid and uncaring. Especially when so much of what she'd tried to do these past five years had been about making sure her mother would be taken care of forever.

"How can you do this to me, Alexa? How can you do this to me?" her mother cried. It went on and on and on, no matter what she or Lillian said.

"I'm sorry, Mom. I wish this didn't have to happen—"

"It doesn't. You can just make up with Grant. Make things better," she said, ringing her hands against the stack of photo albums she'd hauled into her lap. The stacks of magazines and newspapers around her chair had regrown in height since Alexa had cleaned some out just last week. "Then I could keep this house and all my things."

Alexa pushed down the hurt that her mother was more worried about losing her junk than why she and Grant had broken up. Not that Alexa had offered the gory details, but her mother seemingly hadn't even thought to ask. "I can't, Mom. And I won't."

"You could if you wanted to. You could if you cared about me," she said, her voice nearly a shriek. Her sobs and sniffles filled the tense air.

Wearing a pair of khaki pants and a lavender top, Lillian sat on the end of the couch closest to Mom so she could pass her occasional tissues. "Now, Cynthia, you know your daughter's relationship has nothing to do with how she feels about you," she said, trying for the fiftieth time to interject a voice of reason.

"But it does, it does, if she cared about me at all . . ."

"Mom," Alexa said, guilt threatening to swamp her.

Her mother's hand stroked over an album with one of her brother's baby pictures on the cover. "Tyler would never have done this to me."

Alexa flinched, the words impacting her like she'd been struck.

"Enough!" Maverick yelled.

The room went eerily quiet.

He'd been standing just inside the living room by the door to the foyer for the whole conversation offering Alexa silent strength and the certainty that she wasn't alone in all this craziness. He hadn't said a thing through the entire hour-long conversation. Until now.

"Maverick Rylan, don't you raise your voice at me," her mother said with a sniff. But not yelling this time.

"I will raise my voice, because you're not hearing Alexa

and she deserves to be heard. If Tyler were here, he'd be raising his voice, too. So I'm saying what he would say because I know you'd respect him enough to want to hear it." His agitation on her behalf eased some of the sting she felt, and his defense of her made her realize how long it'd been since she'd last had a champion, a defender, someone who'd always have her back. God, it felt good, and it meant everything.

"So, what is it you think he'd say?" Mom asked, dabbing at her eyes.

Maverick stepped up beside Alexa. Frustration rolled off of him, but he did a decent job of reining it in as he spoke. "He'd say Grant Slater is a coldhearted, controlling, abusive bastard. He'd say that Slater hurt your daughter and forcibly threw her out of the house. And he'd say that if those weren't reason enough, Alexa can't go back to Slater for the sheer fact that he's threatening to evict you from here to try to force her to bend to his will. Now I've known you most of my life and I know you've always loved your kids, so I know there's no way you'd want that kind of a man or that kind of a life for your daughter. And that because you're such a great fucking mom, you'll do whatever you can to protect Alexa, too, just like me. No matter how hard it is."

Alexa didn't quite know how to feel about the fact that Maverick had shared all her dirty secrets with her mother, but she had to admit it was the first time since they'd arrived that her mom had stopped yelling and crying. And was actually listening.

"Language, Maverick," her mother said, no heat to the admonishment at all.

"Yes, ma'am," he said.

Her mom looked at her. "Is all that true, baby? Grant hurt you? And he's blackmailing you, over me?"

Alexa swallowed hard, the heat of shame and embarrassment crawling up her face. She nodded and hugged herself, feeling raw and exposed. But at least it was for a good cause, because Alexa could see that Maverick had gotten through to her mother by appealing to her *as* a mother. Smart man.

"Oh," Mom said on a gasp, her hand going to her mouth. "Oh, my poor girl. Why didn't you tell me?"

"I was ashamed for you to know," Alexa said, her gaze dropping to the floor. "For anyone to know." She felt Mav's gaze on her, but couldn't meet it. Not just then.

"Alexa," Lillian said, "how someone treats you is a reflection of them, not you."

"I know that," Alexa said, finally looking at the other woman. "But I also let him get away with an awful lot." She shook her head, refusing to dwell on her mistakes when there was so much she could be doing to try to fix them. "I'm not doing that anymore, though."

Lillian's expression was full of sympathy and approval. "Cynthia, what does learning about the details of Alexa's situation make you feel?"

"Well, I feel terrible, of course. And obviously she can't be with someone like that," Mom said. Regret and trepidation were clear in her voice, but it was as if Maverick's tirade had flipped some sort of reset switch inside her mom's mind. And it was closer to an apology than she usually got from her mom. So there was that.

"So how do you feel about giving this move a chance?" Lillian asked.

After a long moment, Mom nodded. "I guess we have to, don't we?" She nodded again. "So . . . we will." Alexa felt a weight lift off her shoulders, at least a little. And she had Maverick to thank for bringing her mother around.

"Good," Lillian said. "Then how about the four of us come up with a game plan that will make this as easy on you as it can be?"

"Fine," her mother said, a little cantankerousness sliding back into her tone. "But first I'd like to see this new place. Because I can't plan anything without knowing what kind of place I'm going to and how much space it has."

"That we can do," Maverick said. His hand went to Alexa's lower back, and his thumb slowly stroked like he knew she needed the comfort. She did.

Alexa finally looked at him, and the fierce protectiveness blazing from his dark blue eyes absolutely slayed her. Just sliced right open to the heart of her. Which wasn't so hard since her heart clearly beat for him. "Thank you," she mouthed.

He gave her a barely perceptible nod, the intensity of his expression communicating so much. Support. Concern. Need.

"Will you come, Lillian?" her mother asked as she stacked the photo albums on the floor again and rose.

"I'd love to see your new home, Cynthia. Now remember what Alexa said. There's a crew of men there working to fix it up. So it's not quite ready for you yet but it will be," Lillian said. Alexa appreciated the older woman offering the reminder.

"Of course," Mom said. "Let me just get my purse." Making her way through a path lined with boxes and stacks of every possible thing, she disappeared back down the hallway toward her bedroom.

Alexa blew out a long breath. "I can't believe you did that," she said to Maverick, "or that it worked so well."

"I couldn't listen to her continue to berate you when she didn't know all the facts," he said, gravel in his voice. "I'm sorry if you didn't want her to know. But I had to do something."

"I know that was hard, Alexa, but I think she needed to hear it," Lillian said. "It pushed her into a place of acceptance and cooperation, which is a start. But be prepared for there to be setbacks and resistance as all this progresses."

Alexa nodded. "I know." She turned to Maverick. "And don't worry. It's okay." He gave a tight nod just as her mother returned. Alexa donned a bright smile. "Okay, Mom. Let's go see your new house."

She'd only been by Creed's little rancher before, never gone inside, but no matter what it was like, it would be better than here. Better than something Grant could give—or take away. Creed's house would be safer and happier for the both of them.

And that was all Alexa had ever wanted for her mom. And herself.

"THIS WILL DO," Mrs. H said as she, Alexa, and Lillian walked through the rooms of Creed's house for the millionth time. "This will do just fine."

Maverick hung back with Phoenix, wanting to give the women privacy, and not wanting to take his anger out on Al's mom again. He hadn't really intended to interfere or lose his cool, but he could tell what her mother's tantrum was doing to Alexa—he could see it in her posture and hear it in her voice—and he couldn't stand for it to continue for another second, especially when she brought Tyler up that way.

Hanging in the mostly empty living room, he watched as the women went into the kitchen again.

"She took it bad then?" Phoenix asked in a low voice.

Maverick chuffed out a humorless laugh, his gaze tracking Alexa until he couldn't see her anymore. "You could say that."

"Seems like she's come around now, though," he said.

"Yeah," Mav said, his gaze scanning over the space. A dark blue couch, coffee table, and end tables were all that remained. The house was a ranch-style with all the rooms on one floor. It had a big combined den and eat-in kitchen that connected past a breakfast bar to the living room. Two decent-sized bedrooms and a bath sat down the hall. More than enough space for one lady, even one with a shit-ton of, well, shit. "You all worked fast here."

"Wanted to get it emptied out as fast as possible so I could see what work it might need. I called Renner in to help, and I paid the three boys who live next door fifty bucks apiece to haul stuff out to the garbage or the storage pod. Just have to do the master bedroom and I'm done." Phoenix gestured for Mav to follow him down the hall. "We probably don't have time to freshen the paint up for her, but other than cleaning the carpets, this is the main thing that I should probably address before she moves in." He flipped on the bathroom light and knelt by the toilet to pull back the old linoleum. Black mold covered the subflooring underneath. Well, hell. "It's all soft, so something's leaking."

Maverick nodded as his gaze scanned over the old fixtures and the dingy shower. "I got a contractor friend who might be able to help." Maybe he could get the guy to freshen up the whole room, in addition to fixing the water damage. "And I'll pay you back for hiring those kids and whatever else you're laying out."

"Fuck that," Phoenix said, giving him a look. "Like I can't do something nice for your woman?"

The words made desire explode inside Mav's chest. Desire for Alexa to be his, once and for all. "She's not mine. And you're giving her a goddamned house, Phoenix. I'd say that's already above and beyond."

"Coulda fooled me." He smirked and waved his hand. "Anyway, your money's no good to me, and neither is hers." A long moment of silence as Phoenix tugged back more of the ruined linoleum to reveal water stains and more spots of mold.

"Can't claim someone who's not ready to be claimed,"

Maverick finally said in a low voice. "Things are too up in the air."

"Maybe, maybe not. But she looks at you like you hung the fucking moon for her, so maybe she's more ready than you think." He washed his hands.

Mav couldn't entertain that possibility, even with everything that'd happened the past few days. Not yet. So he ignored Phoenix's observation even though it kinda made him want to cheer. "Well, how about I do those rival wheels you and I talked about for your bike. And maybe throw in some custom chrome accents?"

The grin made the deep scar on the side of Phoenix's eye seem less severe. The result of a knife fight back when he'd been a prospect. "Now you're just turning me on."

Chuckling, Mav rolled his eyes. "Bring your ride around any time."

"Hey, there you are," Alexa said, leaning against the doorjamb.

"How's she doing?" Maverick asked. He couldn't help noticing how stressed Al looked. It was in her eyes and the way she hugged herself.

"Honestly? Better than I would've expected given how things started out. She adores the big kitchen and den, so I think that won her over even more." She smiled at Phoenix. "I can't thank you enough."

"You already thanked me. We're good," he said, moving toward the door. "Actually, you can thank me." He slipped behind her and whispered something in her ear.

Alexa's cheeks went pink even as she nodded.

"What the hell was that?" Maverick asked. With Phoenix, you never knew what he might be up to. When she didn't answer right away, he stepped right up to her, pinning her back to the molding. "Tell me."

She peered up at him from under her lashes. "He said . . . that me taking care of you was the only thanks he needed."

Irritation flashed through Mav. "Nosy fucker. Ignore him. You don't need that kind of—"

"No, he's right," Alexa said, grabbing the edges of his cut in her fists. "You're doing so much for me. I want to be there for you, too. I just—"

"What?" he asked, needing to hear what she had to say like he needed his next breath.

"I just need more time."

He probably should've accepted it at that, but something made him push. "And then?"

She swallowed thickly. "And then . . . we'll see if . . . if you think you can forgive me and . . ." She gave a little, uncertain shrug. ". . . whether you maybe want to try again."

He cupped her face as triumph surged through him and then he leaned down so he could look at her eye to eye. "I want."

Her eyes went glassy as she whispered, "You do? After everything? Because I wouldn't blame you—"

"*I. Fucking. Want.*" He didn't try to restrain a bit of the fierceness roughening up his voice. He wanted her to know it. To believe it. To feel it down deep. "You. Us. A future. Our history, even the fucked-up parts. All of it. Understand?"

"Yes," she said on a fast nod, her eyes suddenly brimming with unshed tears.

He caught the wetness with his thumbs. "Don't cry, baby. And don't think you're the only one who has things to apologize for. Because I told you I have regrets, too."

"God, Mav—"

"Alexa?" her mother called from the living room. "Are you ready to go?"

Looking into Alexa's eyes, Maverick loved the hope and affection he saw there. "We'll finish this another time."

"Okay," she said. And then she pushed up on her tiptoes

and threw her arms around him, holding him so tight he could barely breathe. So much unspoken emotion rolled off of her, and it fucking slayed him.

And made him feel hopeful for the first time in a long damn time.

Alexa was going to be his again. Sooner or fucking later. And nothing was going to keep them apart this time.

CHAPTER 23

Want to help me give the cat a bath?" Alexa asked, her face playfully hopeful. Wearing a long black shirt of his, her hair still mussed from sleep, she looked beautiful standing barefoot in the sunlight spilling into his kitchen the next morning.

Leaning against the counter with a cup of coffee in hand, Maverick smirked. "If that's code for getting between your legs, sign me up."

Throwing her head back, Alexa laughed out loud. "Like we need special code for that."

He grinned around another sip. "Good to know."

She rolled her eyes, but it was clear she was enjoying the conversation every bit as much as him. And he was glad after the day she'd had yesterday. After seemingly doing so well at her new place, her mother had fallen into another round of tears when they took her home. They'd ended up being there until nearly nine o'clock, and Alexa had been exhausted by the time they got back here.

"I mean, the *actual* cat," Alexa said, her eyebrow arched. "Not the pussy. Maybe later, though . . ."

Maverick had to adjust himself. "You say shit like that you give me ideas of what to do with that mouth."

Laughing, she disappeared down the hall. The water came on in the bathroom. And then he heard the low murmur of her talking to Lucy. And it occurred to him how much he liked not being here alone. He loved the sounds of Alexa moving around his house. He loved seeing her things sitting with his on the counter. He loved her weird sweater-wearing cat greeting them at the door or jumping up in the bed when they woke up. And it made him realize how much he'd changed in the past five years. How much he valued things now that he'd never thought all that important before—big things like commitment and small things like the sounds of companionship.

Curious, he wandered down the hallway to find Alexa kneeling next to the tub, the cat in her arms, the skull sweater discarded on the counter. Lucy wasn't bolting but she also wasn't looking thrilled with the plan. "She likes baths?"

Alexa chuckled. "She likes it once she's in, but she always gets tense before."

"And why exactly are you torturing—I mean, bathing Lucy?"

Smiling up at him, Alexa shook her head. "Being hairless means her body has no way to absorb the oil from her skin or from when she grooms herself, so she has to be washed pretty regularly. It's worth it for how awesome she is, though. Plus, she's so cute when she plays in the water that I can barely stand it." She pressed her face to the cat's. "You ready, baby?" She leaned over the tub and slowly lowered Lucy in, her arms still cradling the thin, little body as it submerged.

The cat scrambled for a moment, and Maverick prepared to try to block her if she made a break for it, but Alexa just held her there until the animal visibly relaxed.

As he watched, Lucy pushed out of Al's hold and walked a circle through the tub's water. "I thought cats weren't supposed to like water?"

Alexa chuckled. "Just wait."

"For what?" he asked, just as Lucy plopped down on her butt, sat up, and pawed at the top of the water like she was playing the drums. Ten seconds, twenty, thirty, she pawed and pawed, sending up little splashes and shaking her head when they hit her in the face. Grinning, he crouched beside the tub. Alexa met his gaze for a moment, and the happiness in her eyes as she looked at him reached all the way inside him. And grasped hold.

Lucy paced the tub again, stopping to bat at the faucet, the wall-mounted soap dish, and the shower curtain. Alexa grabbed a bag at her side that Mav hadn't noticed and handed it to him. "Line these up on the edge."

He reached inside and found a rubber ducky, a plastic dog, a squeaky mouse that made Lucy turn and look, and a couple of other small toys. "You have bath toys for your cat?" he asked with an arched brow.

"She's my baby," she said, laughing.

One by one, he lined them up as Lucy watched. For a moment, the cat just looked at them. And then she attacked, batting them into the water one at a time like a slugger aiming for the back wall, until they were all floating in the water. And then she pounced on them there again and again.

Maverick couldn't help but chuckle. Because Attack Cat was pretty awesome.

Alexa fished them out once more and together they lined them up. Lucy took them all down a second time until they were both laughing at her antics.

"This is fucking hilarious," Maverick said, gathering the toys and lining them up again.

Lucy didn't wait. She swung for the rubber ducky, knocking it out of the tub and into Maverick's lap.

"This is the coolest cat that ever lived," he said, grinning like an idiot as he replaced the duck on the tub's edge.

"See? I told you." Alexa grinned as Lucy knocked the toy into the water and pounced on it, sending up a big spray of water that got both of them. Alexa let out a little shriek, a belly laugh spilling out of her.

Finally, Al actually got down to the business of washing Lucy, and then she was scooping the cat out and wrapping her in a big towel. "Will you hold her while I do her ears and nails?"

Mav took the bundle into his arms and peered down at the little wet head. This was not an attractive creature by any stretch of the imagination, but now he found that to be part of her appeal. Lucy was kinda like the Ravens— rough-looking on the outside but full of awesome. He grinned at the thought.

"What is that smile for?" Alexa asked as she swiped Q-tips through Lucy's giant ears and, one by one, clipped the cat's nails.

"Was just thinking that Lucy could totally be the club's mascot. You need a biker name, though," he said, hugging Lucy a little tighter to his chest as she tensed at the clipping. "'Lucy' is cute and all but it doesn't really fit our vibe. Or the sweater I bought you. Maybe Lucky or Bones or . . . Slugger. Right?" The cat purred and stared at him. "You like that idea, don't you? Yes, you do, kittykitty."

"You are totally cooing at my cat right now."

"Am not."

"It's turning me on."

"I'm totally cooing at your cat."

Alexa laughed, peering up at him with so much affection. "When you take care of something I care about, you take care of me. It means a lot, Mav."

He handed the cat back and watched as Alexa gave her a rub with the towel and finally set her free. Lucy curled against his leg before wandering out of the bathroom.

He hiked Alexa up to sit on the counter. "It's easy when I care about you so fucking much," he said in a low voice.

"Then I'm the lucky one."

Her words heated his blood and set off a warm, expansive pressure in his chest. His hand cupped her neck as he fit himself in tighter between her thighs. His phone buzzed in his back pocket, but Maverick ignored the fuck out of it as he leaned in and claimed her mouth. Once, twice. "Enjoyed washing your kitty."

She grinned into the kiss, her arms coming around him. "I enjoyed having my kitty washed."

He couldn't help smiling, too. His tongue traced her lips and slipped inside. Guiding her head, he took more, went deeper.

His phone buzzed again.

"Should you check that?" she asked, pulling back, her face so alive with happiness that he just wanted to hide from the world and hold them in this moment. And smash the phone into a million pieces.

"Probably." On a sigh, he pulled the cell from his back pocket to find two missed calls from Caine. Which meant something was up, because the guy never called anyone to shoot the shit. "It was Caine. Better see what—"

The phone rang in his hand, Caine's name on the screen.

"Caine, man. What's—"

"Cops are here. Arresting Dare and Jagger. Come now."

"On my way," Maverick said, anger and outrage welling up inside him. What the actual fuck?

"What's the matter?" Alexa said, all that happiness bleeding out of her expression.

"Dare and Jagger are being arrested," he said, already moving from the bathroom toward the kitchen table, where his cut hung over the back of a chair. "Don't know why. But I'm sure as hell going to find out because this is fucking bullshit."

"I'll be thirty seconds," Alexa said, running to her room.

Mav jammed his feet into his boots, his thoughts racing. What the hell could they be accused of? For being a Raven, Jagger tended to go out of the way to keep his nose clean because so much of the business at the track rode on his shoulders. And Dare was just a little over a week out of the hospital and had hardly left the clubhouse except for the ride to Baltimore . . .

Ice crawled through Mav's blood. Could that be it? But, if so, something didn't add up, because if the attack on the Iron Cross was at the bottom of this, Dare and Jagger wouldn't be the only ones getting hauled in. Maverick couldn't begin to figure it out, except his gut screamed that something wasn't right.

Alexa was good to her word, rushing back in a little navy blue cotton dress and a pair of sandals, no makeup, her hair in a messy knot. Beautiful, especially for the concern she wore on her face. For his brothers.

They jogged out to his bike, and she slipped her hand into his. "I'm sorry."

He gave a tight nod, glad to have her at his side. He drove more aggressively than he otherwise might've, but made it in time to see that goddamned motherfucker Davis shoving a cuffed Jagger into the back of his squad car. Sheriff Martin was there, too, clearly trying to keep Phoenix, Caine, and a few others from losing their shit and earning some one-way tickets to a holding cell.

"I'll be right behind you, D," Caine called out just as Davis grabbed his cousin's injured shoulder and shoved him toward the car. Dare grimaced, and Maverick saw red.

Mav charged, Martin catching him about the shoulders. "He's injured, you fucking asshole," Mav yelled. Davis smirked and pushed Dare into the backseat.

"Don't give him the satisfaction, Maverick. I need you to take care of shit here." Dare nailed him with a hard stare just before the door shut between them.

"What the hell happened?" Mav looked to Caine and

the others, stepping back from the car as Davis started it up.

Caine's expression was set in a lethal scowl that was all rage and hard angles. "Someone dumped a shit-ton of tires and oil out by the drag strip. And then Davis supposedly got an anonymous tip reporting it. Now Dare and Jagger have been charged with multiple counts of illegal dumping."

Head spinning, Mav watched as Davis drove away. The Raven Riders hadn't used the quarter-mile strip where they did occasional car and bike drag races since last summer. This made no goddamned sense. He looked from Caine to Sheriff Martin and back again. "You know Jagger Locke. You know this is bullshit. We've got a fucking licensing inspection tomorrow, and the drag strip is part of that. If we'd dumped the shit, why would we leave it where the inspector might find it? And Dare's been laid up for over a week. Jesus Christ, Martin, you were the one who responded to his shooting. You know he hasn't been hauling anything around."

Martin held up his hands, already nodding. Mav and Dare went way back with Henry Martin, all the way back to high school. Though he'd been a hotshot football player and they were pretty much the same miscreants they were now. "I hear you, Maverick. But it's out of my hands. I'll help where I can but what Dare and Jagger need most now is a lawyer."

"And a private detective," Caine said, his voice like ice.

"Yeah," Maverick said. "Because someone knows who was behind this trumped-up bullshit."

"I'm sorry," Haven said. "But why would illegal dumping cause . . . all this anyway?"

Martin gave her a sympathetic look. "It carries big penalties in Maryland. Fines and jail time." Haven paled.

Maverick looked back to Martin. "Can you find anything out about this supposed anonymous tipper?"

"I'll see what I can do," Martin said, covering his short, wavy brown hair with a sheriff's office baseball cap. "It's odd that Davis didn't call for backup in investigating the tip until after he'd found the dump site. He wouldn't normally risk coming on to your property by himself."

"Yeah, well, I guess he was feeling confident of what he'd find. Which in and of itself is fucking fishy," Caine said.

"Like maybe he already knew," Phoenix said. Nods all around. "And the drag strip is far enough from the club-house and close enough to the highway for someone to get in and out quick without any of us noticing. Especially if they did it in the middle of the night."

Maverick nodded, Phoenix's words sounding more and more like the truth of it. Someone planted this shit to cause trouble for them, maybe even keep them from getting their license renewed . . .

Sonofafuckingbitch.

"The timing of this . . . someone knew about the inspection," Maverick said, his mind racing through the possibilities. And landing on one that made his blood boil.

"Oh, God," Alexa said from behind him.

Mav turned to find her holding a shaken-up Haven's hand, Cora on Haven's other side with an arm around her.

Alexa's face was sheet-white. "Grant," she whispered, giving voice to the same conclusion Maverick had just made. "Grant would be able to find that out. He would . . ." She shook her head, her eyes wide and panicked.

"Christ," Maverick said, his gaze swinging back to Martin. "She's right and you know it."

"Aw, hell," Martin said, planting his hands on his hips. "You can't go accusing Grant Slater of anything without proof. He's one of the mayor's best friends and one of the richest and most influential men in town. If he was behind it—and that's a big if—he certainly wouldn't have dirtied his own hands with it, so you'd be hard-pressed to connect it directly to him anyway."

"He's right," Caine said, palming the knit cap covering his shaved black hair. He shook his head. "He'd hire this out."

"Probably," Mav said, nailing Martin with a hard stare. "But what we can a hundred percent prove is that he's blackmailing Alexa to keep her from calling off their wedding next Saturday. Slater's an abusive, controlling prick, and there's no doubt in my damn mind that this bullshit is part of what he's trying to do to her."

Martin's gaze cut to Alexa, and she gave a nod to confirm what Mav had said. "Damnit," Martin said on a sigh. "Okay, I hear you. I'll dig into this as much as I can."

"Do it," Maverick said, his vision going red the more all the implications of this penetrated his thick skull. "Because if you don't get to the bottom of it, we'll have to. But I'm guessing the fucking body count will be lower if you take the lead."

The sheriff held up his hands and arched a brow. "Let me get out of this conversation before we all regret me being in it." The guy was a friend to them, but he drew the line at knowing anything that might cross a line. And *all kinds* of lines were going to likely have to be crossed to right this mess. Because shit had gone seriously sideways. "I'll get down to the station and keep an eye on your guys. Get a lawyer and get down there." He rounded the back of his squad car.

"Take care of them, Martin," Maverick said, eyeballing the other man. "Anything happens to either of them and there's going to be hell to pay in this town and you know it."

Martin nodded as he opened his door. "Just keep your goddamned heads about you." He got in and drove off, passing a tow truck rumbling into the lot as he did. Slider rushed out, his expression making it clear that he'd heard the news. Phoenix started catching him up as Mav made a call.

James Walter was a personal attorney who Doc had known forever. When Walter answered, Mav quickly explained the situation. The guy agreed to meet them at the station without having to be asked. Next, Mav left a message with the business lawyer they used for matters related to the track.

When he hung up, he turned to the assembled group. The pissed-off expressions on the faces of Caine, Phoenix, Slider, Blake, and Bear looked like Maverick felt. And the worry and sadness he saw on Haven's and Alexa's faces ratcheted up his anger by a factor of about a thousand. "I want a detail up here to guard the women and people at the ready just in case something else happens. Assemble as many Ravens as you can. Caine and I will head down to that goddamned station."

"I'll let everyone know what's going on," Phoenix said, pulling out his phone. "But I want to come, too."

"No, Phoenix. We can't have people losing their shit and possibly making things worse," Maverick said. Because the last thing they needed was more men behind bars. Phoenix gave a tight nod.

"I want to come," Haven said.

"No," Maverick said, feeling bad for her but resolved. "Dare won't want you anywhere near the place. I can guarantee it."

"But—"

"Haven, if he even thinks you're there, it'll make him feel worse," he said, forcing his voice to gentle. "The best thing you can do 'til we get him home is stay here and stay safe."

"We don't know what else might be coming at us," Caine added. Mav nodded.

"Damnit, okay," she said, her voice cracking. "I just . . . if you get to see him . . ."

"He knows," Maverick said, remembering his cousin's words about how close they'd gotten. No doubt Dare was already going out of his mind worrying about how Haven would handle this situation.

"I'm so sorry," Alexa said, shaking fingers pressed to her lips. "This is my fault."

"No, it's not," Haven said at the same time that Maverick said, "No, it's fucking not."

"But Grant did this to get back at me," she said, her hazel eyes a little wild.

Maverick got right in her face. He couldn't tolerate her feeling one more ounce of guilt for what her bastard sleazeball of an ex had done. "That's right. *Slater* did this. Not you. And he did it to get back at us for showing up at the restaurant. I'd put money on it."

"That's what my gut says, too," Caine said. "Look, I'm gonna get down to the station now."

"I'm ready, too," Mav said, nailing Alexa with a stare. "Stay strong for me."

A quick nod. "I will."

"We'll take care of each other," Haven said. "Go. Don't worry about us."

Mav kissed Alexa's forehead and made for his bike.

"I'll get things organized," Phoenix called, his cell pressed to his ear.

Waving, Mav mounted the NRS and brought it to life on a roar. He gave Alexa a look and she nodded. And then he took off.

Way he felt, he was ready to take on the whole goddamned world if he had to, so he'd handle Slater in a fucking heartbeat. One way or the other.

CHAPTER 24

Stunned didn't begin to describe how Alexa felt. Shocked. Horrified. Those got a little closer. "I'm so sorry," she said again as she watched Maverick tear out of the parking lot like a demon made of flesh and steel.

"Hey," Haven said, tugging her hand. "Maverick was right. What your ex has done isn't your fault. In fact, to the extent you believe it is, you're falling into the trap he's trying to set for you. He wants you to feel guilty because then maybe you'll do what he wants. Giving in to his effort to manipulate you would be your fault, but this isn't."

Alexa blinked, surprised at the vehemence of Haven's words. She came across as soft-spoken and easygoing, but the younger woman had a fierceness about her that Alexa hadn't seen before. And that she really admired.

"Okay?" Haven asked.

"Okay," Alexa said with a nod.

"Can you take care of them?" came a gruff voice from

behind Haven. She and Alexa turned to find Slider talking to Cora, two little boys standing close by. Boys who had been much, much smaller the last time Alexa had seen them. "I know I said I didn't need you today—"

"I've got them," Cora said. "They'll be fine. But just so you know, Maverick didn't want anyone else going to the station."

Slider's dark eyes flashed. "Well, he isn't here to stop me."

Cora nodded. "Then go do whatever you need for however long it takes. Right, guys?"

With their brown hair and hazel eyes, the two boys bore a striking resemblance to their father. "Yeah, Dad," the older one said, his forehead set in a wrinkle. "You gotta help Dare and Jagger."

Slider gave Cora a nod and a look, like maybe he wanted to say more, but then he just turned away, gave the boys' hair a ruffle on the way past, and jogged to the tow truck.

"Ahhh, oh, no, it looks like you two are stuck with a bunch of icky *girls* today," Cora said in an exaggerated groan that made the littler boy laugh. "Sam, Ben, this is Maverick's friend, Alexa."

The boys said hello, and Alexa found herself glad for the distraction they might offer her and Haven. "You know, I've met you guys before. You wouldn't remember, because you"—Alexa pointed to Ben, who must've been six or seven—"were just starting to walk. And you"—she smiled at Sam—"were about his size."

"Then why haven't we seen you since?" Ben asked in that way little kids had of asking uncomfortably pointed questions.

"Maverick and I just stopped seeing as much of each other," Alexa said. The boy shrugged, satisfied.

"I think this day is going to require lots of cookies," Haven said on a troubled sigh.

"Awesome!" the boys yelled, barreling up the steps.

"Nothing like kids to offer perspective," Haven said, putting on a brave smile. If she could do it, Alexa would, too.

Phoenix came jogging out. "All right. Blake, Joker, and Meat are here. Mike Renner will be here in a few. Don't leave the clubhouse. Just stay put." He gave them all a look.

Standing next to him, Cora crossed her arms. "We got it. Go do whatever you need to do. And please keep Haven posted if you can."

"Will do," he said, taking off in a rush for his bike. And then he was gone, too.

A few minutes later, the women had gotten the boys set up with a snack and the TV and game console in the rec room, and the three of them took a plate of cookies and a pitcher of strawberry lemonade out onto the big back porch. It was a crystal clear, sunny day, the air fresh and clean, the sky bright blue. The beauty of the day seemed to mock the chaos that had just unfurled out front not a half an hour ago.

Settling into a group of cushioned lounge chairs, they just lay there quietly for a long moment.

"I'm glad you guys are both here," Haven said.

Alexa appreciated the sentiment so much. "Me too. Can I admit something else embarrassing?"

"Something else?" Cora asked, tucking her shoulder-length blond waves behind her ears.

"Something else besides the fact that my ex-fiancé is a controlling psychopath . . ."

"Ah, right. Honestly, there are too many of those running around," Cora said, grabbing a cookie.

"For real," Haven said, turning her bright blue eyes on Alexa. "What's your confession?"

"I haven't had any real friends in a long time." Saying that out loud made her heart race. It sounded so ridiculous, but it had been her reality for years now. She always thought of Christina and the other girls at the office as her *work friends*. It wasn't like she could talk about Grant with them, and since he'd become her whole world, that left her mostly with superficialities. Which defined most of her relationships until these past few days, didn't it? And she wasn't even sure exactly when or how it had happened, only that it had.

Haven reached between their chairs and squeezed her hand. "Cora's pretty much the only friend I've ever had."

"And I'm, like, totally awesome." Cora smirked.

Haven grinned, and so did Alexa. "And she's totally awesome, obviously. But I just mean to say that I'm very glad to have another."

"Me too," Cora said.

"Me three," Alexa said, taking a cookie of her own.

They sat there in silence for a while, enjoying the cookies and the breeze. And Alexa couldn't stop worrying about Dare and Jagger and what Grant might do next. If he was willing to frame the Ravens for something, what the hell else would he be willing to do? She blew out a long breath and tried to gather her spiraling thoughts. She looked from Haven to Cora, and blurted a question. "Cora, how did you come to babysit Sam and Ben?"

Cora and Haven exchanged a look, and Cora chuckled. "It just kinda happened. When we were first here, Slider was in a bind one day and we agreed to watch the boys for him because we didn't really have anything else to do."

"This was before we knew we were going to stay here," Haven said.

"And then once we knew we were staying, Slider asked a few more times and I agreed. So now he's hired me to work for him part-time when he needs. At some point I have to figure out what the heck I'm going to actually do with my life in the long term, but until then, I'm happy to help him out." Cora took another cookie.

"He's changed a lot since I last knew him," Alexa said,

biting into a big chocolate chunk. "Not that I knew him that well, but he was always so outgoing and laid-back."

"*Slider?*" Cora asked, her mouth dropping open. "Like, *my* Slider? Well, not mine, but you know what I mean."

Alexa nodded, not at all blaming the guy, given the way grief had torn her life apart, too.

"Aw, that's even sadder," Haven said, stretching her legs out on the lounge chair. "Dare said his wife died of breast cancer and the poor guy was just devastated."

Cora shook her head. "He's definitely not outgoing and laid-back now."

Haven eyed her friend. "Is he too hard to work for? I don't want you feeling uncomfortable, and no one would expect—"

"No, no," Cora said. "He's fine. He can be gruff and noncommunicative, but he's never mean. It's almost like he just doesn't have it in him to talk or interact. Except with his boys. He must save what he does have for them, because he can be really sweet with them."

"Yeah," Haven said. "Whatever he's going through, he's good with Sam and Ben."

Alexa listened as the friends went back and forth, admiring their closeness, wishing she had a friendship of her own that was as tight as theirs. And of course that made her think of Maverick, who'd been a friend before he became a lover, then more. She couldn't help wonder what was happening down at the police station. She just hoped Maverick managed to keep his temper reined in so he didn't end up sitting next to Dare in a cell.

"So, what are you thinking you might like to do in addition to babysitting?" Alexa asked Cora.

The blonde exchanged a glance with Haven and shrugged. "I'm not sure yet. I was a waitress back home and never expected to leave there, so I never let myself even imagine much before," Cora said, brushing the crumbs off her lap.

"But you've had time to imagine now," Haven said.

Cora nodded and stared off into the distance for a long time. "Okay. So, there's something I always thought would be cool, but I'd just ruled it out as an impossibility for me."

Haven sat forward in a rush. "Really? What is it? I can't believe you haven't said anything."

"It's not like it could happen tomorrow, Haven," Cora said, chuckling.

"So? Tell me." Haven hugged her knees to her chest and stared at her friend.

"I've always loved animals. If money and time weren't any object, I'd love to go to school to become a veterinarian. Even though that would take like a million years since I'd have to go to college first." Cora looked at them from under her hair, like she was afraid they'd laugh at her idea.

"I think that sounds awesome," Alexa said. Cora's plans made her think of the schoolwork she wasn't doing, but in the midst of everything going on, it suddenly seemed so damned unimportant. She pushed the thoughts away. "I love animals, too."

"Oh, Cora, I think that would be amazing," Haven said.

"We'll see," Cora said, clearly uncomfortable to be the focus of their attention. "I did find out that the local animal shelter takes volunteers, so I thought maybe I'd check that out. Just to get a feel for working with animals. See if I really like it. In the meantime, I can keep babysitting for Slider. Or get some other part-time job."

"You totally should volunteer." Haven took another cookie. "This is so exciting."

Cora laughed. "Simmer down. It's just an idea."

"It's a good one," Haven said, arching an eyebrow.

"So is you opening your own bakery," Cora shot back. They looked at each other for a long moment. "Okay, here's the deal. I explore the volunteer position and start looking at schools if you *seriously* look into opening your own business. You have your dad's money coming, so you don't even have lack of start-up funds as an excuse."

Haven's mouth dropped open, and the woman looked to Alexa for help. "She's bribing me."

Al held up her hands, so glad she wasn't alone right now, so glad to have *friends*. "I'm not getting in the middle. Although I think you'd both be crazy not to do those things."

"Okay, then." Haven nodded slowly, like she was coming around to the idea. "Deal."

Grinning, Cora nodded, too. "Fine. Deal." They shook hands.

On a sigh, Haven flopped back against her lounge chair. "Now that we have our lives sorted, I just need my man out of jail and back by my side." The longing in the woman's voice made Alexa think of Maverick. She wanted him by her side, too. And so many things he'd said recently gave her hope that he felt the same exact way. His voice played in her ear.

I. Fucking. Want. You. Us. A future. Our history, even the fucked-up parts. All of it.

Alexa's heart squeezed at the memory of the promising words, the rough determination in his voice, the hot fierceness of his expression.

"I like hearing you call him 'my man,'" Cora said, waggling her brows.

"I do, too," Alexa said. "Never thought I'd see Dare in a relationship. But he obviously adores you. It's really good to see."

Pink filled Haven's cheeks and she chuckled, but it was clear how much she enjoyed hearing it.

Suddenly, Alexa's cell buzzed where it laid on the seat next to her.

Please, let it be good news from Maverick.

It was, quite possibly, the exact opposite.

GRANT: Come home, Alexa.

The words were innocuous enough, but they still made her stomach drop. Because he just wasn't getting it, was he? And on top of what'd happened to Dare and Jagger today, that seemed . . . problematic. Purposely obtuse, at least. Disconnected from reality, at worst.

"Is that Maverick?" Haven asked, hope flaring in her bright blue eyes.

"No," Alexa said, blowing out a breath. "My ex. Asking me to come home again for like the millionth time."

"Home? What part of you having moved out doesn't he get?" Cora asked.

"For real," Haven said. "I thought this guy was supposed to be some high-powered businessman. Because the more I learn about him, the more he kinda seems a little unhinged."

Unhinged . . . suddenly seemed like a really good description of Grant. She thought back over her recent interactions with him. All the little manifestations of his compulsiveness, the mood swings, the paranoia, the refusal to accept reality, the anger. She recalled him stammering and the way his eye had twitched. Alexa shook her head. "He is, but I don't know. It's like me standing up to him pushed him off the deep end."

"Hey," Haven said, grasping her hand. "You're not alone, okay?"

Alexa nodded, appreciating the sentiment so much.

Just then, Alexa's cell rang. "Oh, thank God, now it's Maverick." She put it to her ear and answered. "Hey."

"Hey, Al." Frustration and anger were plain in his voice. "If Haven's there with you, can you put me on speaker?"

She pressed the button. "Yeah, you're on speaker now. What's happening?"

"Haven," Mav said, "we can't get bail hearings for Dare and Jagger until sometime tomorrow."

Haven gasped. "Tomorrow? They have to stay in overnight?"

His rough exhale came down the line. "Fucking judge is probably in Slater's pocket as well. He won't talk to the lawyer until tomorrow."

"Goddamn Grant," Alexa said, emotion welling up inside her. This was so unfair. For Dare and Jagger, for the Ravens, for Haven. For her, too. "I hate him so much I don't know what I'd do if I saw him."

"Tell me about it," Mav bit out.

The lethal tone made Alexa's heart pound with a sudden fear. "No, Maverick. Don't you do anything. Promise me."

"We'll talk about this later, Al. But you gotta know all bets are off. He blackmailed you, he threatened you, and now he's threatening the freedom of two of my brothers and the livelihood of the club. What happened today was a declaration of war."

She understood where he was coming from, she really did, but his words still sent a chill down her spine.

"Haven, the lawyer saw Dare. He said to tell you not to worry, that he's fine, and that he'll be home soon."

"Thank you," Haven said, those two words laden with so much more.

"Listen, I'm sorry to run," Maverick said, "but I want to keep an ear out and catch the lawyer before he goes." After a quick good-bye, they hung up.

"He'll be okay," Cora said, taking Haven's hand. "He's as tough as they come. You know that. And Jagger's there with him."

Haven gave a quick bob of her head. "I know. But he's still hurt, even though he refuses to admit it. And I just hate the idea of him in there."

"So do I," Alexa said. "But Cora's right. It'll just be the one night and then they'll make bail until we can get all this cleared up."

"One night," Haven said, taking a deep breath. "We can make it through one night."

That *we* tugged at Alexa's heartstrings, because it was clear that Haven and Dare really had something special between them. And Alexa wanted it for herself.

With Maverick.

"One night," Cora said. "Easy peasy."

Alexa nodded and put on a brave smile for her new friend. But inside she couldn't help but wonder what other bombs Grant was preparing to launch at them the next day and the day after that—and how much Alexa was willing to let others be hurt and sacrificed for her so that she could escape him once and for all.

ALEXA KNEW SHE was alone the moment she woke up. "Maverick?" she called.

The sheets were cold beside her. Slipping out of bed, she wandered through the house looking for him—his room, the bathroom, the kitchen, the living room. She peered out the front door to check the garage, but it was dark. The LED on the microwave read a little after 4:00 A.M.

Worry sent a shiver over her skin, and Alexa grabbed the fleece throw off the back of the couch and wrapped it around her shoulders. Where could he be?

The Ravens had finally returned from the police station and guard duty around dinnertime, and the meal had been a somber, quiet, tension-filled affair. And it got even more tense when Alexa shared the text she'd received. She'd hated to pour salt into Mav's wounds, but also felt like she shouldn't keep anything from him. Not with so much on the line.

Most of the guys stayed around after dinner to drink and plot against her ex-fiancé, so Alexa had hung with Haven, Cora, and Bunny in the kitchen playing cards until Maverick had finally come in, bleary-eyed and a little unsteady on his feet, and said he was ready to go. When Bunny had said she'd drive them home, he thankfully hadn't argued.

But he also hadn't been interested in talking. When they'd returned to his house, he'd collapsed into her bed and fallen right to sleep, still wearing his Ravens cut and boots and everything. No matter what he'd said earlier in the day, Alexa hadn't been able to fight back the guilt she felt—guilt that he was so upset about his best friend being locked up in jail because of her ex—and she'd been unable to fall asleep.

She'd finally given up and gone out to the couch to work on her project for a couple hours, and part of her was glad that she had—because she was in better shape than she thought she was. A few more solid hours and it would be good enough to turn in. Maybe not her best work ever, but good enough. Right now, that felt like a victory.

A flicker of light out in the backyard caught her eye, and Alexa walked closer to the big picture window. A bright moon sparkled off the pond, and a low flash of red and yellow revealed a small fire.

In bare feet, Alexa crossed the back deck and padded down the sandy trail to the fire pit that sat at the little beach's edge. Maverick sat next to the fire in a white T-shirt and jeans, his feet bare, his elbows braced on drawn-up knees, his eyes focused out over the dark water. He was so beautiful to her that it made her chest ache.

"Hey," she said. The heat of the fire warmed her legs, the sensation a pleasant contrast against the night air.

His gaze cut to her and then dragged down her body. She felt the hungry look like a physical caress. "Hey. Why are you up?" His voice was flat, tired.

"Could ask you the same thing." She came to stand in front of him.

"Too much shit in my head," he said, raking his hands through his hair.

An apology sat on the tip of her tongue, but Alexa bit it back. That wasn't what he needed from her. He needed her to make it better, to make it all go away, even if only for a little while.

"Know what helps that?" She dropped the blanket by his feet, her heart doing a little flip inside her chest. Next, she shed her T-shirt. Then she stepped out of her panties until she finally stood naked in front of him.

The raw need she saw on his face was the greatest thrill and the biggest turn-on. But she wanted to ease his mind before she tended to his body.

She stepped backward, a smile growing on her face. "Midnight skinny-dipping helps that. Like when we were young. Not a care in the world. Just you and me against the world." Backward and backward, until her feet hit the cool water's edge. *Come on, Maverick.*

He tilted his head and his gaze lost some of the blankness from moments before.

Alexa kept going. The water hit her knees, her thighs, her waist. The soft bottom was cold against her feet. But she kept going until she turned her back on him and gently dove toward the streak of moonlight stretching out across the dark, glimmering surface. The temperature was a shock to Alexa's sleep-warmed skin, but it didn't take her long to adjust. And then it was like swimming through silk, soft and slick and tantalizing. The bottom was a little rocky in some places and muddy in others, so Alexa swam out until she could just barely touch . . . and then she floated.

Small splashes sounded out from the water's edge. She smiled up at the star-scattered sky, her heart exploding at the fact that Maverick was getting in, that he'd let her offer a distraction from everything weighing on his mind. Finally, she turned to find him thigh-deep, breathtaking in his nakedness, and heading her way. He dove, giving her a flash of the ink on his back before submerging for a long moment.

She scanned the surface, waiting for him to reemerge. Something grabbed her leg.

Alexa screamed and flailed. Maverick came up wearing a smug smirk, his arm around her waist, his hair appearing dark from the water.

She smacked his shoulder, laughing despite herself. "You scared me!"

"Sorry, baby," he said, his tone clearly not even a little sorry.

Even though he said it playfully, the term of endearment unleashed butterflies through her belly. Until this week, she hadn't heard it in years, and it was both familiar and achingly new after so long. "No you're not. You suck."

He held her tighter, their fronts pressed together from breast to thighs. "Is that an invitation?" His mouth dropped to her neck. Licked. Nipped. Sucked at the soft spot below her ear.

Alexa's chuckle turned into a moan. "A standing invitation."

Maverick's cock hardened between them, feeling deliciously thick. "Did you mean it?" he whispered against her skin.

"What?" she asked, his mouth and wandering hands making it hard for her to do anything but feel, especially when he lifted her to wrap her legs around his waist. The movement lined her core up with his hardness, and he didn't miss the chance to grind against her clit. Small, controlled thrusts that quickly had her panting.

"You and me against the world." Hips still rocking, he grasped her hair in an imitation of a ponytail and forced her head back. And then he licked her from between her breasts to her jaw in a slow, torturous line.

"I meant it," she whispered, her heart thundering. She locked her ankles behind his back to gain more leverage. As close as he was, he wasn't close enough. She needed more. She needed everything.

Maverick kissed her on a groan, his mouth tasting like mint and the earthy cleanness of the water and something that was all him. His hands were in her wet hair, on her breasts, squeezing her ass. He ground his cock against her, the wet slide over her clit driving her hard and fast toward an orgasm. And all Alexa could do was hold on and give herself over to the incredible feelings he was unleashing inside her. Desire. Wonder.

Love.

She loved Maverick Rylan.

She'd *always* loved Maverick. And she knew now what she'd hidden from herself for years—she'd never stopped. Not when Tyler died. Not when Grant made it easier to shove down and ultimately hide from her grief with trips and presents and the excitement of the way he'd chased her. And not when Grant's touch had turned cold and controlling and hurtful.

Feeling the enormity of what she felt right now, she wasn't sure how she'd ever thought she was in love with another man.

Because underneath it all, Maverick had still been there. At the heart and soul of her. Waiting for her to see the truth. Waiting for her to *feel* it.

Her truth.

I love Maverick Rylan.

The admission exploded her apart, destroying the last of her illusions and throwing light onto parts of her she'd ignored for so, so long. Emotion ballooned inside her until it was almost more than she could bear.

"I could get through anything if that was true, Alexa," he said, his forehead pressed to hers, his hips moving maddeningly between her legs.

"It is," she managed, her breath catching.

He pulled back, his eyes searching hers. "Hey, are you crying?"

"No," she said, on a fast shake, despite the fact that her voice was suddenly thick with restrained tears.

"Fuck, am I making you feel pressured?"

She held him tighter with both her arms and her legs. "Not even a little, Maverick. You're making me feel lo"— she swallowed back the word that'd almost spilled from her lips, not sure if it was too much to put out there so fast—"cared for in a way I haven't felt in so long. You're my silver lining in the mess that is my life right now. It all brought me back to you, and I've never been more grateful for something in my entire life."

"Jesus, Alexa," he said, claiming her mouth in a searing, exploring, lingering kiss. "I need you. I need you every way I can have you."

"Then have me," she whispered.

Still kissing her, he turned with her still in his arms and slowly waded back to the water's edge, and then he carried her out. She didn't feel the chill in the air for the heat pouring off Maverick's body and out of his dark blue eyes. The fire had died down but still flickered low among the red coals. Next to it he'd apparently spread out her blanket before he'd joined her in the water.

Maverick lowered her to the brown fleece and came down on top of her, his hips between her thighs, his cock so close to where she yearned for him. But he didn't take her. Not yet. He kissed and licked down her body, his tongue dragging over her sensitive skin until she was squirming and moaning and fisting her fingers in his long hair.

His big shoulders settled between her thighs, spreading them wider. He looked up her body. "I want you to say my name when you come on my tongue." And then that tongue was right there, licking hard and firm over her clit. Driving. Relentless. Mind-blowing.

Her heart racing, Alexa couldn't do anything but chase the orgasm barreling down on her. Hands tighter in his hair, she thrust her hips forward, seeking more of the delicious contact with his lips and tongue. He planted a hard palm against her lower belly and held her, his mouth sucking her clit deep and his tongue driving her over the edge.

"Maverick!" she cried out, her release crashing over her like a tidal wave. Her whole body spasmed at the goodness of it. "Mav . . . oh, God."

On a growl, he crawled up her body and claimed her mouth, his tongue immediately sliding deep. She reveled in the taste of herself on him because she couldn't see the pleasure he'd given her as anything other than a selfless gift. And that was something she hadn't received in such a long time.

"Ride me," he gritted out as he flipped them. He manhandled her until her thighs straddled his hips. "Ride me rough and hard and long, Alexa. Use me up."

"Yes." She grasped his cock and lined it up with her core. She sank down, taking him in inch by rock-hard inch. Her pulse beat so strong she felt it against her skin everywhere. "Oh, yes."

Mav's hands went to her hips. "*Fuuuck.*" When he bottomed out inside her, he held her still, forcing her to take all of him. To keep all of him. She would. God, she would.

Bracing her hands on his chest, Alexa rode him in a slow up and down that had both of them groaning and straining and clutching tight. His eyes were intense blue fire peering up at her, and she couldn't look away. She didn't want to.

"This is where I'm supposed to be," he said. "Deep inside you."

"Yes," she said.

"And this is where *you're* supposed to be." His hands pushed her down harder. "Claiming every inch of me."

"*Yes*," she moaned, grinding her clit against his pubic bone. "Oh, yes."

He pulled her down and hugged her against his chest, his arms banding around her, his hands in her hair. "Say it again," he said, kissing her as much as he could while they moved.

She didn't have to ask what he wanted to hear. "You and me against the world."

His hips moved faster. His arms held tighter. His eyes burned brighter. "Again."

Sensation spiraled hot and low in Alexa's belly. "You and me against the world."

He groaned. "*Again.*"

Her orgasm detonated, stealing her breath. "You and me," she managed.

"That's fucking right," he yelled, his release pulsing inside her and drawing out her own. "You and me, baby. You and me."

When their bodies calmed, he eased out of her but didn't let her go. He settled her at his side, his arm around her shoulders holding their bodies tightly together. He kissed her forehead and sighed, the sound full of satisfaction and ease even as his heart pounded under her hand on his chest.

Or maybe that was her heart she felt, because he'd stolen it totally and completely.

CHAPTER 25

I don't like this," Maverick said as he pulled up in front of the model home where Alexa was working on Monday morning. A number of work trucks filled the driveway of the otherwise empty development. His gaze cut to her, looking so pretty and put together in a pair of navy dress pants and flowy lavender shirt.

"I don't love it, either," she said, giving him a brave smile. "But Grant never comes out here, which is perfect because I can do what I have to do in peace. He won't be here until the walk-through on Wednesday, and then the whole team will be with us. It'll be fine."

Mav clenched his jaw, not wanting to open the argument they'd already had this morning even though everything inside of him demanded he push. For her own good.

Because he wouldn't be able to stand it if anything happened to her. Not when he knew she was in danger. And not when it was on his watch.

It would be him failing his mother all over again—only worse. This time, there'd be no excuses that could absolve him. Unlike then, Maverick knew fully that Alexa was in trouble.

"Look, your guys are nearby, right?" she asked, reaching over and putting her hand on his thigh. He gave a tight nod. Renner and Blake's presence just out of direct sight of the house was the only reason he could entertain the idea of her being out in the world without him all day. "If anything happens that even remotely worries me, I'll call or text them immediately."

You and me against the world.

Her words rang in between Maverick's ears, and he needed them to be true so fucking bad he could hardly stand it. But Alexa needed to be safe in his life and at his side for that to have a chance. For *them* to have a chance.

"Don't even let it get to the point of being worried," he said, arching his brow and nailing her with a stare.

"I won't," she said. "I get it, Maverick. I won't take any chances."

He thought just going back to work was taking one, but they'd already been down that road. No matter how much Maverick wanted to lay down the law and tell her what to do, he couldn't. That was the controlling shit Slater had done and not even a little of what Alexa needed from Mav. He wanted to take care of her, not dictate to her. Damn it all to hell.

Sliding his hand behind her neck, he released a troubled breath. "I need you to come home to me. Safe and sound. You understand?"

Her expression went so soft and sweet. For him. "Aw, I think that's the nicest thing anyone's ever said to me."

He scowled. "I mean it."

"So do I," she whispered. And then she leaned across the big bench seat and kissed him.

He wanted to convince her with his mouth and hands and cock not to go. But he finally released her. "Have a good day," he managed.

She chuckled. "Thanks, even though it sounds like what you meant is, *I sure hope that house burns to the ground.*"

He grinned and nodded. "Pretty much."

She shook her head, and then her expression grew serious. "Keep me posted on Dare and Jagger. I'm really nervous for them."

"I will," Maverick said, his gut in all kinds of knots over the fact that his cousin and one of his best friends had been sitting in a fucking jail cell overnight. At least their bail hearing was today. "We'll get them out on bail and go from there."

"Yeah," she said, sliding out of the truck. She turned and leaned back in. "You and me against the world?"

The words came out sounding like a question, and Maverick looked her right in the eye. "You better fucking believe it."

He watched her walk up the sidewalk through all the brand-new landscaping and disappear inside the big brick colonial. Pulling away and leaving her there was one of the hardest things he'd had to do in a long damn time. Besides Renner and Blake, the only thing that gave Mav any ease of mind was the belief that what Slater wanted more than anything else was to get her back under his control and walking up the aisle to the altar. So she was probably safe for now.

After she left him standing at that altar? All bets were probably off.

"WAITING FUCKING SUCKS," Phoenix said, expressing all of their views as they cooled their heels at the Ravens' clubhouse. Walter had thought that Dare and Jagger would have a better chance of a lower bail if the whole club didn't show up and emphasize the fact that, you know, they were a big fucking motorcycle club. So only Haven, Bunny, and Doc—wearing a suit instead of his colors—had gone.

"Christ, it really does," Maverick said, dropping his head back against the leather couch. This whole day sucked as far as he was concerned. Between his worry about Alexa being at work, the anticipation of hearing from Walter, and the tension ricocheting around this room, Mav felt like a rubber band pulled tight and ready to snap.

"It's gonna be fine," Cora said, sitting on a stool at the bar next to Phoenix. "The hearing will be over any minute and then the guys will be on their way home."

Murmurs of agreement went around the room.

"That's right," Rodeo said, the stress of the situation clearly weighing on the old man—Dare's great-uncle by marriage. It looked like Rodeo had aged five years since Maverick saw him here the night before. Doc had looked even worse.

Maverick heaved a breath. Crossed his ankles on the table. Got up and went to the bathroom. And still the fucking phone didn't ring.

"It's taking too long," Caine said. He'd been leaning up against one of the pool tables, standing statue still and not saying a word since they'd all gathered.

Fuck. The words struck a chord with the feeling of dread stirring in Mav's gut.

Sitting on the coffee table by his feet, Maverick's cell phone finally rang, the ringtone cutting through the thick tension like a knife. He wrenched forward and grabbed it, then held out a hand to quiet everyone as they moved closer. He answered and put the call on speaker. "Mr. Walter, it's about time."

"I'm sorry for the delay, Maverick. The hearing just concluded." Walter's tone deepened that sense of dread.

"And?" he asked, fearing he already knew the answer.

"I have good news and bad news."

"Just say what you have to say," Maverick said, working to restrain the anger welling up inside him.

"Dare's out on fifty thousand dollars bail, but Jagger was denied bail."

The room erupted in angry denunciations of the news.

Maverick held up his hands to quiet them again, his pulse a rushing roar in his ears. "He *what*? Why?"

"It's clear the district attorney has a stronger case against Jagger because he's the track manager and Dare's been laid up because of his injury. And the judge deemed Jagger a flight risk," Walter said.

"Jesus, this is utter fucking bullshit," Maverick said, his thoughts a jumbled mess. Jagger wouldn't run. The guy didn't have it in him. He wouldn't abandon his brothers in the club, his duties at the track that he loved, or his younger sister who lived in Baltimore. "How in the world does illegal dumping warrant all this?" Because fifty grand wasn't chump change. Not that they wouldn't spend it to free Dare—they'd do that in a heartbeat, and then some. But wasn't this all a little excessive?

"Each charge, of which there are two, carries a maximum penalty of five years in prison and a $25,000 fine. And it's clear that the recent shooting at the track played into the judge's decision," Walter added. "He was being a real hard-ass."

Hearing the possible jail time at stake was like getting hit in the gut. With a goddamned baseball bat. "Who's the judge?" Maverick asked, his instincts waving a red flag.

"His name's Harold Brennan."

Mav met Caine's ice-blue eyes and could almost see the same questions in the other man's eyes. What was the likelihood they could discover a connection between Brennan and Slater? What were the chances that Brennan was in Slater's pockets, just like the mayor and Davis? Better than average on both counts, Maverick would bet. Fuck.

They'd sure as shit find out.

Walter passed on a little more information about what would happen from here and they hung up.

Mav rose to his feet and scanned his gaze around the room. Every man's face was more angered and outraged than the last. "Here's what's gonna happen. Caine, you handle getting a private detective on this right fucking now."

"I'd placed some calls this morning," he said. "I'll nail one down right away."

Nodding, Maverick looked to Phoenix. "Hire out whatever work remains on Creed's house. I want you taking over the carnival preparations immediately. Jagger didn't go through all this trouble on the club's behalf so that everything could fall apart three days beforehand, so we can make sure it goes off without a hitch until we can get him home again. And call in whatever help you need. Nothing is a bigger priority."

"Consider it done," Phoenix said, a deep scowl in place of his normally playful, smart-ass expression.

"I can help," Cora said. Phoenix gave her a nod.

"What about the licensing inspection?" Bear asked. The inspector was set to arrive at two o'clock, and they'd learned he wouldn't be alone. An inspector from the environmental crimes unit would be joining him. Who'd have ever thought *that* would be one of their problems? On a sigh, Mav looked at his phone. They had ninety minutes.

"You and I will handle that," Mav said to the older man. "Given what's happened, having two executive board members present might help smooth this situation over. And I want another pair of ears there to make sure we're clear on how to mitigate the environmental damage and begin the cleanup." Bear nodded.

Jesus, this was the last thing they needed when they were trying to repair their reputation in the community. Fucking Slater. Maverick wanted to wrap his hands around the other man's throat and watch the life slowly squeeze out of him.

"Rodeo, I want you to set up a perimeter watch . . ." Mav's words trailed off as the command reminded him of something he hadn't thought of before. "Fuckin' A."

"What is it?" Caine asked, his tone on edge.

"Good news. Maybe." He met his brother's intense gaze. "Remember how the Hard Ink team hacked in to the traffic cameras when we were keeping lookout for Haven's father?" Nods all around. "I wonder if they could go back through the footage and find anyone coming or going from the area of the drag strip?"

"Fuck, that would be good news," Phoenix said. "Worth asking."

"I'll make the call. The rest of you, get to it," Maverick said, meeting the gazes of each of his brothers. "And watch your backs. It's probably Slater, but maybe it's someone else. Either way, we know for sure that someone's gunning for us. And we can't afford another hit."

Two LONG, TENSE, busy days later, Maverick found himself at the track with Phoenix and a bunch of other Ravens helping to organize the carnival. The company had arrived this morning to set up the rides, games, and food trucks. The weekend was supposed to be a scorcher, so they'd hired a tent company to put up a couple of big tents to throw shelter over rows of picnic tables, and those were going up, too.

As for their part, the Ravens were setting up cones to direct traffic in the big parking lot, hanging signage, stringing lighting, roping off areas inside the track where the public could meet and take pictures with the drivers, and otherwise answering a thousand phone calls and questions and putting out fires whenever they arose. Trying to take the heat off of Dare, Maverick had been fielding the phone which wouldn't stop ringing. Only good thing was that being busy made the day fly by. And helped distract him from the fact that Jagger had now been sitting in jail for three days. The injustice of it ate at him like a parasite.

Pausing in the shade under one of the tents, Maverick answered another call. "Maverick, it's Cynthia."

Surprised, he leaned back against a table. It had been years since Alexa's mother had last called him, and then it was usually only to track Tyler down because he wasn't answering his cell. "Mrs. H? You doing okay?"

"Yeah, hon. I was just wondering what time you all were coming over."

"Oh, uh." He swiped at the sweat on his forehead. The work at Creed's was being completed today so they weren't wasting any time—they'd planned to move Alexa's mom and the first load of her belongings tonight. "Alexa gets off around five and then she'll change and we'll be over." Which they'd told her several times this week, but that was a small thing compared to the fact that she hadn't had any more crying jags since Sunday night.

"Oh. Right. Okay. Just wanted to make sure nothing had changed," she said.

"No problem, Mrs. H." Phoenix flagged Mav with a wave and then cut across the grounds to him.

"Sorry to bother you, Maverick. Alexa didn't answer and I wanted to make sure I was ready when you got here."

Didn't answer? Alarm bells threatened to go off, but Maverick also knew Alexa was neck deep in last-minute details today. "You're no bother," he said. "We'll see you soon." They hung up. "Hey," he said to Phoenix.

"Thought you could use a drink," the guy said, handing him an icy bottle of Coke.

"Fuck, yeah. Hot as hell out here today." Maverick popped the top and took a long pull from the bottle. Cold and fizzy and sweet. Then he gave in to the urge clawing up his spine and texted Alexa. *You okay?*

His phone buzzed almost immediately. *Yes, almost done. Breaking for lunch and then that'll be a wrap.*

See? She's fine. He shot off a reply. *Knock 'em dead, baby.* Appeased, Mav slid his phone back into his pocket.

"You did a great job stepping into Jagger's shoes and putting all of this together, Phoenix. He'll be grateful. And so am I."

Phoenix heaved a troubled breath. "I fucking hate that he's in there."

"Me too," Maverick said, the regret he felt a weight on his shoulders that wouldn't go away. And why should it go away when Jagger was locked up for a crime he didn't commit? *That* was a weight.

They sat together for a long time and drank their sodas, both of them clearly lost in their own thoughts. Aside from Jagger sitting in jail, the week was going better than any of them had expected.

Dare was home and no worse for the wear—way more pissed off, but not harmed in any way. The Ravens already had the tires and oil barrels removed from the property, and an environmental firm was treating the small spills that had occurred. A new licensing inspection had been scheduled for tomorrow to review the property after the environmental violations had been addressed. The Hard Ink team had hacked into the traffic camera footage again and was reviewing it, although they said it could take a while. And the P.I. they'd hired had found a social connection between Slater and the judge, confirming their suspicions. Not great news, of course, but at least there was forward fucking motion. Alexa had even managed to finish and submit her schoolwork, and he knew she was feeling good about having that off her plate.

Even better, the illegal dumping story didn't seem to be hampering the carnival at all. Advance ticket sales were strong, local businesses had signed up in droves to sell their food or other products, and the word was getting out. The charity aspect of the carnival was the real selling factor, and it seemed to be getting more play in the press than the dumping story. Thank God for small favors.

Best of all? Grant Slater hadn't bothered Alexa at the model home even once.

"All right," Phoenix said, hopping off of the table. "No rest for the wicked. I'm gonna go find the carnival manager and see where everything stands."

Maverick nodded. "Grab me if you need me. I'll be around until about quarter 'til five." Assuming he could actually sit still for that long when he knew that Slater would be going to the model home today for Alexa's presentation. That fact had him absolutely itching to ride over there and park his bike on all that brand-new grass. They clasped hands, and then Mav sat for another minute and emptied his drink.

Everything was finally coming together—for the carnival. For Mrs. H's move. Even for him and Alexa. His thoughts drifted to the other night, making love to her in the moonlight by the pond. How her words had hit him square in the chest and made him *want*. Her. Them. Everything. More than ever before. They were so close to having her ex behind them that Maverick could taste it. And then he'd be free to lay it all on the line.

So all the news was as good as it could be.

Maverick's gaze scanned over the colorful rides, the bright food carts, and the festive strings of lights swaying in crisscrosses above the whole grounds. Music played over the track's sound system, and men talked and laughed as they worked. Everything was normal. Good. Exactly what it should be.

All of which made him wonder why his gut was still so tied up in knots.

CHAPTER 26

"Thanks Mike," Alexa said, hopping out of the prospect's car in front of the model home. She'd forgotten to pack a lunch this morning, so Mike had run her out to grab a sandwich before the walk-through with Grant, the general contractor, and the sales team. They would all be arriving soon.

"Any time, Alexa," the newest Raven said. "Call us if you need us. We're hanging out two minutes away."

She gave him a nod as he pulled a U-ey in front of the house. Holding her stomach, she frowned. The big rock sitting there at the thought of seeing Grant again said maybe she should've skipped lunch, but she wasn't sure when they were going to fit in eating dinner with moving her mother tonight.

Everything will be fine. You won't be alone with him.

Right.

On a sigh, she made her way inside. The cool air wrapped

around her, helping her stomach just a little, as did the calm, relaxing vibe of the home's design. The place made her want to sit down and stay awhile. And for the four-hundred-thousand-dollar price tag associated with this particular model, she hoped it made a lot of people feel that way.

She stowed her purse and washed her hands, then grabbed her clipboard from the sales office and made another pass through the house. Grant loved perfection. In fact, maybe it was the only thing he truly loved. And in this one instance, she was determined to give it to him. Everything had to be just right for the walk-through. Maybe then he'd see that she could be valuable to him without becoming his wife and just let her go.

She began in the basement, which featured a big rec room, an exercise room, and a media room that looked like a little theater. She checked the finishes, paint job, placement of furniture, and double-checked her punch sheet. Next, she made her way through the living spaces on the main floor. She fixed the plantation shutters on the library windows, making sure all the slats lined up just so because she knew that even one out of place would drive Grant crazy.

Thump.

She froze, her ears going on alert. People were arriving for the walk-through already? She'd thought she had another ten or fifteen minutes. She went to the front door and peered outside, but there weren't any cars in the driveway.

Damn nerves. They had her jumpy and anxious. Feeling time getting away from her, Alexa rushed up the steps to run through the bedrooms, bathrooms, and upstairs laundry room.

At the far end of the hallway, she pushed through the double doors of the master bedroom—and stopped short.

For a moment, her eyes couldn't make sense of what she

was seeing. Rose petals on the bed. Candles flickering on the nightstands and dresser. The low strains of jazz music playing from the built-in stereo system.

What in the world? As it all started to make a crazy, surreal sense to her, she gasped and turned—and ran right into Grant's chest so hard she dropped the clipboard.

"Alexa," he said, his voice casual, happy even.

She reeled back, putting distance between them. "What are . . . what the hell are you doing? What is all this?"

"It's for you," he said, his body filling the doorway.

"For God's sake, Grant, the walk-through starts in ten minutes." Her hands fisted at her sides, hopefully hiding her shakiness.

He shook his head. "I moved it to tomorrow morning."

"What?" She pulled out her cell phone and checked her email. "I didn't get any message about rescheduling."

He grinned. He actually grinned and it was a sickening thing to her. "I wanted to surprise you."

Her mind was spinning, trying to reject the insanity of all this. "With what? Some kind of cheesy seduction scenario? This is my place of work."

"What if it was more than that?" He came closer, his body loose, his mannerisms relaxed.

Still, she retreated further into the big bedroom, her scalp prickling. "Meaning what?" she asked, not sure she really wanted to know.

"What if this place was yours, ours? I know you've always loved it. My house is ours, of course, but I lived there alone first. If we moved here, it could be ours together from the beginning. A fresh start." He said all this like it made perfect sense. And maybe a month ago, it would've. But too much had happened. Too much had changed, for her. Now it just felt . . . creepy.

Unhinged, she heard Haven's voice say.

Get out of here! The thought shivered over her skin.

"I don't even know what to say to you right now." Shaking her head, she pressed her thumb to the fingerprint security button on her phone, bringing it to life. She opened her text messages to send the message already typed out there, the one she'd written just in case but never really thought she'd have to use. Her finger moved for the *Send* button—

Grant swiped the phone from her hand. "Focus, Alexa," he said, slipping her cell into his pocket. "Focus on us. This is important." For the first time, anger slipped into his voice.

"Okay, okay," she said, her voice high and strained. She jumped back from his touch. Shit. *Shitshitshit*. Had her text gone through? If not, she was going to have to run for it. But where would she even go that he couldn't get to her? The office. She could lock herself in and use the business line. But that meant she had to get him farther into the room to create an open path to the door. "Um, I'm just . . . this is a lot."

"I know, babe. But I thought maybe a grand gesture would show you how serious I am, how much I want you back and in my life." He came closer. Her legs hit the mattress and she stumbled, coming to sit on the edge of the bed.

Her ears strained for the sound of a car or motorcycle, but the bedroom was at the back of the house. She didn't hear a thing. Oh, God, what if no one was coming to help?

"It's a thoughtful gesture, Grant," she said, her stomach queasy at sitting among the scattering of red petals. She tried to keep her words kind, her tone placating, unsure exactly what kind of man she was talking to and feeling like maybe she'd never known Grant Slater at all. "But too much has happened. You've scared me on multiple occasions. I can't live like that and I don't feel the same way anymore. You're handsome, successful, and talented. You deserve someone who can love you with her whole heart. Who can be everything you want in a woman. That's not me. And you don't need it to be—women will be lining up to date you—"

"I don't want another woman, Alexa. I want *you*." He stood right in front of her, his knees almost touching hers.

Everything inside her screamed to flee. "Why? I'm nothing, just like you said. I'm a poor girl who was a lowly administrative assistant when we met."

"You're *my* fiancée. That's all there is to it," he said.

She was a possession to him, and that's all she was. One he didn't want to lose. Shaking her head, her thoughts swam. She had to get some space between them. "I, um . . ." She cleared her throat. "I could really use some water."

His expression transformed from angered to pleased, like he was glad that she was asking him for something, anything, and not just rejecting his overtures. "Of course," he said, making for the bathroom. "I knew you'd come around. I knew I had to try. Because I believe in making my own luck, securing my own destiny, not waiting for others to do it for me."

So would she.

She shot off the bed and bolted for the door, time suddenly going all slow-mo even as she raced. Down the hall. Down the stairs. Footsteps pounded after her.

"So help me, Alexa!" Grant bellowed.

OhGodohGodohGod.

Her flat sandal slipped on the tiles in the foyer, but she regained her footing and kept moving. Grant was closing in. She'd never make the office.

She grabbed the front door handle and pulled. It swung open.

Something yanked her hair and she wrenched back. She crashed into Grant, and then they both went down. Pain exploded through her as she crashed in a free fall against the hard floor.

"Ungrateful bitch," he groaned, flipping her over and

crawling on top of her. "You'll learn to do what I say." He ground his erection against her thigh.

Nausea rolled through her as she pushed and twisted with her whole body. "No, Grant. Get off of me. This is crazy. *You're* being crazy."

He pinned her wrists to the floor, squeezing tight. Pain shot through her fingers. "Don't call me that," he growled. "And don't make this harder than it has to be."

He kissed her. Hard. Their teeth knocked, making her mouth throb. He pressed in, trying to force her jaw open. She worked to draw up her knees, to brace the flats of her feet on the floor, to turn her head away. But he held her so tight.

Click.

Grant froze and Alexa's eyelids flipped open. The barrel of a gun dug into Grant's temple.

Alexa nearly cried in relief.

"Get. Off of her. Right now. Before I blow your fucking brains out." Maverick. Maverick was here. Oh, God, Maverick.

When Grant didn't move fast enough, he suddenly flew off of her.

On a groan, Alexa pushed up onto an elbow to see Mike and Blake holding Grant by the shoulders and arms in the doorway. She hurt everywhere.

Maverick crouched at her side and gently helped her stand, his gun still aimed at Grant. "You okay?" he asked her, maybe never looking more fierce in his entire life.

"Yeah. Um, yeah." She was shaking so badly it was hard to think. "I just um . . ." She swayed.

Maverick caught her. "Sit him down and keep him secured," he bit out at the other Ravens. The men manhandled Slater over to the bottom of the stairs and forced him down. "Let's get you outside." Mav helped her onto the little porch.

She sagged down onto the top brick step, unable to do anything else. "If you . . . if you hadn't . . ."

"I'm here. You're good. I've got you." His gaze ran over her face, his expression equal parts enraged and concerned. "Just rest for a minute, okay?" He rose.

"Don't hurt him," she said, her teeth chattering. "Don't do . . . anything that will get you in trouble. He's not worth it."

Maverick scowled but nodded. "Much as I'd love to beat the shit out of him, I have a better plan." He whipped out his cell, swiped his finger over the screen, and put it to his ear. "Yeah, I'd like to report that I've just interrupted an attack on a woman. I have the attacker restrained and need immediate police assistance. And an ambulance." He eyeballed her and moved the phone away from his mouth. "Don't you worry about a thing, Alexa. This time, Slater's fucking done."

Alexa gaped. As if it wasn't miracle enough that Maverick had showed up just when it mattered, his self-restraint in dealing with Grant was frankly a miracle, too. Maverick still had a temper, but five years ago, he'd have solved this problem with his fists first. Now, he was thinking strategically, thinking long-term, which meant he'd grown up a helluva lot in the past five years. But she actually had lots of evidence of that, didn't she? She saw it in the care he took of his house, the way he kept himself in check, the way he was taking care of her and her mom.

It made Alexa feel calmer. Safe. Secure.

Which was all she'd ever wanted.

MAVERICK'S BLOOD WAS boiling, but he wasn't giving Slater the satisfaction of seeing it.

Standing in the front doorway where he could keep an eye on both Slater and Alexa, Mav was doing everything he could to keep himself reined in. Blake and Renner stood on either side of Slater, keeping him from moving a muscle.

Renner had ensured that by pulling down some sort of cord from the dining room curtains and tying Slater's hands to the bannister.

"I am going to sue you each individually and then take your little club for every cent it's got. And then I'm going to bulldoze every inch of the Raven Riders property until no one remembers you even existed." Slater chuffed out a chilling laugh. "I will ruin you and everything you ever cared about. You don't know who you messed with."

Maverick tuned him out. His words just made him angrier, but Mav was already savoring the sweet satisfaction of watching Grant Slater get arrested. That would have to be reward enough.

Instead of taking Slater's bait, Maverick kept his gaze on Alexa. Except for the occasional, random shudders, she sat shock-still on the stoop, her arms around herself.

Jesus, what if he hadn't gotten here when he did? What if he hadn't left the track way earlier than he had to? Knowing Alexa would be seeing Slater at her meeting, Maverick had come to hang with Blake and Renner until it was over, and then he'd planned to drop by here to check on her.

I need your help at the model home right now.

The memory of all three of them receiving that message at the same time still made Maverick's blood run cold.

Sirens sounded in the distance. Closer. Until, finally, three cop cars turned onto the street and parked haphazardly in front of the house.

"Now you're going to pay," Slater bit out. "Home invasion. Carrying a weapon. Assault. False imprisonment. You're done, Rylan. All of you."

"Do you ever shut up?" Maverick muttered, and then he stowed his handgun in a holster against his lower back and went into the yard to meet Martin.

"What happened?" Martin asked, rushing up onto the grass. Davis came running up beside him, a glower covering his weasel face. A rookie cop joined them—Eckstein, his name tag read.

"First, I need to tell you that I have a concealed carry license and I'm carrying at the small of my back," Maverick said, wanting to play this a hundred percent by the book.

Martin nodded. "I know, but thank you. Start talking." Davis threw scowls at both of them.

As an ambulance pulled up, Maverick recounted Alexa's text message and what he'd seen when they'd arrived— Grant, pinning a crying Alexa to the floor of the model home, forcibly kissing her while she struggled and said "no." Saying the words brought the images back to life in his mind's eye, fueling the lethal anger vibrating inside him.

"We tied Slater up inside until you could arrive to arrest him," Maverick said. Davis blanched. They all moved toward the house, following a pair of paramedics who stopped in front of Alexa and started asking questions.

Slater began ranting louder, but Martin didn't pay him any mind. Staying out of the medics' way, the cop sat next to her. "Hey, Alexa. Can you tell me what happened?"

Maverick was torn—he needed to hear it. Every word of it. But no part of him *wanted* to hear it. None of this was about him, though, was it? It was about taking care of Alexa, whatever she needed.

She blinked at them and frowned, her expression almost confused. "Um." She let the paramedics check her vitals, and then she peered at Martin again. "I came back from lunch and found Grant in the master bedroom upstairs. He'd put rose petals on the bed and lit candles." She licked her lips, the sound thick. "He said a bunch of stuff about giving me this house to get me back, and then he took my phone when I tried to text Maverick for help."

"We got the message," Maverick said, trying to send her

encouragement through his eyes. And thank fuck that they had. If Mav had waited to come to the house until after he thought the meeting would be over . . . He couldn't even finish the thought.

"He refuses to accept my decision on calling off our engagement. He just kept trying to convince me that we could start over. The whole thing felt very creepy. When I had the chance, I ran from the room and down the stairs. I managed to get the front door open, but he caught me in the foyer and threw me to the floor." She shuddered.

Slater was a sick fuck, that much was for sure. Between planting the tires and oil on their property, blackmailing her, and now this, the guy was either losing touch with reality or was pure evil. Maverick wasn't sure which was worse. Jesus, this could've been so much worse than it was, and it was already damn bad. He could've lost her. God, he could've lost her.

Emotion welled inside him. Something bigger than the anger and the desire for vengeance. Something brighter. Something far more powerful.

Love.

But more than that. He didn't just love Alexa Harmon; he was head over fucking heels in love with her. He'd known he had feelings for her, of course—hell, they'd never gone away despite their years apart. But what he'd *thought* he'd felt before this moment was the dim sliver of the moon compared to the burning midday sun that he knew for sure he felt for her now.

If he'd have lost her this time, she would've taken him with her.

"Did you hit your head, miss? Can you tell us where it hurts?" one of the paramedics asked.

"Here," she said, gingerly touching the left side of her head. "I fell flat and hard. Everything kinda hurts, but I don't think anything's broken."

"What's this?" the medic asked, taking her hand. Bruises. Her wrist was ringed with bruises.

Rage flashed like molten lava through Maverick's blood. "Sonofabitch," Mav bit out.

Martin held up a hand to him and said in a low voice, "Let's get a picture of that."

"I told him to get off of me but he pinned me to the floor and kissed me and told me not to make it harder than it had to be." Maverick tilted his head as she spoke, noticing how flat and monotone her voice had gone. God, why hadn't he killed Slater when he'd had the chance again? They all could've lied. Called it self-defense. No one would've known otherwise.

The paramedic checked Alexa's eyes, examined her head, and asked her more questions.

"I'm gonna check out the bedroom," Martin said, rising. Davis made for the door as well.

"I'm going, too," Maverick said.

Martin frowned. "Mav—"

"Slater has the mayor, that asshole"—he pointed at Davis—"and at least one judge in his pocket, so if you think I'm not going to see what happened up there with my own eyes before evidence starts disappearing right and left, you're out of your mind." He arched a brow.

Davis put a hand on Martin's chest. "Martin, he can't—"

"Can it, Davis. He's coming. Just don't touch anything, either of you."

Mav could do that. He nailed Davis with a stare that challenged him to do something about it until the fucker finally looked away. Then the three of them went upstairs. Eckstein stayed with Slater, who was getting more and more outraged by the minute because no one had yet spoken to him. Or untied him.

The master bedroom was just as Alexa had described. The rose petals were like blood droplets on the floor and bed, sending a chill over his skin. "Every single thing she said checks out," Maverick said. "She sure as fuck didn't smash her own head against the floor or bruise her own wrists. And Blake, Mike, and I saw him forcing himself on her when we got here, so you've got three witnesses. I don't care how goddamned prominent Slater is in this community, do your jobs." He nailed both cops with a hard stare.

Martin nodded and placed a call on the radio attached to his shoulder, then he looked at the two of them. "Out of the room. I need to take pictures."

After a few minutes, they all made their way back downstairs, and Martin paused in front of Slater. He patted the guy down and found a cell in his pocket.

"That's Alexa's," Maverick said, recognizing the watercolor graphic on the case.

Martin set it aside and nodded. "Grant Slater, you're under arrest for the sexual assault and battery of Alexa Harmon. You have the right to remain silent. Anything you say can and will be used against you in a court of law. You have the right to speak to an attorney, and to have an attorney present during any questioning. Do you understand your rights as I've presented them to you?"

Red-faced, Slater just shook his head like he couldn't believe this wasn't going his way. Martin cuffed Slater, then worked to untie the ropes.

Maverick had seen enough. "Can I get Alexa out of here?"

Martin nodded. "I can follow up with her if I need to."

Outside, Mav found the paramedics packing up their bags. "She's refusing transport to the hospital," one of the men said. "There's a possibility of a head injury, though. She may have a headache, sleepiness, or feel nauseous. Those would all be expected. But if she loses coordination and balance, gets dizzy, or starts vomiting, take her to the emergency department immediately."

"Why don't you go, Alexa?" Maverick asked, crouching down next to her. "Just to be sure."

Just then, Martin hauled Slater out and down the steps. Her ex glared at Alexa, and Maverick put his body between them until he was out of sight, working like hell to keep his own anger under wraps.

Alexa shuddered. "I just want to go home."

"Okay," Maverick said. He gave the medic a nod. "Then let's get you home. This is all over now. Slater can't hurt you anymore."

CHAPTER 27

itting on the couch in Maverick's house, Alexa
hung up the phone. Telling her mother what'd happened was the only way to make her understand why they
couldn't move her tonight. But going through the story and
answering all the questions again left Alexa feeling utterly
drained.

Never in a million years would she have thought Grant
would get that violent . . . or twisted. And who knew what
more he would've done if Maverick and the guys hadn't
shown up?

Maverick sat down beside her and held out a steaming
mug and two little pills. "Here, Al. Try a little of this."

"What is it?" she asked. The ceramic was warm in her
hands, and the heat felt good.

"Just chicken noodle soup and some ibuprofen. I
thought . . ." He shrugged. "I don't know. It might help."

Aw, sweet, sweet man. She tossed back the medicine and

washed it down with a big sip of the salty broth. "It's perfect, Mav." She took another sip, and another, hoping the soup would warm the icy chill that filled her chest. "Aren't you going to eat?"

"I'm not worried about me right now," he said.

"Well, I am."

"Don't be." He tucked her hair behind her ear. "As long as you're good, I'm good."

"I don't know if I'm good or not." Sip.

"You don't have to know right now. But you're here and you're safe and Slater's behind bars. So that's a start." His eyes blazed a dark blue intensity that seemed to peer into her soul.

The fierceness of his words chased off a little of that chill, like he was wielding a pickax and chipping away the pieces of Grant that her ex had left behind inside her. It was a terrifying, nauseating image and immediately chased away her appetite. She set the mug on the coffee table.

"How can I help?" he asked.

She tried to give him a smile. "You already are." Finding it hard to hold his gaze, she ducked her chin and stared at her lap, at the navy capris and sheer patterned blouse over a tank that she'd worn to work today. Knowing Grant had touched the clothing repulsed her. "I want to take a shower."

"Yeah. Okay. That sounds like a good idea." He gave her a hand up and walked her to the bathroom. Worry poured off of him like a waterfall, the force of it too intense and soothing at the same time.

"I won't be long," she said, peering at him around the door.

"However long you need."

Nodding, she pushed it closed. Avoiding her reflection, she undressed. Balled up her clothes and stuffed them in the little trash can. Turned on the water. Waited for it to heat. Got in.

She cleaned herself mechanically, barely feeling the spray against her skin. Her soapy hands found a bruise on her hip. One on her ribs. One on her shoulder. And each little jolt of pain chipped away more pieces of Grant. A bruise on her forehead. On her wrist. On her elbow. *Chip, chip, chip.*

Each piece of him that sloughed off exposed more of her, raw and vulnerable and unbearably sensitive.

It was suddenly like someone had plugged Alexa back into her body. Because all the pieces of *her* snapped into place in one instant so that she felt *everything*. Every bit of it. The fear and the pain and the despair and the disbelief and the shock. Her head throbbed. Her aches were a pulsing agony. It was too much.

Toomuchtoomuchtoomuch.

A sob ripped out of her, and Alexa clapped a hand over her mouth as it folded her in half and finally forced her to her knees. She slid into a ball on the slick bottom of the tub, hugging her legs and burying her face into her knees as she cried. Grant was like a poison inside her she had to release, and every tear cleaned her, disinfected her, set her free.

So she gave herself over to it. One last time. Just until Grant was completely gone from her psyche the way he was from her life. And then she'd never let him have a piece of her again.

"I DON'T KNOW how I didn't kill him," Maverick said into his cell phone. "I probably fucking should've." Rage and regret were like viruses in his blood, running rampant through him and laying waste to everything in their paths. Damnit. He'd known Slater could do something like this. He should've pushed Alexa harder not to go to work. He should've stayed at the house himself. He should've done so many things that might've kept this from happening.

It was failing his mother all over again, only worse.

"I get that," Dare said, "but going after Slater only leads to one result that matters—you locked up. Do I have to worry about you staying smart?"

Pacing the living room, Maverick blew out a frustrated breath. "No. I called the cops and did it by the book. And now he's the one spending a night behind bars, the fucker." The drumming of the shower water sounded out, and Mav had to resist the urge to go to Alexa and reassure himself that she was really there, in his house, safe.

"Good. Because this is probably gonna get messier for her before it gets better." Dare's voice was gruff, tired.

"That much is clear," Maverick agreed. "I'm going to talk to her about filing a protective order in the morning." Though, given who Slater was, who knew how well local law enforcement would follow through on actually, you know, enforcing it. Still, it was better to have the legal paperwork in place. And it would be damn satisfying to imagine Slater getting served.

"Worth doing," Dare said. "But don't count on that to resolve the situation."

"I won't. Not even a little," Maverick said. He stopped in front of the big window that looked out over the backyard and the sunlit pond beyond. He couldn't quite make out the fire pit where he'd made love to Alexa—and where she'd made love to him—he believed that into his very bones. But he didn't have to see it to feel the impact of what they'd shared and what he felt for her.

Everything.

And damnit, he wanted to tell her. That he loved her, that he wanted her for his own, that he wanted forever. With her. But he also didn't want the memory of those declarations to be mired in the pain that Slater had caused. Fuck, he wasn't sure which was the right way to play it.

"Did you hear me?" Dare asked.

"Shit, no. Sorry."

"I asked how she's doing," Dare said.

Maverick shook his head. "I'm not sure. She's mostly holding it together, but I think she's in shock. He slammed her to the ground pretty good, so she's also hurting. Got bruises on the side of her face and some other places." *Afuckinggain.* "She'll be okay, but she's still processing."

"Yeah," Dare said. "Christ. I'm sorry, Maverick. And Haven is, too. She asked me to let Alexa know that she's here for her."

"Thanks. I'm sure she'll appreciate hearing that." And he did, too, the way everyone was embracing Alexa again. It meant a lot to him. A long pause, and everything building up inside him demanded some form of release. "Shit. I'm . . . I'm fighting for her, D. I'm all in. And I'm not letting anything stand in the way this time."

A satisfied sigh, like maybe Dare had been holding his breath, came down the line. "About goddamned time, my brother. About goddamned time." Someone called to Dare in the background. "Listen, I gotta go. Dinner's on. Assume you all aren't coming." It wasn't a question.

"No," Mav said. "And we shifted moving her mother until tomorrow morning, so I won't make it to help finish setting up until later in the day." Maverick wasn't sure whether to regret the carnival's poor timing or hope that it might provide Alexa with a welcome distraction. Either way, the Ravens needed it, and they needed it to be a success.

"We've got it covered. Phoenix pulled this shit together like a boss."

"Yeah, he did," Mav said. "Catch you tomorrow."

"Wait. Mav?"

"Yeah?" he asked.

"Don't you dare blame yourself for this." Dare's voice was gruff, stern, and Maverick could easily imagine the expression that went with it. He'd seen it on his cousin's face a million times. "I know Alexa's situation is probably screwing with your head given what Bunny went through, but this isn't your fault. Wasn't then and it isn't now."

But Maverick couldn't get there. Not yet. Not when Alexa wore fresh bruises he might've prevented. "I hear ya, D." They hung up. Maverick stood there for a long moment, his ears latching onto the sound of the running water once more. Was it just him being an anxious, impatient fucker or had Alexa been in there a long damn time?

Something in his gut twisted, pushing him in the direction of a long damn time.

He made for the bathroom. Knocked. No answer. Knocked again.

His gut went on a free fall.

Maverick opened the bathroom door. Steam hung thick in the air. "Alexa, you okay?"

And that was when he heard it. Crying.

The sound lashed at him and lanced urgency through his blood. He was at the tub's edge in an instant and pulled back the curtain. Seeing her in a tight ball on the floor nearly broke his fucking heart.

In a flash, Maverick turned off the water, grabbed a towel, and draped it around her shoulders. "Come here, baby." He slid his arms under her knees and around her back.

Crying harder, Alexa wound her arms around his neck, making it easier for him to lift her from the tub. "Maverick," she cried, her wet face burrowed into his neck.

"I got you. Don't you worry about a thing."

Water ran from her hair and body, soaking into his shirt and dripping down his arms, but he didn't care. He turned out of the bathroom and carried her down the hall, past the guest bedroom to his own room. Because fuck the guest bedroom. If the two of them were going to make a run at doing this thing again, they were doing it in *his* bed. Their bed, now.

Alexa wasn't a guest to him. She would never be a guest to him. Because this house was where she belonged—and always had. They'd both just gotten lost for a while. But that was all fucking over.

In his room, Maverick settled her on the edge of the bed and pulled back the covers. He kicked off his boots and shrugged off his cut, then settled his gun on the nightstand. "Climb in, Al."

Her breath hitching, she squeezed at the length of her hair with the towel. "But I'm wet."

"You're perfect. Climb in."

She moved to the center and slipped her pretty, long legs under the covers. Masculine satisfaction roared through him at seeing her there, but he had to rein that shit in. Hard. After what'd happened to her today, he wasn't touching her until she indicated that she was ready. Anyway, despite his hard-on, what he needed more than anything was to help Alexa feel safe. Fuck, he needed that more than his next breath. To protect her, to comfort her, to be her shelter in the storm.

Maverick stretched out and pulled her in tight against the side of his body.

Meow.

He looked to the doorway to find Lucy standing there, eyeballing them in her skull sweater.

"Come on, Luce," he said. "Your mama needs us."

The cat padded across the room, hesitated at the side of the bed, then jumped up. She sniffed and stepped, sniffed and stepped, until she stood on his stomach within reach of Alexa's petting hand. And then Lucy curled up on his belly and fell asleep while Alexa stroked her ears.

And Christ, it was probably stupid, but protectiveness roared through Maverick like a demon. Because this felt like his little family. His woman. Their weird-ass cat. Their house.

"Fall asleep if you want to," Maverick said, running his fingers through the loose waves of her damp hair. "I'll wake you up every so often to make sure your head's okay."

"I don't know if I can sleep."

"You can."

She shook her head in a small movement that was just barely perceptible. "I'm afraid."

Her words were like getting sucker punched in the heart. "Don't be," he managed. "Slater's in jail. I've got my gun sitting right here. Nothing's going to hurt you, Alexa, I promise."

"You'll stay awake . . ."

He heard what she didn't say. *You'll stay awake just to be sure?*

"I'll stay awake. You sleep. I'll keep you safe. Count on it."

She drifted off in maybe five seconds, and that had satisfaction roaring through him, too. She was scared, she felt vulnerable, and yet his words and his body had given her the security she needed to let go. The trust and belief that represented staggered him. Just nearly knocked him stupid.

And it made him realize he'd do anything not to break his word.

The conversation with Dare came back to him. Yeah, Maverick would be smart. He wouldn't be the one to start shit. But if Slater came after her again, he sure as hell would be the one to finish it.

CHAPTER 28

Despite being woken up over and over again, Alexa opened her eyes to the early morning sunlight and felt . . . better. Stronger. Freer. For the horrible things Grant had tried to do to her, he was now in jail. And the more she thought about what'd happened yesterday, the more she realized that she'd been stronger and braver than she had in a long, long time. She hadn't caved in to him. She hadn't cowered and fallen apart. She'd schemed. She'd run. She'd fought. And she'd recounted every bit of it to the authorities.

That was more than she ever would've done before.

"Hey. You awake?" Maverick's voice was low, gravelly, sexy.

She shifted to see him better. Dirty blond hair that he'd clearly been running his hands through. Scruff covering his jaw. A face full of hard angles. God, he was beautiful to her. "Yeah. You must be exhausted, though."

He shook his head. "I'm fine. How you feeling?"

Alexa still had some achiness, and she couldn't deny the small throb in the side of her head. But all of that would go away. And she'd still be free of Grant—and that made her freaking ecstatic. "Actually, I feel pretty decent. Nothing some ibuprofen can't fix."

He arched a brow, his gaze running over her face like he was analyzing her words. "Really? I was thinking you could rest here and I could take care of moving your mom. You'd be safe. Dare offered to come hang." He gestured to his cell sitting on the nightstand next to his gun.

She pushed up on an elbow. For a long moment, she just soaked him in. The thoughtfulness of his words shot right to her heart. The raw emotion in his dark blue eyes wrapped around her and made her feel so cared for and safe. And his scruff made her want to feel it against her thighs.

She cupped his face in her hand, settling for feeling the beginnings of his beard against her palm. For now. "That's not necessary, but thank you. I feel a lot better. And honestly? I'm done feeling bad over Grant Slater. Today is all about new beginnings, starting with moving Mom. And I want to be there for her."

His eyes searched hers. After a moment, he nodded and pressed a kiss to her palm. "In case it needs to be said, you handled yesterday like a champ. It about fucking killed me to see—" He shook his head. "But you called us and you ran and you were fighting. When we got there, we saw you. I was terrified but proud of you, too. And I know you're hurting right now but you survived, Alexa. You survived that and you survived him and even if there's other bullshit to deal with, you're out the other side."

His fierceness built her up and bolstered her resolve. "You make me stronger, Maverick."

"You're strong on your own." He kissed her palm again. "Don't forget it."

She swallowed hard, love and need for this man shooting through her fast and urgent. Alexa shifted her naked body on top of his, her knees settling on either side of his hips. "I won't. And you can remind me if I do."

"Better believe I will." As he peered up at her, his eyes flashed hot. His hands landed on the outsides of her thighs. "You sure?"

She ground against the bulge of his cock. "Of this? Of *you*? Always." Bracing her hands on his pillow, she leaned down and kissed him.

The groan he unleashed seemed connected to her clit, because desire suddenly had her aching there. Aching with need and lust and longing. She sucked on his tongue, and his hands went to her hips and ground her down harder against his erection. The rough denim rubbed maddeningly against her clit, making her gasp into the kiss.

"Want you," she whispered into his mouth. "Want you so much."

"Fuck, baby. Lay on your stomach." He helped her push the pillows and covers out of the way, and then she stretched out in the center of the bed. He climbed off and tore his shirt over his head. She watched as he undid his jeans and shoved them down his lean hips, his cock jutting out hard and thick. Looking at her like he wanted to make a meal of her, he wrapped his hand around the base and stroked, once, twice, three times. "Christ, you're beautiful."

"I need you inside of me," she said, licking her lips at the sight of him. Inked and rough and hard. For her.

He came over her, his knees on the outside of her thighs. "You're gonna be so fucking tight like this." His hand slipped between her legs, and she arched her back to give him better access. "Feel that," he said, his fingers finding her wetness, sinking deep. "So wet for me."

"Yes," she said, her voice breathy and needy. "Now, Maverick."

Holding her ass cheeks open, his head lined up with her core and penetrated her pussy inch by mind-blowing inch. A moan spilled out of her as he bottomed out, his hands bracing on her lower back, forcing her to arch further.

"Christ, Alexa, *feel that*." The arousal in his voice spiked her pulse.

"It's so good. But I need you to move. Oh, God. Fuck me. Please." Her words were almost shaky with need.

He withdrew and thrust, withdrew and thrust, slow, dragging movements that had her panting and pushing back against him and aching for him to go deeper, harder, faster. "My cock looks so goddamned good sliding in and out of you."

She felt herself get wetter around him, and it ratcheted up the urgency of her yearning. "More. Give me more."

"More of what, baby?" He came down on top of her, his whole weight covering her, his cock buried deep.

She looked over her shoulder. "More of you. More of everything. Don't hold back, Maverick."

"Al—"

"*Everything.*"

"Fuck." He claimed her mouth in a short, searing kiss. "Everything," he gritted out. And then he did just as she asked. He wrapped his arms around her head and shoulders for leverage and took her like a man possessed. Like a man taking what was his. And that's what she wanted more than anything. His hips flew and slammed against her ass. His cock deliciously battered a spot inside her that had her moaning nonstop. His body covered and claimed every part of hers.

It was the most amazing thing she'd ever felt.

"Christ, I'm gonna come," he rasped.

"Come," she said, wanting to feel him pulsing inside of her. "Come in me, Maverick."

The roar he unleashed shoved her hard in the direction of

her own orgasm, as did the way his cock jerked inside her again and again. And then he was off of her. Flipping her over. Pinning her hips down and planting his mouth right over her clit.

He sucked, *hard*. His tongue flicking and strumming until all she could do was fist her hands in his hair and hold her breath.

Alexa came so hard that her vision blurred around the edges and her heart threatened to pound out of her chest. But still, Maverick didn't let up. He growled against her and continued to tongue her until she was screaming another orgasm and trying to push him off before she lost her mind. She was so sensitive that when he finally released her, her whole body flinched and she couldn't help but laugh as she tried to roll away.

"Where do you think you're going?" he asked as he grabbed and crawled up her, wearing the most smug, satisfied expression perhaps any man had ever worn.

She couldn't help but grin. "Nowhere."

"That's right." He stroked her hair back off her face. "God it's good to hear you laugh."

They stared at each other a long moment, and suddenly their playfulness felt weighted, significant, like the ground was moving beneath their feet. For her, it was. Because emotion ballooned inside her chest until restraining it became simply impossible.

It was bigger than her, more than her. After everything, she had to tell him, and he deserved to know. "Maverick . . . I know we have a lot to figure out, and I know I'm a mess, but I also know that I love you so much that half the time I can barely breathe for holding it in. So I don't want to hold it in anymore. I love you. I'm in love with you." The hammering of her heart had nothing to do with the two incredible orgasms he'd just given her. "So, yeah. I just wanted you to know."

His eyes widened and his lips parted, and then his expression took on a softness she'd absolutely never seen before. "Aw, damn, Alexa. You have no idea what a fucking dream it is for me to hear you say that. I have never stopped loving you. Not one minute of one day. But what I feel now is so much deeper, just bigger, you know? Than anything I've ever felt before. I love you, too. Jesus."

His words—his love—healed every aching place inside her. Just snapped all the broken pieces back into place until she was whole, strong, the Alexa she was always meant to be. He kissed her, intense but gentle, claiming and healing, utter perfection.

"Are you mine, baby? Tell me you're mine," he rasped.

"I'm yours, Maverick." She ran her fingers through his hair, holding it back from his ruggedly handsome face. "I'm so yours."

"You own me. You gotta know that. Christ, I've wanted this for so long." He dropped his head to her shoulder.

The gravel in his voice reached into her chest and squeezed. She wrapped her arms around his big shoulders and held him.

Finally he looked at her again, his eyes bright and so full of love. For her. "This is our new beginning, Alexa. You and me."

"Against the world. I love you," she said, happier than she'd been in years. Happier than she ever thought she'd be again. And, God, she adored the happiness pouring off of him, too. She wasn't naïve enough to think that Grant was going to make her life easy, but there wasn't anything he could do to change this. Because Alexa had finally found herself and, through that, the man she truly needed.

MAVERICK WAS FLYING so goddamned high over the words he and Alexa had shared that not even spending the day with a very anxious Mrs. H schlepping her mountain of crap could touch how good he felt. Unbelievably, that mountain represented maybe a third of what the woman had in her house, but most of what they'd left behind was outright junk.

Only two things put a damper on how he was feeling. First, knowing Jagger was sitting in jail. It ate at Maverick like an itch he couldn't reach. He just had to trust that the Hard Ink guys and their private detective would find the evidence they needed to clear Jagger. It couldn't happen soon enough for Mav—for any of the Ravens. And second, the word that Grant had made bail. They knew it would happen, and they'd taken the time this morning to get the temporary protective order, but it was still a burr in his saddle to know that clearly guilty Grant got to walk while Jagger rotted. Justice was blind, Mav's ass.

At the new place now, they'd just finished unloading the moving truck. He, Alexa, and the movers had managed to get the boxes and furniture in the rooms where they needed to be, but the process of unpacking and really getting the house set up would take a while. At least Mrs. H was out of Slater's place for good.

Mav returned one of the dollies to the now-empty truck parked out in the driveway.

"That was a big job to get done," Alexa said, bringing him a glass of ice cold water. It was another hot one, but the weather was perfect—which boded well for the opening of the carnival tonight. "I'm so glad we got her out of there."

"Me too," he said, taking a big drink. The more ties Alexa severed with Grant, the better. So far that included the restraining order, moving her mother out of his house, and calling in sick to work. She hadn't pulled the trigger yet, but she'd pretty much come around to the conclusion that she was going to have to quit her job. Mav knew how much she liked what she did, and he hated that for her, hated that she was the one who was going to have to walk away when she'd done nothing wrong. "What else would you like to do here today?"

"I'm hoping that we can maybe set up her kitchen, bedroom, and enough of the living room so that she can watch TV. But I don't want to make us late for the carnival." She gingerly prodded the side of her head.

"You hurting?" he asked, his gut twisting.

"Just a little bit of a headache. Not too bad. Honestly, I feel too good from this morning to even care." Her smile was so damn pretty.

"From the orgasms or the *I love yous*?" He grinned and pulled her into his arms.

She chuckled. "Both were very nice."

"Nice? *Nice?* You screamed so loud you almost shattered glass."

Laughing, she smacked him in the shoulder. "I did not."

"Yeah you did. That memory will play in my head for *years*." He arched a brow at her, loving the humor shining from her hazel eyes.

"Okay, I totally did." She ducked her face against his chest.

"That's right. Don't be denying my skills." He kissed her head and grinned again, having too much fun with her. What a difference a fucking day made.

"Oh, my God." She pushed against his chest and retreated, pointing at him, and trying not to smile. "You are too full of yourself."

"I call it like I see it." He followed her toward the house.

She rolled her eyes and turned around, but he could tell her shoulders were shaking. "So, why don't you try your skills on the mess that is the living room? And I'll tackle the kitchen with Mom?"

He winked. "Consider it done. Because, skills."

She threw up her hand and made for the kitchen. Maverick couldn't stop smiling like an idiot. Getting everything you ever wanted did that to a man. No shame in that.

Three hours later, they'd achieved most of what Alexa had hoped for. Everything was put away in the kitchen cabinets and drawers, her mom's bed was made and clothes were all put away, and Maverick got the TV set up, cable connected, and furniture in place so she'd be comfortable. He even found her box of photo albums and set them out on the end table next to her favorite chair.

When he was done, Maverick leaned against the arch to the kitchen. "How's it feeling, Mrs. H?"

"It's a little overwhelming, but it's coming together. You kids did a lot today," she said. "And I know I was a pain in the ass."

He chuckled and winked at Alexa. "A Harmon be a pain in the ass? Never."

Her mom smiled, just what he was going for. "I suppose we have our moments, don't we?"

"Who doesn't?" Mav asked. "What else can I do?"

"I'd love to get all the empty boxes and packing material outside. You're going to have so much space here, Mom. Just wait and see." Alexa tore down one of the boxes, making it flat.

"You got it." He headed for the other end of the house and cleared out the bedroom and hallway first. By the time he emptied the living room, Alexa had taken care of the kitchen.

Smiling, Alexa passed him with an armful of bubble wrap. "We make a good team."

He kissed her. "Damn right we do. Want me to take that out?"

She shook her head. "I got it."

The moment Alexa stepped out the front door, her mom came into the living room. "How's she doing? Really."

"She's strong, Mrs. H. She's okay. You should ask her, though," he said.

"I did, but of course she doesn't want to worry me." She waved a hand. "But I'd like to take that Grant over my knee."

Maverick might pay good money to see that. "I understand the sentiment."

Cynthia eyeballed him. "You're good for her. You always were. Even when you were more of a hellion."

The comment drew a smile from him, but also made him think. "She's good for me, too. And I'm serious about her. That okay with you?"

She nodded. "All I ever wanted was for her to be happy. You make her happy, Maverick. That's more than good enough for me."

Alexa came back in and stopped short. Looking between them, she asked, "What's the matter?"

He chuckled and shook his head. "Nothing's the matter. We're just talking." He managed to keep his voice casual, even though her mom's words added to the high he was riding. Knowing she approved of them—of him—took a load off his mind. Because Maverick was already thinking in terms of forever. What to do with that, he didn't know. But they had time to figure it out.

"You kids should go. I know you have that carnival. I'm pretty beat and think I might just like to put my feet up for a while." She made her way to her chair and sank down. "Aw, look at you putting my books out." She ran her hands over the album on top of the stack and gave him a smile.

Alexa squeezed his arm as she passed him, and then she crouched beside her mother. "You sure you'll be okay by yourself? New house and everything?"

"I'm an old pro at being by myself. You go and have fun. You deserve it after everything." She held out her arms. "Give your mama a hug."

Mrs. H was so much more relaxed than she'd been earlier in the day that it gave Maverick hope that she'd be happy here, and he knew that would make Alexa happy, too.

"Okay," Alexa said, rising. "I'll check on you later."

"You don't have to do that. I'm just gonna watch some

shows and maybe work on unpacking some more." She pulled one of the photo albums into her lap which was something he'd seen her do when she was stressed or upset. So maybe she was hiding how she was feeling until they were gone. Fair enough. She was allowed to be stressed over such a big change—and on such short notice.

"All right then, Mrs. H, we'll get out of your hair for a while. But if you need anything, you call and we'll be here. Simple as." He nailed her with a stare so that she'd know he was serious.

"Don't worry." She pushed back in her recliner and stroked her hand over the album's cover.

Alexa gave her shoulder a squeeze. "I want you to be happy here, Mom."

"I think you did a good thing for me, Alexa. So thank you."

When Alexa turned toward him, the expression on her face nearly sucker punched him. Mrs. H wasn't much known for giving apologies or outwardly showing affection, and she'd given both to Alexa today in one form or another. Maverick knew what that meant and he was glad for her. Alexa deserved it, and she needed it right now, too.

She came right up to him. "So, do I get to dunk your butt tonight or what?"

He smirked. "Nope, I'm on tomorrow. But if you think you can take me down, bring it."

She grinned and arched a brow, her look full of sass. "Oh, I'm gonna take you down all right. But for tonight, I'll settle for you winning me lots of stuffed animals."

He nodded. "Challenge accepted. Let's go."

Outside, they made for his pickup truck. When she got in, Alexa turned to him. "You know, I'm glad the carnival's tonight. We need something happy and fun, a celebration."

He hauled her across the seat and pressed a careful kiss to the side of her head. "Yeah, we fucking do. We all do."

"I'm just sorry Jagger isn't here," she said, squeezing his

thigh. It meant a lot that she thought of his brother, because he felt the same way.

"Me, too, Al. But he's why we have to do this and do it right. We need this to be the big success he knew it could be. Tonight, we'll celebrate brotherhood, club, and family in his honor until we can get him out of there."

She nodded. "Thank you for everything today, Maverick. You were such a huge help and you were so good with Mom. I appreciate it."

"No thanks required, Al. It's what you do for someone you love." He gave her a look.

She leaned her head against his shoulder. "I adore the way that sounds."

So did he. He started the truck. "Good. Get used to it, baby. Because nothing's going to change it. Ever."

CHAPTER 29

'd say we have a huge fucking success on our hands,"
Maverick said, toasting with Dare and Phoenix under
one of the big tents. A bunch of the Ravens had claimed a
few tables where they could take turns grabbing dinner. He
and Alexa had just finished eating burgers and fries, which
might've been a bad decision given she wanted to ride the
Tilt-A-Whirl.

"We can use the good news. It's been a rough few weeks
for everyone," Dare said, looking out over the crowds filling the carnival grounds. Mav's gaze followed, his brain
half scanning for Slater, even though he knew he wasn't
there. They'd had the P.I. put a tail on him the second he
left the police station, and the guy had been directed to
notify them immediately if Slater came anywhere near the
Ravens' property.

Even though it wasn't even quite dark yet, more people
had shown up than they'd expected, and they'd actually had

to rent out the fallow cornfield from the farmer who owned the tract of land across the street from the racetrack for additional parking. That was saying something given the crowds they often entertained on busy race nights.

From the lines in Dare's face, it was clear that Jagger's absence weighed on him. Dare always tended to take the burden of the club's business—and all its members—on his shoulders. Always had. "There'll be more good news to come, too," Maverick said. "You know it."

"I know, but it can't come soon enough." He turned to Haven, sitting next to him on the picnic table bench. "Okay, what rides have you never ridden?"

She grinned like he hung the sun and the moon just for her, and Maverick loved seeing that. His cousin deserved it. And fuck if he hadn't seen a similar expression on Alexa's face when she looked at him. The realization made him feel ten feet tall. "The Tilt-A-Whirl and the Sea Dragon and the spinny thing that plays the music."

"The Gravitron?" he asked. She nodded. Did Dare turn a little green or did Mav imagine it? "Okay. It's a plan."

"Oh, let's ride the Tilt-A-Whirl together," Alexa said. The two women jumped up, excited by the idea.

"First one to hurl owes the other fifty bucks," Maverick said as he and Dare joined the women.

Dare chuckled. "I'm too fucking old for this shit," he said under his breath. "But I'll ride every goddamned thing here twice if it makes her happy."

Maverick understood the sentiment. He took Alexa's hand, linking their fingers. "Then let's do it. I'm curious to see what burgers and fries look like on the way back up."

Alexa and Haven laughed.

"That's disgusting, Maverick," Haven said. He winked at her.

People laughed, music played, bells and buzzers rang out, lights twinkled and flashed against the nearly dark sky.

Standing in line, Mav almost felt like a kid again. Hanging at a carnival on a summer night with his best friend and his girl. Life was good. Anything was possible. He slid his fingers into Alexa's hair and kissed her, long and lingering.

"What was that for?" she asked, smiling.

"Do I need a reason to kiss you?"

"Never," she said.

"Oh, there's Cora," Haven said, waving her arms.

The blonde joined them with Slider's boys in tow.

"My main men," Maverick said, holding up his hand for high fives. Ben jumped to hit his palm, and Sam attempted to put every bit of his strength into it. Maverick laughed at their antics.

"Maverick," Ben said in a rush. "We sat all the way at the back of the Sea Dragon and it feels like you're going to get dumped out of your seat when it's all the way up. It's so cool."

"That sounds awesome, Ben. What else did you ride?" he asked. The six-year-old recounted all his adventures in a fast jumble of words. The boy could barely contain his excitement. Mav was glad to see them happy and having fun. They'd had a rough few years, just like their dad. Speaking of . . . "Is Slider here?" he asked Cora.

"He's working parking right now, so I offered to take the boys around. Who's better to go to a carnival with than some awesome kids?" She grinned at Sam and Ben, and both of them beamed up at her.

"When can we play games?" Sam asked.

"I'm following you two. Just lead the way," she said. As the boys ran off, she threw all of them a wave.

Mav and Dare exchanged a look, and he could read the general tenor of his cousin's thoughts—worry, for Slider. But at least the guy was here. He'd shown up and pitched in. Maverick had no doubt that said as much about his loyalty to Jagger as anything else. And he had to respect that.

"Tickets, please," the man at the head of the line said. They handed them over and found two cars near each other.

"This is going to be so fun." Alexa leaned over and kissed him.

"If you keep doing that, it'll be a fucking blast," he said. She threw her head back and laughed.

Grinning, Maverick pointed at Dare. "Fifty bucks, brother." Dare flipped him off. And then they started moving.

Maverick couldn't remember the last time he'd laughed so hard. He hadn't entirely ruled out the possibility of puking, but between the look on Dare's face, Alexa absolutely howling and screaming in delight, and the way centripetal force glued her to his side, he was having a great damn time.

"That was fucking awesome," he said when they all got off. He clapped a greenish Dare on the back. "What are we riding next?"

They rode the Sea Dragon—though Dare called bullshit on the very back, which Haven was only too happy to accommodate. They rode the spinning teacups, which was a funny sight with them in their Ravens colors sitting in dainty pastel cups. They rode the Gravitron, where the floor dropped out from under them, rock music blaring in their ears. They walked through the house of mirrors, where Haven got stuck in a little path of mirrors and couldn't find her way out—a fact that made her want to go through it a second time. And then they made their way to the bumper cars.

"Now this is more my speed," Dare said.

"But you were so cute in the teacups, see?" She brought up a selfie she'd taken of them on her phone.

"Aw, that is really cute, Dare." Alexa grinned at him.

"Baby, don't show that shit around," Dare said, no heat in his words at all. Maverick busted out laughing. "You have no room to talk, motherfucker." Dare arched a brow at him.

Mav held up his hands, grinning and shaking his head. "I didn't say a word."

They finally got to their cars, each of them taking their own, and then somehow it ended up three on one, everyone coming after Mav.

"What the hell?" he said, laughing and dodging Alexa as she beelined straight for him. "You're supposed to be on my side."

"All's fair in bumper cars, Maverick. Deal with it." She rammed him.

"Aw, you're gonna pay, little girl. Just you wait." He went to turn the car, but Dare hit him next. The guy grinned like an idiot. Mav just shook his head.

After, Alexa wrapped herself around him. "I'm sorry I crashed my car into you."

He feigned a scowl and nailed her with a hot stare. Her playfulness was fucking sexy. "I think I know how you can make it up to me."

"Hey, Haven wants to do the Tilt-A-Whirl again," Dare said. "Catch ya later?"

"You bet," Mav said.

When they were alone, Alexa pushed up on tiptoes and put her mouth to his ear. "Does it involve me sucking your cock?" She gave him an innocent look.

"Jesus Christ," he bit out, the teasing words sending blood rushing south. "You better believe it does now."

She bit her lip, her look so full of desire that he wanted to take her behind one of the rides right this second. "Mmm, I'll look forward to that." She tugged his hand. "But first we need games and stuffed animals. And maybe cotton candy. Or a funnel cake."

"Whatever you want," he said, meaning that in every way he could.

"Oh, I love this one," she said, pulling him toward the game where you shot water into the mouth of a clown to blow up and pop a balloon. They plunked down their money and took up the last two guns side by side.

Alexa lined up her shot like her life depended on it, and then the game began.

Ding ding ding!

"I won! Oh, my God, I won!" she cried.

"Yes, you did," Mav said. "What are you going to pick?"

The man pointed to her three options for an extra-large prize. "You get to pick from the black bear, the dinosaur, or the llama."

She turned to him. "Which one do you like?"

He peered up at them. "I don't know. That llama's ridiculous, though."

"Oh, yay. That's the one I like, too. I'll take the llama."

The man handed it to her, all two and a half feet of fucking weird-ass llama. To go with her cat. Mav chuckled. Who even knew they made llama stuffed animals?

"It's for you," she said.

"You won me a llama?" He looked at it skeptically as she pushed it against his chest. The eyeball on the one side of its head wouldn't stop looking at him.

"Yes! You totally do not have enough llamas in your life." She absolutely glowed with happiness.

"That is true, Al. Thank you. I think." He tucked the huge toy under his arm. People looked at him weird as he carried it around, the tall neck sagging this way and that. He just smiled.

"But now I have to win you something. Let's play that." He pointed to the dart game.

"Pop three in a row, win a large prize," the man yelled. "That's a mighty fine llama you got there."

Chuckling, Maverick laid out his cash. "Fucking llama." His first throw popped a balloon. Alexa cheered. The second one did it again.

"Go, baby!" she said.

Number three . . . And *pop*!

"Yay!" She threw her arms around his neck. "You did it."

"What's it gonna be, little lady?" the man asked, pointing to a row of toys smaller than the llama. Thank God.

"Holy crap, is that a hedgehog?" she asked, her eyes wide.

"Indeed it is," the man said, holding one out to her.

"Is it just me or does this carnival have the weirdest stuffed animals ever?" Maverick asked.

Alexa grinned. "I know. Isn't it amazing? I'll take it. Thanks," she said. And then she turned to him. "I'm so happy I could cry."

Maverick took her face in his hand and leaned in. The llama leaned in, too, which made her giggle. "I'll hold a carnival for you every day if it makes this happy."

"Aw, silly man. It's not the carnival. It's you." She kissed him nice and deep, making him think of her plans for after. When she pulled back, she eyed the llama. "Okay, it's him a little bit, but mostly you."

Maverick laughed. "I guess I can live with that. Then what's next, baby? Because I can't get enough of hearing you laugh and seeing you smile."

"I think we need a funnel cake, Mav," she said, petting her hedgehog.

"Your wish," he said, seeing the food truck in the distance. "Let's go."

"I THINK THIS was my absolute favorite day ever," Alexa said as they made their way back to Maverick's truck. They had their llama, their hedgehog, and bellies full of sweets.

"I love you, Alexa," he said, pinning her to her door. He kissed her slowly, deeply, thoroughly, his tongue leaving no part of her mouth unexplored. Need and lust rose up inside her. She just couldn't get enough of him, and it was the most amazing thing to know that she didn't have to get enough, because he'd always be there. And they'd always be together.

She wound her arms around his neck. "Love you, too," she whispered. "I think we should go check on my mom as quickly as possible so we can get home."

"Mmm." He kissed and licked down her neck. "Yeah, we better, before I take you right fucking here." He pulled away wearing a mischievous grin, his eyes blazing.

She sighed, her body not feeling big enough to contain all the happiness overwhelming her. She wasn't sure she could ever remember a time when life seemed so full of promise, the future so bright. And Maverick had given that to her.

Mav started up the truck and made his way through the parking lot, the line of traffic to get out moving slow.

She thumbed on her phone. "Oh, shoot. I have a voice mail. I didn't hear it ring." She put it to her ear to listen.

Her mother's voice: "Hi, Alexa, it's your mom. I realized there were a few things I forgot so I took a cab over to my house. There's absolutely no rush because I can just take my time gathering some stuff, but drop by and grab me after the carnival. Okay? Bye."

Alexa groaned, frustration flooding through her. Getting her to leave things behind had been a real struggle, despite the fact that most of it was either trash, so old there was no way her mother even remembered owning it, or something nearly identical to what she was already taking. And now, the first minute they left her alone, she ran back for more. "Crap. Mom went back to her house to get more stuff."

"For real?" Maverick asked.

"Yeah." She huffed out a breath. "I'm sorry, but can we go get her?"

"Of course we can. How the hell else is she going to get home?" They finally got to the main road, and he turned in the direction of town.

"Honestly, I think she hoped we'd be a while so she'd have time to collect more things to bring back to the new place. Damnit. I'd really hoped she would see how nice it was without all the clutter and want to keep it that way. Who was I kidding?" Her stomach dropped. She'd been kidding herself, clearly.

"It is what it is, Al. You've given her a nice place, and you can help her keep it up if you want, but you can't force her to change her ways." He took her hand and held it against his thigh.

"I know you're right." And what a difference it was to have someone to help shoulder the burden of dealing with moments like these. She forced a deep breath. It was only some stuff. It would be fine.

Within fifteen minutes, they pulled up to the curb in front of her mom's old place. The driveway was largely blocked off with the most obvious and disgusting of the trash that they'd carried out during the move. Which was going to make schlepping whatever new boxes or bags she'd packed a pain in the butt, but it was too late to worry about that now.

"I'll go get her," Alexa said, opening her door. She caught the smoky scent of a wood fire or a cookout, making her thing of the yummy burgers they'd had at the carnival. God, that had been so much fun.

"You're not going alone, woman. Especially if she has a bunch of shit to carry." He joined her and they made their way up the driveway.

Looking at the house, Alexa couldn't help but think that it seemed dark, although there did seem to be some light—

Not light, a flicker. And a pale haze hung in the air. The scent of wood burning. And then she knew. Oh, God, she knew.

She gasped and bolted. "Maverick, the house is on fire!"

"Alexa, wait!" Maverick yelled.

But she couldn't. Her mother was in there. In that death trap of a house—even with everything they'd removed, it was still loaded down with crap all over the floor. Her heart pounded and her ears rang. The world closed in on her as she burst through the front door—

"Oh, Jesus," she moaned. Smoke hung thick in the dark air, a roiling, looming beast. She stopped short inside the living room. Fire engulfed the kitchen at the back of the house and was crawling into the living room, climbing up the walls, licking at the ceiling, and consuming the piles on the floor. "Mom!"

Maverick was right behind her. "Get out. I'll find her."

"No, I'm not leaving without her," she said, coughing. But at least she could call for help. With shaking hands, Alexa dialed nine-one-one.

"What's your emergency?" the operator answered.

"House fire with injured people inside at 825 Walnut Street. Hurry," she yelled, coughing again. The dispatcher asked a few more questions, but Alexa finally cut her off. "Just hurry." Because the heat was making it hard to breathe.

Maverick turned to her. "Alexa, I'll find her. Go."

"I'm not going without her and we don't have time to argue. This place is going to go up fast so we can't wait for help. Let's just find her and we'll all go together." She turned on the flashlight on her phone, but the light almost reflected off the smoke. "Mom? Answer me!"

"Cover your mouth and nose with your shirt," he said. She did, pulling it up over her face. "Cynthia!" he yelled, as they made their way farther in. He tripped over something he couldn't see, going down on a knee. God, the floor was a hidden debris field.

The fire popped, spraying an arc of embers as the fire found more fuel and spread surprisingly fast. Alexa screamed and ducked, but they had to keep going. Moving slow because they couldn't see what was underfoot, they made for the kitchen. God, this was her nightmare come to life. The thing she'd always most worried about with her mother's hoarding, ever since that fire when she was a kid. They got as close to the kitchen as they could with the fire consuming the doorway.

The heat threatened to sear her skin and wrung sweat from her body. Her chest was so tight that she couldn't get a deep breath, the asthma she hadn't dealt with in so long kicking in. "Mom!" she yelled, finding it harder to project her voice. "What if she's in there?"

He moved past her one more step, the flames stretching out above him now.

A giant *crack* and a big piece of the ceiling caved in. Right above Maverick. The fiery debris rained down on him, taking him to the ground.

Alexa screamed and lurched toward him, thinking of nothing but needing to help him. She grabbed the flaming Sheetrock and lumber and pushed it off of him, the fire lashing at her skin and making her cry out.

"I'm okay," he said, crawling through the debris. Together they beat at his cut and shirt and jeans where they'd caught fire. "I'm okay." But nothing about his voice sounded okay.

"Mav'rick," she moaned, tears from the smoke streaming down her face. And from her realization. "We . . . have to go . . ."

He pushed onto hands and knees. Then stared down the hall. "Fuck, Al, look." He pointed.

And, oh, God, it was her mother, illuminated by the spreading flames. She was sprawled on the floor in front of her bedroom door.

"Stay back," he said. "I'll get her." Maverick rose but stumbled, clearly hurting. He used the wall for support until he finally got to her mom. As she watched, Maverick grabbed her mother by the legs and pulled, stumbling a little as he moved. It felt like forever until he returned to where Alexa waited.

Feeling a little light-headed, Alexa retreated toward the door, almost immediately tripping over something on the floor. She felt around with her hands, finding junk everywhere. She had to try to clear a wider path for her mom. Her chest felt like it could explode from the clenching tightness, but none of that mattered. She grabbed what turned out to be a broken metal table lamp and used the round base of it to shove and push at the piles.

"That's good, baby. Go out. Go on now." Maverick stumbled again.

"I'll help," she said, not sure if he could hear her. She came around and grabbed her mother's arms. Made it a few steps. But dizziness washed over her. She went down to her knees. Damn asthma. "Take her," she yelled as loud as she could. "And come back for me."

"Fuck, Alexa! Follow me, baby. Keep moving." It was like he found a new source of energy, because he was suddenly upright again and pulling her mother hard. "Come on, Alexa!"

She tried. Managed to get one foot underneath herself again. But her breaths were shallowing out and her chest hurt so bad.

"Goddamnit. I'll be right back, baby." He disappeared into the foyer with her mother. Relief flooded through Alexa, because they were getting out. Oh, God, they should be outside by now. The thought made her try to crawl again.

Just keep moving, Al. Mav will be right back to help. She got her other foot underneath her. There.

A voice. There he was, standing in the doorway to the foyer. She held out her hand and looked up, blinking. Her eyes stung like they were filled with crushed glass.

"Imagine my delight at seeing you two arrive. And here

I'd thought I was only going to get the satisfaction of hurting your mother."

Grant?

Rage and hatred surged through her, jolting her to action. She got her feet under her, then finally stood up. "You are . . . a . . . sick . . . bastard," she managed.

"I've actually heard that before," he said with a shrug. "I didn't much like it back then, either."

She glared at him, the firelight throwing demonic shadows across his face. "Why are you doing this?" She forced herself upright, hoping he couldn't tell how unsteady she was. The heat was nearly unbearable.

He held up the neck of a broken bottle, then tossed it aside. Which made her wonder where Maverick was . . . and why he wasn't coming back. Dread snaked ice through her veins. "Because I can. Because I have to," Grant said, an odd flatness in his voice. She shook her head, trying to make sense of the man before her. But failing.

And the fact that Maverick still hadn't come back? Meant Grant had hurt him. She had to face that fact, didn't she? Fury unlike anything she'd ever felt before blasted through her until it became her blood, her cells, her very DNA. She was going to kill him. She was going to revel in it. Even if she died herself.

Oh, God, Maverick! Please, be okay!

Turning, she picked up the lamp again.

He shook his head. "You can barely breathe, let alone lift that thing, Alexa. Face it, I've won. I told you to just give in and do things my way. Now, *this* is my way."

Maybe he had won. Probably. But she moved closer, closer, struggling for enough air to think. But what she was doing didn't require thought. Only instinct. To avenge. To survive.

Lights suddenly flashed outside, and Grant glanced to his side. Which was when Alexa swung the heavy metal lamp with all her might.

The lamp crashed into his right kneecap, and the crunch was a sickening thing. He let out a howl and fell forward, his knee at an unnatural angle. He tried and failed to catch himself, then tripped over the mess covering the floor and went down hard. He moaned and shifted, and she couldn't tell if he was conscious or not. Either way, he was down and her path was clear.

Gasping for breath, she looked at the fire quickly engulfing the living room and closing in on where he lay. And left him to it.

Stumbling to the foyer, Alexa could barely walk. And then she found Maverick lying face down across the threshold of the open front door, something wet darkening his hair. He'd come for her, just like he said. And Grant had hurt him. Oh, God, let him be okay.

But she couldn't focus on her worries just then. She had to get them both out of there.

Using every last piece of herself she could pull together, she stepped clumsily over him and grabbed his feet. She got him clear of the door, and then the world went wavy around her. Wavy and fuzzy. And then there was nothing at all.

CHAPTER 30

Maverick came awake on a gasp that hurt like hell. His throat felt like it'd been scoured with coarse sandpaper, and his body felt like someone had dropped a house on it. He'd been in and out of it a hundred times, but never been able to keep his hold on reality.

The fire. Something . . . hit me. Alexa!

On a moan, he sat up, his hands clumsily pulling at tubes and wires.

"Hey, hey, none of that," a nurse in pink scrubs said, gently stilling his hands. "Just calm down, hon."

"Alexa," he rasped, his voice like gravel. "Alexa Harmon."

"She's right next to you, Mr. Rylan." She pushed the curtain back and revealed an unconscious Alexa propped up in a bed identical to his. Only she had a tube in her mouth and her hands were fully bandaged. "You two have got a lot of, uh, friends out in the waiting room and they pushed hard to get you in the same room. Miss Harmon is gonna

342 • Laura Kaye

be fine but her situation is a bit more serious right at the moment, so I need you to let her rest or I have to move her." She arched a brow at him.

More serious? The pain in the center of his chest had nothing to do with the smoke he'd inhaled. "What's wrong with her?" he asked, his heart fucking breaking. The nurse looked at him like she was debating, so Maverick pushed. He glanced to her name tag. "Erica, I'm going to marry that woman. Please, tell me."

"She had a severe asthma attack exacerbated by the smoke inhalation. Her lungs didn't sufficiently respond to anti-inflammatories, so we had to intubate her to stem the possibility of respiratory failure. Once her lungs are recovered and able to work on their own again, we'll be able to remove the tube. Probably in the morning. She also has burns on her hands and forearms.

Christ, from pulling the burning pieces of ceiling off of him, he bet. Sonofabitch. "But . . . but she's going to be okay?" he asked, needing to hear her say it again.

"She will. You both will. Your burns are minor and your CT scan was clear. You just have a pretty killer bump on your head."

He put his hand to his hair and flinched. Bump? That thing was a fucking mountain. "I don't know how that happened."

She frowned. "When you think you're ready, there's a police officer here who'd like to talk to you. He might be able to tell you more. Want me to send him in?"

Maverick nodded, and she turned to go. "Wait. Alexa's mom. Cynthia Harmon?"

Erica returned to his bedside. "I'm afraid her mother was in severe respiratory distress from prolonged smoke inhalation, and she also had a bump to the head. The doctors are hopeful for a recovery, but we'll know more in the next twelve to twenty-four hours."

"Fuck. Okay." Maverick shook his head, his thoughts a wreck. "Sorry for the language."

She smiled. "Don't worry about it, hon. You've had a rough night." She disappeared out the door. Martin came in shortly after.

"Christ, Maverick. You look like hell," Martin said.

"Fuck you, too," he said.

"We found you and Alexa lying together on the front porch of her mom's house. It looked like Alexa pulled you out before passing out herself."

His gaze cut to her. She'd pulled him out?

He shook his head. "I don't remember. Something hit me, and then—" He shook his head again. Flashes of disconnected images came together, but he couldn't piece them together to make any sense.

Martin sighed. "Grant Slater hit you. With a liquor bottle, as best we can tell. The house is a total loss, so it's going to take us a while to sift through all the evidence. But if I had to guess, I'd say he set the fire."

Rage was a living beast inside Maverick, stalking around and demanding release. "Goddamn Slater," he bit out. "I—"

A moan.

His gaze whipped back to Alexa. Her eyes fluttered, her wrapped hands struggling to move.

"I'm here, Al. I'm right here." He tore the oxygen mask off of his head and slid out of bed. His back and shoulders hurt like a motherfucker, so he grasped the IV pole and used it for support.

Martin reached out a hand. "You sure you should—"

"Try to keep me away from her." He limped to her bed and gently sat on the edge. "I'm here, Alexa. You're safe. I'm so fucking sorry, baby." If he'd taken Slater out at the house after he'd attacked her, this never would've happened. So much for playing it by the books. And trying to be the good guy.

Her eyes swam, then finally fixed on him. He could tell the moment her mind snapped to some semblance of awareness. She moaned again as panic cut lines into her face.

"Stay calm, Al. You're pretty banged up. You burned your hands helping me and your lungs need some time to recover from the severe asthma attack and smoke inhalation. The nurse said the tube can probably come out in the morning." His thoughts raced to what else she needed to know. "Your mom's here, too. She also had pretty bad smoke inhalation. That's all I know so far."

She pointed to his head, her expression full of questions.

"My head?" he asked. She nodded. "I'm good."

She frowned.

"Alexa," Martin said, "do you know how Maverick got hit on the head?"

Her face went white and she moaned, frustration clear in her helpless gestures.

Martin held up a hand. "How about this? I say something, and you just shake your head yes or no?" She nodded.

"Did you see Grant at the house?" She nodded. Surprise flooded through Maverick. Grant had been there the whole time? He looked to Alexa, confusion swamping him.

"Did you talk to him?" Another yes.

"Did he admit anything to you?" Another yes.

"Did he admit or did you see him hit Maverick?" She shrugged, but her expression said she had more to say on the topic. But Maverick knew—the fucker had totally jacked him up. Not only had Maverick not seen him, but he had no memory after the hit.

"Was he inside the house when you came out?" Martin asked.

She nodded. Did that mean . . .

"Did you find a body?" Maverick asked.

Martin nodded. "No positive ID yet. But one deceased in the house."

Slater was dead? Mav's mind reeled, shock and relief warring through him.

Erica pushed back into the room. "Mr. Rylan, what the heck do you think you're doing? Get back in bed and leave Miss Harmon alone."

"Ma'am—"

"That's an order. The rest of this can wait until the woman can fully breathe on her own." She nailed both of the men with a no-nonsense stare.

Maverick pressed a kiss to Alexa's forehead. "I'll be right over there, baby."

Al watched him move away, sadness clear on her face.

"What about this?" Erica said, gesturing at his bed. "Get in, Mr. Rylan."

"Maverick," he said, climbing back in but restless as hell over the ten feet separating them.

"Okay, Maverick. I see how it is, so I have an idea you might like." In that moment, he couldn't do anything but obey her; he was still too shell-shocked by the news that Slater was actually dead. He laid his ass down on a groan. Erica did some rearranging and pushed their beds closer together, leaving just enough narrow space for someone to walk between. "Better?"

"Yeah," he said. "As good as can be in the midst of all this."

"Sometimes that's all you have," Erica said, turning on Martin. "Officer, you're going to have to come back."

He nodded. "I'll let everyone know you're both awake. They're all here."

"Thanks," Maverick said, the comfort of having his brothers, his family, around easing some of the turmoil from the night.

"Now both of you get some rest," the nurse said, dimming the light.

He turned to Alexa, whose big, wide eyes were on him.

"Christ, I love you, Alexa." She laid her bundled hands on her heart and looked at him, so much love shining from her eyes. Just then, that was all he needed. Because he had more to say. So much more. But he'd wait til she could speak, too.

Sleep came to him fitfully. His body ached, his worries focused on Alexa, and his mind kept wandering to any one of a million questions. Had Grant been at the house when Cynthia arrived? Or had he surprised her by arriving while she was packing her things? And why had Grant gone to the house in the first place? What had been the point? Maverick just didn't know. And maybe now they'd never find out.

When he finally did fall, he had dreams over and over again about getting hit in the head just as he'd been on the cusp of running back into the fire to bring Alexa out. He went down hard and stupid just inside the doorway every time, then the dream ended abruptly, making Mav want to scream his frustration.

Was that all that had happened? Was there more? Maybe he'd never know.

And with that, his brain finally shut down. Because his woman was alive and safe. And the man who wanted to take her away from him was gone for good. Just then, that was all Maverick could possibly ask for.

ALEXA DIDN'T THINK anything could surpass the relief of learning from Officer Martin that Grant had died, but then morning had come and they'd removed her breathing tube. And the sheer relief of being able to *breathe* gave that news a good run for its money.

Her lack of grief or even remorse over Grant almost made her wonder if there was something wrong with her, but how could you grieve the loss of someone who only wanted to hurt you, to own you?

She couldn't. That was for sure. Not when her mother still lay unconscious, her prognosis unclear. Alexa felt like she stood at the edge of a tall cliff, her heart and soul set to shatter when it hit bottom, and she wouldn't know whether she'd get to stand or fall until her mother's situation was clearer. After everything she'd tried to do, she hadn't been able to take care of her mother in the end.

How would she ever forgive herself for that?

After getting some scans done, Alexa got wheeled in her bed back to their room, but voices from inside had her asking the orderly to wait a moment.

"I'm so fucking sorry, Mom." Maverick, the sound of his strained, smoked-scoured voice breaking Alexa's heart.

"Oh, son. You have nothing to apologize to me for," Bunny said, her voice strained, too.

"I do. I didn't protect you from my father. And now I've let Alexa get hurt. It's like I can't stop fucking failing the people I care about."

Alexa wanted nothing more than to go inside and set Maverick straight, but she didn't want to intrude on their conversation.

"You listen to me, Maverick Rylan," Bunny said, her words strong and full of certainty. "I *hid* your father's abuse from you. On purpose. So you *wouldn't* know. But the only one of the three of us to blame was your father. You couldn't have changed a thing until I was ready to get out. Tell me you hear me. Tell me you believe it."

A long pause.

"Tell me, hon."

"Fuck," Maverick said. "Okay." The conversation seemed to cut off, or the words they spoke were too quiet to share.

Alexa finally nodded to the orderly, who nodded in return and wheeled her into the room.

She found Dare in a chair beside Maverick's bed and Bunny standing on the other side holding Mav's hand. And, oh, seeing Maverick's incredible dark blue eyes, awake and aware and alive, brought a whole new wave of relief. When she'd dragged his dead weight out the door last night, she'd been afraid he might never look at her again.

"There she is," Bunny said, a big smile on her face.

"Hi," Alexa said, unable to take her gaze off Mav. But having his mother and cousin there was special, too. She never had a big family she could rely on before—and the Ravens were certainly that. Loyal, dependable, protective. Way more than just a club.

Now if her mother would wake up, everything would be as close to perfect as she could ever hope for.

"How are you?" she asked Maverick. She could see him sitting in front of her, of course—living and breathing. But she'd never forget the terror of learning that Grant had hurt Maverick, that he'd wanted to see him die. She'd never be able to unsee the picture of the blood streaking Mav's hair.

"Just some achiness. How about you?" Maverick asked, his eyes locked on her.

Her chest felt like an elephant had sat on it, and maybe was still there. "Same," she said, her voice sounding sultry and low, the result of all the smoke and the tube.

"You're both goddamned liars but I'm so fucking happy you're okay that I don't even care," Dare said. "What the hell happened?"

She and Mav exchanged a look, and then he launched into it.

When he stopped, she jumped in with the things he didn't know. "After you took my mom out, Grant came in and just started ranting. He admitted to intending to hurt my mom and us, too, once we showed up," she said, looking at Maverick, the memory of the terror and despair she'd felt upon realizing he must've been hurt boomeranging through her.

Pain flared in her chest. If he hadn't survived, she wasn't sure she could've, either. Not when she'd just found her way back to him after so long, and not when she loved him so damn much.

"I was so beside myself that he'd hurt you. I grabbed a metal lamp and hit him in the knee so hard it crunched and he fell." She shuddered, a confession welling up inside her, then spilling free. "I . . . I probably could've helped him, but I didn't. I left him."

"Good," Bunny said, that one word so filled with anger that it vibrated through the room.

"I agree," Dare said.

Alexa released a shaky breath and looked at Maverick, and the emotion shining from his eyes reached inside her chest and soothed so much of her pain.

"Shit, I don't remember anything after taking your mom out. But you were so strong, Alexa. You saved us," Maverick said.

Dare braced his elbows on his knees, his gaze going serious. "I hope you don't feel a second of guilt, Alexa. He wasn't behaving rationally. He would've kept coming at you, and he made it into a situation where it was you or him. And the P.I. learned something that I think maybe confirms that." His dark gaze moved to Maverick, then back to her again. "Did you know that Slater spent time in a psychiatric hospital when he was nineteen?"

Alexa gasped. "What? No." She shook her head, barely able to process the information.

Dare nodded. "All the P.I. discovered so far was that it was an involuntary admission. Lasted ten weeks. When Slater got out, he moved away from his hometown and, as best as can be told, never returned."

Shell-shocked, she glanced at Maverick. "That must be why he had no relationship with his parents. Wouldn't talk about it, either." A barrage of questions flooded through her that all boiled down to one—what had Grant been hiding from her? Because Dare was right, Grant had changed these past few weeks from a man always in tight, strict control to one completely out of it. Either way, it really was like she'd been with a stranger all those years. "I don't even know what to say."

"If the P.I. finds out more, I'm sure he'll tell us," Maverick said. "But the most important thing is that it's finally over." He shifted in his bed. "And damnit I want out of this bed."

Dare let loose a small laugh. "Welcome to my world."

Maverick scowled at his cousin, making Dare laugh harder.

"Why don't we let you all rest?" Bunny said, coming to Maverick's bedside. She leaned down and kissed his forehead, and it was the sweetest thing. "You're my favorite son. I don't know what I would've done . . . Well, I'm not even going to entertain that now."

Mav swallowed hard, Bunny's words clearly getting to him. "I'm your *only* son, Bunny."

She managed a small smile and winked. "That's why you're my fave." Next, she came around to Alexa's bed and placed a hand on her shoulder. "I wish I would've had half your strength at your age. You hang in there and take care of each other."

"I will, Bunny." Now she was the one Bunny was getting choked up. "Thank you."

Dare said his good-byes next. Clasping Mav's hand, he said, "This was some fucking extreme lengths to go to in order to get out of your turn in the dunking booth."

Maverick barked out a laugh, and the sound was so amazing to her. Proof of life. Proof of truly living. "Silver linings, man. You gotta embrace 'em where you find 'em."

"Truer words," Dare said, then he came around to Alexa, and leaned down over her so he could look her in the eyes. "You did good, kid."

She blinked back tears and gave a quick nod. And then they were gone, and she and Maverick were finally alone.

"I've had enough of being apart from you," Maverick said, climbing out of bed and shuffling over to her, holding on to his IV stand. A pale blue hospital gown was all he wore, but he didn't care about any of it. About anything other than touching Alexa again.

"Are you naked under there?" Her expression was almost playful, and it made him want to distract her, to help her find a moment of light in all this dark.

He chuffed out a laugh. "You really feeling up to sex?"

Alexa grinned. "No, damnit. But I thought your ass might look cute sticking out."

He shook his head, and then he turned around for her and gave her his bare ass. "Happy?"

"Wow. That is . . . yeah. I'm super happy."

He chuckled and turned back to her.

"I feel *so much better* now," she said. "I might need to see that every once in a while. You know, for purely medicinal purposes."

"You're so full of shit," he said, but he enjoyed her teasing, enjoyed seeing her come back to life, a little at a time. He put down the side railing to her bed. "Let me in." It was a little awkward with her bandaged hands, but she managed to scoot aside enough to make space for him. His back was one giant bruise from where the ceiling had collapsed on him, so he settled on his side facing her. Fuck, that felt good. Satisfying. Exactly where he belonged. "That's better."

"Yes, it is," she said, her breath catching as the smile slid off her face. "I feel happy and sad at the same time."

He cupped her cheek, his thumb brushing under her eye, but there were no tears. "I know, baby. Perfectly reasonable. I'm so sorry your mom is in such bad shape."

"I think I'm going to lose her, Mav. I feel it."

"Don't say that. The doctors don't know anything for sure yet," he said, even though none of the doctors sounded any more hopeful or positive about it than they'd been the night before. Mrs. H had just been in that smoke for so long. "And if the worst happens . . ." He swallowed around a lump. A lump caused by the fact that the first time he'd lost Alexa, it was because she'd lost her brother. What would losing her mother do? "We'll handle it together."

She nodded.

"Promise me," he said.

"Of course we will." She tilted her head. "What's the matter? You look upset."

"It's fucking selfish, given what we're talking about." But that didn't keep him from feeling the anxiety. Christ, he didn't want to have found her again just to lose her so quickly once more.

"We can say anything to each other. Remember?" She rested her bandaged hands against his chest.

"If the worst happens, Alexa, you have to promise to let me help you through it this time. Please." His heart thundered against his breastbone, the heavy beat from a mix of need and fear and worry.

Her breath caught. "Oh. Oh, God, Maverick. You're worried because my grief over Tyler drove me away from you before?" He nodded, a knot lodged in his throat. "I promise. I won't do that again. I'm not that girl anymore. And I've learned so damn much about what love is, and what it isn't."

Relief crashed over him so hard he shuddered. "Like what?"

Her expression went soft and thoughtful. "Love . . . love is the only thing that doesn't hurt. So many people are afraid of it. I think I was five years ago. Afraid that loving you would hurt me, one way or the other. But love doesn't hurt. Abuse hurts, and loneliness hurts, and jealousy hurts, and lies hurt. But love? Love heals. Love puts back together things that were broken before. Which is what you've done for me. So promising you, that's easy. I don't want to be anywhere else but with you. No matter what."

Damn if those words didn't resonate all the way to the bottom of his soul, and make him want things he never thought he'd have. Want them *right fucking now*.

He leaned his forehead against hers. "Marry me." The words almost took him by surprise, but they felt more right than maybe anything he'd ever said. Well, besides that he loved her. "It doesn't have to be right away, but marry me. Say you'll be mine. That we'll ride through this life together, you and me against the world, just like we said. Say you'll let me take care of you and that you'll take care of me, too. Laugh with me and joke with me and fight with me and share your weird cat with me, and *marry me*, Alexa."

Tears made her eyes go glassy, but her smile was like the sun coming out after a storm. Bright and hopeful. "Yes, I'll marry you, Maverick. You are my strength and my home and my truth. Nothing would make me happier than being yours."

"Forever," he said, triumph making his blood sing.

"Forever," she whispered, the first tears slipping free of her pretty eyes.

He kissed her then, a soft pressing promise of lips on lips, and he managed to pull her into his arms. "I didn't exactly plan this today, and I know I need to get you a ring—"

"I don't care about a ring, Mav. I mean, I want to wear your ring, whatever it is, but your heart's the only thing I need." She kissed him again.

"Well, you have that. Because you are my friend and my love and the life I always wanted, Al. My everything." And, damn if that didn't give him an idea for a tattoo. Which made him think of the black-and-purple tribal raven with the red heart at its center. Seeing it on her skin someday was going to bring him to his knees. He already knew that was true.

"Oh, that's perfect, Maverick. Because you're my everything, too."

EPILOGUE

Welcome home, Al," Maverick said, the next afternoon. He had his arm around her shoulders, supporting her weight and helping her across the threshold to his little lake house. They'd been released from the hospital an hour before, but had bowed out of the Saturday afternoon cookout being planned at the Ravens' clubhouse before the final night of the carnival began. Alexa's chest still hurt if she undertook much activity, so that was all more than she was up to just yet.

"I'm so glad to be home," she said. Home. God, that sounded nice. One of the things she'd always wanted but never really been able to find. Lucy came rushing right up to her. "Hi, baby. I bet you were lonely without us."

"Phoenix came by to feed her and keep her company. I told him to line the toys up on the tub to see what she did. He said we can ask him to Lucy-sit any time." He lowered her onto the couch.

She chuckled, her hand rubbing the cat's thin body when she jumped up. "Look at all the new friends you're making."

Maverick grinned. "What can I get you?"

"Nothing at all," she said. "Just be with me."

"My favorite thing." He grabbed the remote and put on HGTV, then settled in next to her.

"Ooh, I adore *Love It or List It*, even though the couple almost always does the opposite of what I would do." She shifted against him, her head finding his shoulder. He put his arm around her, and she felt like she could've purred herself. Besides Jagger being freed, the only thing that could've made this moment better was knowing her mother was well, but there still hadn't been any change in her condition. All Alexa could do was hope and believe.

Mav propped his boots on the coffee table. "I enjoy the rebuild projects. Finding a new home doesn't feel as special as making the old thing you know and love grow with you and work for you in ways you never thought of before."

She nodded, loving how he phrased that. It felt like he was talking about them. And maybe he was. Honestly, what relationship wasn't a fixer-upper? At least the roughest parts of their ride were behind them.

She hoped.

Hours later, Maverick woke her up with a big tray of food. "I made us some dinner."

"You're going to spoil me."

"You're going to be my wife. There's no such thing." He held up a spoonful of mac and cheese to her mouth, since she still didn't have full use of her hands. Part of her was eager for the gauze to come off, but the other feared how bad all that damaged skin was going to hurt when it was exposed to the world. One day at a time, she guessed. "Want?"

She looked past the food to his face. "Want."

He chuckled and winked. "I'm not sure either of us is up to wanting."

Alexa grinned and took a bite. "Probably not. But mac and cheese hand-fed by my man is pretty good, too."

He shook his head and enjoyed a bite for himself.

Something pinged around in her brain that she'd been avoiding all day. She finally gave it voice. "Today . . . today would've been my wedding day."

"I know," he said, grabbing another spoonful to offer her.

"Know what I was thinking?"

His gaze cut to hers, the dark blue so intense. "Tell me."

"Maybe all the bad stuff was supposed to happen to bring me back to you."

He gave a tight nod. "I hate that bad stuff happened to you."

"I have no regrets, Maverick. I want you to know that. Except maybe walking away five years ago."

"Yeah? Well, I've been thinking about that. I've been thinking that neither of us was ready for us five years ago. You pushed me away and I let myself be pushed. Would you do that now?" He gave her a searching stare.

"Absolutely not." She shook her head.

"Me, neither."

They ate the rest of their dinner while watching *The Fast and the Furious*, and then Alexa was too tired to stay awake any longer.

Mav helped her get ready for bed, and got changed himself. And then she walked into the bedroom—and burst out laughing. "This is perfect!" The llama and hedgehog sat on the bed.

"This is your home now. *Our* home," Maverick said. He pointed around the room. "Our bed and our closet and our bathroom and our dresser. I want you to move in, rearrange the furniture, hang pictures, lay your stuff out on the bathroom counter, and leave Lucy's toys in the tub. Whatever makes you feel at home, I want you to do."

"I will, but I don't have to do any of that to feel at home. That's you, Maverick. Just you." She wound her arms around his neck, careful not to put too much pressure there.

"Fuck, I love you, baby." He kissed her on a groan.

"Good, then climb into *our* bed and let me hold you." It took a moment to get situated, but then she was all snuggled up to the long nook along the side of his lean body.

And that's when Alexa knew—*this* was what being home really was. Finding love and belonging and family with one person, one person who could accept her mistakes and hold her tight and be her biggest cheerleader.

Maverick was that for her. She knew that for sure.

And that was everything.

ACKNOWLEDGMENTS

I have a lot of people to thank for this one because sometimes books are hard, like this one was, and those are the ones that take the most support to finish. I have to start by thanking Lea Nolan for all the brainstorming, plotting, and hand-holding, and Christi Barth for reading the draft. I also have to thank my writing partner Stephanie Dray for her incredible patience, and Amanda Bergeron for the same! I also have to thank Amanda for the incredible encouragement she gave me by loving the book, and especially Maverick, as much as I do. It's an amazing experience to work with an editor who gets your worlds and your words and your characters so much, and I appreciate it to the bottom of my heart.

Next, I need to thank my wonderful agent, Kevan Lyon, for everything she did to help me get this one done. And my amazingly supportive husband and daughters for doing so much for me to give me the time I needed to write. I love you guys!

And I also need to thank my Heroes and my Reader Girls for the excitement you all had for the early excerpts I posted from the book—each and every one was a little boost of encouragement and motivation! It's amazing any time a reader mentions that a certain book of yours is their favorite, but a special thank you to every reader who told me *Ride Hard* was your new favorite, because that provided me with such wonderful motivation when the going got tough on this one. I hope you find another story that grabs your heart within these pages.

Finally, a thanks as always to all the readers, who take my characters into their hearts and let them tell their stories over and over again.

~LK

Don't miss the next Raven Riders novel

RIDE WILD
Coming Fall 2017!
Preorder it today.

Wild with grief over the death of his wife, Sam "Slider" Evans lives for his two sons. Nothing else holds his interest anymore, not riding his bike, not even his membership in the Raven Riders Motorcycle Club. And then he hires a new babysitter. . . .

Recently freed from a bad situation by the Ravens, Cora Campbell is determined to bury her past. When Slider offers her a nanny position, she accepts, needing the security and time to figure out what she wants from life. Cora adores his sweet boys, but she never expected the red-hot attraction to their brooding, sexy father that makes her wish he'd notice her. Just once.

Slider sees the beautiful, fun-loving woman he invited into his home. She makes him feel too much, and he hates it and yearns for it, not sure which he feels more, until Cora witnesses something she shouldn't have. Now, the new lives he and Cora have only just found are on the line, and he must claim and protect what's his before it's too late. . . .

And keep reading to enjoy the bonus Hard Ink novella

HARD EVER AFTER

CHAPTER 1

I don't want to let you go," Nick Rixey said, lying on his back in bed with Becca Merritt sprawled half on top of him. Dawn was already around the corner, but neither of them had slept much. At least he wasn't the only one who was a little stressed out about life returning to normal. You'd think it would be the opposite. But it's funny how your body and brain could get used to operating in crisis mode—and resist the reality that the crisis was over.

Becca traced a ticklish pattern across his chest with her fingertips. "I'm just going to work," she said. "I've been off for two months. It's time."

"I know," he said, pressing a kiss to her soft blond waves.

"But we might have time for a proper good-bye before I have to go," she said, a smile plain in her voice.

Nick couldn't help but grin, and Becca was a big part of why that was so much easier to do these days. "Might we now? And what would a proper good-bye look like?" Against his belly, his cock hardened.

"Mmm, a back rub might be nice," she said, her tone full of teasing.

"That's all?" He reached down to stroke his cock, and her head shifted, following the movement. And fuck if her watching him jack himself didn't get him even hotter. How the hell was he supposed to let her out of his sight for a twelve-hour shift at the hospital after they'd been around each other twenty-four/seven for most of the last two months?

"Maybe this, too." Becca slid down his body and joined her hand with his. Her tongue swirled around the head of his cock and her lips sucked at the tip as their hands moved together.

"Fuck, Sunshine. Take all of me," Nick rasped.

She pushed onto her knees, her face so filled with desire—for him—that it blew his mind. Every damn time. Looking him in the eye with those pretty baby blues, she leaned over and swallowed his length inch by maddening inch until he was buried in the back of her throat.

His hand went to her hair and his hips surged. "God, yes." For a few long moments, he savored the pleasure she was pulling out of his body with her lips and tongue and hands. And then he cupped her cheek in his palm. "Lay down," he said.

Smiling at him, Becca stretched out on her belly and laid her head on folded hands. Nick straddled her upper thighs, his cock rubbing against her ass as he smoothed his palms over her beautiful golden skin. To think that for most of the past year he'd been lonely, purposeless, angry, battling with demons so numerous it was hard to believe that they'd mostly been slayed. And it was Becca's walking through the door of his tattoo shop that had put him on the road to getting justice, having his honor restored, and clearing his name—not to mention finding love.

Becca Merritt had saved his life in every way that mattered.

Because of her, he had purpose again in a new business. His surviving Army Special Forces teammates—his family by choice if not by blood—were back working and fighting at his side. And he had hope for the future in a way he hadn't in a very long time, not since a roadside ambush in Afghanistan had killed half his team, sullied the name of his mentor and commander, and ended in the other-than-honorable discharge of Nick and his team. Not to mention injuring him and two of the other survivors. Although, shit, they'd all walked away with soul-deep wounds even if they hadn't been visible to the eye.

But that was all behind them now. After weeks of investigations, fighting, and off-the-books operations against a shit-ton of enemies, he and his team had come out on top and the bad guys were either dead or in custody. And now Nick could see the future stretching out in front of him. And this woman was at the very center of his vision.

"How's that feel?" he asked, kneading at Becca's shoulders. The position tugged at the lingering injuries he bore in his hip and lower back, where he'd taken two rounds during the ambush, but fuck if he was letting his body ruin this perfect moment of peace and closeness between them.

"Really good," she whispered.

He worked his way down her spine in a series of slow, deep massages. When he got to her ass, he pressed his cock between her cheeks and slowly stroked himself against her. Becca moaned. And Nick couldn't wait anymore. He had to get in her. "You wet for me, Sunshine?" He slipped his fingers between her legs and found her hot and slick and more than ready. "Aw, fuck, yeah you are."

"Always wet for you," she said, arching her back.

Straddling her thighs, Nick penetrated her, both of them moaning as he slid home.

"Oh, God, Nick," Becca rasped.

Grasping her cheeks, he began to move, his eyes trained

on where he disappeared inside her. "So good together. Every damn time."

"Yes," she said, arching into him, urging him faster, harder.

Nick braced his arms against the bed and gave her everything he had—his body, his heart, his soul. The sounds of panting breaths and pleasured moans and slapping skin filled the gray-lit room. "Touch yourself," he said. "I want you to come on me."

Becca slid a hand between her legs, and Nick closed every bit of distance between them, his body coming down and covering her from head to toes. He wrapped one arm around her shoulder and another around her head, his fingers tangling in all that beautiful, soft blond hair. "Love you so fucking much," he rasped into her ear.

"Nick," she whispered, her tone tortured and needy. Her movements grew jerky and desperate beneath him, and then she was moaning and coming, her body fisting around him and stealing his sanity.

"Aw, God, Becca," he groaned as his orgasm nailed him in the back. On a series of punctuated thrusts, he sought to get as deep as he could as he poured himself into her.

When their bodies calmed, Nick shifted, but Becca grasped at his hip. "Don't leave yet."

"Don't want to crush you," he said, kissing her temple.

"I like the feeling of you on top of me."

Nick chuffed out a small laugh. "Keep talking like that, and I'm gonna get hard again."

Becca smiled. "I wouldn't complain."

His head resting against hers, Nick sighed. Contentment. Such a foreign feeling. And yet he found it in Becca's arms. And had, from the very beginning, even when he'd been too stubborn and too proud to see everything that she was.

And that was the moment Nick knew what he was doing during Becca's first day back to work. He wanted her in his life. He wanted that life to start now. Hell, to start yesterday. And he wanted it to be forever.

And that meant he needed a ring. The rightness of the idea settled bone-deep inside him. As much as anyone, he knew how life could change in a single unexpected instant. No way did he want to wait even a second more for their future to start.

"Nick?" she said, pulling him from the plans taking shape in his head.

"Yeah?"

"Will you do something for me tonight?"

He finally shifted off her, his body settling alongside hers so he could look at her while they talked. "You can always assume the answer to that will be yes, Sunshine," he said, brushing her hair back off her face.

"I've been thinking about it, and I'd like you to give me a tattoo tonight," she said, bright blue eyes looking up at him with so much warmth.

The request sent his heart beating a little faster. Nick was half owner of Hard Ink Tattoo, though he'd only been working as a tattoo artist on a part-time basis since he'd been discharged from the Army. "You know I've been dying to put my ink on you," he said with a smile.

She grinned. "Well, now's your chance." She pointed toward the drawer on the nightstand. "I printed something out to give you an idea."

Nick couldn't move fast enough. After all the times they'd talked about what she'd want if she ever got a tattoo, and after all the times he'd drawn on her body with skin markers just to put his mark on her—even if only temporarily—he couldn't wait to see what she'd finally decided she wanted on her skin. Forever. He sat on the edge of the bed and unfolded the sheet while Becca knelt behind him, her front pressed tight to his back, her arms wrapped around his stomach.

It was three intertwined cursive words.

Only. Always. Forever.

"Fuck, Sunshine," Nick said, remembering the night he'd shown her the tattoo he'd gotten on his forearm for her and she'd written the word *YOURS* over her heart with a marker. That had set off a raw, urgent lovemaking that had included them writing words of claiming and love and intention all over each other.

Only. Always. Forever.

"What do you think?" she asked.

"I think it's perfect," Nick said, staring at the page. Damn if his throat didn't get a little tight at the thought that she wanted to put their words on her body. "Do you know where you want it?"

She kissed the side of his neck and her breath caressed his ear. "On my right shoulder."

Nodding, Nick could already picture it—and it made him even more certain about what he needed to do today. "It'll look beautiful there, Becca." He shifted to the side so he could wrap her in his arms. "You make me fall in love with you a little more every day. You know that?"

"I think that's the sweetest thing anyone's ever said to me." Her kiss was slow and sweet and lingering. "I don't want to, but I should get moving."

"I know," Nick said, standing and giving her a hand off the bed. He watched her walk into the bathroom, his mind back on his plan for the day. Because he was giving her more than a tattoo tonight. And he couldn't fucking wait.

CHAPTER 2

A few blocks away from the hospital, the nerves Becca had been shoving down all morning finally pushed through. Ridiculous to be nervous about returning to a place where she'd worked for years. But she was. Because the last time she'd been there, a man named Tyrell Woodson had grabbed her from behind, jabbed a knife into her ribs, and tried to abduct her from the staff lounge. Only her struggling—getting cut in the process—and Nick arriving, well, in the nick of time, had saved her from God only knew what horrible fate.

Even worse? The man had gotten away and tried to grab her again, though the team had caught him that time and made sure he wouldn't be a problem anymore. So Becca shouldn't be nervous. She shouldn't be worrying. And she certainly didn't want to let on to Nick that she was.

They caught the red light a block away from the hospital's downtown Baltimore campus, and Nick turned to her from the driver's seat. "I'll pick you up at seven, and then we can grab some dinner and head down to Hard Ink."

"Sounds like a plan," she said with a smile, looking forward so much to finally getting a tattoo—from Nick. He brought their joined hands to his mouth and kissed her knuckles. God, she loved this man. He'd insisted on driving her. Truth be told, she hadn't minded the extra time with him. It was going to be weird to go back to work in the emergency department after all these months off. All the people at Hard Ink had come to feel like her family now in addition to her brother, Charlie, who was in a relationship with Nick's younger brother, Jeremy. She was going to miss seeing them all the time.

Moments later, Nick pulled the car over to the curb in front of the hospital. "Have a great day, Sunshine," he said, leaning over the center console. His kisses made her want to stay. "Be safe."

"I will," she said, ignoring the butterflies in her belly. It really was ridiculous. "Miss you already." And then she was pushing out of the car and crossing the wide sidewalk plaza in front of the hospital's tall glass entrance. She'd purposely arrived close to the beginning of her shift so that she wouldn't have much time before she'd be busy, which she knew would be the perfect cure for her nerves.

A chorus of greetings rose up from the nurse's station of the emergency department. Becca made her way inside and gave a round of hugs. Luckily, things were busy enough with the shift change that no one had time to linger. She headed to the staff lounge to stow her belongings.

Alison Harding came out of the lounge just as Becca reached for the door. "Oh, Becca, it's so good to have you back," the woman said, a hint of sadness in her bright green eyes. Becca had been subbing for Alison the day the attempted abduction had occurred, and Alison had sent more than one guilt-ridden, apologetic text. Not that

Becca blamed her. It was hardly Alison's fault that the undercover military investigation into narcotics smuggling that Becca's father had been investigating in Afghanistan had spilled over into the United States. Or that the bad guys had been selling their heroin to the Church Gang, headquartered just across the city in Baltimore. Or that somehow the bad guys had discovered that Charlie had stumbled onto his father's activities, leading them to grab him and attempt to grab Becca as well.

"It's good to be back," Becca said.

"How are you doing? Did the police ever catch the guy?" Alison asked, tucking a strand of light brown hair behind her ear.

"No, they didn't," Becca said, unable to share what she did know—that Nick's team had caught and interrogated Woodson, and that Nick had threatened the man within an inch of his life. "But I'm good. Really good."

Alison frowned. "God, it's scary that he's still out there, isn't it?"

Becca's belly did a little flip. "No, I really think he's long gone," she said. Marz had taken video of him spilling his guts about the Church Gang's secrets, which Nick had promised to put in the gang leader's hands should Woodson ever come near Becca again. Already beaten up for having failed to capture Becca, Woodson had tripped all over himself promising to stay away for good.

"Well, I hope so." Alison gave her an unconvincing smile. "All right. I'll see you out there." She squeezed Becca's arm and headed down the hall.

Taking a deep breath, Becca pushed into the room where she'd been attacked, worried that it was going to be filled with all kinds of ghosts. Instead, she found a big bouquet of balloons, a sheet cake that read, *Welcome back, Becca!* and a plastic-wrapped bunch of flowers lying on one of the tables. The overhead lights and morning sunshine spilling through the window near the door—the door through which Woodson had tried to drag her—made the room bright and cheery, not the scary, dark place her nightmares sometimes depicted.

Shaking her head at herself, Becca crossed to her locker and ditched her purse. She made a small corner piece of cake with a big pink frosting flower her breakfast, then found herself so immersed in patients that it was noon before she knew it—and time for the other thing she wasn't looking forward to: an appointment with a hospital psychologist. It was standard operating procedure after the attack and the long leave of absence, but Becca wasn't relishing being asked to talk about what had happened. And she was well aware that medical personnel sometimes made the worst patients, herself included. She was way more comfortable taking care of others than being taken care of herself.

She waited in the fifth-floor mental health services suite. Finally, the door to the waiting room opened, and a tall, attractive woman in dress pants and a crisp blouse stepped out. "Becca Merritt?"

"Yes," Becca said, tossing the magazine she'd been skimming to the coffee table.

"I'm Dr. Parker," the woman said. "Please, come in."

Becca had seen her around the hospital a few times but didn't know her well. "Thanks," she said, slipping into the well-appointed office—all warm tones and relaxing landscape prints. She took a seat on the sofa.

The doctor grabbed a pen and folder from her desk, then sat in an armchair and smiled at Becca. "How has your first day back to work been?"

"Fine. Busy. But I'm right back in the swing of things," Becca said, lacing her fingers in her lap.

"Good, I'm glad to hear it. You know this meeting is routine. The hospital just needs to touch base, given the traumatic event that led to your leave of absence." Dr. Parker scanned a sheet inside Becca's folder.

Becca nodded. "I understand." Woodson had somehow managed to gain access to a set of hospital credentials and had posed as a maintenance man, so the hospital had been concerned that Becca would sue. But more than that, traumatic events could lead to bad decision making, which was never an acceptable risk when those decisions were of the life-and-death variety.

"So how are you doing? How are you finding being back in the hospital again?" The doctor's expression was carefully neutral, but Becca didn't doubt for a moment that her reactions were being scrutinized.

So she went for honesty. "I was a little nervous about coming in before I got here this morning, but once I was here, I was fine. As soon as the shift started, everything felt normal. So I think I'm doing pretty good."

Dr. Parker nodded. "I'm glad to hear it. Are you having any nightmares, anxiety, issues with panic, sleep or appetite problems?"

Becca clutched her hands tighter. "I've had occasional nightmares, and for a while I was jumpy if someone approached me from behind, but I haven't had any of the other issues." Frankly, given everything that Nick's team had faced during their investigation into the men who'd killed her father and abducted Charlie, Becca's issues had taken a total backseat. And she'd been fine with that. Because she *had been* fine. And the last thing she'd wanted to do was distract or worry Nick by making him think she was anything but fine. Not when his life had been on the line—so many times. "The whole thing could've turned out a lot worse than it did, so I mostly feel lucky."

"That's a great way to look at it." The doctor scribbled something inside the folder. "Do you have any concerns about being back to work?"

"None," Becca said. "I'm glad to be back." And she was. She'd known she wanted to be a nurse since the age of thirteen, when her mother had died of an aneurysm. The feeling of helplessness Becca had experienced that night had made her determined to be able to help if something similar ever happened again to someone she cared about. She loved what she did.

After a few more questions, Dr. Parker handed her a form. "I'm happy to clear you to return," she said. "Just sign where it's highlighted."

"Great," Becca said. "Thank you." She signed and handed back the form, and then it was time for her lunch break.

Back in the staff lounge, she found a couple of people hanging out around the half-demolished cake. She was glad for the company and conversation as she settled down to the turkey sandwich, chips, and yogurt she'd brought from home, and she was equally glad to find that no one treated her weirdly despite the fact that everyone knew what had happened to her that day. Even if you could keep gossip that juicy under wraps around there, which you couldn't, the hospital had undertaken a security reevaluation and had implemented some new procedures and security mechanisms as a result. So her attack was no secret whatsoever.

Still, as the day progressed and patients were admitted in a nonstop stream, she found it easier and easier to relax. Finally, seven o'clock rolled around, and a bundle of anticipation took root in her belly. She couldn't wait to see Nick, and she really couldn't wait for him to do her first tattoo.

In the staff lounge, she collected her purse from her locker and gathered the flowers to take home. There wasn't much cake left, and she figured the night shift would easily finish it. The balloons made the otherwise plain blue-and-white lounge more cheery, so she decided to leave them there. They wouldn't fit in Nick's sports car anyway.

Not wanting to keep Nick waiting, Becca rushed across the room with her arms full. The door yanked open right in front of her, and a tall, bald man with dark brown skin stepped into the opening, looming over her.

Becca nearly choked on a gasp. Tyrell Woodson. For a moment, she was sucked back into the past so thoroughly that everything around her disappeared.

"Oh, sorry about that," the man said, his voice deep and friendly.

She blinked and swallowed hard. *Not Woodson. Holy shit, not Woodson. What's wrong with me?* Becca forced a smile. "Oh, no. Not your fault," she managed. "I wasn't paying attention." He wore blue scrubs, not a maintenance uniform. And the identification tag clipped to his pocket read *Benton Tucker, Certified Nursing Assistant*. She stepped back to let him in.

He pointed at the flowers. "Are you Becca?"

"Uh, yeah," she said, her heart still racing in her chest. "How'd you know?"

"The cake. I had a piece earlier. When it still said your name," he said with a deep chuckle.

She smiled. "Right. Glad you got some, because it's almost gone. Free food never lasts long."

Another chuckle. "I guess that's right. I'm Ben," he said, extending his hand. "I've only been here for about a month."

"Nice to meet you, Ben," she said, returning the shake and feeling bad for the way she'd reacted to him, which had been not only ridiculous but also embarrassing. Not to mention a little concerning. For a moment, her brain had been entirely convinced that Woodson had been standing in front of her, despite the fact that Ben bore only a superficial resemblance to him. While both men were tall and dark skinned, Ben's head wasn't bald, like Woodson's, but was covered with closely trimmed hair. Ben didn't have any tattoos or scars, whereas Woodson had been covered in them. Ben's face was lean, and he wore a neatly trimmed goatee, where Woodson's face had been round, his cheeks full. And Ben radiated an easygoing good humor, not the menace she'd gotten from Woodson. "Well, hopefully our shifts will overlap soon. Hope you have a good night."

"You, too, Becca." He gave a wave and turned for the cake table.

Becca pushed out into the hall. After she'd successfully battled back her nerves all day, freaking out just because a man had stepped in front of her made her feel defeated and weak and stupid. And that pissed her off. She was stronger than this. And she refused to let a little anxiety get the better of her. Woodson was gone. The Church Gang had been largely destroyed. And Nick and his team had exposed the corruption that had led to her father's death and the team's being railroaded out of the Army. They'd also gotten the justice they deserved.

Everything was good now. The crises were all behind them.

Outside, July heat wrapped around her despite the evening hour, but the only thing Becca cared about was the man sitting in the black car idling at the curb. She rushed across the plaza, the smile on her face growing when Nick noticed her coming.

She couldn't get in the car fast enough. "Hi," she said.

"Sunshine," Nick said, the word filled with so much emotion it made tears prickle against the backs of her eyes. "Missed you." His hand found the back of her neck and pulled her in for a long kiss.

"Missed you, too," she said. His presence chased away the last of her nerves and allowed her to take a deep, cleansing breath. She was fine. No big deal.

He threw the car into gear and eased into traffic. "So, how was your day? Everything go okay?"

"Yeah," Becca said. "Everything went great."

CHAPTER 3

"You made Sloppy Joes," Becca said with a big grin when they got home. The rich, spicy smell of Nick's one and only specialty filled the whole loft apartment—and the gesture filled her heart with so much affection. He'd made her Sloppy Joes the very first night she'd spent there at Hard Ink, back when everything had seemed so uncertain, back when it had seemed like she might lose everyone she had left.

Nick grinned as he moved to the Crock-Pot on the counter and lifted the lid. "I did. Thought you might enjoy something homemade after a long shift."

Becca came up behind him and wrapped her arms around his firm stomach. "You're the sweetest."

He chuckled as he stirred the thick, meaty sauce. "Don't tell anyone."

"Too late," Jeremy said as he walked into the room, Charlie right behind him. The two of them were pretty much attached at the hip these days, which Becca found completely awesome. Her brother had been a loner for so much of his life. He deserved someone as special and fun and loving as Jeremy Rixey.

Eileen loped out after them. Becca had rescued the three-legged German shepherd puppy off the street near the hospital the first week she'd met Nick, back before she'd realized she'd never be returning to her own place again. At first, that was because it hadn't been safe—multiple break-ins had proven that. Now, even though all their mysteries had been solved and threats had been neutralized, it was because her home was here.

"Hey," Becca said, bending down to pet the monster-sized puppy. "You guys are just in time. We're getting ready to eat. Wanna join?"

Jeremy ran his inked hand over his short dark-brown hair, which was still growing out following brain surgery just over a month ago. None of them had emerged unscathed from the investigation into the corruption that had killed her father and blackened his team's reputations. Charlie had been abducted and maimed, two of his fingers cut off to try to make him talk. And Jeremy had been pistol-whipped by a fleeing bad guy who'd attacked them at a funeral. But both of them were doing so much better now. "We already had some," Jeremy said with a grin. "You know I wouldn't miss Nick's Sloppy Joes."

"Pretty much everyone else ate already," Nick said, pressing a kiss against Becca's hair. "Everyone" meaning the other four members of Nick's team and their respective girlfriends, all of whom were crashing in temporary digs here until a huge-scale rebuilding and renovation project was done, which would create six loft-style apartments in the other half of the L-shaped Hard Ink building.

Peering out from between long strands of blond hair, Charlie nodded. "We're gonna catch a movie."

After weeks of being on lockdown here, the idea of just going out to do something as casual and normal as seeing a movie still felt strange to Becca. "Oh, well, that sounds like fun."

"How was work today?" Charlie asked in that quiet way he had.

She came around the counter to him. Sometimes she was completely overwhelmed by her relief that they'd managed to rescue him from the Church Gang. And by her love for him, her only remaining family member. "It was good. Business as usual." Playfully, she pushed his hair back off his face. "I like it long, you know."

"Yeah?" he asked, his gaze a little shy. Even around her. "Me too."

"Me too," Jeremy said in a loaded tone, waggling his eyebrows as he planted a kiss on Charlie's cheek.

Becca laughed and held up her hands as Charlie's cheeks pinked, which was when she noticed the guys' T-shirts. Jeremy's was white with a headless stick figure. It read, *I need head.* Charlie's was blue and read, *I'm Getting Real Tired of Wearing Pants and Having Responsibilities.* Jeremy's innuendo-filled T-shirt collection was legendary around here, and Charlie had been borrowing Jer's clothes ever since he'd been rescued, although he usually picked the least dirty shirts Jeremy had. It was just another thing Becca loved about Jeremy, and about the way he loved and took care of her brother.

"Speaking of responsibilities, how did things go with the construction today?" she asked as Nick passed her two plates. She placed them on the breakfast bar, then grabbed some silverware and napkins.

Jeremy flicked his tongue against the piercing on his bottom lip and braced his hands on the counter. "Inspectors were out this morning and signed off on everything that's been done so far. Contractor's hoping to have the exterior shell totally done before winter. Fingers crossed."

"Considering a few weeks ago there was just a big hole out there, that sounds pretty good," Becca said.

"Yeah," Jeremy said, something dark momentarily passing through his gaze. And Becca didn't have to guess at what it was. There'd been a big hole because the arm of the building that had previously stood in that spot had been destroyed by a military-grade explosive device launched at the building in a predawn attack by the enemies of Nick's team. An attack that had resulted in the deaths of two of Jeremy's friends, members of the Raven Riders Motorcycle Club, which had been helping protect them. On some level, Becca knew Jeremy blamed himself for that. "Well, we better go."

Charlie nodded and made for the door, where he paused for a moment. "Hey, Becca?"

"Yeah?"

For a moment it seemed like he struggled for words. "Have a good night," he finally said, and then he ducked out, Jeremy right behind him.

"Thanks," she said, then turned to Nick. "Was that weird, or is it just me?"

Nick shrugged as he pulled buns out of a bag. "I think he was worried about you being at work today."

"Oh." The thought made her heart squeeze.

Soon, she and Nick were seated at the bar together with overflowing Sloppy Joe sandwiches, some of the pasta salad she'd made over the weekend, and chips. Eileen curled up on the floor next to Becca's tall chair.

"This is the best dinner ever," she said.

"That's because you're easy to please," he said with a smile that brought his dimple out to play. A man with so many rough edges . . . and a dimple. It slayed her every time.

"So how was your day?" she asked.

"Uh, good. Made a lot of progress on the new office," he said. They were turning the previously empty first-floor spot next to their tattoo shop into a high-tech suite of offices for the new security consulting company Nick and his team were opening. "Kinda funny that Jeremy bought this old warehouse because it was cheap, and now it's turned out to be the perfect space for all of us."

Becca smiled. "Yeah. I'm glad everyone is still going to be around here when all the work is done." It had seemed so empty around the building when, earlier in the summer, most of the team had cleared out to return to their homes and pack up their lives to relocate here permanently.

"Me too, Sunshine. This all feels right." Nick wiped up some sauce from his plate with the edge of his bun.

"Where is everyone anyway?" Becca asked. "It's so quiet." With six couples living out of two loft apartments, only one of which had a finished kitchen, it often felt a little like a college dorm around there.

"Shane, Sara, Easy, and Jenna went out to dinner earlier. And I think Beckett, Kat, Marz, and Emilie decided to finish up some painting downstairs."

Becca leaned in for a kiss. "It's weird to be alone."

Nick laughed. "Roger that."

"We could have sex on the counter," Becca said, giving him a seductive look.

He froze with a potato chip halfway to his mouth. "Is this something you've been thinking about?"

"Pretty much if it involves you and sex, you can bet I've thought about it," Becca said, grinning at the expression on his face, part dumbfounded, part aroused. "What can I say? You're very inspiring."

He wiped his mouth and slipped off his stool, then he spun her around to face him, his big body surrounding hers. He tilted up her chin. "Right back atcha, Becca. But nothing is sidetracking me from getting my ink on you tonight. You hear me?"

She rested her hands against his chest. "No sidetracking intended."

His fingers slid into her hair. "Uh-huh. Now, you ready for your tattoo? Because I'm dying to get my hands on you."

WEARING ONLY HER bra and jeans, Becca sat in a chair in the middle of Nick's tattoo room. Since the shop was closed while Jeremy focused on getting the construction on the other half of the building started, they were the only ones down there. The driving beat of a rock song played from the radio as Nick moved around the room getting everything ready.

Cabinets and a long counter filled one wall, which was otherwise decorated with drawings, tattoo designs, posters, and photographs of clients.

Becca had seen Nick work before and loved the dichotomy of this hard-edged, lethal soldier having a soft, artistic side. He was really freaking talented, too.

He handed her three sheets of paper. "I worked up a couple different fonts. What do you think?"

She shifted between the pages. "This one," she said, settling on the cursive design that best interweaved the letters in the words *Only, Always, Forever.*

"That was my favorite, too," he said, giving her a wink. "How is this for size? Bigger? Smaller?"

The total design as he had it on the sheet was about four inches square, the words stacked atop one another. "This looks good to me. What do you think?"

Nick nodded and came behind her. He folded the sheet to focus on the design, then held it against the back of her right shoulder. "Yeah. This is a good size for the space. Gonna be fucking beautiful." He leaned down and pressed a kiss to her skin. "Let me go make the stencil, and we're ready to go."

A few minutes later, he cleaned her skin, affixed the stencil, and let her look at its placement before getting her settled into the chair again.

He pulled her bra strap off to the side. "Ready?"

"Very," she said, butterflies doing a small loop in her belly.

The tattoo machine came to life on a low buzz. "Just relax and let me know if you need a break, okay?" he said, dipping the tip into a little plastic cup of black ink.

"Okay." His gloved hands fell against her skin, and then the needles. Almost a scratching feeling, it didn't hurt nearly as bad as she thought it would. And just like when he'd drawn on her with skin markers, she was already dying to see what it looked like.

"How you doing?" he asked in a voice full of concentration she found utterly sexy. Just the thought that he was permanently altering her skin—just like he'd permanently altered her heart, her life, her very soul—sent a hot thrill through her blood.

"I'm good," she said, relaxing into the sensation of the bite moving across her skin. "Is it weird that I kinda like how it feels?"

He didn't answer right away as the needle moved in a long line. He pulled the machine away and wiped at her shoulder. "Not weird at all," he said, his voice a little gravelly. "Some people like the sensation and even find getting tattoos addictive."

"I can see that," she said. He worked without talking for a stretch, and the combination of the quiet intensity radiating off of him, the driving rock beat, and the buzz of the machine was heady and intoxicating. She found herself breathing a little faster and wanting so much more of him to be touching so much more of her. If she thought he was sexy putting ink on someone else, it was nothing compared to how she felt when he was doing it to her.

"What are you thinking about so hard?" Nick asked, his breath caressing her bare shoulder.

"Really want to know?" she asked, already smiling at what his reaction might be.

"Always," he said, wiping at her skin. He dipped the machine in the ink and leaned in again.

"How turned on this is making me." She really wanted to turn to see his expression but knew she wasn't supposed to move.

He pulled the machine away again. "Jesus, Becca. You're killing me here."

She grinned. "I asked if you really wanted to know."

Nick chuffed out a laugh. "Yeah, well, I've never had a fucking hard-on the entire time I've done a tattoo before, so you're not the only one."

Becca unleashed a small moan. "Now you've got me thinking about your cock, Nick." She couldn't help the hint of a whine in her voice.

"You'll never convince me that that's a bad thing, Sunshine."

"God, I really want to touch you right now," she said, heat spreading over her body.

"Be still," he said, his tone full of a stern command that made her smile.

"Yes, sir."

"Fucking *yes, sir*," he grumbled under his breath.

Another long stretch passed without them talking, but knowing that what they were doing was arousing Nick as much as it was her made her wet and needy and absolutely ready to jump him the minute she could.

Nearly ninety minutes had passed by the time Nick said, "There. It's done." He wiped at her skin and handed her a mirror. "Take a look."

Anticipation made her belly feel like she was looking over the edge of a tall cliff. She crossed to the mirror and turned her back to it, then lifted the hand mirror to see her first tattoo.

"Oh, Nick," she said, her gaze drinking it in. The way the stacked letters intertwined with one another was so beautifully done. "It's . . . gorgeous." Her heart squeezed in her chest. "You are so freaking talented." She looked from the mirror to where he still sat, his gaze glued to her face.

"I think it looks phenomenal on you. You really like it?" he asked.

She looked at her ink again. The stark crispness of the black lettering was so striking against her skin. She adored everything about it—the design, the words, their meaning. "I don't just like it. I love it, Nick. It's perfect. Everything I wanted." Her gaze cut back to him. "Just like you."

"Come here," he said, his voice a little rough. When she stood right in front of him, he pressed a kiss between her breasts. "It was an honor, you letting me do that."

She dragged her hands through his dark brown hair. "Sweet, sweet man," she said, leaning down to kiss him. It started off soft, full of gratitude and love, but quickly flashed hot until they were devouring one another, claiming, wanting, moaning.

"Fuck, Becca," he said, pulling back. "Let me take care of your tattoo."

Wiping the wetness from her lips, she smiled and nodded. "Okay." She sat back in the chair, and Nick cleaned the skin over her tattoo and taped a bandage to it.

"All done," he said. "Now, there's just one more thing I need to do."

CHAPTER 4

Holy hell, had Nick ever been this nervous in his life? He'd faced down warlords, captured terrorists, survived IED explosions, and been shot on multiple occasions. Yet he'd never felt the kind of queasy, can't-quite-manage-a-deep-breath nerves he felt just then.

He retrieved the little black box from the drawer where he'd hidden it, fisted it in his palm, and came to stand in front of Becca. He gave her a hand to stand up, then slowly sank to one knee.

"What are you—" Becca gasped. "Nick?"

"Becca." Looking up at her beautiful face, he grasped her left hand. "When you walked through my door, you changed my whole life. You gave me purpose when I had none. You brought my family back together when I was so alone. You believed in me when no one else did, including myself. You fought for me and loved me and made me a better man." Glassy, bright blue eyes stared down at him with so much love. "You shined light on places inside me I thought would never emerge from the dark, and you helped me reclaim my integrity, my honor, and my life." A knot lodged in Nick's throat. "You saved me from becoming someone I didn't recognize, and because of you I have a life worth living. But only if you'll walk it with me."

"Nick," she rasped, her voice thick with unshed tears.

He flipped open the box and pulled out the diamond and platinum round-cut ring. A halo of smaller stones surrounded the center stone, creating what to him looked like a sun. More accent stones lined the band, giving it a classic, vintage look. He'd known it was the right ring as soon as he'd seen it. Slowly, he slid the diamond onto Becca's ring finger. "I love you with everything that I am, and everything I want to be. Please do me the greatest honor of my life and say you'll be my wife, my partner, my best friend, my companion. Becca Merritt, will you marry me?"

For a split second that felt like eternity, she looked down at her shaking hand. And then she sank to her knees in front of him and grasped his face. "Yes," she said, kissing him. "Only you. Always you. Forever you, Nick. Yes."

"Aw, Sunshine," he said, sliding his hands into her hair. "You make me happier than I ever thought I could be."

"I feel the exact same way," she said, tears finally leaking from the corners of her eyes. "I love you so much."

He kissed her on a groan, his spirit more buoyant and triumphant than it had ever been. Even more than when their records had been cleared and their honor had been restored. That had been exactly what he'd deserved, but this . . . this was more than he ever knew to want.

Becca's hands fisted in his shirt as she sucked hard on his tongue, a needy, desperate moan spilling from her throat. The sound shot right to his cock, making him rock hard in an instant and bringing back every bit of the aching lust he'd felt while he'd been doing her tattoo. Christ, if he thought it was arousing to mark her with his ink, it was nothing compared to what it did to him to know she'd just agreed to be his forever. He was fucking flying.

Nick tore open the button to her jeans. "Need in you."

"Yes," she said, tugging up his shirt. He helped her pull it over his head. For a moment, they were a whirl of shedding clothes and grasping hands and claiming kisses until they were both naked and panting and hot.

He sat in the chair where she'd been sitting and guided her down to his lap, her back to his front. "Take me inside of you, Becca. Ride me so fucking hard."

She took his cock in hand and sank down on him in one slow, slick stroke. "Oh, God," she rasped when he bottomed out inside her. "Needed you so much. All day."

He grasped her hips, his fingers digging into her soft flesh. "I'm here. Right here."

Hands braced on his thighs, Becca lifted herself up and down on his cock, riding him until they were both moaning, desperate, shaking. Her nails bit deliciously into his quads, making him do a double take at the big diamond on her left hand. And *fuck* if that didn't escalate the urgent ache in his balls—to pour himself deep, deep inside her, and never let go.

She threw her head back, sending her long blond waves cascading down his chest. He fisted a thick column of her hair in his hand, forcing her back further against him until she was reclined against his chest and impaled on his cock. "Want you to come all over me," he said, reaching around to stroke her. She arched on contact, but Nick held her fast against him as his fingers pressed firm, quick circles against her clit.

The diamond caught the light as she grasped and kneaded her breasts, her movements growing desperate as she thrust forward against his fingers and back against his cock. On a guttural moan, she held her breath and her core fisted around his length until her muscles were pulsing, sucking, squeezing the sanity from him. A high-pitched moan wrenched out of her as she went slack on his lap, and the languid satisfaction of her body made him feel ten feet tall.

"Holy shit," she rasped.

He smacked her ass. "Kneel on the chair and bend over."

"Ooh. Yes, sir," she said as he helped her stand. He grinned as she got into position and looked back over her shoulder.

Gut instinct had him pulling off the bandage covering her tattoo. "I wanna see this ink while I fuck you." He penetrated her inch by maddening inch, his gaze glued to the words she would wear forever. For him.

Gripping the back of the chair, she peered at the design from the corner of her eye. "You're so good, Nick. All of you. I'm so lucky you're mine."

Her voice lit up places within him that once were so dark. Buried all the way inside her, he leaned over her back and braced his hand on the chair next to hers. Then his hips started to move in small, deep, punctuated thrusts that had her moaning with each stroke and his body screaming for release. As deep as it was, it wasn't deep enough. It would *never* be deep enough. "Fuck, Becca. Just want you so goddamned much."

"You have me, Nick. Oh, God," she rasped as he banded an arm around her ribs and moved faster. The chair screeched against the floor and their skin slapped against the percussive beat of a grinding rock song.

He clutched her left hand on the backrest of the chair, and the diamond bit into his palm. It was the nail in the coffin of his remaining reserve. On a shout, he buried himself balls deep and came until he couldn't help but rest his weight against Becca's back. When his body finally stilled, he wrapped both arms around her and pressed a soft, open-mouthed kiss next to her tattoo. "I love you, Becca. And I always will."

NICK COULD BARELY keep the smile off his face as he opened the apartment door. Him, unable to hold back a smile. If that wasn't life doing a one-eighty, he didn't know what was.

"After you," he said to Becca. As she stepped inside the loft, he flicked on the lights to the main room.

"Surprise!" rang out in a great chorus of voices, along with a few barks. All their friends were there waiting for them—Jeremy and Charlie, Nick's sister, Kat, and all of Nick's teammates and their girlfriends. Baltimore police detective Kyler Vance, who'd been such an ally during their investigation, was there, too. And Nick had even managed to convince Walter and Louis Jackson to come. Walter had been Charlie's landlord and had taken a special interest in helping Becca, even calling in the assistance of his son, Louis, who'd turned out to be an amazing resource for the team as the coordinator of the city's task force on gangs.

"Oh, my God," Becca said with a huge smile on her face. She turned and threw her arms around Nick. "You planned all this?"

Now he could grin. "I did good, huh?"

She laughed and hugged him tighter. "You did amazing."

When they broke apart, he and Becca were surrounded by their friends and family, although the distinction didn't mean much in this room. These people were all their family of choice. Everyone offered words of congratulations as Becca showed off her ring and recounted his proposal.

"Congrats, man. I couldn't be happier for you," Jeremy said, wearing the most unreserved smile Nick had seen on his brother in weeks. Not that Nick could blame him—between recovering from brain surgery, managing the construction on the other half of the Hard Ink building, and grappling with the death of two friends in the attack, the guy had a lot on his plate.

"Thanks, Jeremy. That means a lot," Nick said. He shook

his brother's hand and tugged him in for a quick hug. "I'm happy for you, too. You and Charlie."

Becca arched a brow at Charlie. "So, going to a movie, huh?" Charlie's smile was a little sheepish, where Jer's was a total shit-eating number that said he was pleased with himself for pulling one over on her. "So you were in on all this?" she asked them.

Charlie nodded. "It's nice to have something else to celebrate."

"I couldn't agree more," Nick said as he watched Becca hug the blond-haired man who'd helped make tonight possible when he'd given Nick his blessing to propose to his sister.

Someone touched Nick's arm, and he turned to find Kat standing beside him. Short, with long brown hair, she matched Nick for stubbornness and guts, something she'd proven more than once during the recent investigation. "She's really good for you, Nick. You deserve this. And I'm really proud of you," Kat said. Given the way the two of them butted heads sometimes, the words meant a lot. They hugged, and Nick was reminded yet again just how much he had in his life now. Because of Becca.

"Thanks, Kat. Although all this happiness is really fucking weird," he said.

Rolling her bright green eyes, she shook her head. "Too damn bad. You'll just have to get used to it." She linked arms with Becca. "So when do we get to go dress shopping?"

"I'd love to help, too," Sara Dean said, brushing her red hair back from her face.

"I hadn't even thought about it yet," Becca said, looking between Kat and Sara. Of all the women here, Becca and Sara had known each other the longest. Nick knew that Becca held a special affection for Sara, who'd helped him and the team rescue Charlie from the basement of the strip club where Sara had been forced to work. "I'm off on

Thursday and Friday, so maybe then? Jenna and Emilie can come, too. We'll do a whole girls' day."

"After everything that's happened, isn't it weird to think we can just go shopping?" Sara said. Words of agreement rose up all around, and Nick was glad that Becca had a close group of friends to share all this with.

Shane McCallan came up behind Sara and kissed her on the cheek. "Champagne?" He held out a tray of plastic flutes. Sara looked up at Shane with so much affection on her face, and Nick wondered if he and Becca were that blatant with their feelings. Hell, he guessed they probably were. But everyone in this room deserved a big old slice of happiness, so Nick couldn't begrudge a single one of them.

"You make a good waiter," Nick said to his best friend as he took a glass for Becca and himself. "In case this security business doesn't work out, and all."

"Don't make me tell you to fuck off at your engagement party," Shane said, a hint of his Southern accent coming through.

Nick laughed and shook the guy's free hand. "Thanks again for coming with me today."

"Wouldn't have been anywhere else," Shane said. And Nick knew that was true, despite the initial disbelief and subsequent ribbing Shane had dished out when Nick had told him what he planned to do.

When everyone had a glass of bubbly in their hands, Shane called out, "Hey everyone, gather 'round. I'd like to make a toast."

Standing in a big circle between the loft's open living room and kitchen, everyone quieted. Becca slipped her arm around Nick's back and leaned in tight against his side.

Shane held up his glass. "Nick Rixey is my best friend, my teammate, and my brother, and I know he'd lay down his life for me as quickly as I'd do the same for him."

"Fuckin' A," Nick said, giving Shane a nod. Their other

teammates—Beckett Murda, Derek "Marz" DiMarzio, and Edward "Easy" Cantrell—sent up words of support, too.

"So I couldn't be happier," Shane continued, "to see him getting everything he deserves. Well, maybe even more than he deserves, given how amazing Becca Merritt is."

Against a round of laughter, Nick grinned and nodded, while Becca protested and hugged him.

Shane winked at her. "Becca, you went above and beyond in helping us clear our names, and I will forever be proud to call you my sister." Before things had a chance to turn serious, he added, "So if you ever need any help with this stubborn pain-in-the-ass man with whom you've chosen to spend your life, you just let any of us know." He gestured to the other guys in the room.

"Count me in for that, too," Jeremy said with a big smile. Everyone laughed, and damn, it felt good seeing their friends at such ease.

"So let's raise a glass to the couple who brought us all together. May love, peace, and happiness be your constant companions. To Nick and Becca." Shane raised his glass higher.

"To Nick and Becca," everyone called.

Grinning up at Nick, Becca clicked her plastic flute against his. "I love you," she said.

"Right back atcha, Sunshine," he said, his heart feeling two sizes too big for his chest. They drank.

"Is it time to eat the cake yet?" Marz said to more laughter as he leaned against the breakfast bar. Which was when Nick noticed a big cake with a figurine standing atop it next to Marz's elbow.

"Leave it to Marz to demand food," Beckett said with a smirk. Seeing Beckett relaxed and cutting it up was another big change, because for almost as long as they'd known one another, Beckett had been reserved and quiet, not one to shoot the shit or joke around. Before all this, only Marz had seemed to get behind the big guy's walls. Nick now knew that Kat had had a lot to do with how the man had changed, as much as their relationship had thrown Nick at first.

"Well, he did help me make it," Emilie said, planting a kiss on Marz's cheek. "It was all I could do to keep him from eating all the icing."

"Aw, you made this?" Becca said, stepping up to the counter. The square cake was two layers tall and read, *To Nick and Becca, The Best Is Yet To Come!* Next to the words stood a porcelain figurine of a man in fatigues embracing a blond-haired woman in a wedding dress.

And *that* was officially the first time Nick imagined seeing Becca in her wedding gown—about to get married to him. And hell if the thought of that didn't slay him.

"This is amazing, Emilie," Becca said as the women hugged.

"It really is. Thank you," Nick said, hugging Emilie next. After losing her brother—who'd been the team's enemy—her devotion to everyone in that room was truly amazing. Nick held out his hand to Marz next. "And thank you for not eating the cake before we had a chance to see it." Marz's appetite was pretty damn legendary.

Wearing his trademark grin, Marz nodded. "Dude, it was a close call." Marz could always be counted on to lighten a moment and make them laugh. Despite the fact that he'd borne the most serious injury from their ambush, he never let his amputation hold him back or get him down. Nick fucking admired that, he really did.

For a moment, surrounded by everyone he loved, Nick let himself bask in this moment of such fucking perfect contentment.

The best is yet to come.

Now that all the bullshit was behind them, Nick absolutely believed it. The future was theirs, and nothing could keep him from his happily ever after with Becca now.

"Well, what are we waiting for?" Nick asked. "Let's eat some damn cake."

CHAPTER 5

’m really excited to do this today," Becca said as Nick parked the car along the curb. She'd spent all her free time after work on Tuesday and Wednesday searching local venues, dress shops, caterers, florists, and other things related to planning a wedding. She already had her two days off booked with appointments, just so she could get an idea of what she'd want at her wedding.

Her wedding! Part of Becca could hardly believe it. She and Nick were getting married. She thought back to the stubborn, standoffish man she'd met that first day at Hard Ink all those months ago, and could only marvel at how far they'd come.

"Me too," Nick said. "Besides, whatever makes you happy makes me happy, you know that."

She gave him a look. "Smart man."

He grinned. "Come on. Let's go check it out."

They stepped out onto Front Street, a little cobblestone-paved gem right in the middle of downtown Baltimore. At one end of the block stood the towering 1840s Carrollton Inn and at the other, the historic Carroll Mansion, onetime home to Charles Carroll, Maryland's longest living signer of the Declaration of Independence. A brick-paved courtyard surrounded by lush gardens joined the two.

They'd barely stepped through the wrought-iron gatehouse entrance onto the property before Becca was head over heels in love—with the historic ambiance, the beautiful architecture, the whole romantic setting. A thrill of excitement shot through her. A few months ago, she'd been worried about losing her only remaining family member. Now, she'd gained a huge new family, had her brother firmly back in her life, and was about to become someone's wife. It was amazing how quickly life could change. For the good and for the bad.

"Hello," a tall woman in a smart pants suit said. With her long black hair and warm brown skin, she was strikingly pretty. "I'm Sonya Mayer, the assistant manager of the inn. Welcome." Nick and Becca introduced themselves, and Sonya gave them the tour of the inn's four interior levels and rooms, as well as its outdoor spaces.

"I can't believe I've never noticed this place before. It's just gorgeous," Becca said. The rooms each had their own unique atmosphere and decor, lending elegance to the inn's charming nineteenth-century architecture. And the courtyard would be gorgeous for an outdoor wedding, something she'd always wanted.

"We have our own little enclave back here," Sonya said. "A little oasis of calm and historical charm in the middle of the city."

Becca nodded, struggling to keep her outward cool when inside she was all *I want it I want it and I don't care how much it costs!*

Back downstairs, Sonya guided them to a table where they had a few flower and cake samples laid out. Menus, catalogs, and price lists sat on one corner of the table atop a shiny venue folder.

"Can I offer you a glass of champagne while we talk?" Sonya asked.

"I'd love that," Becca said. "Nick?"

"Sounds great," he said. When Sonya departed, he turned to her. "Okay, tell me how much you want this place."

Becca managed to hold in her enthusiasm for about five seconds. "It's so amazing. Don't you think so? It's pretty and charming and not too big and—"

Nick kissed her. "Done."

"It's pretty expensive, though," she said.

He shook his head, his pale green eyes locked on hers. "I don't care what it costs. If you want it, we're having it. I like it, too. And we deserve the best to start our new life."

"Really?" she asked. "How'd I get so lucky?"

The smile brought out his dimple. "That's my line."

"Here we go," Sonya said, settling two crystal champagne flutes down on the table. She had an iPad tucked under her arm.

"Cheers," Nick said, clinking glasses with Becca. The champagne was sweet and bubbly, absolutely delicious.

"So, have you picked a date?" Sonya asked, bringing the iPad to life in front of her.

Becca looked to Nick. "We only just got engaged," she said. "If we wanted to have the ceremony outside, I suppose we'd need to do it by the fall or wait until the spring?" Nick nodded and gave her hand a squeeze.

"Well, let me see," Sonya said, scrolling through her digital calendar. "We're actually booking a year out right now. I know all the weekend dates in the fall are completely booked. And I think the spring is, too." Becca's shoulders dropped. She shouldn't have been surprised, really, since most people had long engagements to allow them to make their plans. "If you're interested in a shorter engagement, it looks like . . ." The woman focused on the screen for a long moment. "It looks like I only have two options as of this moment. The third Saturday in December, which would preclude an outdoor ceremony. Or, oh, we had a cancellation on Saturday, August eighth. Though if you've only just gotten engaged, I imagine that's much too soon. Otherwise, our next weekend opening is next July."

Becca barely heard anything after the August date. That was three weeks from now. She looked up at Nick. "Is three weeks from now too crazy?"

The smile he gave her made her fall even more in love with him. "Only in the best possible ways, Sunshine."

Tears pricked the backs of her eyes. "I could be your wife in three weeks."

A heated masculine satisfaction slid into those pale green eyes, and Nick turned to Sonya. "We'll take August eighth."

"IT'S A GOOD thing you'd already made an appointment to look at dresses," Emilie said as the five women piled out of Shane's big truck the following day. Sara had sweet-talked him into letting them borrow it for their girls' day out.

"I know, right?" Becca said, still floating over the fact that she was getting married in three weeks. "But the inn was just too perfect to pass up, and neither of us wanted to wait a whole year to get married."

Sara elbowed her in the side. "And you're sure this isn't a shotgun wedding, right?"

Grinning, Becca shook her head. She and Nick had been answering this question ever since they'd returned from the inn yesterday after several hours of choosing food, cake, and flowers for their event. "Nope. There's no bun in this oven, I promise you." Everyone laughed. Becca walked up to the ornate carved desk and greeted the young woman standing there. "Hi, I'm Becca Merritt."

"Welcome, Becca. Please have a seat. Diana will be right out," the woman said.

The five friends sat on the overstuffed cream-colored sofas and nibbled at cookies and fancy wrapped chocolates displayed on plates covering the glass-topped end tables. Becca and Nick might be doing this fast, but it all still felt so special to her. She was glad they weren't waiting.

A woman with short strawberry-blond hair wearing a pretty teal wrap dress approached their group. Diana made quick introductions, then took them to a sitting room where Becca could show off the gowns she tried on. "Do you have a date in mind?" Diana asked.

"I do, and it's really short notice. August eighth," Becca said, not missing the woman's gaze flicker down to her belly and back. Becca almost laughed. "We fell in love with a venue that had a last-minute cancellation, so we went for it."

"Well, we can make this work, Becca. We've got quite a few gowns available in our annual sample sale, so let's see if we can't find something you love. This way, please." She led them into a long rectangular room filled with racks of gowns. "Do you have any preferences for color, silhouette, length?"

"I want to wear a gown that you couldn't wear any other time," Becca said. "Something romantic and full. Maybe sleeveless. And I think I prefer white to ivory."

"Let's start with ball gowns and A-lines, then," Diana said, already pulling a few things off the racks. "Ladies, feel free to pull anything fun that you see."

Becca searched through the gowns, pulling a couple of things that caught her eye. Before long, she was in the dressing room neck deep in satin and lace and tulle. Too much tulle in the case of the first dress, which she obligingly showed to her friends even though she knew it wasn't the one. "What do you think?" she asked as she spun on the dais in front of them.

Kat made a face. "I think it's too young for you."

Sara nodded. "Too froufrou."

Becca laughed. "I agree." She tried on another, this one in a mermaid cut that wasn't at all her style. "Who picked this one?" she asked, laughing.

"What? I thought it was cool," Sara's younger sister, Jenna, said. They both had matching red hair.

"Sadly, I don't have the hips to pull this off. Or the boobs. Or whatever else you need to make this work." Becca rolled her eyes as the women nodded and laughed. The third one was closer—a sleeveless ball-gown style with lots of lace and beading. "This is gorgeous," Becca said. "But it's so heavy I don't know how I'd dance in it."

"I don't know, Becca," Emilie said, tucking her brown hair behind her ears. "That one might be worth suffering for."

It took five more dresses before Becca fell in love. The white ball gown had a sleeveless sweetheart neckline and gorgeous beading at the waist, while the skirt fell in soft layers of satin, full but not poofy. It was two sizes too big and was missing a few buttons down the back, but Diana assured her it could be taken in and repaired in plenty of time. Staring in the mirror, Becca suddenly felt overwhelmed.

Kat was the first one to notice. She crossed from the sofa to stand beside Becca. "You okay?"

Afraid that trying to speak might hasten the threatening tears, Becca just nodded.

"This is the one, isn't it?" Kat met Becca's gaze in the mirror. Despite her petite stature, Kat looked so much like her brothers, with her chocolate brown hair and green eyes—and even a few shared facial expressions—that Becca immediately felt at ease. And she realized there was something she needed to ask Katherine.

"Yeah," Becca managed. "I don't need to look anymore."

She turned to face Kat. "Will you be my maid of honor?" They might not have known each other very long, but in the few months since they'd met, they'd bonded hard and fast, not only over their love for the Rixey men but also because of the way Kat had taken care of Becca during the team's investigation.

Kat's eyes went wide. "You want me?"

"We're going to be sisters, right? I absolutely want you. If you'll do it," Becca said.

Kat hugged her. "I'd love to stand up for you and Nick. I'm so happy for both of you."

"Okay, now. Don't make me cry. I'm having a hard enough time with that as it is," Becca said. Everyone laughed. Becca gave herself one last look in the mirror. "Yeah, this is the one." She turned to see the back of it, all clean, soft lines of satin. On her shoulder, the healing tattoo peeked out through her hair. The design was as beautiful as the words were appropriate, so she had no qualms about the ink showing. She was proud of the gift Nick had given her.

"Well, then," Diana said. "Let's get the tailor to take a look at you, and then we'll get the ladies started on bridesmaid dresses. Any idea what color you'd like?"

"Yes," Becca said. "Kat, can you grab the picture from my purse?" Kat handed Diana the picture of the bridesmaids' bouquets Becca had chosen. "I figured it might be hard to get one bridesmaid dress that works for everyone in the short time we have," Becca continued. "So as long as the gown is a shade of purple that matches these flowers, I don't care what style or length it is. Whatever you guys like."

Diana studied the picture, which showed a bouquet with mauve roses, purple hydrangeas, dark purple irises, berry-colored orchids, burgundy dahlias, and light purple mini carnations. "Oh, yes, we can make this work. I'll grab the tailor for you and show the girls where to look."

In the time it took for Becca to get fitted, everyone found things to try on. And it didn't take long until all four friends decided on dresses that suited their taste and matched Becca's color scheme. Kat chose a sleek, sleeveless dark-purple gown that looked gorgeous with her long brown hair. Emilie picked a mauve V-neck gown with a satin belt at the waist. Sara chose a satin berry-colored sheath with cap sleeves and a sweetheart neckline, while Jenna went with a flirty lavender gown with a drop waist and a fuller skirt that accentuated her curves beautifully.

"You all look stunning," Becca said when they stood before her. "The guys aren't going to know what to do with themselves."

"Shane's never seen me in a dress like this before," Sara said, staring at herself in the mirror. "In fact, I don't think I've ever owned a dress like this before."

Jenna grasped her sister's hand. Despite being the youngest of the five of them, the Dean sisters had been through hell the past few years, especially Sara, who'd borne the burden of repaying her criminal father's debts after he'd died, sometimes in ways too horrible to imagine. "Well, it won't be the last one," Jenna said, smiling. "But, yeah, it's gonna be fun seeing their reactions."

"I think we're all pretty guaranteed to get laid at Becca's wedding," Kat said with a mischievous grin.

They all burst into laughter. "When do you *not* get laid, Kat?" Emilie asked with an arched eyebrow.

"Aw, don't even talk to me, Miss Garza, because you and Marz are loud as hell. Not that I mind, because, *dude,* does he have a mouth on him," Kat said with a big grin.

"Oh, my God," Sara said, her cheeks turning bright pink but her smile saying she was enjoying the teasing.

"He really does." Grinning, Emilie shrugged. "The hazards of sharing an unfinished apartment. Can't be helped." Kat and Beckett had been staying in the room Nick and

Jeremy reserved for her in their apartment until one particularly loud session of lovemaking had apparently caught Jer's ear. His teasing had been relentless. Finally, Kat and Beckett relocated to an empty room upstairs. As much as they all enjoyed each other's company, everyone was going to be thrilled when the new building was done, that was for sure.

Becca could only laugh as the good-natured ribbing went on. "Well, I know I'm getting laid. The rest of you are on your own." By the time they'd all been fitted and had paid for their gowns, Becca was pretty sure they were on the verge of getting thrown out of the store.

They spilled out onto the street, laughing and hungry for lunch. Becca fell behind while she fished for her cell phone in her purse and paused to shoot off a quick text to Nick.

All done dress shopping! I'm gonna knock your socks off! ;)

Nick responded immediately. *Sunshine, you already do.*

Grinning, she glanced down the block—and nearly gasped out loud. Tyrell Woodson stood at the corner, glaring at her.

"Hey, Becca, come on," Kat called. Becca blinked and the man was gone. Vanished. A figment of her imagination. Not that her body seemed to know the difference. Heart racing, she caught up with the group as they made their way to an Italian place they'd agreed on earlier. "You okay?" Kat asked.

"Yeah. Great." Her voice sounded flat to her own ears. She glanced back over her shoulder. Woodson wasn't there. Of course. She let out a long breath. She'd gotten through the whole workweek without another incident like the one she'd had with Ben at the end of her first shift back. Clearly, her subconscious wasn't done worrying about Woodson, though, however unnecessary—and unfounded—that worrying was.

Why was she freaking out about what'd happened to her now? For months, she'd been fine, just an occasional nightmare of being grabbed, being dragged away, being lost and never found. Then again, for most of that time she'd been shut up at Hard Ink with Nick.

They arrived at the restaurant, and Kat paused before she followed the others inside. "Are you sure you're okay?" she asked. "Because you know my brother will kill me if anything happens to you on my watch." Kat arched an eyebrow. Though Becca knew she was joking, there'd been a time not too long before when Kat had in fact been Becca's bodyguard, during a meeting with the man who'd turned out to be responsible for the death of Becca's dad. Nick had gotten angry at both of them when they'd had to deviate from the original plan to get Becca home safely.

"You just survived heart surgery, Kat," Becca said. Kat had gotten shot at the same funeral where Jeremy had been hurt. Watching Nick deal with both of his siblings fighting for their lives was one of the hardest things Becca had ever done. But they'd both pulled through. And now they all deserved a celebration. "Nick is so grateful you're okay that I'm pretty sure you'll be able to get away with absolutely anything for the rest of your life," Becca said with a smile. "And I'm fine, I promise."

"Good," Kat said, giving her a last look. "Then let's eat, because I'm starving."

CHAPTER 6

It happened again the next week. More than once. Most recently, it occurred on her way back to the hospital after grabbing something for lunch. Becca saw Woodson lurking in a doorway farther down the street, but when she looked again, no one was there.

That night, as she and Nick lay in bed, Becca gave voice to the question whose answer she thought might best give her some peace of mind. "Do you know what happened to Tyrell Woodson after you interrogated him?"

Nick shifted to look at her, concern filling his pale green eyes. "Why?"

"I just wondered," she said, feeling a little bad for not sharing what she'd been experiencing. She didn't want to worry him, though, especially when they had so much going on—the construction, setting up his and the team's new business, her work at the ER, planning the wedding. During their off hours this week, they'd managed to send out invitations, find an officiant, hire a DJ, and apply for their marriage license. Luckily, all the guys already had their dress blues from when the Army had held a memorial service for the fallen members of their A-team a few weeks before.

Eyes narrowed, Nick studied her. "You know we sent the harbor police out to that island where we dropped him, but he was gone when they got there. So once Detective Vance joined our investigation, I had him search for Woodson. Just to be on the safe side."

Gone? Becca pushed up onto an elbow. Vance's inquiry was news to her. "So what did he find?"

Nick tucked her hair behind her ear. "Woodson's not in custody anywhere, but he's not here. Vance tracked him to South Carolina using credit card transactions. Apparently he has family down there. Looks like he left town right after everything went down. Marz took that video of him spilling all kinds of secrets. No doubt he wanted to get clear of the city in case we turned it over to Church like we threatened."

Relief flooded through Becca so fast that she sagged back down to her pillow. He wasn't in Baltimore. Hell, he wasn't in Maryland. So it really was her imagination at work. "Oh. That's good."

Leaning over her, Nick cupped Becca's face in his hand. "Shit, Becca. I'm sorry. Have you been worrying about this? I should've said something, but—"

"No, not worried, exactly. I guess I just needed to know. For closure." And it was true. Maybe she could stop seeing ghosts around every corner now.

Nick nodded. "Why don't I have Vance run another trace on him? Make sure he's still out of the picture? I can't imagine why he'd come back with how volatile Baltimore's gang scene is right now. Since the Church Gang imploded, Louis Jackson told us that the word on the street for former

Churchmen is leave or die. It's been open season on them as other gangs fight to consolidate power and take over the heroin trade."

Becca nodded, Nick's words strengthening the bulwarks against her fear. "Yeah, that makes sense. But have Vance run the check. It can't hurt, right?"

"Absolutely. You know I'd do anything to keep you safe, Becca." He nailed her with a stare full of such fierce love that it stole her breath.

"Of course. And so would I," she said.

It only took the weekend before Vance had news. He called Monday night after Becca's shift while everyone was hanging out watching movies in Nick and Jeremy's living room.

"Vance," Nick said as he answered his cell and got up from the couch. "How are you?"

"Want me to pause it?" Jeremy asked, sitting in the corner of the other couch next to Charlie, Eileen attempting to fit her growing body on his lap.

Nick waved him off and headed back down the hall toward his office. Becca followed. "And what did you find?" Nick asked as he settled into the chair at his desk. As Becca looked at him sitting there, memories came rushing back. One of her first nights here. Giving Nick a massage after his back had been hurt when he and Beckett had gotten into a fistfight. How he'd kissed her. "Well, that's good news then."

The words pulled Becca from her thought. Good news had to mean Woodson was still far away, right?

"Okay, sounds like a plan. Thanks, man," Nick said.

"What did he say?" she asked when Nick hung up.

He tossed his cell to the desk and reached out for her, pulling her down to straddle his lap. "As recently as last Wednesday, Woodson got a speeding ticket in South Carolina. Vance is still working on recent credit card transactions. But that's pretty good evidence that he's stayed put." Nick stroked his fingers through Becca's hair. "Vance is going to put out a be-on-the-lookout for Woodson's car with local PD, on the off chance he returns to the area."

Becca nodded. "That all sounds good. Thank you for having him do that."

"A little extra peace of mind never hurts," he said. Hand slipping behind her neck, he gently pulled her down until their lips met. The kiss was slow and soft and exploring, full of the heat that always flared quickly to life between them. "You're gonna be my wife in less than two weeks," he whispered around the edge of the kiss.

The words made her smile. "I am." The kiss deepened. "Yours to do with whatever you want."

Nick's gaze flashed hot. "My thoughts exactly." He urged her to stand up, then he crossed to the door and closed it. When he turned to her, the expression on his face was predatory, so damn sexy she was immediately wet with anticipation. Without a word, he stood in front of her, unbuttoned and pushed down her jeans and panties, and sank to his knees in front of her. "Right now what I want is for you to come all over my tongue."

Becca clutched onto the desk behind her as Nick planted his mouth between her legs, his tongue immediately plunging into her folds and finding her clit. Together they worked her jeans the rest of the way off, then Nick pushed her stance wider and settled his big body in tight between her legs.

He was relentless, his fingers holding her open, his tongue alternating between lapping at her and hard, fast flicks, his mouth sucking.

"Oh, God, Nick," she rasped, her hand falling on his hair and clutching at it. He growled against her, not letting up for a second, and she thrust her hips forward, yearning and seeking and craving even more. She tugged his hair, pulling him in tighter, unable to restrain herself from demanding what she needed.

And it seemed to drive Nick harder, because he worked a thick finger inside her slickness and sucked her in a fast rhythm that had her panting and thrusting and straining. The orgasm hit her like a shock wave, not there one moment and then throwing her head over heels the next. She got light-headed and her knees went soft, forcing her to sag back against the desk.

"Holy shit," she rasped.

Nick eased his hand free of her and looked up, his gaze so full of smug satisfaction that it made her shake her head as she smiled. And then, eyes on hers, he sucked the wetness off his finger and licked his lips. "You taste fucking delicious, Sunshine."

Becca's heart did a little flip as she offered him a hand and he rose. "You know," she said, "if I hadn't already agreed to marry you, I would say yes just based on how good you are at that."

Nick threw his head back and laughed, the kind of free, joyful laughter she'd only heard from him a handful of times. His smile was freaking gorgeous, his dimple a mile deep, and his face so ruggedly beautiful that it made her whole chest ache with how much she loved him. "Good to know," he managed.

Grinning, she wrapped her arms around his neck. "Seriously. A man who can make the best Sloppy Joes on earth, helps total strangers, sings bad eighties anthems, loves his family fiercely, can kill in fifty-two ways if he has to, is smoking hot, *and* eats pussy like he's starved for it is a keeper." She tried to keep a straight face, but laughter was already bubbling up inside her.

"I . . . am really freaking aroused now. Keep talking," he said, his eyebrow arched, that smug smile returning.

She reached for his jeans and tugged the button open.

"About what? Should I talk about how much I love your cock? How amazing it feels inside me?"

Nick licked his lips, a kind of amused disbelief filling his gaze. "Yes, definitely talk about that. Like, a lot."

Grinning, Becca bit her lip and pushed off the desk. Walking backward, she hooked her fingers in the waistband of his jeans and pulled him along with her toward the bedroom. With her other hand, she grasped his hard length, squeezing just enough to wring a grunt out of him. "Come put this inside me, Nick, and I'll say absolutely anything you want."

NICK FELT LIKE he hadn't seen Becca in forever, despite the fact that they'd woken up together this morning. But that had been fifteen hours ago—before he'd spent all day working with the guys to install the carpet in their new offices. As much as possible, they were trying to do the work on the business suite to allow the contractor to stay focused on the much bigger project of the building. Given Jeremy's ability to figure out pretty much any home improvement project, Beckett's electrical know-how, and Marz and Charlie's expertise with all the wiring and secure computer hookups they needed done, they were in pretty good shape.

In the meantime, all of them had been working their contacts to get word out about the new security consulting services they'd be offering. Beckett, Marz, and Shane had already been working in various aspects of the field and had ready clients to reach out to. Having worked for years as a computer security consultant hacking into corporations' systems to find their weaknesses, Charlie turned out to be an amazing asset in making new contacts. All of which was keeping them on track for a targeted post–Labor Day opening date, which would give Nick and Becca two weeks for their honeymoon in Italy and another two for Nick to be back and helping with all the last-minute prep.

Nick's and Beckett's cell phones dinged an incoming message at about the same time, and both of them paused where they knelt on the floor to check their phones. Since Becca and Kat had gone shopping together after Becca's half-day shift, Nick didn't have to guess at who it was.

On the way home. Be there in about twenty! xo

"Aw, look at you two," Shane said, his tone full of sarcasm. "Stop chitchatting with the ladies and let's get this shit finished."

"You are as pussy-whipped as any of us, McCallan, so shut the fuck up," Beckett said as he shoved his phone in his back pocket. Ah, it was so nice that they were all getting along so good again. Just like old times. In all the best ways.

From the next room where Marz and Charlie were working on some wiring, Charlie called, "For the record, I am not as pussy-whipped as the rest of you."

Silence rang out for a moment, and then they all lost their shit. Just flat-out, tear-inducing laughter that had every one of them clutching their guts. Charlie fucking Merritt was coming out of his shell, that was for goddamn sure.

Wiping the tears from his eyes, Nick managed to get to two feet and make it to the doorway, where he found Marz red in the face with hilarity and Jeremy pressing a big kiss to his boyfriend's mouth. The affection his brother and soon-to-be brother-in-law bore for each other made Nick happy, it really did. Because Nick had never seen Jeremy settle down like this before—with a man or a woman, and he'd dated both. And no matter how much Nick admired so many other things about Becca and Charlie's father—the team's former commander—Nick would never understand the homophobic bullshit Frank Merritt had apparently rained down on Charlie from the moment he'd come out. So Charlie deserved this chance to be happy and loved and accepted. By all of them. And, amazingly, they all fit together like clockwork—even Jeremy and Charlie, who hadn't been part of their team.

They were now.

Beckett joined Nick in the doorway, his bright blue eyes gleaming. "Tou-fucking-che, Charlie."

Because he had his hair pulled back in some sort of a bun thing, the red covering Charlie's face was crystal clear, but the guy was smiling as Marz slapped him on the knee.

Everyone got back to work, shooting the shit as they finished up the last of the carpeting.

From where he knelt in the corner, Easy ran his dark hand over his short-trimmed hair and looked around the nearly finished space. "This is all really coming together."

"Yes, it is," Nick said. Right now, it was all plain white walls and industrial gray carpeting, but they'd come a helluva long way from the cement floor, exposed ceilings, and cinder-block walls that had stood there just a few weeks before. "Thanks to the hard work you all have been putting in."

"I'm glad to do it," Easy said. "It's good to be busy. And it's really fucking good to feel like I'm part of something again."

Nick, Easy, Beckett, and Shane all traded looks and nodded. Every one of them felt the same way after the ambush, the other-than-honorable discharge, having their reputations tarnished, and being scattered to the four winds once they'd returned stateside.

"Amen, brother," Shane said, clapping Easy on the shoulder.

When the other three men cleared out, Nick went into the next room to see how the wiring job was coming. "Almost done?" he asked Marz.

"Yeah, hoss. Maybe just another half hour," Marz said. Charlie nodded.

"Anything I can do to help?" Nick asked.

"Nope, we're good. If you see Em, just let her know I'll be up in a bit." Kneeling in front of some cables sticking out of the wall, Marz kneaded absentmindedly at his thigh.

Nick frowned. "You okay?" Sometimes you could almost forget about Marz's amputation because the guy never let it slow him down, even when he should.

"Hmm?" Marz looked up from the complicated jack he was working on. "Oh, yeah. No worries. Damn leg just gets cranky if I spend much time on the floor."

"I told you I'd do that." Charlie paused what he'd been coding on his laptop to look at Marz.

"I'm fine. And this is the last one anyway. Go see your bride-to-be." Marz looked up at Nick with a grin.

Nick nodded. "All right. Later." He stepped through the back door out into the warm July night and nearly walked into Beckett. "Sorry. What's the matter?" Nick asked, noticing the serious expression Beckett wore.

Beckett shook his head. "I just made Becca cry."

Frowning, Nick glanced around the otherwise empty parking lot. Kat's car was there, so they were back. "What?" he asked, heading toward the door to the main part of the Hard Ink building.

Beckett fell into step beside him. "I came up behind her and Kat out here, and when Becca noticed me, she freaked out. Nearly jumped out of her skin. At first she tried to play it off, but then she got upset and ran inside."

Nick punched the code into the keypad, and they stepped into the concrete-and-metal stairwell that led to Hard Ink on the first floor and their apartments and the gym on the upper floors. "Don't worry about it. I'm sure she's fine."

Beckett gave him a doubtful look but nodded. "Let me know if there's anything I can do."

Clapping him on the arm, Nick shook his head. "I'll take care of her." They parted ways as Nick let himself into his apartment and Beckett made his way upstairs. The big open kitchen and living room were empty. "Becca?" he called, an urgent need to see her and make sure she was okay flowing through him.

No answer. He went straight for their rooms at the back of the apartment.

"You need to tell him," someone said. Kat.

"I agree," came another voice. Emilie?

Nick rounded the corner into his office to see Becca sitting on his sofa, her face wet with tears. Kat and Emilie sat on either side of her. Nick's gut dropped to the floor. "Tell me what?"

CHAPTER 7

ick nailed Becca with a stare. As he watched, she
made a valiant effort to button up just how upset she
was, and that made him worry even more. He knelt down
in front of her, his hands on her knees. "What's going on?"

She shook her head, and his heart fucking broke as he
saw her struggle to find her voice and hold back the tears.

Kat grasped something from Becca's lap and held it out
to him. "Someone left this in front of Becca's locker at
work today."

Frowning, Nick accepted the small, floppy, black-and-
brown stuffed animal into his hand. He guessed it was supposed to be a German shepherd, and the damn thing was
missing a leg. It looked like someone had cut the back leg
off and stapled the opening closed. What the hell?

"Look at the neck, Nick," Kat said, her voice serious.

He flipped it around, and that was when he noticed that the
animal was so floppy because the head was connected to the

body only by a thin strip of material along the back. He might not have thought much about that if someone hadn't gone to the trouble of spray painting the torn opening red. As if the neck had been slit. "Sonofabitch," he said, hot prickles running down his back. "Talk to me, Sunshine."

She heaved a deep breath. "I found it at the end of my shift," she said. "I went to get my stuff, and this was sitting upright on the floor in front of my locker. I thought someone had left me a present until . . ."

"This is fucking twisted," Kat bit out.

The words echoed Nick's own thoughts. Twisted and threatening. The removed leg was clearly meant to communicate that the person knew Becca's dog had only three legs, which made the threat personal and specific. "Did you talk to security about this?" he asked, making sure to keep his voice even.

Becca shook her head. "I was so freaked out, I just wanted to get out of there."

"I didn't know about this until just now, or I would've brought us home earlier," Kat said.

"I'm sorry," Becca said, turning to Nick's sister. "I just wanted to forget about it for a few hours."

"I know," Kat said. "You don't have to apologize, but I'm worried about this."

Nick nodded. "Can you think of anyone at the hospital who would do this? Who would have a problem with you?"

"I know some people are upset that I've asked for time off for the wedding and our honeymoon after being on leave for two months." Becca scrubbed her face with her hands. "I overheard some women talking at the nurses' station yesterday. But I can't imagine anyone doing something this cruel. And twisted. Kat's right."

"I don't like it, Becca," Nick said, his hackles all up. "I don't like it at all. I'd like to go with you tomorrow to talk to hospital security. They need to know."

She gave a quick nod. "Okay."

"Is this why you freaked out when Beckett came up behind you out back?" he asked.

Becca sagged back against the couch. "Partly."

Nick frowned, his instincts flaring. "What's the other part?"

The quick look Becca exchanged with Emilie had Nick's gut twisting with worry, especially when Em gave her a small nod. "I know it's ridiculous," Becca said in a small voice, "but I keep thinking I'm seeing Woodson."

The words hung there for a moment and rushed ice through Nick's veins.

Emilie got up and gestured for Nick to sit. He slid onto the couch next to Becca. He'd barely put his arm around her shoulders when she buried her face against his chest, her arm clutching his neck. Her shoulders shook with restrained tears. "Aw, Becca," he said, his heart absolutely aching. How had he not seen this?

"I'm sorry," she rasped.

He locked eyes with Kat, whose expression was every bit as concerned and upset as he felt. "You don't have anything to apologize for. You hear me?"

A quick nod against his chest.

Guilt flooded into his gut. Why hadn't he ever considered that the attempted abductions might have traumatized Becca? She'd been so strong through it all that he'd just assumed she was fine. No wonder she'd asked him what had happened to Woodson. Yet, once again, he hadn't probed deep enough. "Shit, I'm the one who should be apologizing." He stroked her hair.

"No," she said, shaking her head as she pulled away. Her face was red and wet and her eyes were puffy, but she was still the most beautiful thing he'd ever seen. "How could you have known? It just felt so ridiculous that I didn't want to say anything."

"Tell me what's been going on," he said, cupping her cheek in his palm and swiping at her tears with his thumb.

She gave a shy little shrug. "I keep thinking I see him. One minute he's there, and the next he's not. At random times. Around the hospital. On the street. Tonight at the mall I kept feeling like someone was watching me, but of course no one was there. Just like no one's ever there. I was just freaked out about the stuffed animal. After all that, Beckett just scared me and everything kinda crashed in on me." The words spilled out of her in a rush.

"It's not ridiculous, Becca," Emilie said. "It's PTSD." Before all this, Emilie had worked as a clinical psychologist at a local university. Given the shit all of them had been through, she'd been an incredible resource for the whole team these past months.

"But I was fine," Becca said, looking from Nick to Emilie to Kat. "I was fine after it happened."

"The crisis of the investigation probably kept your brain otherwise focused. But then you went back to the scene of the abduction, and you were out on your own for the first time in months." Emilie knelt where Nick had been. "Your nervous system is finally trying to process what happened to you. The anxiety, the reliving of the event, the spontaneous memories, the paranoia. These are all normal given what you went through."

The list of symptoms lashed at Nick's soul. He hated that Becca was hurting. Was the shit that had happened in Afghanistan never going to stop raining down on them? "She's right," Nick said, taking Becca's hand. "How frequently has this been happening?"

Becca frowned, and her gaze went distant. "Maybe a half dozen times since I started back to work."

"Aw, Sunshine," Nick said. He hated that she'd been carrying this all by herself. But no more. "What can I do to help?"

"I don't know," Becca said. "I know it's not real. But I can't seem to make it stop."

"It's gonna take time," Emilie said. "I can help you with some techniques to reduce and combat anxiety. Or you might consider seeing a therapist at the hospital."

"Okay," Becca said. "I'd like to talk to you, I think."

Emilie nodded.

"Maybe you should consider taking off even earlier than you planned," Kat said. Nick could've hugged her, because his thoughts were running in the same direction. But the last thing Becca needed was for him to be an overprotective asshole right now.

"I only have four and a half more shifts," Becca said. "I'd hate to bail on everyone last minute."

"Becca," Kat said, taking her other hand. "You're always taking care of everyone else. You have to let us take care of you, too."

"I know," Becca said in a small voice. "I think if we address this stuffed animal with the hospital and I'm talking to Emilie, I'll feel better."

"That's a good start," Nick said. "But until you take off, I'm walking you in and out of the hospital at the beginning and end of your shifts. If you have wedding errands you need to do, I want to be at your side. And, hey," he said, gently turning her face toward him. "Please talk to me. I can't be there for you if you don't let me know what you need."

Nodding, Becca gave him a look that nearly broke his fucking heart. "I just didn't want to worry you."

He lifted her left hand to his mouth and kissed her ring, then he pressed her hand to his heart. "Taking care of you is my job, Sunshine. For the rest of my life. In good times and in bad, remember?"

Glassiness filled her eyes. "Yeah."

Kat rose, and Emilie followed suit. "We'll give you guys some time alone," Kat said. She leaned over and pressed a kiss against the top of Becca's head. "I had fun shopping with you, sis."

It was the first smile he'd seen from Becca since he'd walked into the room. "I had fun with you, too, Kat," Becca said. "You're going to be the best sister ever."

"Hey, I already am," Kat said with a grin. She and Emilie left.

"Can we get ready for bed?" Becca asked in a small voice. "I'd really like to just lay down with you."

"Of course," Nick said, helping her up. They got changed without talking much, then he climbed into bed and held his arm open to her. Becca crawled in alongside his body and fitted herself tight against his side, like she always did. She fit so fucking perfectly against him. Nick stroked his fingers through her hair. "I don't want you to ever feel like you can't talk to me. About anything."

"I know. I do feel like I can," Becca said, shifting to meet his gaze. Her eyes were so blue. "I should've said something sooner. I'm sorry."

"I get it," Nick said. "I do. But the best thing about having a team is you get help carrying the load. You and me. We're a team now."

Becca smiled. "Always and forever."

"That's fucking right."

"I won't forget again," she said.

"You didn't forget, Sunshine. You're still just getting used to the idea. Me too." He hugged her in against him. "It's hard to lean on someone else when you've been so used to walking on your own."

She nodded. "I love you, Nick."

"I love you, too. There's nothing to worry about. I promise you," he said. And Nick was going to do whatever it took to make that the truth.

WHILE BECCA WAS in the shower the next morning, Nick let the guys know what was going on. Standing around the island in the kitchen, he said, "Becca is dealing with some PTSD from the abduction attempts. Probably triggered by returning to work, the scene of the first attack. And she keeps thinking she's seeing Woodson."

"Damn," Beckett said. "We all saw how roughly he treated her when he tried to grab her the second time. It's no wonder she's struggling."

Nick nodded, the memory souring the coffee in his gut. "Vance has given me some circumstantial evidence that places Woodson in South Carolina, where he's been since we interrogated him, but just keep your eyes open. Be on the lookout. I'm going to do a little more digging there to make sure Becca's not discounting something that's really there."

"Can't be too careful," Beckett said.

"No, not with Becca. That's for damn sure."

"This place is about as secure as we can make it," Marz said. "So we're good here. And the cameras from around the neighborhood are still up and running, so if you have Woodson's vehicle specs, I can keep an eye out. Make sure nothing's hanging around that shouldn't be."

"Do that," Nick said. "Thanks. I'm going to talk to hospital security this morning about this damn thing." He pointed to the stuffed animal, sitting in a plastic bag on the counter.

"Sick fuck," Shane said, glaring at it. "You should let Vance know about this, too."

"I will. I've got a whole to-do list on this today. I'm going to talk to Vance after I leave the hospital, and then I'm going to drop by the inn and work with them to beef up the event security they already provide. I don't want Becca thinking about anything besides having a good time on our wedding day."

Nods all around.

"What am I missing? Can you think of anything else?" Nick asked.

"Would it make her feel any better to carry a weapon?" Shane asked, his gaze serious.

"Good question. I'll talk to her about it. She doesn't have a concealed carry permit, though, and even though some of us flouted that law the past couple of months, I don't know if she'd be comfortable doing so." Though Nick and Beckett had had Maryland permits, the other guys were from out of state and hadn't. Carrying illegally was just one of the ways they'd had to work outside the law to clear their names. Now that they were opening a security firm of their own, all the guys were in compliance. Their business was going to have to be run completely by the book.

"Maybe you should get in contact with Chen," Beckett said. "If Vance can't track Woodson down, Chen sure as hell should be able to. He fucking owes us anyway."

Nick nodded. "True. I'll do that." Chen was the CIA operative who'd first assigned Frank Merritt to the undercover corruption investigation in Afghanistan that had snowballed into the shit storm of the last year. When Nick and his team had rescued Charlie and picked up the investigation, Chen had found them and offered the vital assistance that had finally allowed the team to take down the bad guys and clear their own names. Chen wanted them to work for the CIA from time to time, which meant he was predisposed to do them favors. And Nick wasn't above asking.

"Hey," Becca said, walking into the kitchen. Wearing a set of lavender scrubs, she looked fresh faced and beautiful. His sunshine.

"Hey," Nick said, hugging her in against him. "Want a bagel before we go?"

"Sure," she said.

Nick busied himself with the task, then turned around to find Easy wrapping her in his arms. "I'm here for you, Becca," he said in a quiet voice. One by one, the men repeated the action and the words. *This* was what family looked like. It made Nick fucking proud. And, truth be told, it choked him up. Just a little.

An hour later, they were sitting across the desk from the hospital's chief security officer, a tall, wiry man with graying blond hair and a weather-beaten face. Barry Coleman had served for twenty years in the Marine Corps and worked in security for the past eight, facts that already made Nick feel a little better about leaving Becca there today.

Becca recounted when and how she'd found the stuffed animal, and Coleman asked a series of probing questions. Finally, he said, "Unfortunately, we don't have a security camera inside the staff break room. After Becca's attack, we secured and alarmed that external door, and we put cameras on all the main entrances into the ER, but I'll have one installed in there today. Just for some extra peace of mind. And I'll get my team on reviewing the personnel rosters and camera feeds from yesterday to see if we can pull together a list of people to talk to. This is harassment and intimidation, Becca, and we won't tolerate it for a second. I can promise you."

"Thank you," she said.

"In case it needs to be said, there's no chance Tyrell Woodson could get in here again. We have photographs of him posted at all the monitors. The whole security team knows what he looks like, including the BPD officers stationed in the waiting room," Coleman said.

"We have reason to believe he's out of the area anyway," Nick said. "We heard South Carolina."

Coleman nodded. "That's good to know. We'll get to the bottom of this, I promise."

Nick shook the man's hand, then he and Becca walked out through the back part of the ER. In the break room, Becca stowed her purse in her locker. "You sure you're okay being here?" Nick asked, his hands rubbing her shoulders. "No one would blame you for cutting out a few days early."

"I want to do this," Becca said. "I promise I'm okay. And I wouldn't hesitate to go to Coleman if something happened."

Nick nodded. "Okay. I'll be here at three to walk you out. Have a good day, Sunshine."

She smiled. "You, too. I can't wait to celebrate tonight."

"Me too," Nick said. Tonight all of them were having dinner together at a great local steak house before parting ways for their respective bachelor and bachelorette parties. Nick kissed her for a long moment, and he didn't want to admit how hard he found it to walk away and leave her.

But he had things he needed to do today to give them *both* some peace of mind. Vance, Chen, the inn. Nick also wanted to drive by Woodson's last known address and make sure nothing was going on down there. Anything to help Becca feel better and get past the way his life had exploded all over hers.

It was the least he could do.

CHAPTER 8

That night at dinner, Nick couldn't keep his hands off Becca. Despite the fantastic food, the great company of friends, and the well-deserved celebration, all he wanted was to get Becca alone somewhere so he could flip up the flirty skirt on the stunning little yellow dress she'd worn and get inside her any and every way he could.

Part of it was the top-shelf liquor flowing all around the table, and part of it was the relief Nick felt after all his efforts today had panned out in one way or another. Vance had found a parking ticket on Woodson's car from two days ago in South Carolina, and Chen had agreed to put his considerable resources into not only pinpointing the guy's location but also getting him off the street once and for all. The inn had agreed to additional security, and the head of the security company they used had even made the time to meet with Nick. The guy and his team seemed competent, smart, and savvy, so there was another thing on their side. And Woodson's last known address had not only been quiet as a grave but dust-covered to boot. No one had been there any time recently.

That still left the mystery of the stuffed animal, of course, but Coleman was on it, and Becca's day at work had been incident-free. They'd get to the bottom of that yet.

Becca had been visibly relieved when Nick had filled her in on his day. Now, she seemed so relaxed and happy that it made his fucking heart ache.

Sitting at the dinner table surrounded by their friends, Nick squeezed her thigh. She turned to him wearing a huge smile, a champagne glass in her hand. "Are you feeling frisky, Mr. Rixey?" she asked.

Nick leaned in close. "No, I'm fucking horny. I want to mess up your lipstick and tear off your panties and make my fingers and cock smell like you." He leaned back again, his face carefully neutral.

Her eyes were wide—and full of heat. "Holy shit. How am I supposed to be apart from you the rest of the night after that?"

"Welcome to my world, Sunshine." He threw back a gulp of whiskey.

"Come here. I want to taste that off your tongue," she said.

"Jesus," he gritted out, but it wasn't like he was turning down a kiss. She leaned in, giving him a great view of her cleavage down the front of her sequined strapless dress, and grasped his face in her hand. Her lips were warm, soft, and tasted like champagne and the chocolate mousse cake they'd shared for dessert. Fucking delicious. Her tongue slipped around his, and she pressed herself closer.

"Someone pull those two apart," one of the guys yelled.

Nick grinned even as they continued to kiss. He wasn't voluntarily giving up Becca's mouth, that was for god-damned sure.

"All right," Kat said from the other side of Nick. "We better get the rest of the night underway before we lose the bride and groom." Laughter all around as everyone got up from the table.

"Do you think they'd notice if we snuck away?" Becca asked, her face absolutely glowing.

Beckett grabbed Nick by the shoulders. "Get up, Rix. The tables are waiting for us."

"Apparently," Nick said. "You go have a good time, Sunshine. But you be ready for me later." He arched a brow.

"Oh, I will," Becca said, her tongue licking at her bottom lip.

Shit, he had it bad for her. And he fucking loved it. This woman was going to be his *wife*. How fantastically lucky was he? A man who just months ago would've said he didn't believe in luck, unless it was of the bad kind.

Outside, they found two massive stretch Hummer limousines waiting for them. Beckett had arranged their transportation for the evening through one of the companies he had experience working with—the cars were bulletproof and the drivers were prior military and armed. Nick appreciated the hell out of the gesture.

As the men headed for one vehicle and the women for the other, Nick pulled Becca into his arms. "Have fun, Sunshine. I love you."

"Love you, too, Nick." This kiss was softer, sweeter. Which was good, since all their friends started giving them shit.

"Yeah, yeah," Nick said, flipping the guys the finger. "Before you go, I have something for you," he murmured, then slipped a little wrapped box into Becca's hand. "Wear this and think of me."

"What is it?" she asked.

"I'm not telling," he said. Finding this present had been the other good thing he'd accomplished while she'd been at work.

With a little wave and a big grin, Becca turned to catch up with the women, her skirt twirling out and showing a dangerous amount of thigh. God, she looked gorgeous.

When she was safely tucked inside the Hummer and it pulled away from the curb, Nick got into his own limo and Shane pushed a fresh glass of whiskey into his hand. "Gentlemen, start your livers," Shane called out, loosening his tie and raising a glass of his own.

A round of laughter as everyone drank and the limo started moving. Colored lights ran around the tops of the leather seats, and a fully stocked bar filled one whole side.

Marz sat forward in his seat, a mischievous grin on his face. "If the ocean was vodka and I was a duck, I'd swim to the bottom and drink it all up. But the ocean's not vodka and I'm not a duck, so pass me the bottle and—"

"Let's get fucked up!" they all finished.

"Fuckin' A," Marz said with a laugh.

Beckett rolled up the sleeves of his dress shirt and held up his glass. With a sly grin, he said, "I'll keep mine short and sweet. May all your ups and downs be between the sheets."

"Hear fucking hear," Nick said, taking a drink and laughing at the blush filling Charlie's cheeks. He and Jer were in for a rude awakening—Nick's teammates were fucking fish, and it'd been a damn long time since they'd had a night like this to just cut loose. Hell, it'd been way more than a year since they'd last done it together.

"All right," Easy said, holding up his glass. "I'll play."

"Yes sir, E," Marz said, grinning.

The guy smiled, and it made Nick realize how much Easy had changed in the few months they'd all been back together. A few weeks into their investigation, he'd admitted to them that he'd been badly depressed and battling suicidal thoughts. They'd all been gutted to know how bad Easy had been silently struggling, but they'd banded together around him, and Shane and Emilie had made sure he'd gotten the medicine and therapy he'd needed to fight the demons in his head. "Here's to a long life, and a merry one. A quick death, and an easy one. A pretty girl," he said with a wink at Nick, "and a loyal one. A stiff drink, and another one." Another round of bottoms up. At this rate, they were going to lose every dollar they owned at the casino, and Nick didn't give a shit.

"I'm not good at this," Charlie said with a sheepish smile. "But I'll give it a go." Jeremy grinned at him as Marz clapped him on the back. "To Nick, if you hurt my sister, I'll kill you in your sleep."

For a moment, the words hung there, then everyone burst into guffaws. Yeah, Charlie Merritt fit in just fine.

"No worries. I'll fucking drink to that, Charlie," Nick said, laughing. He took a big gulp of whiskey, enjoying the bite as it went down. "Okay, I've got something to say. First, to nights and friends I'll never forget." Holding his glass high, he looked each man in the eye. "And second, to our enemies."

"*Fuck you!*" they all called out.

"Amen," Nick said. But tonight wasn't a night to worry about enemies. Tonight was a night for celebrating the good things in life. And if Becca hadn't already done it, being with all these guys was making him realize exactly how much good Nick had.

"Ooh, I have a fun idea," Kat said, pulling out her phone. "Everyone take either a cleavage shot or an upskirt shot and text it to your guy. Make 'em remember what they're missing out on tonight." She tugged down the V-neck of her emerald green satin dress and took a picture of herself. A few flicks of her fingers, and she said, "There. Go on, now. Make 'em sweat."

Becca could only laugh as she lifted her skirt and took

a picture of the virginal white panties she wore, complete with glittering sequins. They'd made her feel very bridal. "I love this idea," she said, shooting off a text to Nick. Then again, she'd already been three glasses of champagne into Happyville before they'd left the restaurant, and Kat had given her a fourth when she'd gotten into the limo. So she was prone to love just about any idea just then. "Ooh, I'm sending Nick one of each so he can see how beautiful this necklace is on me," she said, taking a shot down the top of her dress but making sure to get the incredible yellow diamond sun-shaped pendant he'd given her into the frame. She loved him so freaking much.

"Oh, my God," Sara said. "I have no cleavage to speak of, people. But Shane did like these red panties I have on." Awkwardly and with a lot of blushing, she managed to take a picture up the skirt of her little red dress. "You, on the other hand, have great boobs, Jenna," she said to her sister.

"I already sent mine," Jenna said, looking very pleased with herself. She'd worn a form-fitting black dress that gave her the most enviable hourglass shape. On Becca's last day off, they'd gone shopping for new dresses for tonight and the rehearsal dinner, and all the time Becca had gotten to spend with these women was making her fall in love with them even more. She had women she was friendly with at the hospital, but it hadn't been since nursing school that she'd last had truly close friends. Best friends. Now she had four of them.

"I need help with mine," Emilie said, grinning. She handed her phone to Kat, who sat next to her. Laughing, Emilie turned and got on all fours on the seat. She pulled up the bottom of her gold dress just enough to reveal a really tiny pair of satin black panties.

"I knew I liked you," Kat said, taking the picture. "And why am I not surprised that Derek is an ass man?"

"Oh, my. This is going to be a night of TMI, isn't it?" Sara asked, sipping at her champagne.

"Yes," Emilie said, sitting down again. "But if I've discovered anything, it's that life is too damn short and uncertain to hold back."

"I'll drink to that," Becca said, draining her glass.

And that's when all their phones started blowing up. Laughter filled the limo as they all read the guys' reactions to their selfies. Becca couldn't stop grinning—or fantasizing—about Nick's reply.

I'm going to tear those fucking things off with my teeth. Count on it.

His reply to her second selfie made her all warm inside.

You are so beautiful. My sunshine.

"Okay, as much as I want to get you drunk, I also don't want to see you sick." Kat handed Becca a bottle of water and grabbed one for herself. "Drink this before you have any more champagne."

"I will. But why aren't you drinking?" Becca asked. Kat hadn't touched her champagne at dinner, and she was the only one of them without a drink now.

"So I can take care of you," Kat said. "Besides, I'm naturally high on life. Runs in the family. Well, at least with Jeremy and me, anyway."

Becca laughed. Kat and Nick were alike in so many ways, and their stubbornness often had them butting heads. By the time the limo pulled to a stop, Becca had dutifully followed orders and emptied the bottle. "I'm so excited to see what we're doing," she said. The girls had insisted on keeping it a secret.

The driver, an older man named Tony, whose military bearing reminded Becca of her father, opened the door. They spilled out onto the street, and Kat wrapped her arm through Becca's as they walked up to the doors of a posh salon and spa. "We're getting completely pampered. Anything you want. The place is all ours for the night."

"Oh, my God," Becca said. "This is the coolest thing ever." And she didn't know the half of it until they were inside. There was more champagne, a table full of chocolate-covered strawberries and Godiva truffles, and a mountain of presents.

"You never got to have a shower," Emilie said. "So consider tonight your combination shower and bachelorette party."

Becca was completely overwhelmed by the thoughtfulness and perfection of the whole thing. "You shouldn't have done all this," she said. "But I'm really, really glad you did."

They all traded their dresses and heels for robes and slippers and settled in for pedicures. One of the ladies from the spa kept Becca in a continuous stream of drinks and treats and presents. So many presents. A gorgeous lingerie set for her wedding night. A big basket of body lotions and spa products and makeup. A set of pillow cases that read *Mr. Right* and *Mrs. Always Right*. A trio of crystal picture frames. A happily ever after wish jar with their names on it to be put out for people to fill at their wedding. A pair of red satin panties with the words *You got lucky* on the crotch. Sparkling, drop diamond earrings. A beautiful framed print that had Becca and Nick's names, their wedding date, and the words *And they lived happily ever after.*

"I love everything so much," Becca said as the woman put the finishing touches on her purple toe polish. "Not that long ago, I had almost no one in my life. My parents were gone. Charlie had distanced himself. And I threw myself into work just to fill the void. Now, I can't believe everything I have. I'm so grateful for each and every one of you."

"I've never had friends like this before," Sara said, blinking fast. "Sometimes I'm afraid that I'm dreaming and I'll wake up."

"It's not a dream, Sara," Jenna said. "What happened is that you woke up from the nightmare. *This* is your reality now."

"Oh, God, you guys are going to make me cry," Emilie said. "I think we need more champagne. And chocolate."

Kat's pedicure was already done, so she brought the bottle around and refilled everyone's glasses. In all, Becca was treated to a pedicure, a manicure, and a mini facial, and she had her eyebrows shaped. She hadn't felt so relaxed in forever. No doubt everything Nick had learned earlier in the day helped, and for the first time since she'd returned to work, she felt hopeful.

It was after eleven by the time they were all dressed again and had the presents and leftovers packed up to take home. Tony carried everything out to the Hummer for them, then Becca noticed him talking quietly with Kat.

"Is everything okay?" Becca asked, joining them at the front door of the spa.

"Yes, Miss Merritt," Tony said. "There's a man hanging around down the block who's drunk and belligerent. He threw a bottle at a passing car earlier. And he gave me a little bit of guff when I asked him to move away from the Hummer. He left without incident, but I don't want any of you stepping outside until we're ready to get in the vehicle and depart."

Through the haze of champagne and sugar, Becca's gut clenched. "Okay, of course."

"Don't worry," Kat said. "It's just a precaution."

When the other women emerged from the bathroom, Tony said, "Ladies, I'd like you to move directly into the limo once you're outside, please." He went out first, paused as he opened the door, and waved them out.

A half block down the street, a tall, thin man wearing too-big pants and an oversized black hoodie with the hood up skulked in a circle, his arms waving and his body gesticulating like he was having an argument. From this distance, Becca couldn't make out the man's face, but she couldn't deny the relief she felt at the fact that the man was way too thin to be Woodson, who'd been bulky and muscular. Not that she should be worrying about Woodson. Nick's research today really had made her feel a lot better.

Kat bustled Becca into the limo, then climbed in after. As the other women got in, Becca could just make out the man shouting.

"You think you so fucking better than me!" he yelled, his voice full of drunken slur. "Well, you not! You not! And I'm gonna show you! I'm gonna show you!"

The minute Emilie was in, Tony had the door secured behind them, cutting off the rest of the tirade. Almost immediately, the engine started and the Hummer eased away from the curb.

"Please don't let that tarnish your night," Kat said.

Becca smiled. "Not at all. Nothing could tarnish this night. It was fantastic. Perfect. One of the best ever." She meant it, too. And the whipped cream on her cake? In just a few minutes, it would be midnight. And that meant in just one week, Becca was going to be married to the love of her life.

And absolutely nothing could ruin the amazing miracle of that.

CHAPTER 9

"Nick," Chen said when he called on Wednesday morning. "I've got bad news."

"Shit, what is it?" Nick asked. When a guy like Chen said he had bad news, you knew it was *bad*.

From the driver's seat of his truck, Shane frowned, his expression full of questions. He parked the truck in front of the dry cleaner. They'd dropped Becca off at work a half hour before and were picking up their uniforms for the wedding.

"Woodson's in Baltimore. Has been for at least a week, maybe longer."

Nick's gut dropped to the floor, his mind racing. A week? That meant he'd been in town long enough to be responsible for the stuffed animal, for Becca's feeling of being watched at the mall, and maybe even for some of her sightings that they'd thought were impossible and chalked up to her PTSD. "Goddamnit. Are you sure? How do you know?"

"I put a guy on the ground in South Carolina. He learned from some locals that Woodson had left town and traded vehicles with his uncle. I managed to track the uncle's truck to a rest stop near Richmond, where another car had been reported stolen. That car was found abandoned in Baltimore County last week, which we just put together. Otherwise, the guy's been way off the grid. No credit cards. No known vehicles. I have two undercover agents in the city looking for him from within the gang scene. As soon as we locate him, we'll grab him."

"Fuck," Nick said, the weight of this new development crushing in on him. "Thanks for letting me know. Keep me posted." They hung up. "Head back to the hospital. Now," Nick said.

Shane had the truck in reverse and barreling out of the parking lot immediately. "Talk to me."

"Woodson's in town. Has been for over a week. We got fucking outfoxed." Nick dialed Becca. It went to voice mail. "Please call me as soon as you get this, Becca." Ice sloshed into his gut as Nick filled Shane in.

"No one stays off the grid like that unless they fear they're being hunted. Or they don't want to be noticed," Shane said, running the tail end of a yellow light.

Nick appreciated the hell out of his friend's aggressive driving. He really did. "Given the situation in the city, it's probably some of both in this case. But I'm a helluva lot more worried about the latter."

"Roger that," Shane said, darting around other cars as much as he could.

Nick tried Becca's cell again. Voice mail. Damnit. He was about ready to crawl out of his skin. Flipping through the contacts on his phone, he found the number for Barry Coleman at the hospital.

"Mr. Coleman, this is Nick Rixey, Becca Merritt's fiancé," Nick said, his knee bouncing as he scanned his gaze over the street as it flew by.

"Nick, what can I do for you?"

"I need you to find Becca and keep an eye on her until I get there. She's not answering her cell, but I know she might be with a patient. I just got word that Tyrell Woodson is back in town and has been for more than a week. Since we still don't know who pulled the stunt with the stuffed animal, I'd feel better if Becca left early today until we get to the bottom of this and know what Woodson's up to. It seems he took some pains to get back into the city unnoticed."

"I wish I had your connections for intel," Coleman said.

"Yeah, well I wish I didn't need them."

"I hear you," the other man said. "I'll find Becca and stay with her until you get here." They hung up.

In another five minutes, Nick and Shane made it back to the hospital. Nick barely waited for Shane to bring the truck to a stop before he was opening the door. "Pick us up near the ER entrance. It's more sheltered."

"You got it," Shane said.

Nick rushed across the plaza to the main entrance, his gaze scanning the streetscape, the crowd, the sea of faces. He let his guard down for five goddamned seconds, and this was what happened. Becca, potentially exposed to danger and completely unaware.

Inside, he made his way to Coleman's office. Relief flooded through him.

Becca. Sitting across from Coleman at his desk. Her face was a shade too pale, but otherwise she was safe, sound, a fucking sight for sore eyes.

"Nick," she said, rising as soon as she saw him. "He's back?"

Nick cupped her face in his hands. "Yes, but Chen's on it. Woodson won't be free for long. Don't worry, okay?"

She gave him a doubtful look that was like a knife to the gut.

Nick turned to Coleman. "Thanks for your help." They shook hands.

"Anything else you need, you just let me know," the man said.

Taking Becca's hand in his, Nick led her to the main ER entrance, keeping back from the glass until he saw Shane's big black truck pull into the drop-off lane. "That's our ride. Come on."

They jogged toward the truck, Nick's gaze doing a constant scanning circuit as they moved. He got Becca into the truck's backseat, shut her door, and moved to his own—which was when his eye caught it. A glint of morning sun off metal. There at the corner of the building.

Nick opened the passenger door just in time, the report of the gunfire reaching his ears only a second before the round pinged off the door. Close. Too damn close. He dove into the cab. "Go, go!"

"Fuck!" Shane punched the accelerator and pulled the truck into a hard U-ey. Another round hit the back quarter panel.

"Get down, Becca," Nick said as he reached for the Glock at the small of his back. But she was way ahead of him, tucked in a ball on the floor behind his seat. He didn't have a clear shot of anything, especially with chaos already breaking out around the ER's entrance as people dove for cover and the couple of on-site police officers rushed into defensive positions.

In what felt like long minutes but was only a few seconds, they were clear of the area. Shane ran a red light to get them away from the hospital altogether.

Twisting in his seat, Nick looked out the cab's rear window. "Watch for a tail."

"On it," Shane said. "You need to alert the team, Vance, Chen."

"Yeah," Nick said, but first he needed to check on Becca. Christ, every reassurance he'd offered the past week had just been blown to shit. His gut was a wreck, his mind unhelpfully crafting one horror story after another about what might've happened if Chen hadn't called. Or if Nick hadn't returned to the hospital immediately. Or if Coleman hadn't been able to pull Becca off the floor. "Becca, are you okay?"

"I don't know," she said, her voice shaky. When she looked up at him, her skin was ashen.

He reached back and clutched her hand as he dialed Marz.

"Yo, hoss, wassup?" Marz said.

"We've got a situation," Nick said, filling him in. "Let everyone know what's going on. And if you have a chance, scan the security feeds around our neighborhood looking for anything potentially suspicious. We've been keeping an eye out for the wrong damn car."

"You got it," Marz said.

Nick had just hung up when his cell rang again. Chen. Nick put it on speaker.

"I heard about the hospital. You okay?" Chen asked by way of a greeting. Nick wasn't surprised that Chen had information that was only minutes old.

"Yeah, we're in one piece," Nick said. "But it was fucking close. Too close."

"Damnit. Wanted to let you know we have a lead on where Woodson's been staying. Putting together a raid for tonight as we speak."

"Well there's a bit of good news," Nick said. "You need backup?"

"No, you stay hunkered down. I'll let you know when it's done."

"I need you to take this guy out," Nick said, anger lancing through the words. If it had just been him in danger, it would have been one thing. But now it was Becca. Now it was *his family*. And that was a whole other goddamned thing. "I need this situation to go the fuck away."

"I hear you," Chen said. "And I'm working on it." He clicked off.

"If anyone can take care of this, Chen can, right?" Becca asked from the backseat. A little color had returned to her cheeks.

"Yes," Nick and Shane both said at the same time.

When they got back to Hard Ink, Marz had everyone else assembled and briefed in the big unfinished space across from their apartment that was part gym, part war room. It was where they'd run the whole of their investigation against the Church Gang and the mercenaries who'd killed Becca's father and smuggled heroin from Afghanistan into Baltimore. Nick wasn't thrilled at all about the similarity of this meeting to the many they'd held during the investigation they'd thought was done. Closed. Behind them once and for all.

Except it wasn't. Because sometimes the past wouldn't fucking die.

"Chen's people think they've discovered where Woodson has been holing up. They're going after him tonight. His actions at the hospital demonstrate his intention to get revenge, so until we hear from Chen, we're back on lockdown again. I don't want anyone leaving the building today," Nick said.

"What if they don't get him?" Becca asked from where she sat on a folding chair near Marz's improvised desk.

The other team members traded looks with Nick. "I don't know the answer to that yet," Nick said.

Becca nodded. "Do we need to think about postponing the wedding?"

The question was like a punch to the gut, especially because he'd been asking himself the same thing. Fuck. "Not yet," Nick said. A bleak sadness filled Becca's baby blues, and the fact that this scumbag had managed to hurt her yet again lanced boiling hot rage through his blood. Enough was efuckingnough.

The meeting broke up, and the day crawled by like an inchworm moving in reverse.

Nick spent hours worshipping every inch of Becca's body, hoping to keep them both distracted from everything that was at stake as long as he could. The women made six batches of homemade chocolate chip cookies. They watched movies until they were all cross-eyed. And still it wasn't time for the raid.

Finally, a little after ten o'clock, Nick's cell rang with a call from Chen. The devastating news was that they'd apprehended a number of former Churchmen—but Woodson hadn't been among them.

"Well, what's next?" Nick barked into the phone. "This guy came after Becca three times. He's not going to stop."

"I know, Nick," Chen said. "We're interrogating the Churchmen we brought in. We'll find him."

But how fast would they find him? And would Chen find Woodson before Woodson found Becca again?

Because Nick would never survive if something happened to the only woman he'd ever loved.

CHAPTER 10

Chen showed up at Hard Ink Friday morning. His people still hadn't caught Woodson. And Becca was beside herself. She couldn't believe . . . so many things. That Woodson was back. That they might have to cancel the wedding. That maybe she really had seen Woodson some of the times she'd chalked it up to her imagination.

The whole group gathered in the gym, and Chen sat in the middle of them, wearing his usual, nondescript khaki pants and light blue button-down. Chen wasn't his real name, but it was the only one they knew him by—the one that had been on the nametag fastened to the stolen doctor's coat Chen had been wearing the first time Nick had seen him. They'd been at the hospital where Jeremy and Kat had been treated after the funeral.

"I have a proposal for dealing with Woodson," Chen said, scanning the group and finally settling his gaze on Nick and Becca.

"Let's hear it," Nick said.

"I get the word out on the street that Becca is going to be at the restaurant tonight for her rehearsal dinner. We lure Woodson to us rather than wait for him to come at you." Chen's matter-of-fact words hung there for a long moment.

"No," Nick said. Just as matter-of-factly.

This wasn't the first time it had ever been proposed that they use Becca as bait. Nor was it the first time Nick had reacted negatively to the idea. "Nick, Becca said."

"No, Becca. We've been there, done that, and you got hurt," he said. The fierce protectiveness in his gaze made her love him even more.

."I know, but the last time, we also caught Woodson and got information out of him that saved Charlie's life. So it worked," she said. Tension hung so thick in the room you could cut it with a knife. "The alternative is that we cancel the wedding, stay shut up inside the building, and wait it out, right?"

Chen nodded. "We will get him. It's a matter of when, not if."

"I believe you," Becca said. "But when kinda matters a lot right now. The wedding can be rescheduled if we need to, of course, but none of us wants this hanging over our heads. If we can end it tonight, let's end it."

"I agree," Kat said, looking at Nick with sympathy in her eyes.

"So do I," Beckett said. "We'll all be there. We'll all be armed. Nothing's going to happen to Becca or anyone else."

"And my team will be there," Chen said.

"Is this what everyone thinks?" Nick asked, his voice like gravel. He crossed his arms and surveyed the group. Nods and affirmatives all around. "Fuck. Then what's the plan? Because I want it to be goddamned foolproof."

For the next hour, the guys strategized. Chen had brought plans for the Italian restaurant where they were scheduled to go, as well as a big map of the surrounding streets and alleys. He'd arranged to have surveillance on the restaurant starting immediately, to make sure no one arrived early and found a place to lay in wait. When they were done, Chen put in calls to his undercover contacts to get the word out. He was apparently confident enough in the way information moved within and between gangs to think that the word would make it to Woodson in time if in fact he was actively looking for her. Worst-case scenario, it didn't, and he didn't show. And then they were right back to square one, but no further behind.

After Chen left, Becca turned to Nick, where they were all still gathered in the gym. "I want to be armed tonight."

"Me too," Kat said.

Nick and Beckett traded a look, but then Nick nodded. "Everyone who's comfortable handling a weapon should be armed. I want redundancies on top of redundancies where safety is concerned. And for the record, I fucking hate this."

Becca wrapped her arms around Nick and laid her head against his chest. "I do, too. But I hate being scared more."

Nodding, Nick said, "I've got a few calls I want to make. But then I'll be wrapped up here."

"Okay," Becca said. "Maybe I'll go throw together some lunch for everyone." Staying busy was the best way to keep from going crazy. At least, it had worked for her during the team's investigation. No reason why it shouldn't now.

"I'll help," Emilie said.

"Me too," Sara said.

In the end, all four women made their way back to the apartment with Becca, and she appreciated the silent show of support. She really did. They decided on tacos, and everyone got to work chopping veggies and browning the meat. Emilie apparently made a mean spicy Spanish rice, so she took charge of that.

As Becca stood at the stove, the whole thing suddenly crashed over her like a tidal wave. The shooting at the hospital. Knowing everyone would be in danger tonight. The prospect of facing Woodson again—for real this time. "Can you watch this?" Becca asked Emilie, laying down the big spoon with which she'd been stirring the ground beef. "I'll be right back."

She rushed down the hallway and ducked into Kat's sometimes-room rather than her own—the one she shared with Nick. First, because she wanted to be alone in case Nick returned from making his calls. Second, because her wedding gown was in this room, hanging on the outside of the closet door. Luckily, they'd picked up their dresses from the bridal boutique before the lockdown had started, and now it was here waiting for her.

For whenever Nick and Becca were finally able to get married. Because her gut told her it wasn't going to be tomorrow.

Becca sagged down onto the edge of the mattress, her gaze drinking in the gleaming white satin and the sparkling beadwork at the waist. Her lip quivered and her eyes pricked, but she wasn't giving in to tears. She was done crying. Now she was just fucking angry.

It doesn't matter, Becca. The wedding is just one day in a forever that lasts the rest of your life. It's just one day.

And it was. She knew it. But their love had overcome big obstacles—Nick's initial belief that her father had betrayed him, sophisticated and numerous enemies, multiple attempts on their lives. What they had was hard-fought and well-earned. They *deserved* a day of celebration and happily ever afters.

Two soft knocks sounded against the door.

Becca straightened her back, took a deep breath, and said, "Come in."

"Hey," Kat said, leaning in the doorway. "Can I join you?"

"It's your room," Becca said with a small smile.

Kat shut the door and sat down on the bed next to Becca. "It really is an amazing gown. Nick is going to swallow his tongue when he sees you in it."

It might've been the first time all day Becca smiled. "I am looking forward to seeing him see me in it for the first time."

Grasping her hand, Kat nailed her with that Rixey stare. "You just have to hang in for a few more hours. This is almost over."

"I know," Becca said. "I know. But is it bad that I want to be the one to end this asshole's life once and for all? I just want to see the consciousness bleed out of his eyes so I can know it's over for good."

"Not even a little bad," Kat said. "You guys deserve a happily ever after."

Becca chuffed out a humorless laugh. "We all do. But sometimes I'm afraid all we're going to get is . . . a hard ever after. You know?"

Kat's gaze was full of determination. "This guy's going down one way or the other, Becca. And besides, a hard ever after sounds like it could be good to me. I mean, *you know,* hard can be good."

That eked a smile out of Becca, and that smile turned into a chuckle. "Yeah, hard can be good."

"No," Kat said, grinning now. "Hard *is* good. Really fucking good."

It was stupid and childish and ridiculous, but as the hard jokes started flowing out of them, they descended into outright crying giggles and really unattractive snorting that was a helluva better release than tears could ever be.

"Thank you," Becca finally managed. "I really needed that."

"Good. Now come on, let's go eat." Kat pulled her up from the bed.

"I'll catch up," Becca said. "Need to use the bathroom." She headed back toward her room, passing Shane and Sara's on the way. Their door was open, and something caught Becca's eye. She stepped back to the opening and peered in at Shane's big medic case just inside the doorway. Becca shut herself inside the room, knelt, and opened the lid to the case.

When her gaze finally landed on a bottle of injectable diazepam, an idea came to mind. Nick wanted redundancies upon redundancies; well, this certainly fit. And given that Woodson had gotten his hands on her twice before, she wanted a way to hurt him up close if it happened again. Without letting herself question what was probably a totally useless idea, she filled a syringe with a dose guaranteed to induce sleep in a man Woodson's size. Quickly, she put everything away and tucked the syringe into the pocket of her dress, which hung in Nick's closet. No one even had to know the syringe was there.

One thing was for sure, Becca Merritt was done feeling like a victim. She was ready to fight for this life she wanted, once and for freaking all.

THEY ARRIVED AT the inn early for the rehearsal. Before Becca even stepped foot out of the stretch Hummer, Nick wanted to take a look around and discuss a plan with the security he'd brought in extra for the rehearsal. This was the same team who'd be running things at the wedding, so they already understood the nature of the threat from when he'd met with them earlier. To add another layer of security, Chen had arranged to put agents from his detail at either end of the long block on which the inn sat, providing an effective roadblock and a defensive perimeter.

It was all likely overkill. Nick knew it was. The bait would lure Woodson to the restaurant, not here. Hell, they hadn't even published a wedding announcement, so the details of their arrangements could only be known by people with whom they'd shared invitations.

When he was satisfied, he opened the door to the ladies' limousine. "Let's practice us a wedding," he said with a smile. He might be tense as hell inside, but he didn't want to do anything—well, anything *more* than what had to be done—to take away from the joy of the occasion. Becca deserved a happily ever after, and Nick was determined to give her one. No matter what it took.

Becca stepped out of the limo in a stunning long blue dress that made the color of her eyes almost glow. She adjusted the long decorative chain of her purse on her shoulder. He'd given her a small handgun that would fit the bag, and even though she knew how to use it—thanks to her father—Nick really fucking hoped she never had to. But he couldn't have agreed more that she should have the protection on her. It was *always* wise to be prepared for a snafu, that was for damn sure.

Sonya greeted them at the gatehouse and guided the group of them inside. The first floor of the inn was where the cocktail party immediately after the ceremony would take place while they were taking wedding photographs. A tall round table filled with champagne flutes stood in the center of the floor. "Please help yourself while you wait for the minister to arrive."

"Do you want to see the upstairs where we'll hold the reception?" Becca asked the women.

Even though the security team had assured them that the house had been locked up tight all day, with no one coming or going until they and Sonya had arrived to open up for their rehearsal, Nick wasn't comfortable letting Becca go alone. In the end, everyone went along for the tour. It really was a nice place. The kind of place where happy memories were made. Nick wanted that for Becca. For both of them.

They didn't have to wait long for the chaplain to arrive.

Nick didn't know the man personally, but Thomas McAdams was a military chaplain who was a friend of a friend, which was how they'd managed to book him on such short notice. Nick guessed that McAdams was not much older than he was, and the chaplain seemed eager and interested and kind. Nick immediately liked him.

McAdams greeted the whole wedding party, then Sonya gave him a general tour of the outdoor space where the ceremony would take place. They'd process up the brick-lined courtyard between chairs that were already set up for them, and the ceremony itself would take place on a raised brick patio against the backdrop of the rear of the gorgeous Carroll Mansion. A plain wide wooden arch stood there now. Tomorrow it would be decorated with flowers.

As Sonya, McAdams, and Becca spoke, Nick couldn't help but be on the alert. His eyes and ears were wide open, despite the fact that things were quiet. Exactly as they should be. And he wasn't the only one. Every one of his teammates had their game faces on. Nick was fucking glad.

"Okay, now that I have the lay of the land," McAdams said, "I'd like to go over what you all indicated you wanted for the ceremony. Then we'll walk through it as a group, and I'll show you where to walk and stand, all that sort of thing. And then we'll do an actual dry run, music and all if you have it."

"I have it on my phone," Becca said.

"That'll work," McAdams said. For a few moments, they discussed vows, wording for various parts of the ceremony, who was holding the rings, and how they wanted him to introduce them to the audience when the ceremony was complete. "Okay, let's walk through it all. Anyone should feel free to interrupt this time with questions or suggestions. In fact, *now* is the main time to ask questions," he said. "Becca, where do you want to start the procession from?"

Sonya stepped forward. "If I might make a suggestion,"

she said, guiding them back into the first floor of the inn. In the back corner, there were three doors. "There are two private party rooms here we've set up for the bridal party to use before the ceremony." She let them into one and turned on the lights. The rectangular room had a long table that seated eight in the center, with old-fashioned leather armchairs clustered in groupings along one wall. A floor-to-ceiling mirror hung at the far end of the room. "Both rooms are identical. These usually work nicely to allow for last-minute preparations, privacy if the bride doesn't want to be seen by the groom beforehand, and staging for the ceremony itself."

"Yes, that's what we'd discussed. I don't want him to see me until I'm walking down the aisle," Becca said, smiling at him. Nick couldn't fucking wait. "So then we'd be processing from inside?"

"That's right," Sonya said, leading them back out to the main room. "The groomsmen will join Nick at the dais ahead of time. We'll keep these doors shut until it's time for the women to walk. When the music changes, we'll open the doors and the bridesmaids will go one by one. And then the music will change again to whatever song Becca has chosen to walk to, and she'll proceed as well. Is someone walking you down the aisle, Becca?"

"Oh." Without hesitation, she turned to Charlie. "Will you? Please?"

Her brother's face filled with emotion. "Yeah. Of course."

Becca pressed a kiss to Charlie's face. "Thank you. I'm sorry that in all the craziness I didn't think of this sooner." He shook his head, clearly moved by her request.

"Very good," McAdams said. "Let's head outside to see how we'll arrange things at the dais."

As they walked the length of the courtyard, Sonya said, "Remember not to walk too fast, bridesmaids. It's longer than usual, so everyone always wants to run up the aisle."

The women all laughed. When they got to the raised brick porch, Sonya directed each of them to where they should stand for the ceremony itself.

After that, McAdams sped them through the words so they knew what would happen. And then Sonya was guiding them back down the aisle again to show them where to stand for the reception line they were going to form before returning to the porch for group pictures.

This all seemed pretty basic to Nick, and frankly he was a little impatient with it. But that was just the broader situation talking. He tried to block it out as much as he could, especially since Becca seemed to be enjoying herself. And given what they were yet to face at dinner, he didn't want to do anything to ruin that.

"Okay, let's do a full run-through," McAdams said. "Gentlemen, except Charlie, come with me."

Nick frowned and turned to Becca.

She smiled and winked. "Go ahead. I'll be right there."

He gave her a quick kiss. "You're already the prettiest bride there ever was."

"Aw, sweet man. I don't care what anyone says, I'm going to run up this aisle to you," she said as he headed for the door.

"I won't object to that at all," he called over his shoulder as he made his way toward the mansion.

And then Sonya guided the women back inside and closed the doors behind them.

CHAPTER 11

This is so exciting, Becca," Sara said, looking around at the elegant room. "This place is so gorgeous."

"I know. I fell in love immediately," Becca said. The beautiful summer night, the sweet fragrance of the garden flowers, the ambiance provided by the historic architecture. Tomorrow was going to be amazing.

Assuming it happened.

No, it *was* happening. Becca just had to believe it.

"Becca," Sonya said. "If you have your phone, I can hook it up to the sound system so it plays in the courtyard. Just show me what songs you want."

Becca opened her wedding playlist. "This is the music that can play while people are being seated," Becca said, pointing to a list of songs. "This one is for the bridesmaids' procession, and this one is for mine."

"Very good." Sonya hooked up the phone. Classical music immediately filtered in from outside. Sonya had

Becca line the women up in the order in which she wanted them to march, and the music changed for the bridesmaids. "And now we're marching," Sonya said as she opened the doors. The warm twilight air spilled in. White lights twinkled in the trees and on lines strung across the courtyard. It was magical.

One by one, the women walked out the doors. Jenna, Sara, Emilie, then Kat. And then it was just Becca and Charlie left to walk down the aisle. She turned to him. "I'm so lucky to have you as my brother, Charlie. I just want you to know how grateful I am that all of this has brought us closer again." Next to finding Nick, that was one of the brightest silver linings in everything that had happened.

He gave her a small smile. "I feel the same exact way," he said.

"Okay," Sonya said from beside the doors. "Now I'll change to the wedding march, and it'll be your turn."

"Shut the fucking door," came a deep voice from behind them.

Becca whirled. She recognized the voice immediately. Woodson. For real this time.

"Who are you, sir?" Sonya asked. "You can't be in here."

He brandished a gun directly at her. "I *said*, shut the fucking door. Now."

As the blood drained from her face, Sonya hastily pushed the doors closed.

Becca fumbled for her purse, but the decorative metal clasp stuck.

"Don't move, Becca. Don't even fucking breathe. In fact, toss that bag down. Now." Woodson stalked closer.

Which was when Becca realized he'd lost *a lot* of weight since she'd seen him two months ago. His eyes and face had the sunken, haggard look of an addict. He'd let his hair grow back in, too. He was no longer bald. "It was you. On the street the other night."

"Told you I was gonna show you. And when I found out about your wedding, I thought, what better time. Was gonna wait 'til tomorrow. Do it up right for the big crowd. But I figure, I got you now for sure."

Charlie moved just the smallest amount to angle himself in front of her, and Woodson tracked the movement like a hawk. He trained his weapon at Charlie's head and arched an eyebrow. "Get down on the floor," he ordered Becca's brother. "You, too." He glared at Sonya, who rushed to comply. Charlie sank down more slowly, and Becca could feel the anger and frustration rolling off of him.

Becca needed to distract Woodson from whatever he planned to do. Delay him, at the very least. At some point Nick was going to realize something was wrong— she had faith in that into her very bones. He wouldn't let anything happen to her. So she just had to hold on for a short while.

"I told you to drop the bag. Do it *now*," Woodson barked out, punctuating his words by jabbing the gun at the air.

Her belly sinking, Becca dropped the purse next to her feet.

Woodson gave her a droll stare. "Don't fucking play me. Kick it away."

She did, a little of her hope going with it as it slid across the hardwood floor. "How did you know about my wedding?" she asked, wanting to keep him talking.

"Yeah, that was some lucky shit, wasn't it? For me, anyway." He stalked closer, slowly, like he was paranoid despite the fact that he was the one with the weapon. "Little sister of a Churchman who was killed works in housekeeping at the hospital. Guess someone left an invitation out in the staff break room."

"So she's how you got the stuffed animal in to me," she said, her voice shaky. She hadn't been freaking out for nothing after all. Woodson really had been lurking around the edges of her life. For how long she wasn't sure. But what a lesson to trust her instincts.

His grin was sadistic and cruel. "Enjoyed my little calling card, did ya?" He didn't give her the chance to answer, because as soon as he was close enough, he roughly grabbed her arm and tugged her against him. He spun her so her back was to his front, then he dragged her away from Charlie's reach. His forearm pressed savagely into her throat, choking her as she struggled to keep her heels under her. "Because of you," he hissed into her ear, "I lost everything I had. And now you're going to see how that feels, starting with him."

Woodson lifted the gun.

Becca had to do some—

The syringe!

In her rage and terror, it seemed to her that he moved in slow motion. And that she did, too. An eternity seemed to pass as he took aim and she reached into the pocket of her maxi dress. Uncapped the syringe. Jabbed it into Woodson's thigh.

The world froze for an eternity.

Woodson shouted.

The gun fired.

She stumbled as he did, his arm still squeezing her throat.

And then she was falling, falling backward with him, as the gun fired again.

NICK WATCHED AS the women made their way up the aisle. When Kat got closer, she grinned and made a face at him, but then her gaze shifted to his left. To Beckett. And hell if the look his sister was giving his friend wasn't how Becca sometimes looked at Nick. For as much as Nick had been thrown by Beckett's interest in Kat, the two of them had proven to be damn good for each other.

As Kat took her place, Nick searched for Becca. And

found the doors to the first floor closed again. He frowned. Maybe it was to allow the bride to make a grand entrance once the wedding march began? Nick stretched his neck and rolled his shoulders. Probably made him an asshole, but he really wanted this rehearsal to be over.

He stared at the doors. The same music continued on. A prickle ran over his scalp. He looked to his teammates, standing at his left. But his gut had already decided. "I don't like this." No, more than that. "Something's fucking wrong."

The men took off as a unit. "Kat, get everyone in the limo and keep them there," Nick heard Beckett say. "Go."

Becca. Jesus Christ, Becca. Where are you?

Nick full out sprinted down the courtyard. Two security guards spilled out from the gatehouse and filled in behind them.

"Go around to the side and take the shot through a window if you have it," Nick called. Easy and Marz broke off. Guns in hand, the remaining three slowed as they approached the doors. Curtains covered the glass, keeping Nick from seeing inside. In a quiet jog, they hugged the building as they got closer, then Nick used hand signals to communicate the plan. Him on one side, Beckett and Marz on the other. Beckett would force entry, Marz would provide sweeping cover and fire, and Nick would take out the target—assuming he had a shot. There were three friendlies inside.

It was the only way he could think of Becca as his brain shifted to ice-cold operational mode.

Gunfire. One shot. Then another.

And it didn't fucking sound like it had come from the exterior of the building. It had come from inside.

No! Not Becca! Not my sunshine!

With a violent kick, Beckett exploded open the doors. A scream from inside.

Nick swept in to witness something he would never forget for the rest of his life. Becca on the floor on top of Woodson. She wrestled a gun away from him, then rose on stumbling, unsure feet, the gun trained right at the man's head.

Nick didn't know whether to be terrified, proud, or completely fucking dumbfounded.

Gun trained on Woodson, Nick slowly came around so he had a clear view of the man and of Becca's face.

"Becca, are you okay?" Nick asked, his heart a goddamned freight train in his chest. Seriously. The adrenaline coursing through him was strong enough to knock him off his feet, and as strong as the relief he felt at seeing Becca on hers. But she didn't seem to hear him. "Becca."

"I should kill you," she said, the tone of her voice something he'd never heard before. "I should." Despite the shudders racking her body, she gripped the weapon stably, competently. Her finger sat on the trigger.

Nick glanced to Woodson to find him unconscious, then all his focus narrowed in on her, even as his teammates moved around the room. Still vigilant, Nick moved closer. "Becca, it's me. It's over."

She shook her head. "I *should*," she said again, her face crumpling.

God, his heart was fucking breaking. "No, you shouldn't. No matter how much he deserves it, you don't want a death on your hands. Any death. You don't want that. And I don't want that for you."

Beckett moved around behind Becca, poised to disarm her if he needed to, but Nick gave a single shake of his head.

Nick crouched to force himself closer to her line of sight. "Becca. Sunshine. Look at me."

Shattered blue eyes cut to him, but her gun remained trained on the unconscious man who'd wreaked such havoc on their lives. "Is . . . is Charlie . . ."

"I'm okay," Charlie said, sitting up against the wall by the door. "I'm okay, Becca."

Nick spared a quick glance to her brother. Okay, but hit in the shoulder. Shane was taping gauze to the wound from a kit open on the floor beside him. Jeremy was crouched on Charlie's other side, his head against the guy's good shoulder.

"He's okay?" she asked, like she wasn't quite processing the information.

"Yeah. Charlie's okay. It's all over." Slowly, Nick reached out toward her, his hand gesturing for the gun. "You did so good, Becca. You took Woodson out. You saved Charlie. Let me take it from here." The *how* of it all, Nick didn't yet know, but there was no doubting that Becca had saved this fucking day.

Nick's hand fell on the barrel of the gun. Exerted pressure. Forced it down and away.

Finally, she let it go.

It was like the gun had been holding her up.

Her legs went out beneath her. Beckett was right there and caught her as she sagged to the floor.

Nick was to her in an instant. He handed the gun off to Beckett and took Becca into his arms.

"Charlie," she rasped.

"He's right here," Nick said.

She turned within his embrace, a tortured gasp spilling out of her when she saw her brother. Blood had soaked a crimson circle through the gauze.

"It's just a scratch," Charlie said. "I'm fine."

Movement in the doorway. Chen and his team. "I got here as fast as I could," Chen said. "Are you all okay?"

Hell if Nick knew. "Can you stand?" he asked Becca. He wanted to get her out of there, away from Woodson.

"Yeah," she said as he helped her up. She needed the help. Adrenaline had her shaking like she was freezing, and her teeth were chattering.

Nick shrugged out of his suit coat and wrapped it around her.

"What's that?" Chen asked, pointing at the floor by Woodson's leg.

A syringe.

"Diazepam," Becca said in a weak voice.

"Smart," Chen said in that deadpan way he had.

Not smart. Fucking brilliant. When had she done that?

As they watched, one of Chen's men cuffed Woodson's hands.

"Can we go home?" Becca asked, her voice taking on a flat, odd quality. "I just want to go home."

His arm around her, Nick pulled her in against his chest and stroked her hair. He looked to Shane and Charlie.

"He needs stitches, but not surgery. Went clean through the meat above his collarbone," Shane said.

"Can you fix it up at home?" Charlie asked Shane.

Shane pressed his lips into a tight line. "The job will be neater and less painful if we take you to the hospital."

Shaking his head, Charlie looked from Shane to Nick. "I don't care about that. I want to take Becca home."

"Your call," Nick said to his best friend.

"Okay," Shane said after a moment. "Let's get you up." He and Jeremy both helped Charlie stand.

"He was gonna kill all of you. That was his plan," Becca said out of nowhere.

Chen's gaze swung to Becca, as did several of the other men's. "Did he tell you how he knew to come here?"

"Just that someone in housekeeping at the hospital found one of our wedding invitations and gave it to him," Becca said. Well, that answered some questions right there.

"He came from the basement," Sonya said from where she hovered with her security team at the door.

"We'll get to the bottom of it all," Chen said. "Go home. I'll touch base in a while."

"What's your plan with him?" Nick asked, giving Woodson one last glance.

"The less you know, the better." Chen gave him a pointed look.

Nick knew he didn't have to say anything more, so he just nodded and guided Becca toward the door. "Then let's go home."

CHAPTER 12

Becca felt like she was trapped in the dark at the bottom of a well. Somewhere, she knew there was a way out, but as she felt around with blind hands, she couldn't find the ladder. She couldn't find the light.

Despite the fact that, physically, she was functioning.

She answered questions as if by rote. She watched Shane sew up Charlie's wound. She ate part of a piece of pizza that she didn't taste and couldn't finish. She let Nick change her into a pair of pajamas. She felt him touching her, but she couldn't reach him.

She couldn't find the ladder. She couldn't find the light.

But then her friends threw her a rope.

They'd all been sitting around on the couches in the living room for hours, just keeping one another company, just keeping *her* company, when suddenly Kat shot to her feet, her hands fisted, her posture indicating she was waging some great internal debate.

And then she turned to Beckett, who was sitting with his hip resting on the back of the couch behind where she'd been. "I'm pregnant," Kat blurted.

The whole room froze.

Beckett's face was sculpture still. And then his eyes went wide. "Pregnant? Like . . . pregnant?"

"Pregnant like you're going to be a daddy," she said, her voice uncertain.

He came around the couch to her and grasped her face in his hands. And then he gave her a smile that lit up the entire room. "You're pregnant," he whispered, his voice absolutely reverent. One big hand dropped to her stomach. And then he wrapped her in his arms so tightly that it made Kat laugh.

"You're happy," she said.

"I'm terrified," Beckett said. "But I'm also fucking ecstatic."

The whole place erupted in laughter and cheers and words of congratulations, the energy in the room shifting like the planets had just realigned.

Light cracked through the fog clouding Becca's heart and soul.

"I thought I told you there better not be any goddamned children," Nick said.

Kat whirled. "Nick—"

"No, it's okay," Beckett said, his face going serious again.

And then Nick broke out in a deep belly laugh. "I had you. I totally had you." He grasped Beckett's hand and pulled him in for a back-slapping embrace. "Congratulations, man. I'm gonna be the coolest uncle ever. And you're going to be a kick-ass dad."

"Dude, you have no chance of being cooler than me, so give that shit up now," Jeremy said, hugging Kat in beside him.

"You're a fucking asshole," Beckett said as he gave Nick

a playful shove. But that million-dollar smile was back on the guy's face again.

"You totally are," Kat said, reaching up to hug Nick next.

Woodenly, Becca rose from the couch to offer her congratulations.

"Well, shit," Marz said from where he stood next to Beckett. "If we're sharing good news, and why the hell not after this day, then I have to tell you that Emilie agreed to marry me this afternoon." He put his arm around her and kissed her on the temple. "And to be honest, I have no idea how I lasted this long without telling you."

"We were going to share it tomorrow at the reception," Emilie said, her voice cracking. "But I'm glad we did it now. We've been dying."

The smiles on the couple's faces were absolutely brilliant with joy. Another round of jubilation erupted.

The rope was in Becca's hands. The light was burning off the fog.

When everyone had a chance to offer congratulations, Sara called out, "I got accepted into college at Johns Hopkins for the fall. I'm going to finish my degree."

Jenna threw her arms around her sister's shoulders. "Oh, that's amazing, Sara. I'm so proud of you."

More celebrations. More light.

Becca could tell the moment her body finally plugged back in, because suddenly she felt *everything*.

"I'm so happy for all of you," she said, her voice strained. "So, so happy."

Tears exploded out of her. Hot, racking, full-body tears. Sobs that had been stored up since the beginning of time.

Someone wrapped her in their arms and sank down to the couch with her. A hand fell on her shoulder. Another on her back. Another on her knees. Someone grasped her hand.

All she had was rope and light now, even though she

couldn't rein herself in. The tears felt like they released a poison inside her that had to be purged, so she gave herself over to them. Not that she really had a choice.

Finally, *finally,* she managed a deep, shuddering breath. Tears continued to leak from her eyes, but she could see enough to realize she'd literally soaked Easy with her tears. "I'm sorry," she croaked out.

He shook his head. "Don't you worry about a thing. I got you."

She pressed her hand to his heart. "You're a beautiful, beautiful soul, Easy. I'm so glad you're in my life."

The words visibly impacted him. He gave her hand a squeeze.

Becca turned to the others, who'd all formed a tight circle around her. "I feel that way about each and every one of you. I love you and I cherish you and you're just . . . you're all everything to me." At least she wasn't the only one crying, but she was pretty sure she saw only happy tears.

"We feel the same way about you, Becca," Kat said from where she knelt in front of her.

"Yeah," Marz said. "You're da bomb. Then again, I've thought so since you made a MacGyver reference, so . . ." The men groaned. "What?" Marz asked.

Her heart was so, so full. But something still needed to be said. Urgency flooded through her, and she whirled to face Nick, who'd been sitting behind her, holding her and stroking her back. "I want to marry you. Tomorrow," she said. "Just like we planned. I don't want to wait. I don't want to put it off another second." The words rushed out of her. She scrubbed at her face, despite the fact that her eyes seemed set to non-stop.

Nick grasped her hands. "Becca—"

"Please," she said, sensing that his concern for her was going to push him in the direction of caution, of taking things slow. "The best way to fight back the darkness is with love and light. The best way to cheat death is to live life with no regrets, holding nothing back, just throwing yourself into the messy, vibrant, unexpected beauty of it. *That's* what I want. I don't care about what happened. I refuse to let that win. I don't want to wait to be your always and forever. And for you to be mine."

He studied her face for a long moment, his pale eyes shiny and searching hers. Anticipation hung over the room like a balloon about to burst. "I would love nothing more than to make you my wife. As soon as humanly possible. But tomorrow will do."

"BECCA, ARE YOU ready? It's five o'clock, so it's time," Kat said.

Staring at herself in the floor-to-ceiling mirror in the bridal room at the inn, Becca nodded. One by one, her friends formed a tight circle behind her. Kat, one of the bravest, fiercest women she knew. Emilie, one of the strongest and most generous. Sara, one of the most courageous and certainly the most resilient. Jenna, one of the most compassionate, with so much passion for life that she'd helped a broken man rediscover that within himself again.

How lucky was Becca to be surrounded by such extraordinary women? The only one missing was her own mother, and a little part of Becca's heart ached that her parents weren't there to see everything that she and Charlie had become. But that just proved that you had to love and cherish the ones you cared about while they were in your life and never waste a single minute.

"You look gorgeous," Sara said.

"We're all fucking hot," Kat said, making them all laugh.

"We are pretty stunning," Becca said. The gowns, the flowers in their hands and in their hair, the happiness radiating out from every one of their faces. "And I'm ready."

"Let me make sure the coast is clear. My brother has been a total crazy man about not seeing you." Kat winked at her as she made for the door. Becca hadn't seen Nick since they'd departed at noon for the salon. Truth be told, she was at her limit of missing him, too. "Okay, we're good."

They moved out into the main space, where Becca found Charlie waiting for her. The look he gave her was full of pride and affection.

"Are you feeling okay?" she asked him.

"Great," Charlie said. "I'm about to witness my favorite person on earth getting everything she ever wanted. How could I be anything but great?"

"I love you, Charlie," she said, gently hugging him.

"Bridesmaids, it's time to march," Sonya said. The lady had seemed a little rattled when they'd first arrived, but she'd really gone above and beyond in putting Becca at ease. But if Becca was honest, she didn't feel scarred by what had transpired there the day before. She felt freed.

One by one, her friends made their way to the dais at the far end of the courtyard.

"And now it's your turn," Sonya said as the music transitioned to the wedding march. "Congratulations, Becca."

"Thank you," she said as she slipped her arm through Charlie's good one. They stepped through the door and out into the evening sunlight. "I want this for you someday, Charlie. This happiness, this belonging. You deserve it."

He smiled. "I want it, too. And for the first time in my life, I believe I can have it."

"Jeremy is amazing," she said, giving him a little nudge with her elbow.

"Jeremy is everything," Charlie whispered as they neared the back row of chairs. The happiness in the words filled Becca's heart up to overflowing.

The audience all stood. It wasn't a huge gathering—a

handful of Nick's friends from various stages of his life, some of Becca's hospital colleagues and spouses, friends they'd made along the course of the investigation—Detective Vance, Walter and Louis Jackson, Chen. Ike and Jess, who worked at Hard Ink Tattoo, sat to the far side holding Eileen by her leash—the puppy wore a collar with wedding bells hanging off it and a veil that ran down her back. And to top it off, nearly twenty members of the Raven Riders Motorcycle Club had come, some with dates, some without. Before all this, Becca had never before met a person in a motorcycle club, but without them, Nick and his teammates would never have been able to win all the fights that had ultimately allowed the guys to clear their names.

And finally put the past to rest.

Becca was looking forward to getting to know the Ravens more now that all the fighting was behind them.

Looking up, Becca found Nick straight ahead of her, looking as sexy as she'd *ever* seen him. His dress uniform highlighted the strong width of his shoulders and the trim leanness of his waist. Metals hanging on one side of his chest spoke of a man of honor, loyalty, bravery, and so much more. But what she most noticed was the expression on his face. Total, abject, unrestrained love, unconditional devotion, incredible respect.

If you had those things with the person walking through life with you, what more could you possibly want? Becca certainly didn't know.

As she got closer, she could see the men standing up for Nick, standing by his side. Jeremy, who lived life with more pure delight than anyone she knew. Shane, within whom a fire to help and secure justice for others burned so bright. Marz, who was the most positive, loyal person she'd ever known. Easy, who would do anything for anyone, and who was one of the strongest people she'd ever met in her life, even if he didn't yet know it. And Beckett, fierce and self-sacrificing, the quintessential good guy hiding under a gruff exterior. She loved that about him. She loved all of them.

On a table in front of the men stood seven framed photographs. Her father and the six men from their A-team who hadn't survived that ambush on a dusty road in Afghanistan. They were all together again. Just as it should be.

Finally, she and Charlie reached the front. The chaplain asked, "Who presents this woman to be married to this man?"

"I do," Charlie said. He kissed her on the cheek, then turned to take a seat.

Except before he could do so, Kat came down the two brick steps, grabbed his hand, and led him to stand with her. "You should be here, too," she said.

It was the first moment all day that made Becca have to fight back tears.

Nick stepped forward and took her hand, and the glassiness in his eyes hammered the next nail into her effort to make it through the ceremony without smearing her makeup. As he guided her up the steps, he whispered, "I love you, Becca. I am absolutely the luckiest man alive."

"I love you, too, Nick. Always and forever," she whispered back.

And as they exchanged their vows and claimed one another with their rings and confirmed their commitment in front of everyone they loved, Becca knew this was what happily ever after felt like.

"Ladies and gentlemen," the chaplain called out when they'd said everything that needed to be said, "may I present the new mister and missus Nick and Becca Rixey. You may seal your union with a kiss."

As applause erupted, Nick slid his big hand behind her neck and slowly pulled her in. The kiss was deep and soulful and claiming, full of love and heat, the kind of kiss she would remember as an old lady, the kind of kiss that would make her remember that, once, she'd really lived.

But living was what she was all about now. And *this kiss* was what their happily ever after was going to feel like all the time. Full of life and passion and love.

And if they ran into some hard times along the way, they'd fight through them together. Side by side. Surrounded by their friends.

After all, hard ever afters were good, too.

Because hard is good.

At Avon Books, we know your passion for romance—once you finish one of our novels, you find yourself wanting more.

May we tempt you with . . .

- **Excerpts** from our upcoming releases.

- Entertaining **extras**, including authors' personal photo albums and book lists.

- Behind-the-scenes **scoop** on your favorite characters and series.

- **Sweepstakes** for the chance to win free books, romantic getaways, and other fun prizes.

- Writing **tips** from our authors and editors.

- **Blog** with our authors and find out why they love to write romance.

- **Exclusive content** that's not contained within the pages of our novels.

Join us at
www.avonbooks.com